The Inheritors

A Climate Fable

The Inheritors
A Climate Fable

By Eleanor Thorne

LONGSHORE
REBEL

PRESS

Book cover by Eleanor Thorne.

ISBN 979-8-9985500-0-3 (paperback)

First edition April 2025.

After

Chapter 1: Dust and Ultraviolet

September 28, Tallahassee, Florida.

For the first time in three weeks, Anne-Elise Kirby could tell night from day by looking at the sky rather than a clock.

The dust had hung over Tallahassee like a shroud, appropriately enough—sometimes a dull grayish-brown and sometimes the color of clotted blood. It was an apocalyptic sky, a sky of fiery wrath: a heat sky. Yet searing heat was from a different time, the *Before* time.

But the change from one epoch to another was never quite so clean as man-made delineations made it out to be. The searing heat had led directly to the event that had made this omnipresent dust a fact of life for the Florida panhandle. That event had not arisen from nothing. It had a cause, or rather, a two-centuries-long string of causes. The *Before* time had led directly to today, the *After* time. There was no clean division. One smeared into the other like a paintbrush blending colors.

The dust was everywhere. Anne-Elise had all but given up on removing it from her house. As soon as she ran the vacuum cleaner, another layer would seep in through any gap it could find, as if it were water trickling in uncontrollably through a tiny crack to fill a newly empty space. It coalesced on the desktop, the television stand, the coffee table, the surface of her coffee itself. It seasoned her food like a sprinkling of flavorless spice. *The earth has forced us to make this dust part of ourselves,* Anne-Elise thought. *We can't shut out and lock ourselves away from the consequences of our own actions. And considering what some of this dust is....*

But no, she didn't want to think too hard about *that*. That train of thought led to thoughts too grim and dark to entertain, even for her.

The dust was, finally, decreasing somewhat. It was no longer just a dull dark veil over everything, blending day and night into one intolerable, oppressive slurry of timeless, apocalyptic gloom.

But Anne-Elise had no illusions about what *that* meant. The sun was not a friend to the Sunshine State any longer.

As if to mock her, the weatherman on TV announced neutrally, "*The dust over the Gulf Coast is subsiding at last. Visibility has increased in Tallahassee to half a mile as of the top of the hour.*"

The anchor, a cheery blonde, smiled at the meteorologist as the camera panned away from the weather map. "Thank you, Jake! It does feel like we have been in mourning, and Mother Earth has mourned with us, but now the black veil is lifting. We may even see the sun again in a few days!"

For some reason, no doubt to avoid calling his colleague out as a blithering idiot, the weatherman merely half-grimaced, half-smiled at this absurdly rosy anthropomorphism.

Fools, Anne-Elise thought. *Utter fools. The atmosphere is a physical, nonliving system. It's not mourning anything. If it had feelings, they would be feelings of vengeance, not grief. And if you think the sun is benevolent now, you should be left out beneath its rays for a while.*

It made a certain demented kind of sense that people would revert to quasi-religious anthropomorphism of "Mother Earth" and the sun, Anne-Elise supposed. In the anti-science epoch into which the country had decided to catapult itself, that really made *eminent* sense, in a way.

She tried to focus. It wasn't as if it mattered what nonsense these fools on television babbled. Their parent company could switch them out for someone else and few in the audience would care. Given enough time, few would even remember much of the long line of predecessors of their current anchors. They certainly wouldn't remember specific idiotic comments that any of the anchors made. Media personalities were temporary, disposable, throwaways like everything else.

Anne-Elise grabbed her coat, a solid black polyester trench coat designed for rain, and pulled it on over her heavy gray sweater. The absurdity of such clothing in September in Florida briefly crossed her mind, but she dismissed that at once. Such thoughts were another artifact of *Before*. This was *After*, and the requirements of *After* were different: direr and grimmer. Wearing summer clothing was a luxury that people here no longer had.

Now ready to face the conditions outside, she reached for her car keys, leaving the television on. Let them babble into the void, for all she cared.

As soon as she opened her patio door, a cough seized her. *Perhaps I'm not ready after all to face the outside just yet.* Anne-Elise sputtered over the pavement, feeling a metallic tang in her throat that did not particularly surprise her. She fumbled in her purse for her face mask. It wasn't perfect, but some filtering was better than none.

*   *   *

The dust had made Anne-Elise's dishwater-blonde hair feel chalky and voluminous by the time she had reached her car. Scowling, she got into the vehicle and ran the windshield wipers, releasing some fluid to attempt to clean them. It wouldn't last—the windshield would be coated again by the time she reached the lab—but at least that layer wouldn't be quite as thick, with the speed of the vehicle and air resistance blowing some of it off.

As she drove down Interstate 10 toward the lab, she passed a billboard that made her scowl. A cartoon astronaut with palms raised stood beneath an inappropriately cheery yellow sun on a dark blue field. The product announced its name, claims, and slogan in a "golden age of science fiction"-type font that evoked a happier, more optimistic era.

Don't let decreased ozone put you out of yo' zone!

SPACE SUIT IN A BOTTLE

All all-new proprietary & patented SPF 500 sunscreen for our changed world

Join the Early Tester Program and get SPACE SUIT IN A BOTTLE for the low, low price of only $49.99/16 oz bottle

Anne-Elise shook her head. *Less than three weeks and the parasites have already arrived. If there is one thing humans do marvelously well, it's exploit each other.*

The next billboard she passed was starker. Simple black text on a white field read,

SAY THE WORDS

This billboard had been vandalized already with a message filling two lines, "HYPE STORM / CLIMATE LIE." For a moment Anne-Elise wondered if her brother-in-law knew who had done this. Most likely not. He was now in DC full-time, far from here.

I hope it was all worth it to you, Chelsea, Anne-Elise thought. Her older sister's self-righteous visage flitted through her memories. Years of that face dominating and blighting her life. *You cost Edward and me our parents. You destroyed not one, but two of your own families. You guilted us for holding a grudge against you and not forgiving you, when the terms of forgiveness were to accede to your loathsome politics at the cost of our own careers.*

And you won. You got your brass ring, the thing you've craved your entire self-absorbed life: importance. I hope it was worth it, you selfish bitch. Of course, knowing you, it probably was.

Fresh memories of the new president's press conference then filled her mind.

"The Vice President's Blue Ribbon Storm Reanalysis Panel has quickly determined that intensity claims about Hurricane Leonard made by the National Hurricane Center during the previous administration were exaggerated to the point of scientific fraud...."

As if scientists could reanalyze an unprecedented storm in a matter of days. But then, the Blue Ribbon Panel's members weren't field experts. They were computer programmers and engineers barely out of college—sometimes college dropouts—rather than experts in the field of tropical meteorology or *any* subject area of meteorology.

But because they were young and had destroyed their prospects for any other career by being involved in this disgraceful venture, they were utterly loyal to the new president and vice president. They had done exactly as they were supposed to do, provided that one understood that they were motivated by politics rather than science. The Vice President himself had even gone on that horrid political show, *Attack Dog*, before the storm had even made landfall, to baselessly accuse the Hurricane Center of lying about its unprecedented intensity and the equally unprecedented type of storm that they were declaring it.

And the liar had gotten away with it because the data—the Hurricane Hunters—they—they had—*Edward*—

Anne-Elise shoved that thought out of her mind at once. No. No.

She chose instead to recall the Space Suit in a Bottle billboard. *Even if it doesn't work—which it very likely doesn't—why do we need SPF 500 sunscreen now, President Gilbertson? Why did you even approve such a product to go on the market? Federal regulations used to cap it at SPF 60. Why'd you change that?*

Why is everyone wearing a sweater and a coat in September in Florida? Why is this cloud of dust everywhere over your home state's capital? Where did the dust come from? And why did the storm that generated it form? The answers are all words that the government can't say now.

This sarcastic turn of her thoughts subsided as she approached the Intensity Labs Advanced Fusion Testbed. Flashing her ID badge at the guard, she drove through the gates and into the parking lot. Another pair of guards stood at the door: Karl Parnell and Chris Hayward. Anne-Elise knew them well.

"Director," Parnell said as she approached. "It's good to see you. It's been hard, but what you and your people have here is *hope*."

Anne-Elise wasn't in the mood for this resolute sunniness. Idiomatic usage itself would need to change, she reflected briefly, since the sun was a menace now. She glared at Parnell. "This is like offering a 'miracle cure' for cancer when the patient has been wheeled into the morgue," she snapped.

Parnell was visibly taken aback at this cynical statement. He was clearly uncomfortable contradicting the lab director, but his colleague Hayward managed, "That may be so for that one, but other cancer patients could still benefit."

Anne-Elise faced him down with another steely glare. "The cancer patient in the metaphor is not just a single individual."

And with that, she entered the fusion lab.

*　　*　　*

"Director," Dr. Bobby Gleason said when Anne-Elise passed through the lounge. He raised a coffee cup to her, a sad smile on his face. "Surprised to see you at such a late hour. Though perhaps it's not so surprising, really. It's been hard in the... outside world. This is a sanctuary."

Dr. Gleason was the Deputy Director, five years younger than Anne-Elise's forty-five. A bespectacled Black man from California, he had been—like Anne-Elise herself—a dedicated environmentalist in grad school, but also like her, he had been a pragmatist and a firm believer in innovation. That mix of realism and idealism had led both the future Director and the future Deputy Director of Intensity Labs to major in nuclear physics. From each coast—MIT and Caltech—they had found their purpose here. They had always gotten on well and had a healthy professional friendship... at least in the *Before* time.

"We've had a stable net-positive process for seven days," Dr. Gleason remarked as Anne-Elise logged into the computer with her access card and biometrics. "Your process is just as efficient as it was supposed to be...." He broke off. "It's ironic, really, that *ultraviolet* laser light could be our salvation, given what has happened... but I really think we've got it. The future of power generation is here. We've been through hell lately—you especially—but things are going to get better now."

"You think so?" Anne-Elise said listlessly, waiting for the screen to load.

"I do. There's certainly something bittersweet about this happening *now*, of course, but... better late than never, right?"

"No, I'm not sure it is. There's 'late' and then there's 'too late.'"

Dr. Gleason didn't know what to say for a moment. But unlike the guards, he realized what was truly troubling Dr. Kirby, or at least he thought he did. "You're referring to the new administration's policies. It's rough going that federal workers aren't supposed to say"—he scowled at the computer screen—"'climate change.' But we're an academic-private partnership."

Anne-Elise gave him a deeply cynical look. "My brother-in-law is the new White House Press Secretary. You don't know how these people think like I do. You're fortunate there, by the way. Anyway, they're going all-in on dead-dinosaur fuel. It'll be heavily subsidized, and all green power—nuclear included—will be *Catch-22*'d into oblivion. And that's if they don't go for an outright ban."

"A *ban*?"

"Yes. That's what my brother-in-law gloated—that I'd 'better look for new work soon.'"

"Your *brother-in-law* said that to you? That's what he's focused on now, after his daughter—"

"Yes." Anne-Elise stared at her colleague. "He did. That is what these people are like, Bobby. And let's not hold up Vera as some sort of heroine either. She's just as bad in a different way."

"But that's...." Dr. Gleason struggled to find words. "I'm almost at a loss for what to say. A policy of deliberately crushing energy innovation is just asinine."

"Yes, well...." Anne-Elise trailed off pointedly.

"But why?"

"Culture war. They support anything that will stick it to 'their enemies.' Simple as that."

"Well, I can't resign myself to that kind of bleakness," Dr. Gleason said, getting up from his chair. "What did we work for all this time, if a handful of politicians can render it all for nothing?"

"If people don't want what we offer them, we worked in vain. We may not like to face that, but that doesn't make it untrue."

Dr. Gleason sighed as he headed for the door. He gave her a wave farewell with a sad half-smile on his face. When the door clicked shut behind him, Anne-Elise focused fully on her computer at last.

She withdrew a USB stick from her purse and stuck it into the port. A window appeared showing the contents of the drive. One particular file stood out to her. She opened a command terminal and typed the path and filename into it, then sat back and stared at the screen as the cursor flashed.

How am I even considering this? she thought. *How did it come to this?*

Before:
Tropical
Disturbance

Chapter 2: The Sunshine State

August 29, one month earlier, Tallahassee.

Just touched down. Spare a ride?

The text message from her twin brother Edward stared back at Anne-Elise as her phone hummed.

Edward Kirby worked as a forecaster at the Hurricane Center in Miami and flew into storms occasionally as a Hurricane Hunter pilot, leaving from Lakeland Linder Airport in Polk County. But the season was in an uncharacteristic lull at the moment, despite the fact that it was August, so he had been granted a few days of leave to visit with his family.

Anne-Elise looked forward to Edward's visits, but she also knew the argument that would ensue every time he flew up to Tallahassee in "Sallie," his Cessna 172 Skyhawk. Their niece Vera Mellor, the daughter of their older sister Chelsea and her husband Richard, would raise hell about its carbon footprint.

Edward loved that plane. It was his grown-up toy, and only Nature itself could conceivably part him from it. And he loved the persona that stepping out of it gave him, the Platonic ideal of the cocky aviator in his brown leather jacket and glasses.

Even the name of the thing was—but Anne-Elise had to push that out of her mind. The real-life Sallie was his coworker Sallie Evans in the National Hurricane Center in Miami, a postdoctoral scientist not even out of her twenties. Anne-Elise's lips thinned as she contemplated that... situation. Edward believed that Dr. Evans had a crush on him. Anne-Elise had visited their workplace before, and she had never seen any evidence of it.

Then again, Edward had two failed marriages under his belt. In both cases, his wives had initiated the divorce, and he had been taken completely by surprise. He seemed oblivious to women's cues, convinced as he was of his own genius, coolness, and sexual magnetism. Her brother's romantic life was the one thing about him that irked Anne-Elise. Otherwise it sometimes seemed to her that they were as emotionally close as they had been physically close in the eight months in which they had shared their mother's womb. They had been united against the world—beginning with their own parents and their sister Chelsea—from childhood....

She brought her thoughts back to the present as she typed her answer to Edward's text. **On the way.**

* * *

Dear God, it was hot. Anne-Elise wiped the sweat off her forehead. There was little point in wearing makeup. At this moment, she really couldn't blame Edward for traveling well above the sweltering ground.

There he was, wearing that brown jacket and those glasses again. Anne-Elise had to acknowledge that he did take on the exact look that he wanted, the look of characters like Indiana Jones or Ian Malcolm, a scientist who was also a glamorous, cocky, sarcastic adventurer—far too cool to hide all the time in the lab or the office. His brown hair, dyed to hide the streaks of gray, was perfectly shined to match his youthful persona, a persona at odds with his age of forty-five years. He grinned at his twin sister as she approached the airport hangar where personal aircraft were stored.

"VFR all the way," he announced. "A perfect flight, the water glittering like diamonds, the sun reflecting off Sallie like gold." He smiled. "But it *is* the Sunshine State."

"Indeed. The Sunshine State," Anne-Elise replied mockingly. "More like the state of gators, mosquitoes, stupid politicians, air thick enough to swim in, and Florida Man." She smirked.

Edward raised his eyebrows. "Actually, humid air has lower pressure than dry air at the same ambient temperature—"

"Shut it, Florida Man," she teased.

"I'm not Florida Man."

"You are a man, born in Florida, living in Florida," Anne-Elise said with a click of her tongue. "You are quite literally Florida Man."

"Florida Man is an aesthetic—a personality—" He gazed down at his aviator jacket and gave a cocky shrug. "I don't

16

think I have it."

"Taking one's personal small plane out for a flight is as 'Florida Man' a thing to do as taking out one's boat."

Edward chuckled as they got into Anne-Elise's SUV. "Speaking of stupid Florida politicians, are we going to have to deal with Richard tonight?"

Anne-Elise turned the keys in the ignition, started the vehicle, and began to back out. "Unfortunately we're going to have to deal with the whole family."

"Even Vera? She hates her parents more than we hated Mom and Dad."

Anne-Elise exited the airport parking lot and entered the highway. The bustle of traffic set her teeth on edge. *All these vehicles. Odds are that some of these drivers are distracted... or intoxicated. And why did you have to bring up Mom and Dad—*

She tried to focus on the conversation topic as Edward had raised it rather than on her own mental digression. "That is exactly what draws her to a scene: being able to show how much she hates it and looks upon it with self-righteous contempt. She'll be here to criticize every one of us, mark my words," she declared. "She thinks you and I are just as bad for 'the cause'—*any* cause, *whatever* might be the cause du jour— as Chelsea and Richard."

"She'll be on me about Sallie again."

"Oh, yes." *And how sad it is that I know he means the plane, not the woman,* she thought. *But Vera won't care a bit about the woman.*

"You know," he said, considering, "factually, she's right. I do have a larger carbon footprint by burning fuel than I would by taking my Prius. I just like to fly." He leaned back in his seat, smiling. "We've all been on passenger jets, but until you sit in the pilot's seat of your own aircraft, flying like a bird, doing what most generations of humanity only dreamed of doing, soaring around the clouds and at one with the sky, I don't think you can understand. Pleasure and sublime joy have a certain innate value that, I think, often outweighs whatever comparatively small negative they carry."

"I suppose that makes sense. I was thinking earlier about how utterly miserable it is with this heat and how much nicer it must be to fly amid the clouds." She gazed out, where the heat waves rippled visibly from the road.

"It's a record heat wave in several ways," he said, his smile fading. "Duration, intensity, and extent. The high has been at least ninety-six for two months, over a hundred for half that time, and the Gulf is scarily hot."

"We're at, what, J? For the next storm?"

"L. The next name is Leonard."

"That's a lot of storms, but not many for us, and those few were all early and weak, if I recall right."

"You do. It's been rough for the Caribbean and Central America since then, though. There's been a high-pressure system steering them into that region: the same one that has also caused the record heat wave and turned the Gulf into...." He became very grave. "I'd say 'rocket fuel,' but...."

Anne-Elise gave him a momentary raised eyebrow and quickly reverted her gaze back to the highway. "I'm sure the Gulf can support a Category Five."

"The Gulf can support a hell of a lot worse than a Category Five at the moment," he said quietly.

"I didn't think there was anything worse than a Category Five."

He didn't want to respond, so she raised her eyebrows again.

"*Theoretically*," he ground out, "tropical cyclones can become... *very* intense. I've modeled it. Let's hope it remains merely theoretical. It requires certain upper-atmosphere conditions too, not just high sea temperatures. But," he collected himself, "yes, for me, aviation is about pleasure, and I think that's a part of being human. And in the case of my Sallie, the negative effect *is* comparatively small. My plane isn't what's injected the atmosphere with steroids, so to speak. It's the fossil-fuel industry and big ag, which Richard constantly goes on camera to defend for his boss. And where's the pleasure and sublime joy in *that*?"

18

"People like our sister and brother-in-law—and our niece, for that matter—take pleasure in petty things," Anne-Elise said acidly. "In spite, in self-righteousness, in making others uncomfortable, in *taking away* whatever it is that gives them that sublime joy." She sighed. "I envy you in this, Edward. You have found that in your work and your hobby."

"I thought you liked your job. Cracking the atom open and unlocking its power...."

She raised her eyebrows. "Actually," she said in exactly the same tone that he had used when he had begun to correct her about air pressure, "I'm *smashing atoms together* rather than cracking them open—"

Edward chuckled. "Fair point."

Her smile faded as she steered the vehicle toward the restaurant where they would be having dinner with their relatives. "I believe in the potential, and I'd like to think it'll make a difference for humanity someday. But then I encounter people like... well, like the rest of our family."

He nodded, not requiring further elucidation. "Maybe you should take up a hobby."

"I read. That's hobby enough for me."

He subsided, not wanting to argue with her about her books. They had been her refuge for as long as he could remember. It would never change.

Anne-Elise pulled into the parking lot of Eileen's, an American fine-dining restaurant. She scowled at the sight of the red BMW that she knew to be Chelsea and Richard's, and then the sticker-plastered bike locked to the bicycle rack of the surf shop next door, since the owners of a place like Eileen's had clearly never even considered that any of their customers might arrive on bicycle. But Vera Mellor's was unmistakable. Anne-Elise sighed at the sights.

"They're here already," she muttered. "All three. So it's really a miracle that there isn't a cop in front of this place to arrest one or more of them."

"They'll probably all behave themselves until *we* show up," he said. "That's when the performance should start."

"You're probably right."

Trying to keep scowls of dread off their faces, the fraternal twins entered the restaurant. "Mellor and Kirby, party of five in total," Anne-Elise announced to the staff. "I think the other three are here already."

"Yes, they are waiting for you. Your table is this way."

*   *   *

Anne-Elise regarded her older sister with a mix of derision and envy. Chelsea was four years older than she and Edward, but she did not look it. Her hair remained naturally golden-blonde, her face unlined. As far as Anne-Elise knew, that too was natural—though she would not put it past Chelsea's chauvinist husband to expect her to get cosmetic surgery or Botox. But Anne-Elise thought she could tell if Chelsea had done that. Instead, the only indication that she was not in the bloom of youth was the faintly visible pattern of pores over her skin that became more evident with her slight plumpness, and even her shape could be considered "voluptuous" rather than actually overweight to any real degree. But a forty-nine-year-old could not carry the same weight as a twenty-five-year-old without giving some indication of her age. For Chelsea it was that her skin was no longer perfectly shiny and smooth. On the other hand, Anne-Elise knew that her own face did bear wrinkles.

At *least I look my age*, she thought bitterly as she joined the rest of her family at their table. *Chelsea looks almost like she did as a teenager, the high school beauty queen that every straight boy wanted, and look where that role and that sense of entitlement got her.*

Vera, Chelsea's daughter, looked like her mother only in her body type. Both were curvaceous. But Vera's hair was dark like her father Richard's, and she had cut it very short and dyed it with pink streaks. Her clothing was also markedly different from that of her parents. Whereas they were dressed in a crisp blue suit and a red sheath dress respectively, Vera wore jeans and a loose-fitting t-shirt. A tattoo of leaves and daisies peered out above her collar. It was obvious to Anne-Elise that Chelsea disapproved of her daughter's style choices, but Vera was twenty-three and could dress and look as she saw fit.

"Edward. I'm so glad that you made it in safely," Chelsea said as the twins sat down. But before they could begin their conversation, a waiter approached to take their orders.

Edward ordered beer, but no one else in the family had an alcoholic drink. Chelsea pursed her lips in muted disapproval. Even Anne-Elise thinned her lips, but she did not say anything.

"Right," Chelsea finally said as their drinks were set down before them. "As I was saying, I worry about that plane...."

"It's quite safe in my hands," he dismissed, taking a sip of beer. "Don't forget that I fly hurricane eyes, Chel."

"In planes that are specially beefed up for the job! Your 'Sallie' is not like one of those Hurricane Hunters that you fly."

The National Oceanic and Atmospheric Administration had two Lockheed Martin C-130J Super Hercules aircraft specially modified for the use of hurricane meteorologists who needed to conduct reconnaissance missions into storms to determine their precise structure and intensity.

"And that is why I don't take her into hurricanes. But the experience I have in such conditions makes me very confident that I can handle a beautiful day like today," Edward said, amused.

Vera, who had been shifting impatiently in her seat, then spoke up hotly. "Your plane is a problem because of its fuel usage, as you well know! Aviation is a terrible contributor to the climate crisis—"

"Vera," Edward said heavily, "we've had this debate before. My plane is a drop in the bucket compared to industry emissions. Individual actions will not make any discernible difference. I've run climate models. I can prove it. The only reason—the *only reason*—to do them is to make *yourself* feel better."

"But you are setting a good example. Others might reduce their emissions by making similar sacrifices."

"Right, because private aircraft are as ubiquitous as cars, and cars are just as easy to give up without major inconvenience. Gotcha."

"You still set a good example," she said stubbornly.

Anne-Elise turned to her brother. "Edward, I forgot to tell you. I had solar panels put on the roof, since the fusion lab is still probably a year from hooking up to the grid." She turned theatrically to her niece. "Your household did that recently, I understand? What kind of power savings are you seeing?"

Vera glowered and stammered. "We... haven't decided on the brand yet...."

"Oh? That's surprising." Her tone radiated insincerity. "Is the father of that one guy... what's his name...."

"If you mean the one of us who holds the mortgage, it's Mike."

"Right. Is Mike's father having financial trouble? I thought he was loaded."

Chelsea then cut in. "Many people have financial difficulties. We shouldn't judge."

"That's exactly what I say. We shouldn't judge," Edward agreed. "Including my plane. If I didn't take it, I'd have to drive the length of the state to visit our family. If we had gone electric years ago, that would be the obvious choice. But we didn't."

Chelsea interrupted again, trying to smooth things over. "I'm glad that we have this chance to visit, even though I worry for your safety in that plane."

"Driving is far riskier, statistically speaking. As we all know."

They fell silent at that. Nobody wanted to speak of the deceased Kirby parents.

"Well," Chelsea finally said, "I do worry about that plane, but you'll do what you want, of course. You don't have to take *my* concerns into account, even if I wish you would."

"Yes, he'll do what he wants as a grown man without respect to someone else's concerns. You of all people should understand that," Anne-Elise cut in.

Richard set his fork down and glared. "Was that necessary?"

Anne-Elise was provoked now and not inclined to back down, even though Edward was giving her looks of dismay and protest. "At this point, yes, I think it was. 'Let's all pile on Edward for his plane' was okay—we can judge for *that*, whether because it uses airplane fuel or because you imagine it's unsafe—but you are off-limits?" She glared back. "If you're going to pick on him, you should expect your actions to be scrutinized too. All of you."

Richard turned to his wife. "There you have it. It's as I've always told you: She will not get off her judgmental high horse. Decades later, and she still judges and condemns you for a pair of teenage mistakes, one of which your mother pressured you to do."

"I don't judge or condemn her in the least for the thing you're alluding to. And if you think I'm judging her for what she did at sixteen, rather than a few years later, that says more about what *you* would consider judgment-worthy than what I would."

"If we are going to dredge up my sins from over thirty years ago, yours will be fair game too," Chelsea said. "And I have shown contrition and turned my life around. There isn't a day that goes by that I don't regret... that act. Do you regret anything *you* did as a teen when Mom and Dad were spiraling? Or *said*?" she added with a pointed look at Anne-Elise. "Either of you? Or are you proud of it all to this very day?" She did not wait for an answer. "I merely wanted to express my satisfaction that we *are* having this family night out. It's so rare that we ever get that chance."

"I wonder why," Richard said sarcastically.

The waiter then brought out their food, setting the plates in front of each of them. Richard had ordered steak, served well-done with steak sauce slathered over it like a flood. The waiter visibly disapproved, but had the courtesy not to criticize a customer. Anne-Elise had a chicken dish, Edward a seafood plate, Chelsea a large bowl of fettucine alfredo, and

23

Vera a vegan salad. Richard cut into his meat slab with a vengeance, as if it had personally offended him.

I do think it personally offended the waiter, Anne-Elise thought, slicing her chicken into pieces.

As she glanced furtively at Richard, her eyes involuntarily widened at the sight of a gnat around his plate. Gnats didn't fly fast, but they were so small that they seemed to flit in and out of existence. *Like elementary particles and their inherent quantum uncertainty,* Anne-Elise thought. *Do they exist or not? But it's not a firm answer, of course. They have a probability of existence. And if it were possible for me to see one, that would mean it definitely existed. That would collapse the probabilities.*

Schrödinger's gnat, she thought. *Are you going to land on that sauce-slathered hockey puck and drown? Is my pig of a brother-in-law going to eat you? Or will you escape this restaurant to live another day?*

The gnat, however, did not appear in Anne-Elise's line of sight again. She supposed it was fitting. *For now I'll choose to think it left our table. And who could blame it?*

She regarded her shredded chicken for a moment before addressing her brother-in-law.

"Did you see the news story last week about the woman in Miami who put her baby into a wood chipper?"

Chelsea's fork clattered to the tabletop as she glared at her younger sister. Richard threw his knife down, infuriated.

Anne-Elise continued undaunted. "I read that they were only able to identify it as her offspring by DNA," she said. "Can you imagine?"

"What is wrong with you tonight?" Chelsea snapped.

"It's just gruesomely interesting," Anne-Elise said. "The depths of human depravity are always perversely fascinating to me."

"That says something about you," Richard growled. "For the last time: Leave her alone."

"I'm not talking about *her,* Richard. Unless she was pregnant at forty-nine and threw the fetus into a wood

24

chipper too."

"You know full well—"

"Richard, leave it," Chelsea finally said. She glared at Anne-Elise again. "She knows what she is doing. You shouldn't take her bait."

"It's a real story," Anne-Elise insisted, reaching for her phone ingenuously. "Look, I'll show you—"

"I believe you. That's not what I mean."

"This is why I hate family gatherings," Vera commented. "In fact, I consider my real family to be my polycule."

"You've used this word many a time," Anne-Elise said, "and I still don't understand it. Are you all in a relationship together?"

Chelsea shuddered as Vera explained. "No. There are different kinds, and some include sexual relationships, but ours is ace."

Anne-Elise did understand this shorthand for asexuality, at least. But that just raised a question of its own.

"So in what respect does it differ from a group of friends?" she asked. "It sounds like just a fancy way of saying 'friends.'"

"If I did explain the nuance, you would just scoff," Vera retorted sullenly.

Richard sneered. "Doesn't matter to me what it's called. They're not your kin. That's all that matters."

*   *   *

Edward had managed to eat the majority of his fish by now, listening to the "conversation" in silent, passive amusement after they had mercifully ceased to talk about him and his plane. *They are horrible,* he thought, *and I don't really blame Anne-Elise for calling out their hypocrisy and baiting them with comments like this, but it isn't a good look for her either. She needs to let go of the past like I have. It's as I advised her: She needs a hobby.*

They managed to return to their meals for a few minutes. The sounds of lips smacking and silverware clattering replaced the sounds of spiteful conversation. But then they began to pick at the remainders of food and their pace of eating slowed to a crawl. Knives and forks squealed against flatware, a soundtrack of impending doom gathering volume as a sense of dread filled Edward. The topic he had wanted to avoid—politics—was about to burst out.

*　　*　　*

Anne-Elise had not wanted to discuss politics either, but unlike her brother's passive dread of the subject, her dislike was aggressive. She prepared herself to argue again with her sister and brother-in-law.

Chelsea spoke first. "Speaker Gilbertson will be a guest on *Attack Dog* tonight. A prerecorded interview that will air, I mean. I was hoping that we could all watch as a family. Richard coached him well, I thought."

Her voice needled, pitched to try to make others feel guilty and obligated. With Anne-Elise, it had the exact opposite effect. *I have too much experience with her victim routine to fall for it anymore*, she thought.

"You know full well that I don't watch that crap," she said as sharply as she could, "and the presence of Hal Gilbertson is not an inducement to me to change my ways. I can't imagine that Edward feels any differently."

Chelsea frowned like a disappointed schoolteacher trying to shame an errant student. "I know that you wouldn't want to watch it for political reasons, but since we *are* your family, I had hoped that you would support Richard's work for our sake."

"Leave me out of it," Vera muttered.

Anne-Elise glared at them. "Richard's work consists of coaching and managing press appearances for a politician that I have voted against every time he has run for office."

"You shouldn't expect them to support us, Chelsea," Richard said gruffly, eyeing Anne-Elise. "And I don't know why you brought it up either. But since you did, I'll point out that it *was* a good appearance."

"It wouldn't be that hard to put in a good appearance when the point of comparison is 'Mad Chad' or whatever he calls himself," Edward said.

"Mad *Dog*," Richard corrected officiously.

"Right, because nothing says 'mad dog' like a curly-haired, baby-faced, shrieking dweeb in a tie. Anyway, what did Gilbertson actually talk about?"

"The energy crisis and his proposal to address it."

"What energy crisis?" Anne-Elise spat.

"You know what I mean. The dust storms out West and the blackouts that they cause to *certain* parts of the grid."

"It's a problem, yes, but 'energy crisis' is hyperbolic. Of course, I'm sure that's his point: call it a crisis to demonize clean power."

"It is a rather good proposal," Chelsea cut in before they could fight. "I think even you will like it. It will benefit you."

Anne-Elise's hackles were instantly up. "I'll decide that for myself. Whatever Gilbertson is up to, he did it without soliciting any comment or discussion from my lab. I'm the Director, so I would know. No one from his office approached us. And that suggests to me that whatever he is doing, it *won't* help Intensity Labs, and will probably have the opposite effect. By deliberate intention, at that."

"My friends are organizing against Gilbertson's bill," Vera put in.

"I think you should keep your powder dry for another fight," Edward advised. "This has to be just a performative stunt by Gilbertson. Unless he's working with Phillips to get something they both support—which I assume he isn't, since there's been nothing in the news about it—this is just a messaging bill for his base. You shouldn't waste your time on that."

"I'm not inclined to take advice from a *hurricane scientist* who insists on flying a *personal aircraft*. If even *you* refuse to modify your behavior when *you know* the problem is real, why should activists take your advice about tactics? Even the so-called experts aren't taking it seriously!"

"The last time your friends 'organized' anything, it consisted of screaming at commuters and marauding around city parks with spray paint," Anne-Elise said. "That's what people remember about it: what *you* did rather than whatever you were protesting."

"And I assure you the bill is quite real," Chelsea said. "Even if Phillips does veto it, a future administration could take one up with the same text."

"Are you not going to explain what this bill *does*?" Anne-Elise snapped.

Richard cut in again. "He'll explain it on *Attack Dog* better than anyone."

"I thought *you* were his press secretary and could answer questions about his work. Guess not."

"Sister," Chelsea began.

Oh, you're playing that card now? Anne-Elise thought grumpily.

"We don't usually have the opportunity to do anything as a family. Vera doesn't want to visit us at our house—"

"Because I am a grown woman, but *he* insists on ordering me about as if I'm a child whenever I am there—" Vera began.

"My house, my rules," Richard cut in.

"Nonetheless," Chelsea needled, "your house is something of a neutral zone, sister—and Edward is staying with you anyway—and it's the closest of all our homes to the restaurant. Your house, your rules, as my husband said. I just wanted us to have some time together. I know we... don't all share political views... but perhaps in *your* house, we could have a normal, healthy discussion."

Anne-Elise eyed them. "Fine. Since, according to you, I control the DMZ, we'll have a ceasefire and negotiations there. But 'my house, my rules,' as you and your husband said. Remember that, because I certainly will."

She threw her fork on her now-empty plate. Indifferent to the expected behavioral code in the restaurant—after all, the entire conversation had been a verbal war—she waved her hand for a waiter to return to present them with their checks. She had had more than enough of her sister, brother-in-law, and even their daughter for one night.

But unfortunately, the night was just beginning. They

would all decamp to Anne-Elise's townhouse afterward to watch a show that three of them despised.

Richard Mellor was not a person who withdrew from a fight, so Anne-Elise had fully expected him to continue arguing with her. When he instead remained silent, she could not help but glance at him to find out why.

He was staring at his plate, which was empty of everything except vegetable juice and extra sauce. His face was curdled in disgust. "There's a *bug* in my food!" he exclaimed.

Chelsea peered over, trying to comfort him as he stifled a gag. "It's all right," she soothed. "It probably was just flying around and happened to land there after you were finished. I doubt there are bugs in the kitchen."

"This is a good restaurant! Insects—"

"Even the best restaurants have doors to the outside."

Anne-Elise felt a momentary pang of disappointment for the gnat that hadn't made it after all, but the hilarity of the situation was too much. She laughed, not even trying to stifle the chuckles.

Her male-chauvinist brother-in-law, who fancied himself the manliest of men, was turning green at the sight of the tiniest dead insect in food that he had not even consumed.

And it was, after all, only a gnat, and it had been too intoxicated with the scent of food that was inconceivably luxurious to an insect and too stupid to avoid drowning in an attempt to gorge itself. *On a creep's dinner plate in a Florida restaurant is an entire Greek tragicomedy,* Anne-Elise thought. *And next up is disintegration in the dishwasher.*

Yes, that was funny.

Chapter 3: Mad Chad or Whatever

The ride to Anne-Elise's townhouse was too long for even the most dedicated carbon-emission purist, which Vera Mellor liked to pretend to be when it suited her, to make with just pedal power. But when faced with the choice of riding in her parents' vehicle or that of her aunt, she reluctantly loaded her bike onto Anne-Elise's SUV's rack and got into the backseat, scowling visibly in the rear-view mirror as she stared at some app on her phone.

Without a word, Anne-Elise left the parking lot and drove toward her house. *Why am I doing this?* she asked herself as the city lights flashed by. *If Chelsea and her vile husband want to watch that show, they should be forced to do it in their own place.*

Her niece was resolutely silent, and Edward also looked sour at the prospect. She sighed. Vera annoyed her, but at least in this, all three of them would presumably be on the same page. *They can impose themselves in my home tonight, but they'll pay for it,* she vowed. *They'll regret it. This is a passive-aggressive act by Richard Mellor, but I know a thing or two about passive-aggressiveness myself. They can watch his damn boss on that damn show, but if they do it in my house, they won't get to do it in peace.*

They arrived at the townhouse and filed inside. Anne-Elise had furnished it stylishly in Mid-Century Modern Centennial Revival style. *Sci-fi glam with a hint of nuclear apocalypse a century ago,* she thought as the reproduction Space Age lights turned on to reveal a living room in gold, chrome, shiny black, off-white, navy blue, and turquoise. *Now it's sci-fi glam with a hint of climate apocalypse.*

"Damnia, TV on," she called out. The flatscreen on the wall flashed on as the AI assistant complied. Edward stifled a laugh.

"Why did you rename your assistant that?" Chelsea disapproved.

"My house, my rules," Anne-Elise replied pointedly. The truth was, she had told Omnia—the name for the most ubiquitous brand of voice assistant these days—to answer to the mildly profane name just today, for the sole purpose of annoying her relatives. But they didn't need to know.

Richard scowled as he sat down on the sofa next to his wife. "Childish."

"Damnia," Anne-Elise said, ignoring him, "stream the most recent episode of *Attack Dog*."

"Understood. *Attack Dog with Mad Dog Chadleigh* will begin after advertisements from sponsors."

"Oh—and don't save this in the algorithm. I don't like this stupid show, but my relatives want to see it."

"Understood," the renamed AI said personably. "I won't use the stupid show for recommendations because it is a gift for stupid relatives."

Edward burst out laughing, and even Vera cracked a smile as her parents became red-faced and huffed with indignation.

"Is that what you've told it we are?" Chelsea exclaimed.

"Nope. It deduced that itself, it would seem."

"Shouldn't be allowed to use AI this way," Richard muttered.

"My house, my rules. And who's going to stop me?" she challenged. "Your unrequited crush, Hal Gilbertson?"

He ignored that. "What you teach it goes into the cloud."

"What I teach it affects what it presents to *me*, not anyone else."

"I do know that's what they *claim*," he said darkly, "but I don't believe it."

Chelsea interrupted them before they could argue further. "Look," she said, pointing at the television. "That might be a fun vacation idea. Very different from Florida!"

An advertisement for "Northwest Passage Luxury Cruises" was streaming. Frank Sinatra's version of "Fly Me to the Moon" played in the background. Happy, smiling cruise-goers laughed, danced, and raised drinks as the ship passed by picturesque, but disturbingly green, Arctic shores and islands. Skaters flew gracefully across the ice on the ship's indoor rink. Affectionate couples and happy children threw snowballs in "North Pole Park," the ship's snow machine generating a steady flow of the white stuff—the only snow in sight. A Santa Claus actor put in a "surprise" appearance to a group of delighted children playing in the artificial snow. Finally, as the camera cut back to a view of the ship sailing down the Alaskan coast, an AI-generated polar bear emerged onshore to flashing cameras and waved a paw at the ship to close out the cheery ad.

"That was obviously not real," Chelsea said, oblivious to the appalled looks on the faces of her daughter and siblings, "but I *have* heard that it's easier to see polar bears than it used to be."

"They've been driven onto land because of ice melt," Anne-Elise said. "It's not a good thing."

"But from the safe distance of a cruise ship, the danger would be nonexistent."

"I meant for the bears," she replied in withering tones.

"Well, I think humans are more important," Chelsea said piously.

But before they could carry the argument further, the ad break ended and the show itself began streaming.

A hard drumbeat punctuated by the snarls and growls of dogs began. The camera angle shifted, momentarily settling on the bright multicolored spotlights, before panning down to a stage. Between two leather chairs stood a life-size painted model of a bulldog and a wooden doghouse. Wood-slat fencing and a "BEWARE OF DOG" sign bounded the back wall.

Then, to the thunderous applause of either a real audience or a computer-generated one, Madison Chadleigh himself pranced onstage. A clean-shaven white man in his thirties with curly brown locks, he almost always wore a navy blue suit and a red tie for his show, and tonight was no exception. He was clearly hamming it up for the camera and enjoying every second of his introduction, but he still clenched his fists and teeth in affected rage.

"Mad Dog, indeed," Anne-Elise muttered in derision as this effete man sat down in the first chair.

The host faced the cameras, his hairless face twisting in fury—whether real or acted was unclear to Anne-Elise. "Welcome to *Attack Dog!* The watchdog, the guard dog, of real America!" He raised his clenched fists.

The cheers sounded. In Anne-Elise's living room, three people rolled their eyes and two gazed on in rapture.

"Friends," Chadleigh barked, "we have a very special guest tonight—yes, we do"—more cheering at these words—"but before we talk to him, I have to get something off my chest!"

The camera cut to a video montage of sweaty, muscular, brawny men of all different hues and ethnicities laboring away as an instrumental performance of the national anthem played. Waves splashed and the sun bore down on an offshore oil rig, as shirtless men worked the machinery and chattered genially to each other, their voices inaudible. Then the montage cut to an oil field in what appeared to be Alaska. The men wore flannels and jeans now, but they looked similar to the previous set.

In fact, I think some of them are identical, Anne-Elise thought cynically. *AI-generated footage, no doubt.*

The montage then switched to a coal mine, which was lit up brightly by workers' helmet lamps and glaring LEDs mounted in the mines. They used obsolete manual picks, which confirmed to Anne-Elise that it was not real footage. But the men were the same: rugged, handsome, and perfectly fit.

Then it switched to a natural gas plant, flames shooting into the sky as the camera angle swooped down to men working the equipment. More sweat beads, more rolled-up sleeves, more handsome beefcakes.

"How very homoerotic," Anne-Elise remarked as the montage concluded with a waving American flag. "Is Mad Chad going to make a special personal announcement tonight before bringing on Gilbertson?" She cast a malicious gaze at Richard. "I'm afraid you may have competition."

Edward laughed. Richard flushed red in anger, sputtering as he tried to think of a reply.

Vera, however, beat him to it. Frowning deeply and humorlessly, she scowled at her aunt. "I really had hoped that *our* side had moved past using queerness to mock our political opponents."

"Oh, lighten up," Edward said. "Your aunt has nothing against gay people, and you can't deny that that's an awful lot of sweaty, beefy men."

"Hush, all of you," Chelsea said authoritatively as the show continued. "He's going to explain it!"

The camera had switched back to the *Attack Dog* studio, where Chadleigh glowered. "That," he practically shouted, "is the heart and soul of America! Red-blooded American men, of every race and color, toiling in field, factory, and mine! The satisfaction of useful manual labor! These men can go home to their wives every night knowing that their work powers this great country. When they turn on the living room lamp, they can know that it was *their own hands* that made this possible!"

The crowd erupted, and with that brief lull, Anne-Elise could not stop herself. "Actually," she said in acid tones, "I think that when *those* men 'go home,' it's with a program command of 'return' or 'exit.'"

Edward laughed again. "Yeah, I thought some of the faces looked awfully similar."

"He is making a rhetorical point," Richard said pedantically.

"Do you deny that it is AI video?" Anne-Elise challenged.

"I mean... I'm sure it is... but the point stands!"

"No, it doesn't," she disagreed. "If he has to use AI to get that footage, it means he can't get *real* footage showing that stuff. Which means that America has changed and moved on!"

The applause subsided on the show, so she fell silent as Chadleigh continued his harangue. "But now," he snarled, "there are people who want to send these real, red-blooded American men—"

Anne-Elise snorted.

"—to the misery of unemployment! To turn those muscles into flab, to shorten those lifespans by decades from diabetes, drug use, alcoholism, and even suicide." He paused as the audience booed. "It sounds like a comic-book villain, doesn't it? What kind of evil mastermind would want to destroy healthy, fit men in the prime of life?"

On TV, a projection appeared next to Chadleigh as if he were a news anchor: a comic book cover depicting a buff, impossibly fit Captain America fighting against a malevolent Dr. Zola. The audience laughed—or a laugh track played; it was impossible to tell which it was.

Chadleigh's signature scowl was gone, replaced by a jovial chuckle. At this point, Anne-Elise realized why he had any appeal: He mixed anger and humor.

"Yes, point taken," Chadleigh said, pretending to speak to an offstage crew. "But sometimes reality mirrors fiction—and this is one of those times!" The scowl was back as he clenched his fist again and pounded it on the right armrest of his chair. "The evil masterminds who want to destroy hardworking American men *are* just like that—trembling stick figures in lab coats, who glow green by the light of their screens!"

Anne-Elise's own scowl returned too. "Ah yes, the scientists are the bad guys. I should've known."

"These people think that they're smarter than the working man. And you know?" Chadleigh asked rhetorically. "Maybe they are. Maybe, because they have degrees from such-and-such *Institute of Technology*, because they have three special letters behind their name, maybe they *are* high IQ. But there are things that no 'Tech' Ph. D. can provide. If you spend your life in a lab, you turn into a glow-in-the-dark night-crawler."

The projection next to Chadleigh depicted a glowing whitish-green lizard-person crawling on all fours, to audience laughter. Anne-Elise scowled. *Yes, I do see why this man has viewers.*

Chadleigh chuckled, shaking his head. "Oh no, now our

opponents are going to say that nobody is *actually* a lizard-person, and they'll dismiss everything I say because of that image," he pretended to scold his audio-video crew, even though the entire scene was obviously choreographed for comedy. The audience—or track—applauded. "Back to the point!" The projection vanished. "When people turn into *figurative* night-crawlers, rather than interacting with *real* people like those men in the clip you just saw—"

Anne-Elise and Edward rolled their eyes.

"—they get detached from humanity! My friends," he demagogued, "we have two major human crises in America today: a crisis of masculinity and a crisis of solitude. They feed each other. People living their lives isolated from each other, their eyes adapted to Dark Mode, their brains wired for screen-scrolling rather than fellowship with other human beings."

"You can't really disagree with him about that," Chelsea said to her siblings. She narrowed her eyes at Vera, who was pointedly ignoring the show, glued to her phone, lips pursed.

Anne-Elise had been thinking something similar: that, however much she derided his focus on *men* in this harangue, he did have a decent point about social alienation and technology. *That,* she thought, *is another reason he's so dangerous. He says a few things that aren't crazy. Like a horoscope, he's right occasionally, so people focus on the anthill he gets right while ignoring the mountain that he gets wrong.*

Chadleigh continued. "The tech lifestyle turns men away from their natural urges to use their hands, to see the physical fruits of their labors... to find good wives and start beautiful families. These things are what men *naturally* are driven to do. The physical!" He pounded his armrests. "The *real*! When they're denied that, even if they don't even know that they need it, even if they think they *don't* need it, it shrivels their manhood—and not just metaphorically!"

Anne-Elise sighed. "'Looking at computers shrivels your balls.' He goes from something somewhat reasonable to a ridiculous conspiracy theory."

"I wouldn't be so sure," Richard objected. "I've heard that radio waves from our devices are—"

"They're not shrinking our gonads, Richard," Edward said with a roll of his eyes.

"But if all this radiation gets into our cells, how could it not do something? X-rays, nuclear radiation, UV rays—even microwave radiation."

"But not the whole electromagnetic spectrum," Anne-Elise said. "Edward and I know about this, Richard. He's a meteorologist and I'm a nuclear physicist. Longwave is safe."

"Hush," Chelsea said again, pointing to the screen. "You're missing it!"

Chadleigh was still ranting about solitude and masculinity. "If a man and a woman meet in high school or college, or church, and they want to get married in their twenties and start a family, with their own biological children, conceived by sexual intercourse, they're seen as *freaks!*"

"What the—" Edward began laughing.

"The night-crawlers would have everyone meeting by screen when they're too old to conceive healthy children. Old, damaged eggs and low sperm counts. So what's the solution that the night-crawlers offer? More technology. Devices, injections, stab stab stab right in the gonads to get those cells out, mess with them, stick them back in. Or, if that doesn't work, they tell you to reject your own genes, to end your biological line, and take in a stranger's child while pretending it's your own."

What a way to describe adoption, Anne-Elise thought. But her sister was gazing at the screen as if she agreed with every word.

"That's the norm now!" Chadleigh ranted. "That's what they expect of everyone. And those who break with it and follow nature, who become husbands and wives, mothers and fathers, the natural way, are seen as antisocial freaks."

"Okay," Edward said, turning to his relatives, "who let him take LSD and then read *Brave New World*? Because none of this is true." He smirked wryly. "I have two ex-wives, both of whom I met in person, to back me up. And working on getting number three, also in person."

Anne-Elise had been amused at his comment about *Brave New World*, but the smile faded when he alluded to his young colleague.

"And those young people who don't get sucked into the void of the screen?" Chadleigh continued. "They have to live in the world amid those who do, adrift, feeling lost. When this world is *theirs* by nature. It is!" he exclaimed, thumping his chair again. "It's meant for *humans*, not glow-in-the-dark night-crawlers."

"This is dehumanizing," Anne-Elise said.

"These people like their numbers, their screens, their *theories* better than they like people, when it comes down to it," Chadleigh continued. "They're *anti*-human. So when they destroy the physical, the manual, the real-life interactions, it's serving their goal of destroying *us*."

The audience—or the recording—booed.

Chadleigh paused, a faint smile forming on his face. "But all is not lost. There are leaders who are trying to stop this agenda, in all its forms. And that brings me to our guest tonight—to speak with us about energy, Speaker of the House Hal Gilbertson!"

The Speaker, Florida Representative Gilbertson, walked onstage to thunderous applause. He was a Hispanic-heritage white man of age sixty-two, bearing a faint stubble and thick salt-and-pepper hair. He winked and smiled asymmetrically as he strode across the stage, raising one hand in a two-fingered "V for victory" gesture. Chadleigh rose from his chair to greet him. They shook hands like old friends, and Gilbertson sat down in the other chair on the opposite side of the bulldog and doghouse.

"Speaker, it's an honor to have you here again," Chadleigh said.

"It's an honor to *be* here again. I always like coming on *Attack Dog*."

"I understand you have a bill in the works that'll try to

save physical sources of American energy and the good jobs they provide."

"Yes," Gilbertson said, smiling a glittery white smile. "We're going to cut federal subsidies for unproven energy sources and increase them for tried-and-true ones."

"Unproven, meaning—in the context of your bill—"

"Well, we thought about requiring twenty years of no blackouts, no accidents—but that kind of requirement could have unintended, harmful collateral damage, you understand."

Chadleigh nodded.

"You mean it would hit fossil fuels if you required 'no accidents,'" Anne-Elise muttered.

"So the bill provides for an independent panel to periodically assess the reliability and safety of each possible energy firm," Gilbertson said. "The panel would have a 'viewpoint balance' requirement so that the climate lobby couldn't sabotage it with ideologues." He chuckled. "Just like the evil mastermind night-crawlers you were just talking about!"

Chadleigh shook his head in denial. "Oh no, Speaker, it's as I said—we mustn't talk about that, because our opponents will say we're claiming that lizard-people exist."

"Oh, of course, you're right," Gilbertson agreed with a wink.

"I'll have to have a talk with my A/V crew about it. We'd better make sure to stick strictly to cold, dry facts that nobody can dispute, since our opponents have no sense of humor!"

The audience, or recording, laughed.

"You're right, sir; you're quite right," Gilbertson agreed sycophantically. "But for my bill, I won't let... *figurative* night-crawlers... slither their way in!"

They continued their interview, Gilbertson agreeing with Chadleigh's assertions about masculinity. Anne-Elise stopped paying attention at this point. She turned instead to her relatives, indignant.

"This is what you thought would be a good bill that would

benefit me?" she charged her sister and brother-in-law.

Richard bristled. "To the best of my knowledge, Intensity doesn't receive direct federal funding. It comes from private endowments and the academic sector. There may be federal funding for the universities, but it's not direct to your lab."

"That's right." Anne-Elise's voice was taut.

"So you have to compete with companies that *do* get direct federal subsidies."

She glared at him. "Is this the spin Gilbertson gave you to tell me? It sounds like it. 'Tell her this to avoid a fracture to the family,' no doubt." She scoffed. "You are uninformed. Intensity isn't marketing its power. We're *research* still. We're not *competing* in the private sector. Yet." She raised her eyebrows at him and Chelsea. "When we achieve net-positive power generation, then we will start that transition. And we don't think we'll need government subsidy to compete."

"Then the Speaker's bill doesn't affect you at all," Richard said triumphantly. "So why are you getting hysterical about it?"

Anne-Elise tamped down her profound irritation at this man, whom she knew to be a male chauvinist, patronizing her like this. She was a nuclear physicist with a Ph. D., damn it!

She swallowed her ire in her response. "He is going after green power as a matter of ideology," she said. "He isn't trying to make the market 'fair to all' or help innovative research by reducing government payoffs to existing market players. He's doing it because he wants to help fossil fuels. We all know it. And fossil fuel companies *are* my foe."

"They are merely a source of energy. If your cold fusion—"

"It's not cold fusion," she interrupted. "That is a pie-in-the-sky dream. We are working on the only *proven* kind of fusion, *hot* fusion, because we're *realists.*"

Richard continued. "Whatever you're doing, if it gets on the market someday, some people will still want to stick with what they know and trust, what's been used for two hundred years now. A lot of people are frightened of nuclear power. Your market base will be different. Different customers. Fossil fuels aren't a threat to you."

"They are lobbying politicians like Gilbertson to use the government, the power of the state, to crush their competition," she replied tartly. "And those elected officials do it, not for the money—maybe that used to be the case, but it's not anymore—but because they want to stick it to people they dislike. It's not about being bought off. Not anymore. Now everything is about sticking it to the people a politician's base disapproves of." She scowled. "It was actually more hopeful when it *was* about money and bribery, because a better offer could flip them."

"That is breathtakingly cynical," Chelsea said disapprovingly. "You don't think it is better that politicians fight for what they believe in? Even if you don't share that belief?"

"No, in this case, I do not," Anne-Elise replied. "And that's what Gilbertson is doing. He's throwing red meat to his base, which thinks climate science is bunk. And so does he. That's why he's doing this."

"We have a difference of opinion," Richard said coldly. "And since I know him and you do not, you should defer to me."

Anne-Elise barked a cutting laugh. "But you don't have to defer to me about my knowledge of the clean power sector? Or even my knowledge of *what we do at my own workplace?*"

Richard ignored this.

Edward interceded at once, turning to his niece. "You've been silent throughout this discussion," he said to Vera. "You can't approve either."

Vera scowled as well. "I do not. But I also don't think nuclear power should be subsidized. We should stick to solar and wind."

"They aren't going to be sufficient," Anne-Elise said. "Wind is not viable in the Southeast, and solar doesn't scale well in a lot of regions. It's fine for individual houses, but it's hard to mass-produce."

Vera looked outraged. "The single-family house is an

environmental disaster! Dense housing is clean housing. But American suburbanites like their big yards and huge mansions—"

"How are you going to scale up solar collection if everyone is packed into human beehives?" Anne-Elise challenged.

"Rooftop solar panels take in far more energy than the house actually requires...." Vera trailed off reciting her activist talking points, realizing something. Her face fell.

Anne-Elise pounced. "That is true if they are providing power for a single household. If they're mounted on a high-rise condo building, the power needs are hundreds of times greater, aren't they?"

"But then a lot of open country is freed up for massive solar farms...."

"So you're going to deforest the East?"

"The Plains and desert West have enough space to power the country with solar and wind...."

"And if anything goes wrong at one of the source farms, like a dust storm or a fire, every part of the grid depending on that site is blacked out. We've been seeing this all summer. We need reliable *locally generated* sources, and a source that isn't subject to the vagaries of weather. Nuclear is a necessary piece in the clean-energy puzzle, and once we get fusion, there won't even be the issue of radioactive waste disposal."

Richard cut in, scoffing. "This is irrelevant. Harry Phillips is going to lose—all these dust storms and fires have happened on *his* watch—"

"So you think he's responsible for the weather?" Edward exclaimed in derision. "We made our bed decades ago—we put the charges on the climatic credit card, and now the bill is due—"

"It doesn't matter! He's going to *lose* next year. He looks like a flabby wimp on camera. His much-vaunted veto pen won't be an obstacle then." He leaned in aggressively. "The Speaker's bill *is* going to become law, so you'd better figure out a way to live with it!"

42

"What date is it? Did I fall into a coma for a year while the next election occurred without my vote?" Anne-Elise said with heavy sarcasm. "I wasn't aware that Gilbertson had already been anointed as a nominee, let alone an election winner."

"Primary season is already underway, and he's leading in the polls. Either he or Jim Barnett Hale is likely to be *your* next president, and given that choice, you would do better with Gilbertson."

"I'm not sure I would. Hale is an ignorant buffoon, but he doesn't have it in for green power like Gilbertson does. I'm sure he *prefers* fossil fuels, but he hasn't used the governorship of Texas to throttle alternative energy."

"Hale is crazy. You can tell by how he looks. Going around cosplaying in that cowboy hat and spurs and pretending he's some Old West badass. It's pathetic. You saw Gilbertson. He's a reasonable man, a photogenic man. Even if you disagree with him, you have to see that."

"He's good at *looking* reasonable and photogenic, but so is Mad Chad."

"Mad *Dog*."

Anne-Elise continued as he had not interrupted. "And that's what makes him so dangerous! Hale is a joke. I disagree with most of his policies, but he seems less likely to me to *specifically target* my job with state power."

"Hale is a lunatic. He ordered a state investigation into the public schools' Gay-Straight Alliances on the basis of a conspiracy theory about child molestation."

Seeing an opening to pivot to another argument, Anne-Elise leaned in pointedly and gave Richard a look. "Yes, he did, and yes, that's a lunatic thing to do. And why did he do it? *The Attack Dog show.* Its illustrious host, Mr. Madison Chadleigh, spread the rumor that there were older gay teens sexually abusing underage boys in those clubs."

"He didn't spread the rumor," Richard objected. "He mentioned that the rumor *existed* and that he wasn't taking a position on its truthfulness."

"He did it that way to avoid being sued for libel. What millions of people watching his show heard was that teenagers were having gay molestation orgies in the schoolroom. Which is exactly what he intended his viewers to hear. His little wink-wink tonight about the 'lizard-people' image is the same thing. He does this, it seems. Insinuates something and then backs off, wink-wink. But my point is, *that* is why Jim Hale wasted taxpayer resources on that stupidity: Mr. Madison Chadleigh."

"I suppose there is some point you're trying to make by saying his full name?"

"She thinks it's a 'gay' name," Vera cut in, oblivious to the fact that she was siding with her far-right father over her aunt. "That's her 'point'!"

"Apparently *he* thinks it's a 'gay' name, since he doesn't go by his actual name onscreen," Anne-Elise countered. "Take it up with him! Unless, of course, it's easier to go after me instead," she added pointedly.

"This is silly," Richard said. "The point is, Hale is a credulous fool and a cowboy-cosplaying peacock. Speaker Gilbertson has gravitas."

"What if I said that I don't think gravitas is a positive in this choice? In my view, Gilbertson is every bit as suggestible as Hale. He's just better at hiding it." She leaned forward aggressively. "And as to your original comment, that I would 'do better' with your boss—no, I wouldn't. Hale is a performative idiot. Gilbertson is a true believer, and his beliefs would harm my profession and field."

"Hmph," Richard huffed. "Well, he's leading in the polls. You'd better make peace with him."

Chapter 4: Generation Climate Catastrophe

Vera Mellor did not like her surname—or, more to the point, she did not like bearing the surname of her far-right parents. But she also did not want to take her mother's maiden name. *My aunt and uncle on the Kirby side think they're not like my mom and dad,* she thought, *and I suppose that's technically true... but that does not mean that they are better. They like their personal comforts and privilege too much to want to do the real work, make the real sacrifices, that activism requires.*

My uncle is a hurricane scientist, but he won't even give up that airplane. My aunt likes being a lab director too much to advocate for truly clean energy. And that's just one issue. They don't care a bit, either one of them, about other causes. My aunt even insults right-wingers by queerphobic insinuations.

Vera had decided some time ago that, with neither "Mellor" nor "Kirby" as an acceptable surname, she would be better off inventing her own. She had unofficially changed her surname a couple of times already, but currently she was going by the name Vera Hope.

Her driver's license and official documents still contained the name Mellor. She had not gone to court to have her name changed. She wanted to be sure that this was the name she wanted to keep. But all her friends knew to use it.

Her family, of course, did not.

She had to admit that her aunt and uncle didn't know about it. But her parents did know, and they pointedly refused to use it.

I wonder sometimes why I even continue to participate in family events, she thought that evening. *They are horrible people. But I suppose there is value in knowing what the enemy thinks. I have an inside track on what Hal Gilbertson is doing, with my fa—with Richard Mellor in the position he's in, and I should use my privilege for the greater good. Richard Mellor's money, paid to him for supporting Hal Gilbertson—and, before that, various right-wing think tanks—paid for all of my expenses as a child and even in college. I should try to make amends. I*

*should use the information Richard Mellor insists that I hear in
order to undermine him and his employer.*

These were the justifications passing through her mind as
she waited for her ride back to the house in which her
polycule lived. They were her found family, her *real* family,
regardless of what her fa—what Richard Mellor had to say, in
that patronizing, authoritarian tone of his. The house had
been too far for her to ride on her bike, but Mike was driving
here to pick her up.

The SUV stopped on the narrow street, idling as Mike
parallel-parked. Vera eagerly loaded her bike onto the rack
and got into the vehicle. Inside were the other three
members of the polycule: Channing, a basic white girl like
Vera humbly acknowledged herself to be; Butterfly, a
nonbinary femme; and Sohrab, a white atheist Muslim
convert. They all greeted her as a smile broke over her face
and she crowded herself in.

When Vera had first met Sohrab, she had wondered how
someone could be both a convert to Islam and an atheist. She
understood the concept of being "culturally" of a specific
religion—raised in that faith—but leaving it behind while
retaining some of the cultural markers or holiday
observances. But Sohrab had been raised a plain American
white guy named Bradley Nelson. He had, like Vera and
Butterfly, changed his name. He did read parts of the Quran;
she had seen him streaming live to his social-media followers
as he did so, but he never entered a mosque, and he was very
insistent that he did not believe in the existence of Allah and
remained an atheist while also being a Muslim.

It didn't make logical sense to Vera, even to this day.
Every now and then, the unkind, privileged thought surfaced
that *Sohrab wants to claim the label "Muslim" without having
to do anything Muslim,* but she always tried to tamp that
down, scolding herself that it was not for her to question his
self-definition of his identity.

Channing elbowed her, a wry grin on her face. "Do we
have to scrub you down when we get back to the house?" she

teased. The rest of her friends laughed.

Vera grimaced, laughing along with them. "I do feel that I should take a bath," she said. "But it's psychological dirtiness rather than physical!"

They fell silent then, contemplating the city. Channing drew her phone out of her Chloé bag and began scrolling. Vera considered for a moment before doing the same.

Their eyes glazed over at once, and while the feelings of outrage and indignation at social media news flared up in their brains like fireflies illuminating their abdomens in spring, the *causes* of their outrage disappeared from their short-term memories almost as soon as a firefly's bioluminescence, leaving behind only the unfocused anger itself. Her fingers smearing the screen with each swipe, Vera knew that she *was* angry, but it was hard to recall exactly why. *The volume of outrage is so great, it's hard to focus on one thing*, she thought. *The problem is the entire system. It needs to be dismantled to the very foundation.* Yes, that had to be the reason she couldn't focus. She continued scrolling, reading single-sentence calls to action and indignant headlines in rapid fire, forgetting everything that she had seen thirty seconds before except for the most egregious ones—or the most clickbait ones.

Finally Mike turned the SUV down the last street. The house was a three-bedroom single-family residence in a cul-de-sac. Mike, as the most well-to-do of the polycule, held the mortgage, a gift from his parents when he had graduated from college, and the rest of them paid rent to him. He parked and they all got out of the SUV.

God, it was muggy. Vera was accustomed to heat and humidity as a native Floridian, but this record heat wave was something else. It should not be ninety degrees at ten o'clock at night, but her phone told her that it was, and she had no difficulty believing it.

Vera stumbled over a crack, focused on her phone, only for Butterfly to catch her. As she righted herself, her gaze caught the roof of the left-side neighbor's house and the solar array mounted on it. Her lips thinned as she recalled the conversation she'd had with her relatives.

"Mike," she said as he unlocked the front door, "shouldn't we look into setting up solar panels at last?"

He hurried his friends inside, trying to avoid letting mosquitoes in as well, then shut and locked the door. "If we spend money on an array, that's money we won't have for other things."

"Yes," Sohrab chimed in, "we have to determine how we can do the most good for the most people with our money."

"The *most* effective altruism," Butterfly added, smiling.

"And if we put money toward a solar array, it'll help our carbon footprint, but *our* carbon footprint is barely anything compared to the effect of fossil-fuel power production," Mike continued. "It's a drop in the bucket. Putting up solar would make *us* feel better, but that's all it'd do."

Vera nodded. This argument made perfect sense to her.

"I think we would do better to spend the money on a big protest," Channing said. "Let's protest Gilbertson's bill. That's why you wanted to see the Mellors, wasn't it? To learn about that?"

"Yes," Vera said. She sat down on a sofa and sighed, realizing that she needed to charge her phone. At least the side table had a USB outlet. She hooked it up, hoping it would charge fast so that she could quickly get back to reading her feed. Something might happen—indeed, something undoubtedly *would* happen—and she might not learn about it until it was too late to do anything.

"Well, let's arrange something," Mike said.

"A major climate action day," Butterfly said. "We'll work our way around town until we reach Gilbertson's Tallahassee office."

"Actually, let's make it more than just us five. Let's make it everyone in GCCF," Mike said, naming a local activist group of which they were all members. "We'll plan our attack as one!"

"Sounds like a plan," Vera agreed.

*   *   *

It didn't take long to organize the protest, which was scheduled for the thirty-first: the day after the next. Generation Climate Catastrophe Florida was a self-organized nonprofit with a total of fifteen members, five of whom already wanted to protest. There was no official leadership —"*we're an anarchist collective, not a hierarchical structure*," Mike always insisted—but the members rapidly agreed to hold a roving protest. They spent the preparation day purchasing supplies and making their plans for where to go, what posters to hold up at each site, what other methods of protest to employ at certain places, and how to get media attention.

Butterfly—who had chosen that name partly to reference a caterpillar's transformation, but also to evoke the phrase "social butterfly"—decided to spread word on social media throughout the day. In addition, Mike had ideas for how to *ensure* that people took notice. As they all gathered in the house the evening of August 30 to finalize their plans, he explained.

"They ought to take notice when we block traffic on Highway 90," he said. "And if they don't, they will when we hit the university campus!"

Butterfly grinned and leaped gracelessly in the air, landing with a hard thud. "They should certainly take notice of *me!*"

She—no, Vera scolded herself fiercely, *they*—had decided to become the symbol of the protest, wearing a set of monarch butterfly wings attached to their back. It had been a little expensive to have the wings delivered by same-day drone service from a warehouse, and the other GCCF members expressed concern about the carbon footprint of such a means of acquisition. But the alternatives, Butterfly sadly assured them, had been to drive around Tallahassee looking for an off-the-shelf costume piece or the supplies to make one. And then, unfortunately, Butterfly would have spent their time cutting, sewing, and applying orange, silver, and black glitter rather than doing important public-outreach work on social media all day.

The glitter itself was a concern for many people in the group. Microplastics had a detrimental effect on health—both animal and human—and the environment. Surely Butterfly would drop pieces of glitter everywhere that GCCF took their protest on foot? But sh—they said that the glittery wings would be much more eye-catching than wings made with plain fabric. They reassured GCCF that they would lacquer the glitter down firmly. That had now been done. The wings were damp and smelly, but they should be dry by the following day. Whether the scent would vanish was another question.

Channing wrinkled her nose. "Those wings reek, Butterfly," she said. "I hope they don't smell like that tomorrow. If it were winter, that would be one thing, but in this heat and humidity, that'll be horrible."

"But I can't drop glitter everywhere."

"True, true. Well," she concluded stoutly, "we'll make it work."

Vera had a concern of her own, which had struck her when they had decided on a traffic halt.

"Some of the drivers will probably worry that they'll be fired for being late," she said hesitantly. As that occurred to her, she had a moment of doubt that this was truly the best thing to do. Then another dire concern struck her. "And some might need to get to the airport—"

"Let them miss a flight! Let them reflect on what airplane fuel does," Mike snapped.

"Fair enough," she conceded, recalling her disapproval of her uncle's plane. "But some might need to go to the hospital. Should we really do this? Maybe we should protest on the side of the highway instead."

Channing and Sohrab had also hesitated at this representation, an angle that had not occurred to them until now. But Mike, again, had the decisive argument.

"We need to do it this way. People will ignore us if we stick to the median and shoulders. They'll be driving too fast to even see our signs, probably, and if they are going slow enough, people just look away. They don't want to see. So we have to force them to look." He smiled patronizingly. "We'll get out of the way for an ambulance or a fire truck."

"Or police?" Channing suggested ingenuously.

"No. We don't move for cops. Unless they threaten to shoot us," Mike ruled. "But we'll clear out for an emergency vehicle."

Vera still was not fully satisfied. "But some people could be fired for being late... and it seems that they're disproportionately likely to be marginalized people...."

"If they're working for that kind of boss, they are propping up a bad system," Mike dismissed. "Someone who'll get fired from Walmart for being late one day should see it as an opportunity to find a job with a better employer. Our theme is anti-consumption and anti-capitalism, after all."

They accepted this, heads nodding in agreement—or acceptance.

Bzzzt! Mike picked up his phone. "Oh—Dad just sent us an additional two hundred dollars. Look." He showed the message to them, which depicted a dollar sign and a plant emoji. "'Green for green.' I get it."

"That's nice of him," Channing said. "We may need it if anyone gets arrested."

"Now let's all get some sleep," Sohrab urged. "There's a busy day ahead."

*   *   *

August 31.

Automobile horns, cursing drivers, and stereo systems turned up to maximum volume blasted through the air. The cacophonous din competed with the screams and shouts of Generation Climate Catastrophe Florida, whose members stood in the inbound lanes, spread out to fill the road and block all traffic on that side.

Some of the GCCF members held the line, unmoving, carrying orange traffic cones that they had picked up from a road construction work site nearby. These cones served the additional purpose of letting the human protesters meander through the stalled traffic to interact with drivers. Vera had worried about that; it was not at all unusual in Florida for people to carry guns in their vehicles. But Mike had a plan.

"Yeah," he said—or rather, shouted in order to be heard—to Vera as they carried their signs. He eyed a pickup truck's rear bumper, which bore a "Hal Gilbertson for President" sticker. "No point in talking to that one. And they're the ones most likely to pack heat."

"He's got his phone out, probably recording us," Butterfly said.

"Let him. The more exposure, the better."

As Mike had stated at the previous night's meeting, GCCF had settled on a theme of anti-consumption and anti-capitalism. They all had made signs with messages fitting this theme. Channing's read, "*Growth Is a Ponzi Scheme.*" Vera and Mike held up two that were meant to be two parts of a whole, so they had to march together. Mike's said "*Capitalism Caused the Problem*" and Vera's said "*It Can't Be the Solution!*"

She worried that the drivers would not immediately understand how this theme related to climate change, fixated on their personal concerns as they would be. Many people did not choose to see that *every* act of consumption, every form of participation in a predator economy, had a carbon footprint. They liked their expensive luxury items too much. Vera scowled at the sight of all the stopped vehicles, so many of them with only one person inside. It didn't even *occur* to them how unnecessary and harmful that was. Why didn't they carpool, commute by bike, or just move closer to their workplaces? *Nobody ever thinks that their consumption is excessive, unnecessary, and harmful,* she thought.

The day was as hot as every day for the past two months had been, and Vera was sweaty even though it was just morning rush hour. The plastic stake taped to the back of the poster slipped in her sweaty hand as she almost dropped it onto scalding asphalt. Passing the poster to Mike for a moment, Vera reached into her Balenciaga bag and took out a microfiber towel to dry her palms. It was monogrammed VM rather than VH. She frowned; she would have to get a new one soon to reflect her new name.

Butterfly sallied through the stopped traffic and furious drivers, wings flapping and fluttering, lacquered glitter sparkling in the sunlight. As Vera's gaze followed her friend's dance, she caught a glimpse of a car that inspired a solution for her conundrum. "Look," she said, fixing on this car: a hybrid sedan. "*That* one."

"Why that one?" Channing asked, confused.

Mike understood Vera's reasoning, though. "Because they want to make it *look* like they care while only going halfway," he sneered.

"And look at their bumper sticker," Vera agreed. "Imagining that they're doing enough!"

The car bore a weathered "Phillips/Romano '48" sticker, indicating the driver's support for the incumbent moderate Democratic president and vice president. Vera's gaze narrowed as they strode toward the vehicle.

"*Your car is killing the planet!*" she roared at the startled—and now enraged—driver.

The woman behind the wheel rolled down her window, glaring. "Why are you picking on *me*?" she roared. "I'm on your side!"

"Then prove it! Get an EV!" Mike shouted. "Or better yet, take the bus! Or get a bike! No more half measures!"

She blew her horn. "Go to hell!" Her window rolled back up.

They were unsure for a moment what to do—whether to tap on her window and continue to shout at her, or select another driver—when Butterfly danced up to them, wings swaying.

"The cops are en route," Butterfly reported. "I think we should clear out before they arrest us. We have a lot to do today."

Blue flashing lights appeared in the distance. "You're right," Mike said, stepping away from the hybrid.

"But I thought we weren't going to move for cops,"

Channing said.

"We weren't going to move out of their way if they were headed to harass someone else," he said. "But they're coming after *us*."

"Kick the traffic cones to the side," Sohrab called out to the GCCF members forming the line, "and let's all head out of here!"

"FSU campus is next!" Channing chortled as they piled into their SUVs.

*　　*　　*

Florida State University had a renowned meteorology department, which had for decades had a strong focus on tropical meteorology—an important aspect of Florida weather, to put it mildly. FSU graduates had a long history of supporting hurricane research and forecasting. As GCCF's three SUVs parked in a guest lot, Vera reflected on the fact that her own Uncle Edward was one such.

He forecasts hurricanes and does some sort of research into extreme ones, but I am doing more to actually help the climate, she thought smugly. And that thought gave her another idea.

"Let's get these students out here with us!" she called out, pointing at the sign identifying the meteorology department.

The others instantly took her meaning. Cheering and shouting in glee, they clustered together outside the building and held up their signs.

"*Out of the classroom, into the street!*" Mike shouted. It was a variation of a cry that another activist group had made when they had protested outside a scientific conference in Atlanta: "*Out of the lab, into the street!*" Mike and the others had been impressed enough to adopt it themselves.

From above, the blinds of several windows presumably in meteorology classrooms—fluttered open, and faces appeared briefly in these windows. Vera noticed several scowls on these faces, and, to her indignation, at least one person actually rolled their eyes. The blinds closed again.

How could students *studying the weather* not care? *For the same reason that my uncle keeps flying that plane,* Vera thought, *and I must remember that he isn't marching with us today either. They think that they're doing enough already. That and these students probably think their grades are more important than the future of this planet, so they won't leave the classroom to stand with us.*

Whatever the reason, this clearly called for heavier artillery. Vera liked the rhythm of Mike's cry, but they could do better. As she considered what to chant, it suddenly came to her with a brilliant stroke of inspiration.

"*Off your ass, on your feet!*" she called out between chants of Mike's cry. Her friends paused, realizing how well it would fit with just a very slight modification. "*Out of class, into the street!*"

They began stomping and clapping their hands—though this required staking their posters into the earth while they did so. Butterfly's wings flapped, the lacquer coat cracking now from the stress of repetitive motion and glitter flakes sprinkling to the grass. Several people who were passing through campus paused to stare at them as they stomped, clapped, and chanted. "*Off your ass, on your feet! Out of class, into the street!*"

They continued doing this for several more minutes, but no one emerged from the building to join them. Even the most enthusiastic, such as Butterfly, were becoming demoralized.

Mike was the first to stop the chant. He sighed, reaching down to uproot his poster from the ground. "We're wasting our time here. Nobody seems to care... or they're too scared to stand with us."

Vera sighed as the handful of students passing over the green gave them curious looks and—in the case of Butterfly—suppressed snickers. She wasn't quite as cynical as Mike, but she did wonder where everyone was. Why were they mostly hiding indoors? Surely not *everyone* had class... and there would always be some who skipped. It was a summer day... and... oh.

"Butterfly," Vera said suddenly, "when you were on social

yesterday, was there truly any interest in this?"

"I thought there was."

"Then I wonder what happened? Could it just be too hot and humid for anyone to get out and look?"

"Maybe. It *is* really gross. But that's all the more reason why people should *notice* us and *think* about what we're saying!"

"We may have left more of a mark than it seems," Sohrab put in. "We definitely left behind a memorable impression on the commuters. I bet they'll remember us and remember *why* we protested. And even here, we've made an impression."

"Yes, but I had hoped we would get interviews of some sort."

"I thought we *would*," Butterfly said. "Let me look at my phone... oh... oops. There were some podcasts and streaming shows that were interested in us, but they expected us to be at Gilbertson's office."

"Well, let's get over there, then!" Channing exclaimed impatiently.

"Wait," Butterfly continued, scrolling. "It says... Gilbertson has left."

"Left?" Vera said. "What do you mean?"

"He's flown up to his office in Washington, DC." Butterfly scowled. "He posted about it on his accounts. '*Back at the House and ready to do the People's work.*' Coward! This is because of *us*! He's afraid of us! Why else would he go?"

No one disputed this argument. All the other members of GCCF nodded their heads in agreement.

"Well," Mike finally said, "we'll just have to change our plans. We'll pick another site for our main protest."

They fell silent again as everyone considered where that should be. Someone suggested the city parks, and there was some momentary interest in this idea—until Vera suddenly had a better one occur to her.

"Let's go to my aunt's workplace," she said. "Intensity Labs Fusion Testbed."

"Ooooh," Butterfly agreed, wings shaking, "that's a good

idea!"

"Where is it?" Sohrab asked. "Aren't they university-affiliated?"

"Yes, but because they're a *nuclear* site, they aren't on campus." Vera smirked. "My aunt loves to boast about how 'safe' it is, but if it's so safe, why can't they do their work *here*?" She gestured around.

"There's probably a permitting requirement," Channing mumbled. Vera shot her a hard look, and she added at once, "But why would such a thing exist if there wasn't a good reason for it? You're right. The fact that it isn't on campus is evidence enough that it's too dangerous!"

"And we really shouldn't be spending money on unproven sources of power when we have two that we know work," Mike said, unknowingly echoing the very words of Hal Gilbertson's bill.

Channing nodded firmly. "Fusion is a *distraction.* It's a dream people have been chasing for *decades* when we have had two perfectly viable clean power sources before us all along. I agree: Let's go to this testbed!"

"Butterfly," Vera said, "let whatever media sources you've spoken to know about our change of plans, so that they can be ready for us there."

"Yes, ma'am!" Butterfly replied cheerfully.

*   *   *

Back in Mike's SUV, the five polycule members set down the signs that they had made for Hal Gilbertson's office and quickly scrambled new ones together. They had purchased far more poster board and stakes than they actually needed, so they had a surplus.

Although the fusion lab had a public entrance for guests and media, the protesters took it as a personal insult when the security guards menacingly turned them away at the checkpoint for credentialed employees, relegating them to the parking lot.

"Segregation!" exclaimed Ash, one of the younger GCCF members. "This is just a way to keep the public from seeing what they're doing!"

"We need to consider if we want to risk arrest by defying their cops or if we want to wait for the media to show up so that we can at least be heard. Butterfly," Vera turned to her friend, "what's the word on that? Who are we expecting, and when?"

"On the way, I reached out to several podcasts and shows," Butterfly said. "Most of them couldn't come here on such short notice, but there was one that intended to. A streaming channel called 'Earth@600 Report.'"

"What does that mean?" Ash asked. "Oh-six hundred hours, like that?"

Butterfly shrugged. "I don't know."

Vera cut in then. She did know this. She'd heard about it enough from her aunt and uncle. "No, it refers to parts per million of carbon dioxide."

"My God, is that where we're at now?"

"Yeah, we hit the 'milestone' last year, like people have been predicting for thirty years that we would." She shook her head. "We did it right on schedule! Go us." Heavy sarcasm filled her words. Shaking her head, she held up her newly-made sign, which read *We Can't Invent Our Way Out of Disaster.* "Yes, we are at the right place! People have been chasing fantasies for *far* too long."

Ash was still unsure. "I think we should have a more traditional protest. We shouldn't let them bully us."

"Some of us need to give an interview," Vera said. "But if you want to protest the site instead, just be careful. Don't let them hurt you."

"We'll be fine."

The group then split in two, some of them going with Ash to approach the security checkpoint again and others following Vera, Mike, and the polycule to the public entrance.

There they finally saw that the streaming show that had taken an interest in their protest had been there all along, waiting for them to arrive.

The Earth@600 Report was a rather professional-looking

outfit, Vera thought. They had a logo, an easily recognizable globe of green, brown, and blue with a translucent tan "glow" surrounding it. Their show's name read in bold text below the planet symbol. They had quickly obtained media credentials from the Intensity Labs staff, and they had also been granted permission to set up a camera at the public entrance. The camera crew had already mounted the equipment, and the hosts—a pair of young men who seemed to be close, Vera thought—held microphones, eagerly awaiting the protest. Their eyes lit up at the visible approach of GCCF, and one of them instantly approached Mike and Vera, who were at the head of the group.

"Patrick Gardinier, Earth@600 Report," he introduced himself, holding out the mic. "This is my partner, Felix Parrera. We learned about your protest on social media—"

Butterfly cut in eagerly, bouncing on the balls of their feet, wings still flapping and crackling—albeit now showing signs of wear. "I'm social media outreach! You spoke to me!"

Gardinier blinked, overwhelmed. "Right. We had some questions for you, and it's our hope that we'll have a good talk...."

Mike tensed. "Oh yeah? What questions?"

"We understand that you originally intended to protest Speaker Gilbertson's new bill at his local office, but that after he returned to DC, you changed your venue. Protesting Gilbertson's office needed no explanation," he said with a chuckle, "but we were wondering, after that fell through, what made you select Intensity Labs to protest?"

Mike spoke up first. "Intensity Labs is funded in part by FSU," he said, "but it's not on campus. If nuclear fusion is so safe, why isn't it?"

The other interviewer, Felix Parrera, interjected. "There are strict regulations about it," he said. "But they were meant for obsolete methods of nuclear *fission*, which does, of course, produce radioactive waste."

"But why not change them, if that's the case?" Mike challenged.

"Well, as we all know, the process of government can be very slow." Gardinier raised his eyebrows. "Did you have a specific objection to this power source, and that is why it was your alternative protest venue? If so, could you share your objection with us? We're interested in hearing what the climate activist community has to say about energy."

Vera raised her protest sign pointedly. "We cannot invent our way out of disaster," she repeated. "That is our real objection. Fundamentally, it doesn't *matter* if fusion is as clean as a whistle!"

"Why doesn't it?" Parrera challenged. "Don't take it personally," he added at once when she bristled. "This is our job as independent media, to ask challenging questions."

"Of course," she said, trying to keep irritation out of her tone. She took a deep breath, recalling the many arguments and discussions that she had had with her relatives and friends on the subject. "The theme of our protest today was opposition to consumption and opposition to this capitalist, predatory economy that encourages unnecessary consumption."

"That almost *requires* unnecessary consumption," Channing agreed.

"We are facing *climate catastrophe* because of this consumer society," Vera continued earnestly, getting into the swing of it now. "Your own show name proves that! 600 parts per million? That's a disgrace! It is a shame upon the previous generations that left us with this."

"Yes. We are 'Generation Climate Catastrophe' for a reason," Channing said, "just as you are Earth@600 for a reason! We are the ones paying the price. It's not fair. But here we are." She flexed her shoulders, which were aching from holding up the poster.

"Fusion power has been an unfulfilled promise for a long time," Vera said, "a shiny object to chase, when we've had reliable green energy all along. But even if Intensity Labs catches the shiny object at last, how is that a good thing? This would just allow the pattern of consumption to continue. It's a *moral hazard* that would allow people to continue the behavioral patterns that caused climate change."

"There are some who would say that burning fossil fuels and unsustainable big agriculture are the 'behavioral patterns that caused climate change.'"

Mike then cut in rather aggressively. "I had thought that your outlet would be friendly to us, not biased."

"We are one of the top climate-related streaming channels in the world," Parrera replied. "But we ask tough questions to *everyone*, because the climate crisis itself has no easy answers. If you think clean fusion is not part of the answer, we are going to ask you why."

"You want to know why? Here's why," Mike snarled. "A 'perfect' fix would just mean that nobody has to change what they do in a meaningful way. It'll just continue the power structure that caused the crisis."

"Exactly," Vera agreed. "It needs to be dismantled, not propped up indefinitely with an injection of—of fusion energy," she concluded lamely, not remembering the specific atomic products of fusion reactions.

"We want revolutionary change," Mike said. "We don't want an indefinite continuation of the behaviors that made the crisis happen." He scowled. "Our generation, *Generation Climate Catastrophe*, you might say, has suffered more than anyone. We deal with anxiety about this crisis every day of our lives, and those who caused it don't care! That's why the entire system needs to be dismantled."

Parrera and Gardinier were about to question them further on this assertion, but shouts, sirens, and a pair of building security guards interrupted the interview.

"Are these also with that... group?" the female security guard sneered at Vera's associates.

"I hear sirens," Mike snarled back. "What's going on?"

"Your friends have been detained for vandalizing the building with spray paint and trying to trespass," she snapped.

The Earth@600 Report crew backed away at once. "We

were not involved in this," Gardinier assured them. "We have press credentials. We were going to interview this activist group...."

An official from the lobby of the public entrance then emerged through the automatic door. "You all need to leave," he announced. He gave Vera, Mike, and their companions a hard look. "Security has told us that the paint your pals used on our south wing is easily washed off, so we won't press charges for vandalism. But they *did* try to trespass into a secure facility. If you all get out of here now, that's all that we'll ask the police to pursue."

Mike looked as if he wanted to argue, but Vera and Channing realized, at once, that now was not the time for his spite and arrogance. "We'll be off at once," Channing chirped. She gave an apologetic look to the Earth@600 Report team. "Sorry we couldn't talk much. Maybe another time."

As they headed away from the building, Vera asked the others quietly, "Do we still have enough money left to pay their bail and fines?"

"Yes," Mike said. "We do."

Vera was relieved. Ash and her associates would have to appear in court and pay the fine, but the money that they had set aside for this protest would cover it. Mike had been right: *This* was a good use of the money. *Putting up four solar panels on our roof wouldn't have done much*, she thought, *but this? How many people did we touch today with our protest? How many minds did we change? How many people are now aware because of us? I think this will make a real difference.*

Chapter 5: Perturbium Laser

Anne-Elise knew that the climate protest had come to her lab. Dr. Bobby Gleason, the Deputy Director, had informed her that the Earth@600 podcast had been granted press credentials and clearance to wait for the protesters in the public lobby. The group's own arrival later reached her ears, but only after it had broken up.

"I wish I could say it surprised me that my viper of a niece chose this lab to protest when Hal Gilbertson left town," she told Dr. Gleason, who grimaced at her epithet for Vera, "but it doesn't."

"Well, it surprises *me*. What's their problem with us?" he asked.

"Frankly? They are a passel of self-righteous hypocrites who want everyone else to suffer while falling far short of their own claimed standard," she replied cuttingly. "That's what my niece said to that podcast, that they regard clean fusion as a 'moral hazard.' And their leader is even worse. They don't want to solve the crisis in any way except one that causes hardship."

"Hardship?" Dr. Gleason scoffed. "I saw the two-thousand-dollar handbag that one of them was carrying—and all the glitter that the costumed one left on the sidewalk—"

"Let alone the money spent on *bail* and *fines*," she agreed. "You don't want me to get started on them. You really don't."

"Who were they trying to win over, anyway? Who does this appeal to?"

"Themselves and people like them."

Dr. Gleason rolled his eyes. "They'll continue to be irrelevant in the big picture if they keep this up."

"That's okay with them, I think. They'll get to regard themselves as righteous victims that nobody listened to. It's not as desirable as inflicting hardship on others, but it's a nice consolation prize."

He shook his head again. "I guess we'd better just focus on our own work and not worry about them."

"You're right."

*　　　*　　　*

Anne-Elise came home that evening to an unpleasant surprise.

"I've been called back to Miami," Edward said glumly. "Gotta leave tomorrow. There's an invest in the Bay of Campeche that they want everyone back in the office to work."

Anne-Elise knew, by now, that the term "invest" meant a tropical disturbance of particular note to the National Hurricane Center, because it was showing signs of organization, threatening land, or computer models showed it developing—or all of the above. "Is it looking like a U. S. problem?" she asked him.

"Yes, most likely. Whose problem, and how big a problem, are the questions at the moment. There's a trough coming, which will probably break the heat wave—"

"Well, thank God for that."

"Don't thank God yet, because we don't know what else He has in store. The seawater is still going to be hot after the frontal passage, but suddenly there's cooler and drier air above it if the trough is strong."

"Ouch," Anne-Elise said, understanding well the explosive nature of the thermodynamics in such a scenario.

"Ouch is right," Edward said grimly. "So—the storm's path and intensity depend on the trough's strength. If it's weak, this system will be steered weakly toward the north, and it probably avoids the east Gulf hot pool. It still recurves to the east, but it's over land by then, merging with the front. But if the trough is strong enough to pull the storm east while it remains at sea, then it goes right over the hot spot, and that's a big problem."

"'A big problem,' meaning for the Florida panhandle?"

"Too early to say." He cringed. *Yes*, he thought. *It's the most likely landfall site in that scenario. Don't lie to her.* "Probably, though. Anyway, this could be a big deal, and they want us all back at NHC."

"Well," she said philosophically, "I regret that our visits are

64

always short, but so it is. We're both doing very important work, and duty calls. Rest up tonight, so that you'll be in top form to fly tomorrow."

*   *   *

Anne-Elise took the morning off to drive Edward to the airport where his Cessna was waiting for him. The Hurricane Center had already informed the aviation authorities about his situation, and he had a takeoff slot allotted for him.

"I'll keep in touch!" he called out, putting that leather coat and glasses on despite the heat. He winked. "Don't believe everything you hear on social media. If there's cause for alarm, I'll tell you!"

Anne-Elise waved goodbye to him reluctantly. *I never get enough time with him anymore. We used to be so close. It was us against the world, or at least against the rest of our family. It still is, but now we have to oppose them from opposite ends of the state.*

She was heading for her car when her phone buzzed loudly, indicating the arrival of an important email. The sender was Dr. Gleason.

Anne-Elise,

Very important. You've been summoned to DC to give an account of our work to the House Energy Committee. That's the one Gilbertson used to lead, you know. Apparently someone watched Mad Dog.

I already asked if it could be done virtually. They said no. You have to fly up there—at their expense, at least—to do it in person. Absolutely ridiculous in this day and age.

I know this is going to infuriate you. It's infuriated me. But with any luck, you can convince them that we're not trying to do... whatever they think we're trying to do. From what I heard of that show, it seems that they may believe we're trying to create nuclear lizard-person mutants. I'm not sure.

65

It's profoundly frustrating, considering how close to sustained breakeven that we are. This country could soon undergo an energy revolution, and it's ridiculous that a demagogic comedian could upend that. I hate even putting this in writing, but perhaps if you could pull some strings with your BIL? Nothing unethical, of course.

Bobby

If you had any idea what my relationship with Richard Mellor was like, Anne-Elise thought, *you wouldn't have asked that. Talking to him is as useless as talking to the wall.*

Actually, it's more useless. There might be devices on the wall that do as you ask or even answer back.

She sighed at Dr. Gleason's feeble attempt at humor. *I wish we were trying to create nuclear lizard-person mutants,* she thought. *Then we could just set our mutant army on these morons. I know you're trying to joke, but it's too serious for humor.*

This was not the first time Anne-Elise had been to DC to testify before Congress. Although Intensity Labs did not receive federal dollars directly, it still had to report on its activities as a nuclear site, and occasionally she had had to give a summarized presentation of the report. But she had never faced a decidedly hostile audience, and from the tone of Dr. Gleason's email, it appeared that this time there would be one.

Because of that idiot and his show, she thought. *The people's representatives are taking direction from performers and talking heads. But then, this is nothing new. This sort of thing has been going on my whole life. I don't remember a time when it wasn't the case.*

She had learned in college that this hadn't always been so. In the early years of her childhood, the seeds were already being sown, but before she and Edward had been born, political leaders actually did listen to subject-matter experts rather than hearkening to the rants of demagogic

66

entertainers.

Sometimes those experts could be compromised, of course. Anne-Elise recalled the histories of scientists in the pay of the fossil-fuel industry who downplayed the effects of their employers' activities on the climate, or doctors paid off by the tobacco industry to dismiss the harms of smoking, or other such accounts.

But the very fact that these industries needed to corrupt scientists to their side meant that the society of that time respected scientists' opinions on their areas of expertise, she thought. *These companies couldn't just present a carnival barker to argue for their side. They had to have the veneer of expert respectability. Now, we are regarded with suspicion rather than respect. The fact that everything and everyone is online is what's caused this. The "wisdom of crowds"—ha! Crowds have proven beyond doubt that they choose entertainment, radicalization, and self-assured reinforcement. I don't think people like Madison Chadleigh even have to accept money from the interests that their rants benefit. They really and truly believe a lot of what they say, so they say it without financial remuneration.*

That, she thought, was profoundly depressing. She recalled telling Richard that she thought it was better when politicians could be bought off, because then it was just a matter of putting up more cash or influence than the other side.

If the mid-century American version of "honesty in politics" means honest idiocy and honest self-righteous ignorance, I'd take good old-fashioned corruption instead, she thought.

But there was nothing for it. She would have to fly up to DC and testify before the House Energy Committee that Madison Chadleigh's brain-dead rants about clean energy were merely paranoid fantasies.

As she got into her car, she scowled to herself at the thought of the Chair of that committee. CG Taverner, *the Dishonorable Gentleman from Indiana,* she thought in derision. Despite being from a very different region of the country, he and Gilbertson had a history. Taverner was quite young, merely thirty-seven years old, and the sixty-two-year-old Gilbertson had taken him on as a protégé—and his replacement voice in the committees—as he ascended the ranks of House leadership. But Taverner's true inspiration and mentor was Madison Chadleigh.

The young representative was a major proponent of fossil fuels, but he also swallowed Chadleigh's ideas about "masculinity" and his conspiracy theories about "educated elites" hook, line, and sinker, despite being a graduate of an Ivy League college himself. He had been admitted on scholarship, and apparently, as a poor nobody from the Midwest, he had never truly been welcomed into the social scene of the blueblood legacy-admission kids. In Anne-Elise's opinion, he carried his grudge into his political career, and this was what motivated his populist attacks on "elites."

In any case, CG Taverner was a true product of the new culture that had formed and taken shape in the age of the Internet, about which Anne-Elise had just been thinking. Unlike Gilbertson, he had never known anything else. During his first campaign for high office, he had even acknowledged having been active on the now-defunct troll forum 4chan as a teen. This admission had, according to post-election polling data, earned him a tsunami of votes from similar-minded young men. Some users of the successors to that still-infamous site had even generated an AI-video mockumentary about their hero called *Mr. /b Goes to Washington*. The modern hyper-atomized media system was all that Taverner knew.

Anne-Elise was a product of that system herself, but she supposed she was intelligent enough to see its severe faults. Taverner must have taken some of the same kinds of social history classes that she had in college, but he had undoubtedly dismissed their lessons and implications.

She did not look forward to appearing before his House Committee to defend her work. As Dr. Gleason had said, they were expected to reach net-positive power generation any day now, and unlike previous fusion labs' accomplishments in that respect, Intensity's next-generation ytterbium ultraviolet lasers were expected to keep the reactions net-positive once they reached the milestone. Very quickly, the power expended to start the laser would be zeroed out and then blown away by what was generated. If all proceeded according to expectations, this would be historic.

Since becoming Director, Anne-Elise herself had, to her regret, been somewhat removed from the details of engineering and physics, and more focused by necessity on the annoying nonsense of management—and politics. But she understood the processes thoroughly and had contributed significantly to the design when she was just a nuclear engineer. This was still *her* baby, *her* project.

And I have to defend my life's work to a smirking twerp who gets his information from a political talk-show host.

She sighed as the lab came in sight. It was what it was.

*   *   *

September 3, Washington, DC.

Anne-Elise scowled at Representative Taverner, the smug, arrogant Chair of the House Committee on Energy and Commerce. A conventionally attractive white man with brilliant blue eyes and dark blond hair almost the color of Anne-Elise's own, he marred his natural good looks with the obnoxious expressions he kept on his face. At this moment, she had to give it to her brother-in-law. Compared with this twit, Speaker Gilbertson did show maturity and gravitas.

"Miss Kirby," Taverner began.

"Dr. Kirby," Anne-Elise corrected at once. The nameplate identifying her also used the wrong honorific. She was quite sure it was intentional, a way for this product of the bro-world of right-wing social media to diminish and demean her.

Taverner raised his eyebrows in feigned surprise, but he did not offer an apology, nor did he accede. "The information we received said that you were *Miss* Kirby."

"The information you received is wrong, then, and if you could be in error about such a basic and readily verifiable matter as my educational credentials, it does offer a possible explanation for why you called me here to explain my lab's activities."

"Now, Miss Kirby, this isn't a very good beginning. In any case, even if you did have a doctorate—"

"I *do* have a doctorate."

"—you would still be an unmarried woman." He smirked fully.

"That is disingenuous, Congressman. You know the rules of honorifics, and I insist on being addressed properly. Your staff can check my biography on the lab's website right now if they like. Or they can give MIT a call, if they don't believe the site."

"I see no reason for that. We aren't asking questions that require a doctoral degree to answer." He shuffled his papers officiously, then raised his immaculately groomed eyebrows again. "I understand that Intensity Advanced Fusion Testbed, your lab, received two million in funding from Florida State."

"That is correct."

"And that this grant was partly paid to the university with federal funds."

"Are you insinuating misuse of taxpayer dollars?" she snapped.

"Oh, no, not *misuse*. I merely question if this particular *use* of tax money is a good one."

"If rooting out questionable expenditures is your goal, I would imagine you have far bigger fish to fry than a paltry two million, which are, quite frankly, likely to pay extremely high dividends for the nation soon. We have a very promising ultraviolet laser design. Past neodymium solid-state lasers have resulted in technically net-positive fusion power generation, but it wasn't breakeven at all when the energy required to power these lasers was considered. With fast ignition and our high-performance ytterbium laser—"

Taverner interrupted her with a quick, contemptuous laugh. "Come now, Miss Kirby, we're not here for you to spout incomprehensible jargon. What concerns me is not *ytterbium*, but, you might say, *perturbium*."

"You should save the jokes for the Madison Chadleigh show, Congressman, except that they're so bad he might *feed* you to his dogs. Unless they are as artificial as his videos, of course."

"You are out of order," he said smilingly. "But this *is* a good digression to my main point. I am the Chairman of the House Energy Committee and even I don't understand this jargon."

"If I were you, I wouldn't be so proud of that as to boastfully enter it into the Congressional Record."

He shook his head, clicking his tongue in reproof. "Let us *try* to keep this hearing civil. I don't want to dock your time, Miss Kirby."

"Doctor."

"My point is, the fact that your 'work'"—he actually raised his index and middle finger on each hand beside his head in the gesture of mock quotes, Anne-Elise observed with derision and growing fury—"is incomprehensible even to *me* means that it cannot possibly replace the good jobs in the fossil-fuel industry that so many average working-class Americans still hold."

Anne-Elise sensed an opening. "Do you mean to imply that the average working-class American is too stupid to work for a fusion lab or other clean-power source?" She knew that this hearing was being televised and that clips of various moments would spread all over the Internet, and would probably also find their way to shows such as *Attack Dog*. She knew she had to make this good. "I think better of American workers than you seem to, Congressman. You shouldn't project your own failings upon them."

"You truly think that coal miners or oilfield workers can just waltz into your lab and understand what's what?" he said with derision. "This shows just how elitist and out-of-touch the so-called scientific enterprise has truly become."

"I don't think that and I didn't say it," she said. "Those are your words, Congressman. But I don't think they are all *too stupid* to learn. The immediate problem they might face is one of"—she flailed for a better-sounding word than "ignorance," finally settling on—"training. Not capacity. Could they design the lasers for an advanced fusion lab? Probably not. But there are other sources of clean power. Fusion is but one piece in the puzzle," she said, using the same expression she had used with Vera. "Could they work in a wind or solar farm? After on-the-job training, why not? Even people who were the greatest geniuses of their times, like Sir Isaac Newton, would have a lot of catching up to do if they suddenly came back to life today. There's no shame in it."

That went well, she thought, considering the camera as she sat back in her chair. *I held my temper and made a good point, which he'll be hard put to refute. I loathe the omnipresence of "viral moments" and the distillation of complex matters into sound bites, but if this is the world we have, damned if I won't hold my own in it.*

Taverner sighed theatrically, leaning back in his seat. He shook his head and clicked his tongue again, folding his palms together atop his table. Faux sorrow filled his voice as he replied.

"It is very easy for people like you to say 'just get retrained.' Very easy indeed. But to the thousands of workers who have spent their lives working on the oil field or the natural gas plant, being told that they have to learn something new if they want to stay employed is a serious hardship. Especially when, as the Speaker has indicated with the introduction of his new bill, this change is not even a natural market-driven change, but is being foisted upon the population by government subsidy."

"You have it exactly backwards, Congressman. We should have transitioned to green power decades ago. The only reason *fossil fuels* are still viable is government subsidy for *them.* Clean power holds its own in a free market. We saw this in earlier years. In the 2010s and 2020s, it looked as if clean power might obtain a dominant market share simply by its own virtues. All that time, government was subsidizing *fossil fuels.* Clean power still did well." She also leaned back in her chair, meeting his gaze stare for supercilious stare. "And then government stepped in to *punish* clean power. Revocations of wind farm permits, punitive taxes on electric vehicles and solar panels, spurious 'corruption' and 'fraud' investigations of green-power companies, and massive cuts to scientific research, including nuclear, during the late '20s. But try as it might, it didn't kill off clean energy. It just prolonged the natural decline of fossil fuels."

A gleam had appeared in Taverner's eyes at the mention of that reactionary period. No doubt to him it was a "golden age." Anne-Elise suppressed an annoyed sigh as he took his turn again.

And, sure enough—"We should have continued those policies," he said. "During that period, the masculinity crisis and solitude crisis—which began during the 2010s that you think were so glorious—began to retreat a bit. More men were working fixed shifts with known, predictable hours, which allowed them to set aside time for their families." He gazed at the cameras, aware of his true audience. "Traditional shift work with fixed hours and predictable tasks is the only way that men can be sure they will have that time, and when it comes to energy, this can only be feasible with proven energy sources that have stood the test of time. Experimental work such as your fusion lab requires strange, unpredictable hours. It harms the American family when the breadwinner cannot be sure if he will be called away to work at a moment's notice."

Anne-Elise chose, as a matter of maintaining focus, to set aside his sexist fixation on the idea that families had to have a male breadwinner. Instead she decided to call out his double standard. *The real audience will yawn at a dry policy debate, but a personal attack could go viral*, she thought, hating that she was playing this game, but unable in a way to stop herself.

"I'd point out that, once fusion becomes—as you say—*proven*, there won't be any strange or unpredictable hours required, because it will be just as routine as gas plant work.

But more to the immediate point, if you're so concerned about families, may I suggest that you look at the one before you? You know full well who I am in relation to the Speaker's press secretary. This kind of inquisition is creating political rifts in *my* family." She leaned back again, grimly smug.

The thought momentarily crossed her mind that it wasn't entirely just a matter of perceived necessity that she was doing this. No, she realized, *a part of me likes wrestling in the mud just as much as Taverner himself does. I hate it, but I am a product of this era too.*

Taverner, however, just shook his head again. "That is a personal attack, and I'm afraid you have forced me to dock you a minute of speaking time." He paused to let it sink in before continuing. "But as it happens, I *do* know who your family is. The problem, though, is not your brother-in-law. It's your twin." He leaned forward, resting his chin on his clenched left fist in supposed thoughtfulness. "The mere fact that you are financially and professionally vested in this unproven fusion lab raises questions about conflicts of interest in your brother's work."

Anne-Elise could not believe her ears. "My brother's work —as a hurricane forecaster?" she sputtered. "You're insinuating things about his scientific credibility because of my work, but not about my brother-in-law's political loyalty?"

"Dock Miss Kirby another minute of speaking time for that interruption," he said. She gaped in fury at him as he continued. "I am well aware of the 'political rift' between you and your sister. The very existence of that rift is why your brother-in-law and sister are *not* conflicted. Your brother, though...." He raised his eyebrows. "A green-energy researcher, whose lab takes in up to two million dollars indirectly from the federal government, and whose twin— whose *exceedingly close* twin, from what I'm told—is a *weather* scientist? Yes, this raises questions." He paused, smirking for the cameras. "You may respond."

Anne-Elise managed to suppress her temper. How *dare* this weasel insinuate anything inappropriate involving her and Edward, either personally or professionally! *Once an Internet troll, always an Internet troll,* she thought in utter contempt. *Only a bottom-feeder of the Dark Web would make an incest allusion in the Congressional Record. And he accused me of personal attacks!*

She took a deep breath before addressing him. "Your insinuations are vile and utterly beneath your dignity as a Member of Congress," she said. "And also off topic. You are concerned, for some reason, that jobs in science, engineering, and advanced power would be bad for families. I would like to reassure you that a clear majority of the staff at Intensity Labs have spouses, children, or both. They and the single childless members of the lab's staff, such as myself, all have good relationships with at least some other members of their families, such as siblings and aging parents. They are all proud to support their families with the good pay of these challenging jobs and equally proud to be working toward a brighter, sustainable future for the younger generations of their families."

This was also a good line, she thought—and Taverner seemed to know it. He smirked superciliously at her. "I don't doubt that, Miss Kirby. But the question is, would it be a good thing for *America* for traditional energy-sector jobs to be replaced with difficult lab jobs? Would it be a good thing for *America* for large numbers of workers to bear the stress of knowing that, if they screwed up, it wouldn't just cause a mild fire, but a radioactive meltdown?"

"Fusion power doesn't carry that risk. At Intensity Labs, our next focus of research will be efficiently producing the proton-boron fusion reaction. It's been done before, but not with net energy gain. And it doesn't have the issue I'm about to describe—"

Wait, what? Don't describe it, you fool! Don't describe it, a voice in her head protested—

"—but for now, we're doing conventional deuterium-tritium fusion with an eye for a commercial product. And with that reaction, there is—"

No, *no*, *don't say it*, *do not say it*—but her honesty as a scientist and urge to explain her passion won out over her better judgment.

"—a free neutron produced with each successful reaction, but they are captured."

Why did you say that? she beat herself up immediately, even as Taverner's eyes widened in surprise. *Why the hell did you say that? What a moment to play the eager, impeccably honest scientist!*

"So there *is* a risk of neutron radiation?" Taverner repeated. "So much for the claim that this power source is clean!" He shook his head. "For half a century, climate scientists have been warning about dire, bleak consequences from burning fossil fuels. But all I can see is that we have longer summers!"

"Which cause deadly heat waves, such as the one we've been in for two months, and *wildfires*, such as those out West."

"Fires that have damaged the parts of the power grid connecting to wind and solar farms."

"Which is why we need nuclear in the picture. My point is that climate change is not benign, Congressman. It's not an extended summer vacation."

"Change always seems scary," he said condescendingly. "And that is assuming that all these 'records' are real. But let us say, for the sake of argument, that climate change is real and carbon emissions caused it. If so, it seems that the choice we face is a mild, slow warmup—which we can adapt to—or a power grid dependent on unreliable windmills and panels, with a source subject to *radiation leak* as the 'backup.' And for what? For putting multiple generations of hardworking American men out of work, plunging their wives and children into poverty and despair?" He shook his head one last time as the time allotted for the hearing dwindled. "If climate change is real, it couldn't do anything worse than that."

*　　　*　　　*

Why, why, why did you say that? Anne-Elise continued to beat herself up. *What the hell were you thinking? You won that argument. Your opponent was knocked down. And then, rather than finishing the bastard, you decided to give him a new knife to use.*

The thought momentarily crossed her mind that it was kind of dark to consider a debate of public importance in the manner of a boxing ring or video-game boss fight. But she couldn't help it.

Why did you do that? Now that's the clip that will be everywhere.

Her thoughts turned bleakly to the smug, smarmy man's concluding remark. *Oh, I bet climate change could do a lot worse than that.* She thought of Edward, far away in Miami, looking at the storm that had called him away from Tallahassee. *The storm that he fears might become a Category Five, from what I could read between the lines. Or—what was it that he said when he flew in? "A hell of a lot worse than a Category Five," whatever he means by that. I suppose he has his professional obsession and I have mine, and we each understand only the basics about each other's work. But he wouldn't view me, let alone treat me, with the contempt that that ass did today....*

She wondered then just what that storm was doing. Had it been declared and named yet? She opened the lid to her laptop and looked.

Her eyes widened in shock at what she was seeing online, spread all over social media by weather hobbyists. *Edward has told me that sometimes the models go crazy with storms early in their development, but this is next-level crazy.*

Chapter 6: Hurricane Leonard

September 3, Miami.

The National Hurricane Center was in a state of barely controlled chaos.

The invest that had brought them all back to headquarters was no longer a mere tropical disturbance. Now a tropical storm in the Bay of Campeche, it had been named Leonard. The models had not been especially impressed with Leonard when it was merely "Invest 91L," because they had all shown the possible heat-wave-breaking trough staying weak and the storm itself intensifying to a respectable but—in this era of rapid intensification—basically unremarkable low-end Category Four before hitting east Texas.

And what an indictment of humanity it is that a Category Four is "unremarkable," Edward thought amid the bustle. Category Five hurricanes occurred most years, and there was usually a beast of at least 180 miles per hour at least every other year. For decades, a small group of people had argued that these beasts merited the creation of a new "Category Six," with winds beginning at 192 miles per hour, but the Hurricane Center resolutely opposed this idea.

"*The creation of a 'Category Six' would lessen the significance of 'Category Five,'*" Dr. Vinay Chandra, Director of the NHC, had always said. "*If there is suddenly a category greater than Five, that means that 'Five' doesn't carry the punch in the minds of the general public that it ought. We already face this with 'Category Four,' especially with Fives being more prevalent than they used to be. 'Category Four' often unofficially and silently becomes 'only Category Four.' We don't want that for 'Category Five.'*"

Edward agreed with the Director, but that was partly for his own professional reasons. His pet project, his passion, was the extreme tropical-cyclone model that he and some academics at Florida State's meteorology department—for he worked in a research partnership with them during hurricane offseason— had created specifically to model the most extreme kinds of tropical cyclones that the planet could potentially generate.

It had always been just a research project, a source of interesting but niche scientific journal articles. Edward was still a member of the old research group and still had an account on FSU's supercomputer, so he could run the research model there as he liked rather than taking up government resources improperly. It was—he had to admit it —kind of fun every now and then to do that just to see what the model could spin up with various extreme initial conditions. Conditions that hadn't ever actually *occurred* all at the same time. The planet would have to draw the inside straight from hell. It was all theoretical, and so, yes, kind of fun.

It was still kind of fun, even though those conditions were no longer looking so theoretical. Edward had not yet dared to initialize a run of his Supercritical Tropical Cyclone Research System, or STCRS—pronounced "stackers"—on FSU's computers. But what the government's official operational models were showing indicated that maybe he ought. Maybe. If this pattern continued. Just to see.

The models had not gone wild with Leonard when it had been merely Invest 91L, but now that it was a named storm with a well-defined core and winds already at fifty miles an hour, they had suddenly taken more interest in it. The much-vaunted cold front that Gulf state residents were eagerly hoping would break their interminable, hellish heat wave would also create a groove in the atmosphere for Leonard to slip into like water running into a ditch. In the new runs since Leonard's naming, models were now showing the trough catching the storm and lofting it north.

Straight into the record-warm, record-warm-depth water of the central Gulf of Mexico. Straight over the Gulf Loop Current.

But the air temperature, which had been at or above one hundred degrees Fahrenheit for the greater part of two months, would no longer be the same temperature as the sea. It would suddenly be fifteen or twenty degrees cooler and significantly drier. Thermodynamically, it was like a spark to kindling. And after the disruptive, shearing frontal passage—which Leonard itself would not be under, as it would merely find a weakness that the trough created—the winds would calm down, leaving nothing to weaken the storm as it continued to ride the weakness northeast toward the east-central Gulf Coast.

The hurricane component of NOAA's Unified Forecast System, the Hurricane Analysis and Forecasting System—or HAFS—was showing the extremely well-organized Tropical Storm Leonard intensifying rapidly to Category Five, with winds over two hundred miles an hour in two days and central pressure of 840 hectopascals or millibars. That would be a new world record.

Predictably, the shocking output of this model run had made the rounds of social media the previous night. Little did Edward know that his twin sister had seen it before he had.

And that was what Dr. Chandra had gone into the office that morning to face. He knew better than anyone that it would be chaos. He just tried to keep it at *controlled* chaos.

There was a staff meeting in one minute. Edward reluctantly took himself away from his computer to attend. He really wanted to run his STCRS model... and if he could impress his postdoc trainee, Sallie Evans, with some wild output, even better....

"All of you!" Director Chandra barked at the forecasters and interns as they entered the conference room. "We've all seen what the HAFS is doing, of course."

"What's your take on that, Director?" Dr. Evans herself asked. Edward gazed admiringly at her. Such a smart girl. Woman, he corrected himself in his thoughts. She's *twenty-nine.*

Dr. Chandra did not mince words. "I think it is possible," he said, grim-faced. Groans and gasps filled the room. "And it is for that reason that I ask all of you to exercise extra professionalism during this time. If this storm does what it most definitely *could* do, some area along the Gulf Coast will be in for a world of hurt, and it is up to us to give them all the information they need to minimize that hurt. I know we cannot control what the weather weenies and fanboys say on social media, but I don't want to see any of you encouraging hype and inappropriate 'cheering' for extreme hurricanes under your professional, identifiable accounts. And I hope you don't do it even anonymously," he added.

"You can count on us," Edward called out.

Dr. Chandra gave him a look. "I know you have access to that experimental model at your university. You are not obligated, as NOAA is, to provide your model output to the public. Therefore, I don't want to see it happening."

"I wouldn't do that," he said. "I don't want to give the weenies fodder either."

"Good." The Director turned back to the group. "If Leonard does become a major threat, I will unfortunately have to ask that you all work extra hours. This type of event is why we are here."

No one objected.

"And of course, we will be flying Leonard nonstop. However strong it becomes, we know that this is going to be a rapid intensifier—"

"What isn't these days?" someone muttered.

Dr. Chandra nodded grimly. "Yes. And so we need data. Those of you who aren't in the Hurricane Hunter crew, you may be asked to step in as forecasters when your colleagues are flying."

"Understood, sir," someone said.

Edward's heart had soared at these words. *That's me. I'm a Hurricane Hunter. This could be a chance to fly a world-record storm! To be in the eye itself at that historic moment!*

The Director continued, transitioning to his morning briefing. There wasn't much to say that they didn't all know, though. Forecasting Category Fives was an annual ritual here, sometimes more frequently than annual. But forecasting a potential world-record-holder—*possibly in kind as well as degree*, thought Edward—was another matter. They all knew that the next few days would be the most important of their lives.

*   *   *

The next model runs continued to show a world-record Category Five hurricane being picked up by the trough and zeroing in on the east-central Gulf Coast for an eventual landfall, and Leonard itself steadily intensified for the next six hours. At this pace, it would be a hurricane by the next update. Its core was immaculate. The growing central dense overcast, the precursor to an eye, towered up vertically as perfectly aligned as the chimneys that meteorologists often used as metaphor.

The first flight was already tasked and en route to the storm from Lakeland. Edward was not going to be on that flight, but he was all right with that. Better to reserve him for when—and he did indeed think it would be *when*—Leonard rapidly intensified.

Instead he analyzed the data coming in from their stationary sensors and satellites. There were buoys and ship reports to supplement the satellite estimates, though aircraft reconnaissance would be needed to get the storm's true intensity.

He also watched the models as they generated their output every three hours. Edward vaguely recalled from his youth the days when many weather models ran six hours apart. Computers were slower then. Now, they updated and ran much more frequently, allowing them to adapt for new data that they ingested.

Of course, there was no "ground-truth" data to *be* ingested just yet. The most recent reconnaissance report was from when the storm became a tropical storm. That was well out of date now. It didn't stop Edward—and every other meteorologist in the building—from following the models' output religiously, though.

Sallie Evans, Edward's postdoctoral trainee, came to his desk with a cup of coffee for each of them. His was in his favorite mug, one from the Air and Space Museum in DC with

82

a print of the *Wright Flyer*. He gave her what he believed was a flirtatious wink, not seeing the momentary flicker of annoyance pass over her face as she sat down. He had the well-cushioned, wheeled, reclining, swivel executive chair and she had a stationary side chair with stiff scratchy fabric on the cushions, but he did not notice that either.

She saw what he had pulled up on his monitor and smiled, this time a real smile. He did notice that.

"It's really something, isn't it?" he said to her, gesturing at the screen with a wave of his hand.

Her smile faded and became thin. "It is that," she conceded. "But how much value does it really have with the aircraft data so out of date? I think we'd all do better to wait and see what the models show after the next recon dataset gets ingested."

"Well, sure," he said, mildly disappointed that she didn't share his enthusiasm, "but it's what we have *now*. And in any case, you should take a look at the recon that's coming in. They're in the storm now."

"It's not yet a hurricane, last I checked."

"It's on the verge. I bet it becomes one before they leave."

She nodded. "A classic case of rapid intensification."

"There's also an upper-air mission." He suddenly sat upright in his chair, narrowly avoiding splashing coffee over his lap. That would have been *rather* unpleasant, he thought, hurriedly setting the mug down. "In many ways, that's equally important. Maybe more so. I should take a look at what it's finding, but I forgot."

"You mean the tropopause temperature."

Edward was pleased that she understood exactly where his mind had gone. *Such a smart girl, and she knows my research background very well.* His imagination quickly fixed upon the explanation that he most wanted to be the case—she had learned a lot about his research background because she was interested in him personally—but he had to admit that it was equally likely to be because she was, after all, his postdoc, and postdocs were famously eager to please their mentors by becoming founts of knowledge about their mentors' specialties.

That's still a promising beginning, he thought—and then finally returned to the actual conversation, though only a few seconds had elapsed since she had spoken.

"You've seen the sea temps," he said. "Thirty-seven degrees in a Loop Current eddy. Body temp. And in the theory, which is older than either of us—certainly older than *you*," he said with another wink, still not seeing how her lips thinned, "even older than a middle-aged loser like me"—he paused for a millisecond, waiting for her to disclaim that appellation—

"It would be hard to call an aviator and renowned scientist a 'loser,'" she said almost rotely.

He beamed. "Well, thank you. In any case, the theory isn't quite as old as my *lamented* parents would be if they hadn't driven their van into a ditch... but to get to my point, with thirty-seven-degree water and humid surface air, we'd need... I believe... tropopause temperatures lower than seventy-five below zero for, ah, *my research* to become applicable to the situation."

Dr. Evans frowned. "I wouldn't think Director Chandra would approve of this sort of speculation...."

"It's just between us," he said, dashed. "Two professionals talking to each other about theory. Anyway," he added, recalling something, "*you* confirmed that you were thinking of the tropopause temperature." He smiled pointedly.

"It's a relevant factor for any tropical cyclone." She picked up her own coffee mug. "I had better get back to my desk."

He sighed as she left, observing her figure admiringly in the fitted sheath dress and blazer she wore. She dressed well, unlike most of the staff, minus the Director himself, who wore basic polo shirts and trousers. She stood out, but Edward found nothing to complain about when he saw her. It was rather the opposite.

Yes, she's very smart, but she's too cautious in many ways. She needs to loosen up a bit and break the rules a little.

Chandra's a good guy, and he does look out for us, but he didn't mean—or tell—us not to talk about storm hypotheticals among each other. She's over-complying. Trying not to sound like an overexcited newbie in front of her boss. That's all it is. She thinks she has to be as "sedate" as her elders—more sedate, in this case—or we won't respect her.

It's unfortunate. She has no reason to believe I don't respect her.

Ah well. I remember being young and fresh. It can't be helped. What's important is that I know she privately shares my passion, even if she's ashamed to admit it.

He was certain he had the correct view of it. With this conclusion for consolation, Edward returned to monitoring data.

*   *   *

As the flight crews continued to send data, Edward shifted between monitoring that, monitoring the models, and conferring with his colleagues.

For run after run, the HAFS stubbornly insisted on a world-record Category Five. The other models still included a few—*the Canadian model, of course,* Edward thought with mild amusement—that showed the cold front weak and the storm meandering toward a Category Three or Four landfall in Texas or Louisiana, a humdrum event these days. But even those were showing the trough stronger with each successive run. And most of the global and regional models had jumped on the bandwagon that HAFS had begun, showing the trough eroding the high-pressure system significantly, breaking the record heat wave at last—but also providing a gap for Leonard to enter the most thermodynamically explosive environment on the planet at this time.

The entire Gulf of Mexico was very warm, at least thirty-three Celsius, but there was a very hot spot, a Loop Current eddy: the site of those thirty-seven-degree seas. *Human body temperature,* Edward thought again. The models, HAFS included, were sending Leonard into a hot area, because the entire east-central Gulf and Gulf Loop Current were hot, but the models were not taking it directly over the worst spot.

He navigated to some images of the upper atmosphere, wondering what that was forecast to be after the cool-down. *Eighty below zero Celsius,* he noted. *No idea what it is currently. The upper-air mission will find that out. But if the forecast is for eighty below, that means this simulation isn't even hitting its maximum potential intensity. With eighty below at the top and thirty-four-degree seas, the pressure should be lower than 840 millibars.* A quick inspection of wind images showed him the reason. The model was also spinning up turbulent flow around the hurricane's periphery from the storm's own rapid intensification that sheared it a bit.

That shouldn't happen, he thought. *They can entrain dry air if they intensify very fast—if there is dry air around—but they don't shear themselves. It's a feedback problem with the model, I think.*

He really wanted to run his own model. It could deal with what he now suspected was going on. The storm was trying to intensify too fast for the HAFS to handle well, so the model was generating artificial ripples of heat flux from the storm's excess. It was then producing artificial thunderstorms, ringing the hurricane and popping up in the model field like popcorn, from the highly thermodynamic environment. These simulated storms were creating shear that shouldn't actually exist, and they might also be artificially raising the tropopause temperature before Leonard could fully utilize the extreme gradient to intensify itself.

Edward considered the situation as an expert. HAFS, like other operational models, had a fixed configuration that had been determined by scientific peer review to be the best for the *general* case for which the model would be used. Certain configurations modeled severe thunderstorms well; others handled most tropical cyclones better.

But there are always edge cases, Edward thought. *And that's where my model would come in.* STCRS, like other research models, could be configured in a wide variety of ways. Edward also had a default configuration for it, curated for the type of phenomenon that it was meant to handle, and he would try that first, but he could also tweak it if something about the output seemed wrong.

The sooner his shift ended, the better. He knew that if he logged into the FSU supercomputer now and set a run, he wouldn't be able to look away from it.

He had distractions enough as it was. He didn't like to admit it, because it seemed like a weakness, but he also kept a close eye on social media just to see what the weather hobbyist community had to say about the insanity that the models persistently predicted, even if, in his opinion, those models were missing some things.

Edward rolled his eyes as he scrolled his feeds. *Ah yes, the same old same old. The newer, usually younger amateurs and students getting super-excited about these model runs, posting images enthusiastically, while the "sedate elders" tell them to settle down and that the models are just "guidance."*

That they are, but that can cut in both directions.

A cry and a din of voices suddenly erupted. Edward popped up from his cubicle like a prairie dog.

"Hurricane-force winds!" someone called out. "Recon just found them!"

Edward smiled. *Speaking of excitement. We all get excited, even us seasoned professionals. The most humdrum and expected event in the world, a tropical storm becoming a hurricane, but we still get excited when it happens.*

"Good," he said. "We all knew it was going to happen, and better that it'll make it into the five o'clock update."

"What about the intensity forecast?" a middle-aged woman asked. "Even now, I still cringe at forecasting Category Five for a storm that has just been upgraded to a hurricane... but with the model trend being what it is...."

Dr. Chandra swept into the room. He had overheard the conversation. "The model data is out there, and as you say, Fisher, it is what it is. We should follow the data, wherever that leads us."

Eyes widened throughout the room.

"So... we're going there?"

"Your name will be on this forecast, Fisher. If you folks want to forecast a Five, you have plenty of model support for it."

They were all rather surprised. It was a rarity for the cautious, stern Director to so quickly approve such a remarkable move as forecasting Category Five for a newly declared hurricane. *The Director believes this is going to be bad,* Edward thought. *He called everyone in for a reason. He believes the models... or if he doesn't, it's because he thinks they may not be strong enough.*

"I think it would be a bit of a joke *not* to, Director," Adela Fisher was saying. "Everyone can see what the models are doing. They're public. I'm not saying we have to forecast two-hundred-mile-an-hour winds like some of these things are showing, but if we don't forecast a Five, we had better show Leonard missing the weakness in the high. It is indefensible otherwise."

"And the models that were showing it missing the weakness are starting to change their tune," Edward finally chimed in. "Go for it, Fisher. I think we all expect it. Take the plunge."

The meteorologist gave a quick nod. "You're right."

*　　*　　*

Edward wondered what the upper-air aircraft mission had found for tropopause temperatures. He pulled up that dataset and examined it.

Seventy below zero Celsius, he noted. *A bit too warm. But that's just what it is now. HAFS has it hitting eighty below after the heat wave breaks. I suspect that may be underdone, warmed up by "heat" released by thunderstorms that shouldn't really exist. Yes, I need to run STCRS when I get home.*

He wondered why, even in his own thoughts, he was dancing around the term—the type of storm for which he and his FSU team had developed STCRS. *Seventy below is a bit too warm, I just thought, but too warm for what? On one side of*

88

that invisible boundary are extremely intense, but thermodynamically conventional, hurricanes. And on the other side?

He supposed that there was still some residual embarrassment at the idea of seeming too "excitable." He had once been one of the weather hobbyists like those he had monitored off and on all day. Indeed, as a true child of the social-media age like his twin, he had never known anything else. And he had known well what happened—what kind of shaming, spread to potentially thousands of strangers' eyes, would ensue if he expressed "too much" enthusiasm and interest in his passion, such as posting model output depicting a world-record tropical cyclone.

Or thinking the word "hypercane." There, that wasn't so hard.

He had coded a model to simulate extreme tropical cyclones, including—*those.* He had done dozens of simulations with this model. He had written papers about these simulations.

But somehow, it was different when it was no longer just research. One could build castles in the air, write about them, and other fiction writers would accept this approvingly. Or one could build apocalyptic storms in the computer system, write about them, and the world of theoretical research would accept it.

Things were different when it might not be theoretical. *When the stakes are higher, and we're potentially talking about a real storm and real people, we do need to be responsible and judicious,* he reasoned. *But sometimes we may take that too far and shame ourselves for even considering possibilities.*

I'll run the model, he resolved. *That'll provide some clarity.*

*　　*　　*

At last, with his shift ended, Edward headed home to his condo. He was preoccupied all the way and barely avoided a car accident in Miami. *That wouldn't have happened in my plane,* he thought sourly, swerving away from the irate driver he had nearly hit. *But I can't exactly fly from home to work.*

God, "the future" sucks. We were supposed to have flying cars.

Anne-Elise had left him several furious text messages about her experience before the House Energy Committee and that obnoxious, smirking creep who chaired it. Edward would reply to her in a bit. She was too worried about those fools, he thought. Admittedly, they had summoned her to explain her work based on the ravings of a demagogue on a streaming show, so he could understand her point of view. But people like Gilbertson and Taverner just liked to posture for their obsessively online base.

Edward opened a can of cold beer, taking a long chug and momentarily relishing the rebellious defiance of his older sister's moral disapproval—really, the disapproval of *both* of his sisters, he reflected. He wasn't his father. *My "drug" is the plane*, he thought.

He sat down at his home desk, and logged onto the FSU supercomputer, where the STCRS model awaited. He downloaded the current observations and environmental data, initializing a vortex for Hurricane Leonard. Holding his breath, he executed the command to run the model.

Edward had developed STCRS for a world with climate change. It was not meant for general tropical cyclone use, but rather, to handle extraordinarily intense storms that past research had predicted could occur in a warmed world: the kinds of hurricanes that certain people wanted to call "Category Six," the hurricane-hypercane transition, and hypercanes themselves.

In theory, hypercanes would have—not *different* physics, precisely, but under extreme conditions, the processes controlling a storm's intensity would shift. Under certain conditions of near-surface humidity and temperature, the temperature differential between the ocean and the upper atmosphere would be too great for a storm to achieve an equilibrium by normal means. It would take in more heat than it could dissipate by the usual tropical-cyclone processes of rainfall, venting up through the "chimney" of the eyewall, and surface vapor fluxes. This was the meaning of "supercritical" in the model's name.

Of course, infinite intensification was impossible. There was always a limiting factor. But in supercritical conditions, that limiting factor would be the storm's own internal friction. It was slower and far less efficient at dissipating heat, so the storm could get much, *much* stronger. Such was the theory, which atmospheric scientists had known since the 1980s.

The question was whether Leonard's environment would be supercritical. The upper-air crew had found that temperatures in Leonard's projected path were currently minus seventy Celsius. Even if Leonard went over the hottest spot in the Gulf, seventy below zero at the tropopause would not be cold enough to make the environment supercritical. The cold front's passage would lower the upper-air temperature, but by how much? The HAFS didn't predict a supercritical environment even then, because it didn't take Leonard over the hottest eddy. Eighty below and thirty-five-degree seas didn't *quite* make the cut either. As extreme as the HAFS-simulated storm was, it was not a—

Edward took a deep breath. *Simmer down,* he told himself. *Don't get excited. See what the model shows first.*

The phone rang with the ringtone that Edward had set specifically for calls from Anne-Elise: "Atomic" by Blondie. She would have plenty to rant about, he supposed. This would probably be a long conversation. The model might even be finished by the time he got back to his desk.

*   *   *

The run had indeed finished quickly, so Edward's script set the next task going. The STCRS post-processing software automatically generated images of the raw model output, an image of each predicted variable for each height level from the surface to the top of the output field. STCRS produced output all the way to the fifty-kilometer level, well into the stratosphere. For normal tropical cyclones, this would be unnecessary, a waste of computing resources, as they did not extend that high into the atmosphere. But STCRS was not designed for normal tropical cyclones.

At this reflection, he considered the pronunciation that his team had decided upon. *We could have pronounced it* "stickers" *or* "stockers," he thought, *but there's a dark allusion in pronouncing it as we do. This is the* "stacker" *model.*

As the output directory filled up with folders and images, Edward gazed at the images in his viewer.

Meteorologists had to understand and consider many different variables that laypeople did not often know about because they didn't need to know about them. Edward would look at these when he had the time. They were important for understanding the structure and physical processes of the hypothetical storm. But even meteorologists—or perhaps *especially* meteorologists—also just wanted to see the big, splashy fields.

He clicked the menu in his image viewer and selected "Surface Pressure." The software instantly rendered a timeline of images for him. He pressed the right arrow key repeatedly, advancing the modeled evolution of Hurricane Leonard as it quickly became Major Hurricane Leonard—*no surprise there*, he thought—then headed northeast, picked up by the forecast trough—entered the east-central Gulf of Mexico, the hottest sea temperatures in the world at the moment—continued to intensify—reached the intensity of—

Edward's eyes popped. He gaped at the modeled projection.

It stared back at him pitilessly, almost defiantly. The simulated eye of Leonard glared out from his screen, contoured with a pressure value in dark, dark blue. *A pressure value of 730 millibars.*

His pupils flitted away from the monitor.

He tried to calm his beating heart. He had seen simulations of storms with this intensity before.

But only in research. Only in simulations of hypothetical storms that we added to the model ourselves as baseline vortexes just to see what was possible. This is a real storm. This exists. It has a name.

Edward took a deep breath. *It's the output of a computer program. This happens sometimes. Even the operational models can go hog-wild sometimes, producing forecasts far stronger than the storms actually end up becoming. It's been happening for, what, forty years? This particular computer model stunt is almost as old as I am. And this is a research model, an experimental model. It belongs to my FSU group, so we have no obligation to release anything to the public. The Director is absolutely right about that. It would be grossly irresponsible of me to dump this to the Internet.*

I'll see what the operational models do first. They're missing something, I think, but I may be wrong and they may be right. Time will tell.

Edward forced himself to think of the word he had been avoiding. *Anyway, even in this simulation, it's not a hypercane.*

Not quite.

He closed the STCRS image viewer and tried to forget about it. *I need a nap,* he thought, getting up. *I'm not a young man anymore, and the past few days have been hard on me. And if I may be called back to the office at any time, I should nab what sleep I can.*

*   *   *

Edward's dream—a flight dream, as was often the case for him—was suddenly and rather rudely interrupted. Edward blearily reached for his phone, trying to silence the sounds of "Surfing in a Hurricane" by the late, great Jimmy Buffett. This was the ringtone he had set for Dr. Vinay Chandra, and the Director only called when there was a critical situation.

"Hello? Director?"

There was a pause. "Edward, did you get any sleep?"

"I've been asleep since eight. What time is it?"

"It's two in the morning." Chandra paused again. "I'm glad you got some rest, because we need you back at the office."

Edward suppressed a groan, scrambling to clear his eyes. "Immediately?"

"As soon as you're able to drive safely."

"What's going on?" he said.

93

"The recon crew in Leonard just found that it's a Category Five."

"*What?*" Edward was suddenly wide awake. He stumbled out of bed. Fortunately, he had only changed out of his trousers for pajama bottoms. He slept shirtless these days. It was just too hot to wear a top under sheets. "But it was just upgraded to a hurricane...." He quickly did the math in his head. "Nine hours ago."

"It's happened before," Chandra said grimly. "But the problem is, we have no reason to believe it's finished."

"Well, no. All the good models were saying that." *Mine included.* "What's the current intensity?"

"914 millibars and 180 miles an hour."

Edward whistled as he pulled on some socks. "Gotcha. I'll be over as soon as I can." He paused, unable to resist adding, "I don't suppose you want to know what STCRS did with it?"

"Not particularly. Get over to the office, Kirby."

"Aye, aye, Cap'n." Edward knew that when the Director called him by his surname alone, rather than his first name or even his surname and honorific "Dr.," it meant he was not in a mirthful mood. "I'll be there."

*   *   *

It was Labor Day weekend. Technically, Edward supposed, it was Labor Day itself now. The cold front was forming out west, but it was still quite warm. The late hour did not prevent Miami's streets from being packed with revelers, beach-goers, partiers, vacationers.... *How many of them know what's in the Bay of Campeche?* Edward wondered. There were so many people out and about that it took him almost an hour to get to the NHC.

He finally made it to the center and strode in once he got past security. Everyone inside looked very serious. Several people were gaping at their screens.

"Intensification has continued, I take it?" Edward asked.

"It's 881 millibars and 195 miles an hour," Adela Fisher replied.

Edward's eyes widened. "So almost a hundred millibars in

ten hours. Thirty-three in just one. We're in big trouble, aren't we?" That prediction from STCRS came roaring back to his mind.

Director Chandra scowled, but neither he nor anyone else could dispute the point.

Before: sowing the wind

Chapter 7: A Long Walk to Hell

Thirty-two years ago, Panama City, Florida.

The Ford Escape ambled down U. S. Highway 98 twenty miles per hour below the posted speed limit.

This wasn't a wholly unusual occurrence in Florida, where there were so many elderly drivers, but the reason for it in this specific case was something else. In the driver's and front passenger's seats sat Vernon and Jacqueline Kirby, both in middle age. The car was weaving and shifting—not gears, but direction—at a speed that would have been considered leisurely if the driver had been doing it intentionally.

In the super-sized cup holder, two empty beer cans rattled. Several more rolled back and forth on the floorboards.

Jacqueline lurched in her seat as her husband swerved the car almost onto the shoulder. "You drive like shit," she snarled, choking down a surge of bile from intoxication and carsickness.

Vernon jerked the car back toward the center line—and about a foot over it into the passing lane—as if the car were a weapon in his hands. "You want to take the wheel? All you do is bitch and whine and drink—"

Jacqueline laughed sharply. "That's a riot coming from you. You drink up your money and you're too lazy to have any ambition for more." She took a deep breath and reached for her purse, taking out a bright red lipstick and applying it sloppily.

"You look like a whore. That your plan to get more money?" Vernon snapped. He eyed the middle seat, swerving the car again. "It's clear where that one got it from—"

Smack! Jacqueline reached across the shift stick and cup holder to slap her husband in the face. He jerked—and with him, so did the car, just as they crossed onto a bridge. Tires squealed as he tried to avoid an impact with the concrete half-walls. Jacqueline swore again.

Seventeen-year-old Chelsea Kirby, sitting alone on the middle seat in the state of numbness or ostensible catatonia in which she had existed for the past two weeks, ignored the beer cans, her father's intoxicated driving, and her mother's equally intoxicated rage by sheer force of will. But in the back seat, fourteen-year-old Edward and Anne-Elise sat tensely, staring ahead as though expecting the car to crash at any moment.

When their father nearly crashed into the bridge, Anne-Elise couldn't take it anymore. Her heart was pounding and she was absolutely certain that she was going to die if she remained in this car. She shouted out above her parents' venom.

"You're drunk! You're both *drunk*, and you're going to kill us all! Stop the car and let Chelsea drive!" she shouted.

Their parents' argument did cease at this. The tires squealed again as Vernon slammed the brakes, the Escape halfway across the bridge. It made a quarter-turn in an arc. Anne-Elise clutched her seat desperately, though she knew it would make no difference if the vehicle went off the bridge. The car ground to a sudden halt. All the voices within fell silent as well.

In that terrible moment, Anne-Elise feared that her father, in drunken idiocy, would slam the gas again and drive the car off the bridge intentionally just to spite her. But the moment passed.

"So your parents' driving isn't good enough for your royal highness?" he snarled, his tone icy cold and terrifying. "Your mother and I chauffeur you and your brother anywhere you need to go, and it's suddenly not good enough for you?"

"Not as *cool* as having your seventeen-year-old sister drive you?" Jacqueline added, her own fury with her husband forgotten when they had the chance now to team up against their own child. She barked a nasty, spiteful laugh, meeting Chelsea's eyes in the rear-view mirror. "I'm not letting either of you go off with *her*. You'd probably come back the same as her, *pregnant*, and your brother would be a perpetrator—"

In her incandescent fury and terror, Anne-Elise was certain that her mother's attack was an allusion to incest. "You're disgusting!" she shouted. "How could you say that to us? You're vile and disgusting, so *fuck you!*"

Edward's eyes widened. This was not the first time he had heard his twin sister use that word, but it was certainly the first time he had heard her direct it at one of their parents.

"How *dare* you speak that way to your mother?" Vernon bellowed. His voice was so loud that it hurt the teenagers' ears. "You either apologize to her or you can get out and figure out your own way home!"

Chelsea, Edward, and Anne-Elise all gaped wide-eyed at the threat.

Vernon saw their reactions and continued, encouraged by this response to his abusive bullying. "Same if my driving isn't good enough for you! You can find your own way home then too. Make your choice and make it now!"

Another terrible pause ensued, and it was clear that Vernon and Jacqueline Kirby were certain that Anne-Elise would cower, cringe, and apologize. After all, what fourteen-year-old would voluntarily step out of the family vehicle on the Hathaway Bridge, the mile-long stretch connecting Panama City's east and west?

But Anne-Elise had arrived at a resolution in those few seconds. For the past six months—ever since Chelsea had been increasingly getting into trouble, staying out too late, going missing with wild "friends," finally tearfully admitting that she had become pregnant, and then riding out of state across the country to get a mid-term abortion—Anne-Elise had been veering closer to an emotional ledge. Her parents had been drinking more and more heavily. Their fights had been getting worse and worse. Those fights had increasingly often invoked the names of their children, either as cudgels or as examples of how one or the other parent had failed terribly as a parent.

And at last, Anne-Elise had had enough. She could not have articulated it precisely, but something just seemed to shatter and vaporize inside her. The feelings of affection and loyalty that she had thought she felt for her parents, even through the ugliest fights and drunken scenes of the past few months, suddenly just... didn't seem to be there anymore. Anne-Elise felt numbness instead. It was odd, unnerving, disorienting. These were her parents. Wasn't she supposed to feel something?

But unlike those feelings of affection and loyalty, numbness was no barrier to doing what she knew she wanted to do.

"Fine," she said in remarkably cool and calm tones. She reached for the door handle, unbuckled her seatbelt, and picked up her small purse. "I'll get out, then." She unlocked the door and tried to lift the handle.

Jacqueline and Vernon could hardly believe their ears. He practically turned red. "You think you're going to *walk* home?" he shouted.

"I'll walk across the bridge and call an Uber." Anne-Elise opened the door.

Her parents snarled and screamed incoherently. "Like hell you will! You won't tell anyone about this!" Jacqueline raged, reaching for her door. Anne-Elise darted out, but unfortunately she was on the right side of the vehicle, same as her mother. Jacqueline stumbled over and grabbed Anne-Elise's phone out of her hands.

Once the initial step had been taken, it was easier to take more. Anne-Elise did not hesitate or think twice this time. At this moment, this was *not* her mother. This was a drunk, vicious adult who was trying to steal from her, control her, and endanger her safety. This was a person who was threatening Anne-Elise.

Fight, flight, freeze, fawn. Until now, Anne-Elise had never had to consider which would be her default reaction in a threatening situation. And now that she was in that kind of situation, she didn't think about it at all. She just acted.

As Jacqueline grabbed the phone out of Anne-Elise's hand, the teenager reached upward, fingernails out. Jacqueline screamed as her daughter's nails raked over her arm, drawing blood.

"You little *bitch!*" Jacqueline raged, slapping Anne-Elise

across the face. The teenager glared back, a red mark rising on her left cheek, but her other cheek was pink too from the fury that she no longer had her phone. The device was in her mo—in *this woman's* triumphant hands.

From inside the car, Edward had been watching the entire proceedings, his heart palpitating in shock, adrenaline, and dread. Vernon was observing too, a smugly satisfied smile forming on his face as Jacqueline triumphed. That smirk was too much for Edward. He unbuckled his seatbelt and reached for the handle of his door too.

"You think you're going to walk her home?" Vernon laughed. "Hand it over, then."

"I'm not giving you my phone." He gave his father a level stare. "If you want it, you'll have to take it from me."

"You think I won't? If Jac can, I certainly can." He clenched and unclenched his fists pointedly. "In a few years, you could take me. Probably win. But not yet. You haven't hit puberty yet."

Edward's face fell at the realization that, indeed, his father was much bigger and stronger than he was. It embarrassed him that he was fourteen and had not yet had the growth spurt, muscle development, beginnings of facial hair, or... other changes... that a few of the boys in his P. E. class boasted in the locker room. He was still a scrawny, short nerd with a voice that had only just begun to deepen. Even with his father drunk off his ass, Edward knew that he couldn't defeat Vernon Kirby in a physical fight.

"Please, if you're going to walk with her, please just hand it over," Chelsea begged from the middle seat, turning around to face him.

He scowled. "Finally decided to get involved?"

"Please just give me your phone, Edward," she said. "Please don't fight him."

"You heard her," Vernon said as Jacqueline got back into the car with Anne-Elise's phone in her hand. "You can either be quiet and ride home, or you'll be put out of the vehicle too."

101

There was no choice for Edward. Whatever had snapped and broken in his twin had now done the same inside him. He gave Chelsea a look of profound disappointment and derision for her cowardice and submission, but he did hand her the phone. It was better than being hit by a large man.

"*Coward*," he hissed at her, making her flinch.

He opened the door, stepped out, and slammed it as hard as he could. The Escape's tires squealed again as Vernon pulled it back onto the highway and roared down the length of the bridge.

With the vehicle no longer between them, Anne-Elise and Edward walked over to each other. They stared at the retreating rear window as the family vehicle got smaller and smaller.

"I hate them," Anne-Elise declared. She took a deep breath. "And I've hated them for a long time. I just didn't realize it until now."

It was on the tip of Edward's tongue to tell her, "No, *you don't*," but he did not. It was inconsiderate, for one, to imply that she did not know her own feelings best. And for another, the rational side of him knew that she was telling the truth.

I hate them too, he realized. *And why shouldn't I? What kind of parents would put their own children out of the car, take their phones away to deny them any way to get home other than walking, insult and strike them, all because they were drunk and their children didn't want to be in a vehicle with one of them driving?*

"I hope he wrecks the car and *kills* himself and *her*," Anne-Elise added, hatred and spite curling her lips.

Edward also refrained from saying "*You don't mean that.*" Maybe she didn't... but maybe she did. In a way, it would only be returning a like sentiment, just perhaps with more intention and purpose. Their parents were certainly indifferent enough to their welfare. *They tried to make us ride in a vehicle with a drunk driver. When we refused, they took our phones away so that we couldn't call for a safe ride. They forced us to walk ten miles home on a major highway in a city, with no way to call for help. They may not have wanted to kill us, but they definitely didn't think about our safety or our lives.*

"What about Chelsea?" he said instead.

Anne-Elise paused, considering that, as some of the fury melted from her face. "I don't want her to die," she finally said. "I hope *she* is okay. But she is weak."

Edward fell silent at that, as the long road stretched out ahead of them. He took a deep breath and girded himself for the walk. He didn't really want to begin just yet. It was so discouraging.

Anne-Elise seemed to be thinking in the same way. "It's a long walk, but at least we'll be safe." She reconsidered. "As long as nobody sees two teens walking alone and tries to hurt us, we'll be safe. And we're more in control of what happens than we would've been in that car."

That, Edward realized, was what was most important to her: control. He couldn't much blame her. "There are very few people who would abduct random children," he said to her. "Most of the time it's a parent in a custody battle who kidnaps a child."

"So that'll be *them* in a few years."

Edward sighed. He couldn't deny the fact that their parents did seem to be careening toward a divorce.

"Actually, no, I'm wrong," Anne-Elise said suddenly. "They wouldn't fight over us. They'd fight over who got to *not* have custody. They don't want us."

Edward blanched at her dark cynicism. "You really think so?"

"I'm sure of it. Edward, Mo—our mo—*that woman* said that if we did anything with Chelsea, I'd come back pregnant and you would have been the one to do it!" She scowled in disgust. "How could a parent say that? *She* said, to your face, that you would—that we would—be incestuous—" She shook her head, unable to even get the words out. "And if she does think that's happening, what kind of a mother is she—what kind of a father is *he*—to make awful comments about it rather than trying to stop it?"

"I don't think she meant that, Anne-Elise," Edward said. "I think she meant that I would get some random girl pregnant. Not *you.*"

Anne-Elise reconsidered the horrible moment in her mind. "You may be right. But that doesn't make it okay. That's still an awful thing to say to one's children."

Edward could not say a word against that conclusion. "It is," he agreed. "And she's wrong about what she did mean—what I think she meant. I'm not going to go through my life using and dropping girls—or women, when I'm grown up—like Chelsea did with boys, and I'm not going to drink like *them.* I won't be *anything* like the other people in this family."

"Neither will I," Anne-Elise vowed. "I'll never treat my family the way they treated us today! I don't know if I even want kids of my own, but I'll never treat a niece or nephew like this."

Edward extended his hand to her for a shake, which she gladly gave. They then turned and faced the rest of the bridge, a bleak and monotonous beginning for the first leg of their walk. But they had no choice now. They began the trek.

"This is because of *her,*" Anne-Elise said suddenly and savagely as they walked on. "Chelsea. She goes around getting in trouble, hanging out with wild people, getting *pregnant,* and it's provoking them to say things that they'd normally keep to themselves."

"They're responsible for their own words," Edward objected. "Chelsea is a teen like us. They're adults."

"They are responsible for what they said, but it's still partly her fault. They can't handle her and so they take it out on *us.* They see that they screwed up with her and so they don't want any of us anymore. And that's why I don't think either of them would want us if, or maybe *when,* they get divorced."

He didn't want to argue, since, after all, neither of them could know the truth—yet. Instead he changed the subject back to the walk ahead of them. "We might not have to walk all the way," he said. "Someone nice will probably stop for us and offer us a ride home. Or call the police, and the police will offer us a ride."

"I guess we'll find out." Anne-Elise seemed doubtful, but she was too focused on her hate for their parents to think about anything else.

*　　*　　*

They trudged on as cars passed, one after the other. They might as well have been self-driving, for all the attention that they gave to two kids walking the side of the road.

"The cops will show up," Edward said again, as if to convince himself more than her. "Too many cars have gone by for *someone* not to call them."

Anne-Elise gave him a skeptical look. "We have to keep going anyway."

"When the cops come," he insisted, fixed upon that idea, "we can tell them why we had to do this. Things will change then."

Anne-Elise then realized why her brother was focused on this idea. It was a lifeline to him, the chance to tell someone about the awful situation at home. "The cops have to come first."

"Well," he said stubbornly, "if they don't, we can tell the counselor at school. Someone needs to be told, Anne-Elise. This isn't normal and it isn't okay. They put us in danger."

"Who will believe us?" she exclaimed despondently. "It sounds so extreme and crazy! 'We didn't want to ride in the family SUV when our parents were driving drunk, so they ordered us out, *fought* with me, and took our phones away so we couldn't call for a ride—or report them.' That sounds nuts. And they would deny it, of course." She sighed. "I hope the cops come too. They wouldn't be able to argue with the fact that we *were* walking the side of the road without our phones, and when they tracked down our parents, they would give a breathalyzer test. The evidence would still be fresh. We'd be believed. But if we wait...." She trailed off unhappily.

Edward nodded. Nothing more needed to be said.

They walked on, their legs getting tired and their feet starting to hurt, but there was still a long way to go, and there was nothing along the way except subdivision after subdivision: a typical model of development for Florida. If they wanted to stop at a business to make a call, they would have to take a significant detour without a clear idea of where they were going, since they didn't have their phones.

But one good thing was that traffic had finally thinned out as they walked through residential areas. Anne-Elise breathed a sigh of relief—

"What are you doing in this neighborhood?" a woman's sharp voice popped at them.

The twins halted, looking around for the source. On the front entry of one of the cookie-cutter houses stood a suspicious-looking woman. A burly man, presumably her husband, stood beside her—and he carried an AR-15-style rifle in his hands. Anne-Elise's heart nearly stopped. Was this lunatic going to *shoot* them? Taking aim at pedestrians simply walking through the neighborhood was murder... *but him going to the execution chamber ten years from now is cold comfort if he splatters our brains across the sidewalk,* Anne-Elise thought. *Our parents wouldn't even mourn us. They'd only care about what would happen to them when it came out about why we were in this area at all.*

"We're stranded and having to walk home," Edward said, trying to soothe the couple.

The woman glared. "Why can't you call a ride?"

"We don't have our phones."

"Tell them *why,* Edward," Anne-Elise muttered.

"How," the man barked, still holding his menacing gun, "do two teenagers in the year of our Lord twenty-nineteen end up walking the streets without phones?"

"You tell them," his wife chimed in. She turned to the twins, scowling. "I don't know what you're doing, but I'm sure it's nothing good."

"Probably trying to rob the neighborhood," her husband said.

"Or sell fentanyl to someone here."

"Yep. That's probably why they have no phones. They can't be tracked that way."

"Our parents took our phones away and ordered us out of the car!" Anne-Elise exclaimed hotly.

"Bullshit," the man snapped. "No parent would do that." He hefted his gun. "You're wild youth, unruly teens, up to no good—"

His words brought their hated sister to mind for Anne-Elise. It was too much. Her resolution to let her more diplomatic brother handle the situation evaporated. "Call the police if you want to. We don't mind. We can tell *them* what happened."

The man then laughed darkly. "You must think I'm stupid." He hefted his gun and fired.

Anne-Elise screamed, but the bullet pinged off the street instead of hitting either of them. He had deliberately missed, firing a warning shot. Surely that was still illegal, since they were just walking harmlessly along the sidewalks... but in this moment, Anne-Elise didn't much care. These people were crazy—and armed.

"Get out of this neighborhood if you know your own good!" he shouted. "And tell your gang that the next time they send someone into *this* subdivision, we won't miss!"

"Come on," Edward said anxiously to her, tugging her sleeve. "Let's just go. These people are nuts."

Anne-Elise did not want to turn her back to them, but she knew she had no choice. She turned aside, doubling back with him the way they had come. "They must have had a drug dealer in that area before," she said quietly, "so they think any teen stranger in there is one now." Her gaze hardened. "They're still insane, though."

"You were right," he suddenly said as they reached the edge of the subdivision and reentered an artery road. "People are *scum*. They're selfish and crazy! Nobody is going to offer us a ride or even call the cops. Instead they try to shoot at us! For nothing! We were just walking! We have a right to walk on the sidewalks."

"Yes, Florida Man and Florida Woman are crazy and dangerous, and you never know where you'll find them," Anne-Elise muttered. "You'd expect to find them in the swamps, or a trailer park... but you're just as likely to find them in a pretty, 'respectable' suburb like that."

"Horrible, nasty people can have money."

"Well, yes. We know that from personal experience, don't we?"

He gave her a silent, curt nod. They continued walking, making sure to avoid the next subdivision.

*　　*　　*

The extra distance to walk meant that they took much longer to finally get home—and had to go through neighborhoods where the residents increasingly kept to themselves behind locked doors and barred windows. Anne-Elise and Edward were sweaty, exhausted, and almost numb from the shock and fear when they finally entered their familiar street.

The driveway of the Kirby house came into view as the sun fell low in the sky and the shadows lengthened. Anne-Elise glowered as their carport became visible—and the vehicle within.

The Escape was intact. Their father had not crashed it, and there was no indication that he had been arrested for DUI and detained.

"Well," Edward remarked upon the sight of the family car, "at least they're safe...."

"There is no justice in this world."

He raised his eyebrows at her, shocked—but perhaps, he supposed, he was less shocked than before. The long, traumatizing walk had done that to him. Perhaps she even had a point.

Yes, perhaps his sister really did mean those harsh words. *If she does,* he thought, *she has more in common with them than she would want to admit, wishing harm on others for their wrongdoing.*

But he still couldn't entirely blame her. They reached the door and entered the house, bracing themselves.

*   *   *

The house was oddly, disturbingly quiet except for the low murmur of the television. The white tile floor, white walls, stylish minimalist Scandinavian furniture, abstract art reproductions, and stark LED lighting created an atmosphere that Anne-Elise had never cared for, and now, the starkness of this house's interior seemed almost like a horror-movie set. Anne-Elise half expected to walk into one of these rooms and find blood and gore spattered all over the white tile, like a jump scare in a movie. *The way Mom and Dad are going, it'll happen someday,* she thought darkly.

And to make matters worse, it wasn't even immaculately clean. Anne-Elise saw spots of dirt, liquor stains, mildew, and grimy shoe prints disfiguring the floor and furniture. She shuddered. Definitely like a horror-movie set. She liked modern styles herself, but not like *this*.

Almost any style can be made to look creepy, she thought, *but Victorian, medieval, Gothic, things like that—they are at least cozy even when they are creepy at the same time. There's nothing cozy about modern minimalism when it's made creepy. It's just gross and disturbing. Blood, gore, and filth on stark white.*

But Art Deco can't really be made creepy, she thought. *Art Deco and Mid-century Modern aren't creepy. That's stuff like starbursts, spheres, other geometric shapes, and science imagery. Science-fiction things, sometimes. It was a golden age for science. It was the dawn of the space age and the atomic age. Not exactly the stuff of horror. That's why it can't be made creepy, and that's what I'll make my house look like someday. A beautiful golden future, no horrors from the past. It will look nothing like this, anyway.*

Chelsea passed the twins, looking away from them, not meeting either's eyes. Anne-Elise scowled at her older sister, her mind distracted at once from plans for a distant future when she was free of this place and these parents.

"You made it home," Jacqueline Kirby said, coming out from the kitchen. She hiccuped, making Anne-Elise scowl even more. "I'm glad." She reached into her pocket and produced their cell phones. "Here you go."

The living room furniture creaked as their father rose. "You two seem to be intact. Sweaty, though. Get cleaned up and we'll order in a pizza for dinner tonight. You get to pick the toppings."

It was as if nothing had happened. Both of their parents were acting... normal. Not apologetic, but instead they seemed to be pretending that the horrible scene and the despicable abandonment had not taken place.

What the hell? Anne-Elise thought as she and Edward went to their respective bathrooms to wash their faces. They passed their older sister again, who was in her room.

"I just wanted to tell you," Chelsea began, "they're going to buy us all new laptops tomorrow."

"What for?" Edward snapped. "I don't need a new computer."

"Unless they smashed our existing ones in a drunken fit while we were away," Anne-Elise spat.

"They didn't," Chelsea said repressively, "and that's horrible to say." She turned to her brother. "You could probably ask them for something else. I expect they'll get you whatever you want."

"Why?"

"I think they're sorry and want us to forgive them," she said. "We should. It's the right thing to do. I've been reading the Bible since... the abortion... it's been a comfort to me... and forgiving them is what we should do."

Anne Elise had very different ideas of their parents' motives. "I think that's delusional. They're trying to buy our silence. There's an old Pat Benatar song about it. You talk about the Bible, but this is actually like 'Hell Is for Children.' They don't care about us. They care about protecting themselves. That's all it is."

Chelsea scowled. "You are far too bitter and cynical for a

fourteen-year-old."

"No, you are just blind and stupid. But of course you are. That's how you got into *your* situation, isn't it? You didn't think it could happen to you." Without waiting for Chelsea to snap back, Anne-Elise flounced into the bathroom to clean up.

I will never be like them or her, she vowed to her reflection. *They won't win. I will survive this household, I will be successful, I will become something better and more important than any of them, and when that day comes, I'll tell all three of them to go to hell. I will be a survivor, not a victim— no matter what it takes.*

Chapter 8: The Wages of Sin

Thirty-one years ago, Tuscaloosa, Alabama.

Chelsea Kirby strode across the University of Alabama campus, heading for her car. The campus was practically shut down, both for Christmas break and for COVID-19, but Chelsea herself would not be going home.

Her first semester in college—the pandemic semester—had been bizarre, nothing like she had expected. Surely quarantines, isolation, and remote classes were not the typical college experience? But they had been that for her this term.

However, if she went home to Panama City, she would probably get the virus. Anne-Elise and Edward both had it at the moment, and their parents had quarantined them in their own home. The twins were not allowed to leave their bedrooms, according to the text messages that they sent their older sister in fury. Their parents gave them their meals by quickly opening their bedroom doors, shoving trays of food through, then slamming the doors again.

Chelsea remembered the most recent text Anne-Elise had sent her. **They say that they have to protect themselves because they're older and sick,** she had scoffed, adding an emoji with censor symbols over its mouth. **They're sick because they're a pair of drunks. If anyone should get COVID, it's them. They might die and then we would all be better off.** A skull emoji had followed this.

Chelsea had refrained from scolding her younger sister for wishing ill upon their parents. Anne-Elise was sick with a terrible virus and, with her brother, was being treated like a criminal in her own home. Chelsea could make allowances. After all, it wasn't as if Anne-Elise *meant* these spiteful things she often said. She was just angry a lot. That was all there was to it. She didn't mean it. She *couldn't* mean it.

Chelsea felt sorry for her siblings, but she didn't want to return to that herself. *Fortunately,* she thought, *I don't have to. I have another option: the one bright light this semester.*

During fall of last year, as a high school senior, she had

looked forward to college, because she would be in a different state, well away from the disaster that was home. She wouldn't have to think about the increasingly vicious fights of Vernon and Jacqueline Kirby, nor their alarming descent into pronounced alcoholism. She wouldn't have to live with her foulmouthed fifteen-year-old sister or the venomous invective that Anne-Elise often spewed. That was a good thing. *If I had to live with her all the time, I might start to think she did mean the stuff she says,* Chelsea thought.

She wouldn't have to remember what she had done just a year and a half ago. Moving to Tuscaloosa for college was supposed to be a clean slate. She wouldn't be around any of the boys from high school. She wouldn't have to face any of her "boyfriends" from that era or consider what had followed their attentions to her.

The pandemic had made Chelsea's first semester of college a disappointment, but she had to acknowledge that it was certainly *not* a disappointment in terms of being a clean break from the past.

And then there was her one bright light: her boyfriend, Richard Mellor. Finally, Chelsea had found a worthwhile boy—no, she corrected herself, *man.* Richard was a sophomore studying political science, but despite being just a year older than she, he was mature beyond his years. Unlike the high school boys that Chelsea had known, he did not expect sex.

Chelsea had enjoyed her awakening as a sexual being. It had been fun to discover that part of herself. *But there was a price,* she thought, cranking her car. *Many prices, really. The obvious one—*

She sighed. *Forgive me. I did what my parents wanted, and at the time, I thought it was what I wanted too, but it was wrong. It was a sin. It was homicide, even if the law doesn't call it that, and I will have to live with that for the rest of my life. In a way, it's worse to have to live with the punishment of one's own conscience than to suffer punishment from the law.*

There were other prices that she had to pay as well. Now, her first time could never be with Richard. He knew that she had a past, and he had accepted her anyway, but she still regretted that she wouldn't get to discover this with him.

Eight different boys from high school, she thought, driving toward Richard's parents' house, *and I'll have to go through my life knowing that every one of them has memories like—that —of me.* She burned with shame at the thought.

There was nothing to be done now, of course. It had happened, and the past was immutable. She would just have to move forward and take comfort where she could. She did not like to talk about it with her family, because none of them would understand, but she had found some comfort in the story of the "woman who had lived a sinful life" in the Bible.

The Kirbys were not a religiously observant family, so she had no real idea how to look for a house of worship that would suit her. She had read about the different branches of Christianity and still had no clear notion which one was the one for her, so she had focused on reading the Bible in solitude.

Then she had met Richard. It had been a chance meeting at a line to pick up fast food. They had been the only two students there at that moment, and Chelsea was having to balance a handbag, a backpack, and her food. When Chelsea's order almost overwhelmed her, Richard gallantly defied the social-distancing orders to assist her. They had then defied the masking orders as they introduced themselves and shared their meal together.

Richard was from a religious family, but it was not a churchgoing one either. The Mellors had stopped attending after their former church had decided to follow COVID guidelines and switched to televised sermons. Instead they held home prayer meetings in their living room with a handful of like-minded people. *"Rather than being told what to think by some preacher who's corrupted by the world, we'll decide what God's Word means ourselves,"* Richard's mother had said. It was a revelation to Chelsea—and, as Richard had told her, why shouldn't they do so? Every church had originally formed by splitting off from another one.

114

She would be spending Christmas with his family, and she looked forward to it. Richard's parents had plans to fly up to Washington to attend some sort of demonstration during the first week of January, and Chelsea didn't know much about that, but they would be back at the university campus by then anyway.

She was only nineteen years old, but Chelsea believed she had found the man she wanted to marry. Richard had been a source of stability, and in his family, she had found the family she had always wanted for herself.

She had reached the house. After she pulled into the Mellors' driveway and parked, Richard stepped out to greet her in a hug. She hurried inside, letting him remove her suitcases from the vehicle like the gentleman he meant to be.

Mr. and Mrs. Mellor then welcomed her inside with smiles and the promise of hot chocolate. She smiled as well as she stepped in.

*   *   *

The Mellors' house was very different from the Kirbys' in several ways. The furnishings and décor were a little dated and generic, unlike the hyper-modern minimalist look of the Kirby home. But they were also homier, and the shabbiness of the Mellor home was not disturbing like the dirt and stains in the Kirby house were. *It's because this is just normal wear,* Chelsea thought, sitting down contentedly on a plush sofa. *It isn't signs of abuse and alcoholism.*

Richard sat down in the living room next to her as his mother brought them all mugs of warm hot chocolate.

Amelia Mellor was gentle-faced. She had clearly never been a bombshell beauty, but she was a pretty enough woman in middle age. She wore her mouse-brown hair long, falling in waves on her shoulders, and donned comfortable trousers and a holiday sweater at home. She was not troubled in the least by the presence of an outsider in their home during a pandemic.

"I'm so glad that Richard brought you home," she said, hugging Chelsea after carefully setting the hot chocolate on a side table. "You're a beautiful, beautiful young lady. And I was so sorry to hear about all that you have suffered. Please, my dear, know that you are welcome among us for as long as you remain in Richard's life—and I hope that is for a long time!"

Chelsea was embarrassed. "I don't deserve your compassion," she mumbled.

"You're quite wrong there, dear. We are called upon to show compassion. We may not deserve *God's* compassion, but He grants it anyway, so we should do the same for each other." She patted Chelsea's shoulder, smiling. "Nonetheless, the fact that you say this of yourself means that you know it was wrong, what was done to you. You blame yourself, but you mustn't—not entirely."

"I wasn't... forced. I mean...." Her face was red. "Raped." The word seemed harsh, unsuitable for conversation with this gentle woman, but it was better, she supposed, to just say outright what she meant so there was no mistake.

"Well, no, but I meant what came later. You were a minor. You were under your parents' control. They wanted to get rid of an embarrassment to *them* without concern for what it would mean to *you*. Your parents were selfish, and I will pray for them."

"I don't know...." Something was still troubling Chelsea, and she felt that she could confide in this woman. Perhaps it was that she had never known another female friend or relative in whom she could confide about serious matters—or perhaps she'd never wanted to confide in anyone about serious matters—but she trusted Amelia Mellor. "If I had become a single mother, would I have gone to college? Would Richard have even looked at me?"

She sipped her hot chocolate gravely. "I cannot say if you would have gone to college, but if you had met Richard, it would not have mattered to him. And if God has plans for the two of you together, you would still have met him, even if it wasn't at college."

Chelsea's heart thumped. "You think—you truly think—that this could all be a plan? I've started reading the Bible, you know, but I don't know what to make of some of it. I mean... God may have had great plans for people in the Bible *then*, but now? For me?"

"God has plans for everyone, dear." Mrs. Mellor smiled again. "Richard is very taken with you. And I see why. You are sweet. You deserve better than your blood family." She raised her eyebrows as Chelsea, embarrassed, sipped her own hot chocolate to avoid answering immediately. "I understood from Richard that your parents have locked up your teenage siblings because they supposedly have COVID?"

Chelsea set her mug down, unsure how to answer that. *Supposedly* had COVID? "They tested positive," she said uneasily, "and they do have symptoms. Anne-Elise and Edward have texted me themselves to say so. So our parents haven't locked them up on false pretense. But I don't think they should have done it at all. It's cruel."

Mrs. Mellor nodded. "It is. Have they looked into ivermectin?"

"I don't know. I don't think so."

"They should. When Gary had it a couple of months ago, I got that for him, and he recovered in just two weeks!" She lowered her voice. "*They* don't want us to know about that, you know. So I suppose that if your parents are worldly, they may not believe it even if they are told about it. I feel sorry for your brother and sister. We have a little left over, though. You could mail it to them. Unless your parents are confiscating their mail."

"I really don't know. I think they're on the mend now. My sister's texts seem to have more anger and less defeated misery, for sure! I'm just afraid they are still contagious."

Anne-Elise and Edward weren't sick for two weeks, she suddenly thought. *They have had symptoms for just one. Did this medicine actually do anything at all for Mr. Mellor? Maybe he was just sicker, though.*

She didn't say that to her hostess, of course. Mr. Mellor probably had just had a bad case. She supposed that, since *she* hadn't lived in this house or observed his progress with the virus, she wouldn't know as well as someone who had. No doubt the medication really had helped him. Mrs. Mellor, who had been his primary nurse and had observed his case more closely than anyone, surely wouldn't have claimed that it had helped when it hadn't.

Mrs. Mellor nodded. "I will pray that they recover fully, then. And I'll still mail the ivermectin! A Christmas present for them. It won't do *us* much good now."

At this, almost as if on cue, the men of the house entered the living room, talking boisterously.

"If you still feel weak, Dad, I'll get the branches down tomorrow and check the roof," Richard said. He sat down on the sofa next to Chelsea and flung an arm around her as his father took the classic brown leather armchair that even Chelsea recognized as his.

"Branches?" she spoke up. "What happened?"

"A thunderstorm broke some tree branches and they fell on the roof," he explained. "Dad's worried it got damaged."

"I'm not weak, though," Gary Mellor said. "I can manage it."

"Mrs. Mellor was telling me about how you were sick with COVID," Chelsea ventured. "Do you think you might have long-term symptoms?"

He scoffed. "No. It's just being in my fifties. That's all!"

"Don't believe everything you hear," Mrs. Mellor scolded her. "There is no such thing as 'long COVID.' It's just an excuse for lazy people not to work!"

Richard agreed with his mother. "As if they didn't have money handed to them on a silver platter with telework! Lazy, entitled, and spoiled."

"But not in *this* house!" Mr. Mellor said. "I'll get the branches down."

"I'll still walk around on the roof, Dad."

"All right," he conceded. "You can do that."

They lapsed into silence, the women sipping their hot chocolate as the men found a football game on television. Chelsea finished her cocoa before it got cold, and Mrs. Mellor got up to make more, including cups for her husband and son. The men declined.

Finally, during halftime, Richard broached the subject of his father's strength again. "Are you sure you're up to this trip to DC that you two have planned for January? It's likely to be cold."

"I think we can handle a bit of cold. Son," Mr. Mellor said very seriously, "there are times when we are called upon to take risks and make sacrifices for the greater good. We have to be there."

"The future of this country is at stake," Mrs. Mellor added gravely. "We are living in dark times."

That seemed very dramatic to Chelsea. Weren't they just attending an election protest? She had been to an anti-abortion event this semester, so she was one of the last people who would say that protests didn't matter, but surely it was putting an extreme spin on it to say that the future of the country was at stake.

She didn't say that to her hosts either, of course. *These are lovely, kind, welcoming people,* she thought. *I like this family so much more than my own. In fact... yes. I want this to become my family. I shouldn't be rude to them. They're much wiser than I am, obviously. They haven't made the mistakes that I did.*

Instead she leaned into Richard, cradling her hot chocolate as he pulled her close. They watched the rest of the football game together, his parents observing serenely. It was a perfect picture of domestic tranquility, and Chelsea vowed that, if Richard would have her, she would create this with him too someday.

*　　*　　*

Thirty years ago, Orange Beach, Alabama.

Chelsea clutched her bouquet close and smiled, closing her eyes in bliss as the sea breeze kissed her face. Thirty feet ahead, the white-topped waves of the Gulf crashed ashore. The famous soft white sand of this stretch of coastline filled her white strap sandals, but she didn't mind. That was part of having a beach wedding.

Today, Chelsea thought, was a white day. Her dress was

also white, of course, something that she wouldn't have been allowed to wear a century or more ago, but the color now basically meant "new start" rather than "virginity," so that worked well for her. White was new paper, clean linen. Clouds. This beautiful sand. *And the next phase of my life,* she thought.

Two years ago, I wouldn't have thought that I would be getting married. It wouldn't even have been something I wanted. I would have been horrified, actually. I wouldn't have wanted to think of being "chained down" or "losing my freedom." What a counterfeit that freedom was, though. This is better. This is right.

She regretted that Richard's parents wouldn't be here, but they were, unfortunately, in prison for their part in the— events—of a year ago, the protest that they had attended after her Christmas visit. It was hard for Chelsea to imagine the mild, parental Mellors screaming at cops, smashing windows with a pole, and such things, but there was video of them doing so.

She still considered it shocking and cruel for them not to be allowed to attend their only child's wedding. Couldn't they be guarded and given ankle bracelets, if the administration deemed them—this normal, middle-class couple—such a terrible danger? Richard agreed.

"*It's an attack on the American family,*" he had said, "*but that's the kind of enemy we face. The fight for the traditional family is the fight of our lives.*"

Chelsea saw his point. Since becoming close to the Mellors, she was becoming more interested in politics than she ever had been. *I have come to care about something bigger than own personal pleasure,* she thought. It was such a pleasant, gratifying feeling, far more pleasurable and satisfying than the cheap thrills of high-school wild-girl revels. This family truly had helped her to turn her life around and become a totally different person.

She had decided that, to make amends for the abortion, she had to get involved in the anti-abortion movement on campus, and they had welcomed her with open arms. They particularly valued her personal experience. *"There's no voice as strong as that of a survivor,"* the organization's president had said. Chelsea now understood that she *was* a survivor rather than purely a perpetrator. Her parents had all but forced her to get one—but no, that was mainly her mother, because it usually was the mother who pressured a daughter into an abortion, the organization's leadership had explained to her. Fathers usually didn't want to destroy their children or grandchildren. It was almost always the mother—or grandmother, in the case of a pregnant teen. Chelsea now understood that she had been a victim of her mother, but she could not absolve herself either. She had not, after all, been raped. To make up for her own part, she was becoming more involved in pro-family political issues. Her wedding today would make her an even better spokeswoman for the topic of family.

Richard's parents couldn't be here, but his college advisor, Professor Hal Gilbertson, a leadership figure in the Department of Political Science, would fill the traditional role of the groom's family. A native of Florida rather than Alabama, he was planning to leave the University after the spring semester and run for office in his home state, so he wanted to do this for his favorite student. Professor Gilbertson believed that the Mellors and others in their predicament would be released from prison before they served their full sentences. Chelsea and Richard hoped he was right.

In the meantime, their house was Richard's in trust. He and Chelsea would be living there. It was more appropriate and adult than married-student housing. She vowed to take good care of the house for as long as it was theirs.

"Stay out of the water, you idiot! You think you're going to go for a swim now? You'll freeze!"

Chelsea closed her eyes again, but this time it was in dread and disgust rather than bliss. Her wretched mother was approaching, and from the sounds of it, she had already been into the mimosas.

Jacqueline Kirby staggered up to her bridal daughter, kicking sand as she did. "Well!" she half-spat. Chelsea drew back; sure enough, she held a champagne flute with the telltale orange drink in it, and the scent of alcohol was on her breath. "You look nice. Pity that your husband's family is a pack of criminal morons, but I guess your original family isn't so great either."

Chelsea sneered at her mother. "Are you unable to be civil even *today*?"

Mrs. Kirby shrugged. "The truth's the truth."

"I don't want to discuss the plight of Richard's parents," Chelsea said tautly.

Mrs. Kirby burst out laughing. "Their *plight*, is it? Their self-inflicted plight? Exactly whose fault is it that they aren't here?"

"The administration's, for targeting them."

Mrs. Kirby shook her head. "What have they been doing to you that you believe this shit too now?" She chuckled nastily. "If they were 'targeted,' why weren't you and your groom targeted too? Oh yeah, because *you weren't there*. You and your man didn't *do* the shit his stupid parents did. I repeat myself: They brought this upon themselves." In a dark, yet oddly self-aware gesture, she raised her mimosa to the cloudy sky. "As do we all. Sometimes it takes less time and sometimes more, but we all reap what we sow in the end."

"Mom," Chelsea said, alarmed, "you don't have to think this fatalistically. You could stop drinking. Both of you. You're going to be dead in ten years or sooner otherwise."

She laughed again. "I know I'm going to die young. It's not a problem. The world is going to hell, and I don't want to be an old woman in it."

"It's not for us to decide when our time here is at an end."

"Sure it is. Who else has the right?" She stared at Chelsea. "You know what your brother told me? He said there'll be places on Earth in a few decades where people literally cannot survive."

"That sounds like climate alarmism to me."

122

"Is that term a Mellor family special? They're wrong, then. Your brother knows this stuff. He's started studying it and is talking about majoring in it. And I see it myself. Just a couple of years ago, Michael was a Category Five, but nobody even remembers it unless they were there where it hit, because bad storms are so common now. Your brother's right, and this is not going to get better. And it isn't just the climate. The world is going to pot in every way, and I see no reason to want to become old." She put the champagne flute to her painted lips as the perfectly nihilistic coda to this statement. "Bottoms up, daughter dearest."

And with that, she drained her glass, dropped it into the sand, turned her back, and stalked off.

Chelsea picked up the sand-encrusted glass, sighing. She took a deep breath to calm herself. As she did, she finally realized that the person her mother had yelled at over the cold water was her father. He *was* walking awfully close to the waves.

She decided to speak to him. He was her father, after all, and this was her wedding day. And if he was also drunk, as seemed likely, he might fall into the water. That would necessitate an ambulance, and it would certainly disrupt and delay her wedding. She didn't want that.

It had been just two years since Chelsea had last seen him, but Vernon Kirby had not aged well. His eyes were bloodshot and yellowish-tinted, and he had developed a large beer belly. He stared at the waves, something indefinably dark in his gaze as he fixed upon Chelsea knew not what. It sent chills down her spine. Her mother's mood was clearly cynical, but there was at least some bitter self-awareness to it. Her father looked like a man already planning his departure from the world.

The idea that he might be gazing upon the waves with precisely that intention frightened Chelsea. She hurried to his side, took his arm, and gently, subtly steered him away from the waves.

He didn't object, either verbally or with his motions, but

that also seemed creepily passive. Finally, when she had helped him up the nearest embankment to dry sand, he turned to her to speak.

To Chelsea, his expression and gaze seemed apologetic and regretful. Was he going to say that he was sorry for the past few years? She recalled the Mellors' prayers—and her own—and hoped for a moment that this might be that moment at last—

"Why the hell do you want to do this?"

Chelsea couldn't believe she had heard him right at first. She blinked. "I'm sorry?"

"You're a sophomore in college. If you get pregnant again, I'm sure that man will force you to carry it to term, and that'll be the end of any chance to get your degree."

Chelsea bristled, her hopes of her father's repentance shattered. "We are going to use contraception," she said coldly.

He snorted. "Didn't think Bible-thumpers approved of the Pill."

"There are lots of views about it among Christians, and the Mellors don't see it as a sin for married couples, as long as they aren't using it to avoid *ever* having children."

Vernon Kirby snorted again. "Convenient, I guess. Well, I hope it works. Don't forget to take it." He scowled. "But this is still a bad idea for other reasons. You're twenty years old. Even your mom and I didn't get hitched that young, and look what marriage did to *us*."

"I told Mom this, and now I'll try telling you. Seek counseling and put down the bottle. You can fix this. It doesn't have to end the way you think it does."

"It's already ended. We just haven't buried the corpse yet."

"You are legally married, and you're both alive and attending my wedding!" she insisted. "It's *not* over while you still draw breath!"

"It's over, Chelsea. The die is cast. Frankly, I regret ever marrying your mother, and I know she feels the same."

"The twins and I exist because you and Mother married!"

"Countless people would've existed if this or that couple had paired off, but because they didn't, those people *don't* exist. And it doesn't hurt them, does it? Because there *is* no 'them.' There's no anything, just a possibility that didn't happen."

Chelsea could not believe her ears. "Are you truly implying to me on my wedding day that you wish I had never been born?" she exclaimed. She shook her head. "I am sorry that you are this depressed, Dad. But consider. Richard's parents don't regret the fact that I exist. They love and value me."

"They're crazy, Chelsea, and they're in prison for acting on their craziness."

So they love me because they're crazy? Is that your implication? Provoked at last, Chelsea spat her response. "Before they were made *political prisoners*, they were better parents to me than you and Mom ever were. And that's why, today, I'm proud to change my name and become a Mellor. *They* are my real family." She glared at him. "After today, I must ask you to stay out of my life until you fix yourself. I'm praying for you, but *you* have to make the decision."

Without even waiting for a response, she walked off.

She passed the twins as she headed toward the site where the wedding decorations were being set up. It had been two years since she had seen them in person, and although she had had some preparation from the selfies and videos that they had sent over the years, it was still different to see the changes in the flesh. They both looked drastically different, having gone through puberty.

Edward was significantly taller than he had been at fourteen. He was quite a looker, too. He had discarded his glasses for contacts, it seemed, and was fit and muscled, no longer a scrawny geek. Chelsea knew from his texts that he had taken up swimming and competed with the high school swim team. He was contemplating numerous career options, including the Navy and Air Force, but he was also very interested in the weather. The keys to his first car jangled in his pocket.

Anne-Elise looked different too. She was at least five feet nine inches, rather tall for a girl or woman, and she had filled out in... other ways. She looked at least twenty, Chelsea's own age, and she had become pretty, but Chelsea knew that her sister's looks were not as striking as her own had been. *I don't mean that as vanity,* she thought. *It's just true. But Anne-Elise's personality and interests are very different from mine when I was her age, so I doubt she cares... and that's a good thing. It worked out okay for me, but I don't want them to go through what I did.* Her sister's texts and messages were mostly about her science fair projects, scholastic bowl, and the video game series *Fallout*.

Anne-Elise shot her older sister a glare as Chelsea passed. She winced. That look was one of hatred. *Does she truly resent my absence so much as that?* Chelsea wondered.

For a brief moment, Chelsea considered stopping beside the twins to talk—maybe even offering them houseroom in her and Richard's house, since the elder Mellors were in prison for the foreseeable future and there was a surfeit of bedrooms.

But no, that's a breach of trust. I shouldn't open their house to other people without their consent. She considered. The Mellors probably wouldn't mind Anne-Elise and Edward's presence, actually. They had not approved of the elder Kirbys, but they had always been sorry for the twins. *But I haven't discussed this with Richard. I shouldn't invite them without asking my husband first. And Mom and Dad could legally petition to have them back. They are minors. No, it's better not to even bring up the subject.*

The moment passed, and she continued by her siblings without a word.

*   *   *

Twenty-one years ago, Pensacola, Florida.

No one was crying at the funeral home. The guests who were distant relations or former colleagues of the departed did not know quite what to make of the fact that the three siblings were all dry-eyed, but so it was. With two coffins in the room, one ordinarily would have expected a large crowd of mourners, but there were not even many guests, and Chelsea had the bitter thought that, in fact, there were no true *mourners* at all.

In the interest of propriety, she and Richard had brought their two-year-old daughter, Vera, to the funeral. She had never known her Kirby grandparents, and now she never would. She did understand that she was to be quiet, at least.

Twenty-year-old photographs of Vernon and Jacqueline Kirby adorned the tables where the coffins rested. The coffins themselves were closed. There was no help for it.

"*Mom's head was basically severed when she was thrown partly through the front windshield. But since it wasn't all the way, her neck was right over the broken glass,*" Anne-Elise had said. She had put a finger to her own throat and had mimed cutting her head off, to Chelsea's shock. "*Dad's legs were bent backwards at both knees, and his neck was broken and his skull smashed in from the car roof's collapse.*"

Chelsea had tried to be compassionate rather than judgmental. Anne-Elise had flown down at once from Boston —or rather Cambridge, where she was in school. Despite the distance, it had actually been easier for her to get there quickly. Edward was working on his thesis defense, and Chelsea had been coordinating an important meeting between newly elected *United States Representative* Hal Gilbertson and a pro-family group. Anne-Elise had been the one forced to confirm the identity of their parents' bodies in the morgue after they were pulled from the wreckage of their SUV. It must have been an unbelievably traumatic experience for a twenty-four-year-old, as the twins now were. But she had been disgusted and shocked at how graphically explicit her younger sister had been in describing the bodies' condition. Did she truly feel *nothing* for their parents even after their violent deaths?

Forcing her thoughts back to the present scene, Chelsea watched blankly as her younger sister picked up a cup of coffee and sipped it.

"They're not even cold in the ground, but we already have an offer on the house," Anne-Elise said tonelessly, her black dress sheathing her figure in the dim light of the funeral home. "I'll say this for them. They did keep their home very desirable as a piece of real estate."

"About the only good thing they did for us," Edward muttered.

"With the proceeds, we'll be able to pay off their outstanding debts, and it will leave us with a hundred and eighty thousand. I have no objection to splitting it equally three ways."

Chelsea felt the crassness of discussing this at the visitation, but she still did not want to provoke a scene by scolding her siblings for it. *And Anne-Elise and Edward had to live with them for years after I left home. I guess... she did mean it all along when she said she hated them.* Guilt tugged at her. *I might have been able to stop this if I'd just invited them to Richard's parents' home. Maybe they would have shaped up once they lost all their kids. Maybe—*

Anne-Elise drained her coffee and picked up another cup, though she didn't seem to be enjoying it. To Chelsea's eyes, it was an act of compulsion, or perhaps a defiance of the alcoholism that had finally cost their parents their lives. Anne-Elise raised the second coffee cup, heavy irony and profound bitterness on her still-young face. "Neither of you object either? Good. Then here's to our *inheritance.*"

Chapter 9: A Beautiful Golden Future

Eighteen years ago, Cambridge, Massachusetts.

Anne-Elise knew she was supposed to be smiling, but at this point her graduation photos were more an assertion of defiance.

She glared.

Her gaze was fierce as the camera flash snapped. I *did it*, she thought, staring at the vague blur of the graduation crowd. She couldn't identify any of her guests there, but it didn't matter. The ones who could be there were.

And the ones for whom Anne-Elise had perhaps most intended her defiance could never be anywhere on Earth again.

I *did it*, she thought anyway, the grotesque images of Vernon and Jacqueline Kirby's dead bodies flashing through her memory in time with the camera. I *beat you. I broke free of you. You kicked me down, but I got back up. Now I am standing and walking across the stage of the best university in the country, and you'll never get up ever again.*

Today, Anne-Elise graduated with her doctoral degree in Plasma Physics. Her research assistantship at the Massachusetts Institute of Technology's Plasma Science and Fusion Center had given her a window into a brighter future, and she was now going to take her expertise into the private sector. A startup venture, Intensity Labs Advanced Fusion Testbed, had hired her as a chief engineer to design next-generation lasers.

Her work as a graduate student at MIT would not be directly applicable to her new career. MIT's PSFC focused on the torus tokamak option for fusion development, whereas Intensity Labs' approach was laser-mediated inertial confinement fusion. But for every meaningful job, there was always something to be learned and applied, even if the application was not direct. Anne-Elise knew that well. She had some ideas of her own for laser design already.

If Intensity Labs could meet its immediate goals, there was the promise of a major infusion of funding from Florida State.

Best of all, Intensity Labs was located just outside Tallahassee, not exactly where she had grown up—and there were too many unpleasant memories of Panama City for her to even *want* that now—but close enough that it would immediately feel like home.

Anne-Elise walked across the stage to shake the hand of the university president and departmental deans. Away from the popping flash of the camera, now she did notice her relatives in the crowd.

Her smile momentarily faltered. The one fly in the ointment, so to speak, of Intensity's location was that it was not Miami. And that was where Edward worked now.

He had obtained a doctoral degree too—his was in atmospheric science, with an emphasis in tropical meteorology—but he had managed to do it a year earlier than she had, and since then, he had obtained his pilot's license and begun his dream job as a forecaster at the National Hurricane Center.

Anne-Elise liked to tease him—good-naturedly, of course —that the reason it took her longer to get her degree was that nuclear physics and plasma physics were much more challenging fields than "weather forecasting." He never failed to rise to the bait, even though he knew well that it *was* bait and that she actually did not hold his profession or major in contempt in the least.

"*We're actually working hand-in-hand on the same problem, if you look at it in a certain way,*" she had told him several times. "*You're trying to prepare people for the world we currently have, and I'm trying to change that world.*"

"*But my job will always be needed, even if we solved climate change tomorrow,*" Edward would then argue. "*There will always be hurricanes. What's changed is how many bad ones there are.*"

"*Well,*" she would say, "*I'm about to get on that problem.*"

Anne-Elise smiled fully again. It would be all right. When Edward had saved enough money to achieve his *other* big dream and buy a small aircraft for himself, he could even fly from Miami to Tallahassee whenever his work allowed. They would see each other.

She stepped off the stage, her time in the spotlight at her graduation already over. There were many graduates, and each one could only have a fraction of a minute.

But graduation is a blink of the eye compared to a lifetime. It is just a stepping-stone. It's not the destination. At last, I am about to build that beautiful golden future I've dreamed of since I was a kid.

*   *   *

The crowd had broken up into a chaotic, disorderly mass of people. Anne-Elise hurried through the chaos to find her family. Her major professor had wanted to speak with her and his other students to wish them all well and congratulate them, but that was done now.

Still wearing her academic robes and carrying her diploma, she found her family. Her smile faltered again at the sight of Richard and Chelsea Mellor.

She supposed she would have been far angrier if they had snubbed her. It was... appropriate... for them to attend, especially since her parents were dead. And their daughter Vera, now five years old, was a cute little girl.

That thought had barely passed through Anne-Elise's brain when Vera herself curled her face, stamped her foot on the ground, and began to shout.

"I'm *hungry*! I want a sandwich! I got a headache!"

SMACK!

To Anne-Elise's shock and immediate contempt, Richard Mellor bent down and walloped her bottom—*hard.*

Vera's face screwed up in pain.

"You be quiet!" Richard snapped at her. "If you cry out, I'll spank you again!"

Vera bit her lip to avoid this retaliation, but she could not stop the tears from silently pouring down her cheeks.

Anne-Elise glared at him. "She's had to sit in the stands for hours. She probably *is* hungry."

"Don't tell me how to manage my family," he retorted.

131

Anne-Elise gave her sister a look of disgust for putting up with this. Chelsea finally had to intervene. "She's probably right, though," she said mildly. "Children do need to be fed."

Richard scoffed. "Nobody will be able to get any food anywhere for hours, with this crowd dispersing."

"Boston is a large city," Anne-Elise said. "If we took the T, we could even get to the harbor and have some seafood...."

"I'm not getting on the subway. You're liable to get stabbed."

"No, you aren't."

"I see videos of it on the Internet all the time."

"They're probably not even real. Most viral videos are fake now. Anyway, I've lived here for six years and I've never even witnessed an attack, let alone had one happen to me."

"*You* can ride like a hobo if you want," he said, "but I'm not going to, and neither will my family."

"Ah, so it's about classism, not fear of crime. I see."

Richard threw his arms up in the air. "You go on and do as you like! But I'm hiring an Uber."

"To a restaurant, I hope. Your daughter is hungry."

"She was given the option of staying with her grandparents—since *you* didn't invite them—"

"Why should I have invited your parents?" Anne-Elise scoffed. "They're nothing to me and that is how I want it." She gave him a pointed look as she readied her next barb. She knew well how to devise quick sound bites and "owns," as a child of the social-media age. "I'm only glad that they decided not to force their way in with baseball bats and pokers."

"They are free and clear. Get over it."

"Doesn't change the past. In any case, you should feed your daughter, not beat her for acting out because she's hungry."

"Anne-Elise," Chelsea cut in, "there's nothing I can do right now. We all see the crowd. She'll have to wait."

Anne-Elise sighed. "I have a granola bar in my purse. Vera, will that do for now? We'll eat lunch in a bit."

Sniffling, Vera accepted the granola bar. But she gave it

one look and then sneered back at her aunt, to Anne-Elise's shock. That look was *precisely* Richard's look of contempt in feminine miniature. "No!" Vera declared. "I don't want *that!*"

"We buy a brand called American Heartland Naturals," Chelsea put in unhelpfully.

"Well," Anne-Elise spat, "I support my university when I can." She turned to Vera again. "There's nothing wrong with it. The brand of this granola bar is Cambridge Plasma. It's made right here on campus, and it's just as good as the kind you like."

"No!" Vera shouted.

Exasperated, Anne-Elise took the granola bar back. "You see all these people?" She gestured around. "They're *all* hungry. They're mostly all going to go to restaurants. That means we'll have to wait for anything else. You can eat this granola bar now, or you'll be hungry and have a headache for a while!"

Vera pouted. "My headache's gone now. I'll just be hungry. I'm not eating *your* gross stuff."

Anne-Elise had had enough. *I never want children,* she vowed. "Fine," she said to the little girl. "If you change your mind, come back to me. But I'm going to talk to your uncle and other aunt now."

She turned aside from Richard Mellor—God, *why did Chelsea marry this horrible man?*—and looked instead to Edward, who had been silent through the whole awful interaction.

And to the woman with Edward, whom she was meeting in person for the first time. *His new wife, Emma MacArthur.*

"I'm very sorry about that," she apologized to Emma as the Mellors mercifully stepped aside. "I should have introduced myself to you first."

"It's fine! I understand," Emma said, Edward taking her hand in his and squeezing it proudly. "Children's needs come first." She pulled her hand free of Edward's and extended it to Anne-Elise for a handshake.

She doesn't look like me, Anne-Elise thought as she shook Emma's hand. *She's tiny, short, and has short dark hair. I am average build, tall, and have long dirty-blonde hair.*

She questioned herself about why that bothered her. What difference should it make that Edward's wife didn't resemble his sister? *I've heard about mothers who are possessive of their sons and see their wives as some messed up sort of "competition,"* she scolded herself. *Mom is dead now, and she never cared much about Edward—or me—anyway. But it could happen with a sister too when it's a very close emotional connection. That's why,* she resolved. *I'm troubled that Emma doesn't look like me because it's a sign that Edward "rejected" me. But he hasn't. We are siblings, and she is his wife. It's supposed to be different. It would actually be kind of weird if she did look too much like me.*

"Edward told me that you met at a conference," she said to Emma, "but that you don't work at the NHC."

"No," Emma agreed. "I work at the University of Miami. But we did meet at AMS—that's the American Meteorological Society," she explained. "I'm a research climatologist."

"Is it 'Doctor'?" Anne-Elise asked her. "I just want to be sure I address you right." She chuckled. "Since I now have personal knowledge of how important that is."

"Heh. No, I just have a Master's."

"No shame in that," Anne-Elise rallied. "It's good to meet you at last. Edward has spoken a lot about you."

Edward then interjected, somewhat embarrassed—but there was also brazen boldness mixed in, the same kind that Anne-Elise herself had exhibited as she walked across the stage. "We just wanted a quiet, private wedding," he explained. "Neither of us saw any point in a big ceremony. A Justice of the Peace gets the job done just as legally."

And you probably don't put any stock in "weddings" after the disaster that was our parents' marriage, Anne-Elise thought. But she didn't say that. Instead she she silently but pointedly raised her eyebrows in an unspoken question.

They instantly took her meaning. "Oh, God, no, what a horrible thought," Edward said, with a momentary shuddering glance at Vera Mellor. "Nothing like that. We just wanted to get hitched."

Emma, Anne-Elise noticed, appeared a little dashed at her new husband's clear revulsion at the idea of children. *They don't share views on that?* Anne-Elise wondered. *Or actually... it looks like they haven't even discussed it. Or if they did, he didn't listen to her. That's not a good beginning, either way.*

I share Edward's opinion of the little monsters. The thought had intruded before she even knew it.

She tried to shove it aside. "Well, it's an honor to welcome you to the family—such as it is," she managed self-deprecatingly. "Now let's get some of that delicious Boston seafood!"

*   *   *

Twelve years ago.

"Your performance has been outstanding," Director Vince Hailey said to Anne-Elise. "This is a new record for the time that a fusion lab can maintain breakeven energy."

Anne-Elise smiled. "Thank you," she said, "but I'm not satisfied yet. The laser is still far too expensive to power up. We may be at breakeven on the reaction itself, but not when the power used in the laser is counted."

Dr. Hailey nodded sympathetically. "Yes, it's a tough nut to crack. But you know about Edison himself! And all the false starts a century ago in quantum physics and designing the bomb."

She nodded. "I have some ideas of how to resolve the issue. I think, for one, we need to have two laser types."

Hailey raised an eyebrow. "You're talking about fast ignition."

"Yes. And I think we should switch to an ytterbium-doped laser."

"Neodymium glass is better-tested and easier to get."

"And so everyone, it seems, is using it," she said, "but nobody is experiencing a major breakthrough. I think we need to do something different."

"Ytterbium has issues—"

"I know, but it's still extremely efficient for most uses. The issues arise with the typical fusion application. But if we used *fast* ignition, specifically the cone method...."

"That also has issues. You're introducing a new element very, very close to the fuel itself."

Anne-Elise was excited now and eager to show off her idea. "I know that too, but I have an idea to leverage magnetic fields for shielding."

"So a combination of the principles behind the tokamak approach and ours? That's... certainly an interesting challenge."

She yielded. "It's easier to show you than to explain it."

She turned to her computer, where an atomic simulation program was running. She set a visualization of her simulation going and gestured for her boss to take control of the mouse to look at what he liked. The Director interacted with the simulation, eyes getting wider by the moment, as he quickly examined rendered diagrams and numerical results.

"Holy mackerel," he finally said.

Anne-Elise smothered a smile. *How wholesome. Such stark contrast with my potty mouth.*

He turned back to her. "You've sold me. Now make it work."

"It may take years," she cautioned. "I am certain that problems will arise that the simulation didn't discover. They always do. I think that we need to do it in stages."

"Of course. But this is the ultimate goal."

*   *   *

Ten years ago, Tallahassee.

Anne-Elise stepped into the office of the Director of Intensity Labs. This had been a commonplace event for a long time, but for the first time, it meant stepping into *her* office. Dr. Hailey had unexpectedly passed away, and the Engineering Division Chief, one Anne-Elise Kirby, was the obvious and unanimous choice to succeed him.

As she sat down at the desk, she reflected on her time and work here. The lab still had not perfected her brilliant design of two years ago, but the reactor had achieved a new record for energy production with ytterbium-doped solid-state lasers using fast ignition. They had not yet figured out how to shield the reaction from interaction with the element in the cone, but Anne-Elise had always expected that to be the most difficult part.

She gave the photo of the late Director Hailey a sad smile. At least he had lived to see everything in her design succeed except that.

"I'll do it," she vowed to the man who had been a professional mentor exceeding the mentorship of her graduate committee. "Not for you, because you would understand well that it's not about one person. But for that beautiful golden future I promised myself long ago."

She sighed and rubbed her eyes as she sat down in the chair, *her* chair. It was a shame about Dr. Hailey. He had only been seventy-one. It was too young for a great scientist to die, but it had been too *old* for either of them to consider the other as a partner in anything beyond work. Dr. Hailey had, in some ways, been like the father that Vernon Kirby never had been for her, and she believed he had seen her as a daughter of sorts. But if he had been younger, closer to her own age, she wondered if it could have been different. She had always known him as a widower, his wife having died in the COVID pandemic years ago. They had already been too old to have children, and he had never remarried.

It wasn't in the cards, Anne-Elise concluded philosophically. *We were of different generations. I'm just glad to have had him as a mentor and a father figure.*

Her phone rang. It was Edward. Why was he calling? He knew that she was at work. Fearing what she was to hear, she answered the phone.

He was pacing around. She could hear his very footsteps. "Emma has *left* me!" he exclaimed. "She's filed for divorce and taken all her things out!"

Oh. Anne-Elise was at a loss for words, not because this was a shock to her, but because she had no idea how to convey her lack of surprise to him.

"I had no idea she was so unhappy!" he continued.

I *did*, Anne-Elise thought.

She and Emma had never become especially close. Emma had regarded Anne-Elise with a certain degree of suspicion and wariness, almost as if she saw her as a rival. But she was as isolated as the Kirby siblings themselves always had been, being estranged from her family over politics. Perhaps due to a lack of anyone else, Emma had confided in her about Edward's attitudes.

Emma told me that she couldn't ever get him to hear her when she talked to him. She wanted children, for some Godforsaken reason, but he didn't... and then there were other things. His supposed "flippancy." I don't think he's flippant.

Her conscience then nagged at her. *Okay, he can be too cocky and devil-may-care. I'll admit that. And some people just can't deal with people like that. She is apparently one of them.*

He's always listened to me. He didn't always agree with me, but he always heard what I had to say. Ever since we were kids, it was like that. That long, horrible walk home....

I suppose I could have told him what Emma confided to me, she thought. *He might have listened if it had come from me.*

But why was that my responsibility? She was his wife. It was her responsibility to make sure her husband heard her... and act accordingly if he didn't.

And that's exactly what she did. I didn't sabotage his marriage. It was never my duty to fix it in the first place.

Finally she addressed him. "Sorry. Just—taking in the shock myself," she lied. "I'm really sorry, Edward. Truly. You know that I'll always be there for you, though, right?"

He sighed over the phone. "Yes. You were always different."

"So if you want to get anything off your chest at any point, just... drop me an email or a text, okay? I can't promise I'll always be able to answer the phone, but I don't want that to prevent you from telling me anything that you want me to hear."

He heaved a weary sigh. "I'll keep that in mind. God," he

burst out. "What happened? How did it go wrong and I had *no idea?*"

*   *   *

Seven years ago, Tallahassee.

Edward was getting married again, and this time, he was having a ceremony. It was a small one, but he and his new bride had informed the family in advance this time, so there were guests and the meals, events, and accommodations that one would expect at a wedding—just a smaller-than-average number of them.

The Mellors were present, of course. Vera was there, but she was paying little attention to anything except her phone. At age sixteen, she was thoroughly in rebellion against her right-wing parents and had adopted all manner of progressive values. Some of them, Anne-Elise found ridiculous, little more than a rediscovery of the same extreme social-justice progressivism that had been in vogue briefly during her own youth. It was unnerving to see this girl profess the same things that Anne-Elise had heard in her own high-school years. *Does this mean I'm officially old?* she wondered. *I'm only thirty-eight. That's not old enough to be old.*

But the groom's relatives and coworkers were not the only guests at this wedding. This time around, in stark contrast with Emma MacArthur, the bride, Corrine Grant, had a very extensive and obviously very affectionate family.

Are you trying to do what Chelsea did? Anne-Elise thought grouchily as she stood off by herself in the reception hall after the ceremony. *Get yourself a new family, a better family, by marrying into it? I hope you've exercised better judgment than she did, then.*

Corrine and Anne-Elise had rubbed along well enough during their handful of meetings. Corrine was an emergency manager and Navy veteran, and she had met Edward in the aftermath of a hurricane. She was an experienced captain and lifeguard, and there was a no-nonsense toughness about her that Anne-Elise respected.

She just wasn't sure how well Edward would take it once he had to live with such a strong personality. *And interact regularly with all her family*, she thought.

Corrine's family was a mix of every possible hue and ethnicity, and Corrine herself was Black. Her race made no difference to Anne-Elise or Vera, and in this instance, Anne-Elise couldn't find fault with Vera's political ideology.

I suppose I'm being a little unfair. Chelsea has never really acted racist that I've ever seen, either, but Richard's behavior today has been shameful.

She glanced up at the new couple, who were both smiling as they talked with guests—including their brother-in-law, though their smiles looked a little strained with him. Corrine was lovely in her wedding gown, and she wore her long hair in a twist of two dozen braids with little white roses attached at the ends. Richard, however, was acting like a robot. Even from fifteen feet away, Anne-Elise could tell that he was abrupt, curt, and trying not to stare at Corrine's hair. It was appallingly rude, and, yes, racist.

He works for a Hispanic man, Anne-Elise thought in disgust. *But then, Hal Gilbertson looks white, and he doesn't have a Spanish name. Corrine is a Black woman. That's what bothers Richard. He can't pretend she isn't. And he doesn't know how to relate to Black people, particularly women.*

She really, really doesn't look like me.

There was that thought again.

I hope he listens more to Corrine than he did to Emma. She gazed at Edward's new wife. *Good luck to you. You'll need it.*

*   *   *

December 26, last year.

"I'm worried about Edward," Chelsea said. "It was sad when Emma left him, but he reacted relatively healthily to it. He got a hobby, that plane of his. But with Corrine, this is different." Her expression became grave. "He brought beer. I've never seen him drink before. It reminds me of Mom and Dad—"

The words were out of Anne-Elise's mouth before she

could stop herself. "Don't act like you care about our well-being."

"Are you referring to your teen years? Really? It's been decades."

"You're only proving my point by acting like it stopped mattering just because you *wanted* it to stop mattering. If anything did happen to him, you'd just be glad to inherit some of his money, like you were when Mom and Dad ran the Explorer into a gully. You don't care about anyone but yourself."

Chelsea scowled. "I cleaned up my life. They could have too. I'm not responsible when grown people ruin their lives."

"You drove them to it with your behavior."

Chelsea glared again as her gaze turned into a sneer of supercilious contempt. "I've always thought that your judgment is just a front for something else, like it is with every judgmental Puritan. You were just jealous of me. Jealous of my boyfriends, resentful that you were a nerd and a virgin while I was hot, popular, and boys wanted to have sex with me."

"Oh, and also jealous of the shredded red flesh that that doctor drew out of you? Keep telling yourself that," Anne-Elise sneered. "I made something of my life and I didn't have to push anything out of my vagina, living or dead, or rely on any man, to become a successful person! I did it all by myself, with no one giving me a boost. Not even Edward, and certainly not you."

* * *

August 28, seven days ago.

Anne-Elise shook her head. That wasn't how it had happened. As satisfying as it was to imagine her sister having said those things, because it would have been just cause for resentment, it hadn't happened that way. And as equally satisfying as it would have been to have that comeback herself, she hadn't done that either.

* * *

Chelsea scowled. "I cleaned up my life. They could have too. I'm not responsible when grown people ruin their lives."

141

"You drove them to it with your behavior."

Chelsea glared again as her gaze darkened into something just as malicious as Anne-Elise's own expression. "You want to talk about driving people to a bitter divorce for selfish reasons? Let's, then. When Edward went to Miami, leaving you behind, and married Emma and then Corrine, you resented it. And frankly, it came across as jealousy."

"Jealousy?"

"You never did want any other female to have anything to do with him. You see him as yours and always have. It's bizarre, and it really makes me wonder." Her voice had transformed into a snarl.

"What are you insinuating?" Anne-Elise snarled back.

"It was always you and him by yourselves, even when you were too old for that to be appropriate. You've always been creepily possessive of him. So I have to wonder. When you and Edward were teenagers, did you?"

"Did we what?"

"I think you know what."

"Say it. If you are depraved enough to think it, then say it!"

*   *   *

It hadn't happened that way either.

I can't rewrite this memory, Anne-Elise told herself sternly. *That way lies madness. If I re-imagine this conversation often enough, I may forget the real memory and start believing the imagined one. That's terrifying.*

And I'm the depraved one to imagine such a conversation. Mom put it into my head all those years ago on that awful car ride, and she might not even have insinuated what I thought she did. I'll never know for sure now. But whatever Mom meant, Chelsea never said these things at all.

*   *   *

Chelsea scowled. "I cleaned up my life. They could have too. I'm not responsible when grown people ruin their lives."

"You drove them to it with your behavior."

"You know, if this is the standard you insist on, you'll fall short too. Emma and Corrine confided in you about things

142

Edward did that frustrated them. And they knew how close you two always had been, as twins. They knew that if he listened to anyone, it would be you. But you didn't tell him anything."

"If they couldn't make him understand their complaints themselves, it wasn't my fault. It wasn't my job to play marriage counselor."

"But it is my fault that our parents drank themselves to death?"

Anne-Elise knew that she was defeated on this point. But she couldn't forgive her sister. She just couldn't. There was more to it than just their parents' behavior. "They *were* drinking themselves to death, and they were doing it for many years," she almost choked out. "They were so focused on hating each other that they weren't being parents. And you were the oldest child—four years older than Edward and me—and you weren't there for us either." Her voice almost broke as she shook her head.

"If it wasn't your job to be Edward's marriage counselor in your thirties and forties, how was it my job to be your replacement mom at seventeen? They weren't there for me either at that time."

"We were supposed to be there for *each other*, as siblings. And you *weren't*. Other people were always more important to you."

"I'm sorry, Anne-Elise. But I was *seventeen*. I should have focused on you and Edward, I know. But I was young too."

"And we were younger. *You* could drive. *You* could get a job. After your abortion, *you* could make plans for college. And then you did. You went off to college and barely communicated with any of us. Remember 'COVID Christmas,' Chelsea? Edward and I were being locked up in our own home, but you ran off to Richard's crazy-ass parents that year. And then you two got married in school, so we hardly even *saw* you until Mom and Dad died." She suppressed the crack in her voice at these words. "*You* escaped, but Edward and I had to keep living with it for years and years."

"I *said* I was sorry."

Anne-Elise's temper finally snapped. "You *really* sound sincere."

"Believe me sincere or not, but I do want us to be a family now, at last."

"You want us to be a family on *your* terms. You demand that we listen to your politics and let your husband lecture us all about his views. You insist that every get-together must be what *you* want. You try to tell me what to do in my own house! You're not our mother, Chelsea, and we are not children anymore. You want to fix what happened by turning back the clock, in a way. You could have acted like a mother when you were eighteen or nineteen and Edward and I were still underage. We needed one then. But it's too damn late for it now."

With that, Anne-Elise stalked out of her sister's house, slamming the door behind her.

*   *   *

That was what had happened.

To this day, she didn't think she had been wrong to call her sister out about what she was doing and why she was doing it. But Chelsea had still pointed out some truths that Anne-Elise found very uncomfortable, and it was no easier for Anne-Elise to face those truths than it had been for Chelsea to face her own.

Edward's wives *had* entrusted her with their own frustrations with him, drawing on their close relationship as twins who had been by each other's side through trauma, and Anne-Elise had said nothing to Edward about it. There *had* been a subconscious part of her that had not wanted to share him with any other woman.

She scowled. *I was right when I told Chelsea that it wasn't my job to fix his marriage, either of them. It doesn't matter what other motive I might have had. And am I really wrong to have had that motive? His wives didn't want to be with him, in the end. They weren't loyal to him like I am. I will always value him, because he's the only one who was there for me.*

144

And that's why I sneer and insult her for the abortion, she realized suddenly. *It's not that I am against abortion. I'm not. It was the right choice for her at age seventeen. I insult her in graphically, explicitly violent ways over the abortion because it is a proxy for the other "motherhood" that she rejected. I don't have a problem with her abortion. I resent that she didn't act as a mother to us when we needed one.*

And now it's too late. She had her chance, and she left Edward and me to our biological parents' violence instead. I won't let her forget that. She doesn't get to play mother now.

We're middle-aged adults now. All the toxicity and abuse that we took in then has become a part of us. It can't be ripped out now.

It was never alien to us, either. It didn't come from outside our system. It came from us. We created it and took it into ourselves. We let it grow up with us, and it's become part of us now. In an ideal world, it shouldn't have happened, but that's not the world we have.

It's too late, far too late, to undo the damage. We'll all just have to live with the consequences.

Before:
Reaping the
whirlwind

Chapter 10: A Four-Letter Word

Present day, September 4.

Edward was heartily glad that he had managed to get six hours of sleep, because it was going to be a long night—and morning—at the Hurricane Center.

He had arrived at the center around three A.M., when Hurricane Leonard had already reached a stunning intensity level for the Atlantic. Just a few decades ago, an intensity of 881 millibars and 195 miles an hour would have been a basin record. But it was definitely not finished, as Chandra had feared in his phone call.

The meteorologists continued to stare at their feeds of incoming data as the Hurricane Hunter kept sampling the storm. The next full advisory was set to go out at five o'clock—four o'clock local time for the time zone in which Leonard currently churned—and, barring some reason to issue a Special Advisory sooner than the standard six hours apart, that was what they would do. There seemed little point in doing otherwise now.

Dr. Evans, Edward's trainee, mused aloud bleakly on that very subject. "What even *warrants* a Special Advisory anymore?" she said. "We issued one at two o'clock when it became a Five. And before that, at eight P.M. when it was upgraded to a Two just three hours after becoming a hurricane." She chuckled. "Category Two. How quaint. But what else is *left* for Leonard to do that would justify a Special Advisory? The world record, I guess."

Edward momentarily reflected on the fact that she was speaking of it as a *fait accompli* that Leonard would break the world record. *Well, of course it will,* he thought. No one questioned that now. It wasn't even a controversial forecast anymore. *But my statements and allusions are still controversial.*

The idea seemed rebellious, roguish, and dangerous to him—very much of a piece with the persona he believed himself to possess. "That, yes," he agreed with her, reclining in his chair. "I can think of a couple of other milestones, too."

Dr. Evans cringed. "I'd rather not go there."

"We may not get a choice." In spite of his dark tone, Edward was excited—and fully awake. He was becoming increasingly convinced that his research hobbyhorse was about to become reality.

He had remembered to bring in his personal laptop, mindful of not logging into the FSU supercomputer on government resources. Dr. Chandra probably wouldn't mind, at this point, but Edward was starting to feel a certain possessiveness about this situation. This was *his* model, and he was going to run it from *his* computer.

To simulate my storm, his brain supplied. He suppressed a wry smile at the thought that he was starting to think of Leonard as his own too.

Upon arriving at the office, he had kicked off another run of STCRS with the latest observational data, both of the storm and of its surrounding environment. He had decided to run it in rapid-fire mode, with a truncated forecast simulation period. The most important thing to know, he believed, was the immediate future. The next forty-eight hours were what mattered most, so he set the simulation to run for that short time, producing output for each hour of the forecast. This meant that the model would finish quickly and he could start a new simulation within the hour, allowing him to ingest new data into it.

By four o'clock in the morning, Leonard's eye pressure had dropped to 864 millibars and its winds had increased to 205 miles per hour. They would wait a bit longer for additional readings before issuing the five A.M. advisory, because the Hurricane Hunter crew was reporting no indication that the storm was about to stop.

Frequent lightning and hail in the eyewall, their vortex report read. Those products of severe thunderstorms only happened in hurricanes when they were rapidly intensifying. Leonard's intensity was in a very special class already, but it was still getting stronger.

The forecasters seemed to divide into two groups: those

who were too shell-shocked—or perhaps just too sleepy—to react to what was happening and wandered around the office as if in a daze, and those who might have manifested right off social media's most "excitable" weather-weenie groups.

While waiting for STCRS to finish, Edward got up and went to the lounge to get himself some coffee. He tried to be above both groups. *I'm the one who best understands what's probably coming,* he thought as he poured the hot Joe into his Wright Brothers mug. *I shouldn't let myself get hyper. No, I'll leave that to my storm.*

Suppressing a smile at his own joke, he returned to his desk. His model had finished running.

He pulled up his image viewer and clicked through the images. His eyes widened in spite of his resolution to stay cool.

When he had run it at home, the STCRS model had not sent Leonard straight over the thirty-seven-Celsius Loop Current hot eddy. It had entered the broader hot area of the Gulf, which had enabled the storm to intensify to 730 millibars in that simulation, but it had avoided the worst spot.

The storm in this run had not done that.

Edward gaped as the model—his model, which had simulated so many intense but imaginary storms for research —sent this all-too-real system directly over the body-temperature water. The modeled "Leonard" broke the barrier, reaching 687 millibars in this run. *Assuming the theory is correct and sub-700 pressures indicate hypercanes,* Edward thought. *I'll check the other fields for additional evidence to be sure.*

The surface winds were modeled at 370 miles an hour. That was devilishly difficult to achieve on Earth. The only thing that could overcome the frictional drag was an extremely strong forcing mechanism... *such as a pressure low enough to give someone altitude sickness,* he thought excitedly.

He checked the modeled vertical velocity, and his eyes widened again. At some hours of the simulation, the model predicted Leonard to have over forty meters per second in vertical updrafts. That was comparable to the kinds of numbers one might see in severe thunderstorms, but it was unheard of in hurricanes. *The plane can take the g-force that'll produce, though,* he thought. *The Super Hercules is a beast.*

I want to fly that storm when it does this, he resolved. *I will be in the cockpit. I will make certain of it.*

He then heard another human breathing and realized that Dr. Evans had been at his cubicle all along. Surprised that his storm could immerse him so thoroughly that he had not noticed her, he turned around, smiling at her.

"You see what I see, then," he remarked, gesturing to the screen. He took a sip of coffee cockily and raised an eyebrow at her. "If STCRS is right—and I think it is—then this storm isn't anywhere *near* finished." He pulled up his viewer and clicked eagerly through the various meteorological fields. "Right now we're looking at simulated forty-two-meter-per-second verticals... that'll jostle the plane good, make it quite a fun ride for the lucky pilot and crew who get to fly it." He winked knowingly at her, oblivious to the look on her face. "Here," he continued, navigating to the surface winds, "we see winds that would embarrass a Hollywood twister. And here's the crown jewel: sub-700." He leaned back again.

Dr. Evans gaped at him in disbelief that she could not hide. "Dr. Kirby, with all due respect, you seem to be treating that model run as a video game for which you've just achieved a high score. Or a badge saying 'Achievement Unlocked: Hypercane.'"

"Oh, come on," he argued, smiling. "You have to admit, it's cool."

"If that actually plays out, it will be horrible for someone."

Oh, will you stop throwing cold water over everything with this eternal caution and virtue-signaling? he thought in exasperation. *Just admit why you're actually here!*

"Yes, landfall is horrible," he said with an aborted roll of his eyes. "We're all trained to say it. To pretend that the reason we're in this field is that we *hate* extreme weather and want to *never see it again.* To be ashamed of our lifelong interest, usually formed in childhood, and to acknowledge, like a damn land acknowledgment, how guilty we are supposed to feel about being meteorologists. You know what?" he said, an idea suddenly hitting him. "Let's propose something just for us to serve that purpose of virtue-signaled shame. We'll call it the *landfall acknowledgment.* 'Leonard is a terrible, *terrible* storm, and I'm a *bad person* for enjoying a potentially unique event in the field that I studied rather than obsessing over what it'll do if people don't get out of its way!'"

Dr. Evans shrank back. "I didn't mean—"

Edward picked up his coffee mug and took a defiant sip. "I will wear my devil horns openly. A hypercane would be cool."

He had not realized that his voice had been getting louder and louder with this harangue, and that several of his colleagues had been eavesdropping. With his utterance of that word, the unspoken oath of silence that they had taken shattered into pieces.

"Do you really have a model showing that?" someone asked, approaching his desk.

"It's that Florida State one he's published on," said Fisher. "Yep—I recognize that image viewer from your papers. What've you got? Is it really modeling a hypercane?"

An excited chatter broke out among the forecasters as they clustered around Edward's personal laptop. Proudly he demonstrated his model results to them.

"How do you know it really is one?" Fisher asked. "I know the pressure and wind values are in line with what you'd expect, but do the processes truly meet the definition?"

"With the input fields what they are, the theory predicts that the storm should qualify," he said. "This took it right over the body-temp eddy, and at the top of the troposphere it was eighty-two below. That'll do it. Barely, but it'll do it. And this pressure is indeed 'barely.'" He couldn't resist adding, "But is that word actually appropriate for numbers like this?"

"Why aren't the operational models showing anything like this?" another forecaster asked skeptically. "Your STCRS is...

well, it won't be two hundred millibars deeper than anything else anymore, but surely to God it'll be at least one hundred...."

"They're not taking it over the hot eddy, and I'm not sure they're correctly modeling the tropopause either," Edward explained. "The HAFS was doing some things with popup thunderstorms that looked nonphysical to me." He raised an eyebrow. "But we've seen HAFS simulate a sub-800 storm before."

"Yeah, but it's never been accurate when it did."

"Yet," Fisher muttered.

"Exactly. Yet. And here's the thing. My theory is that those artificial thunderstorms are choking off Leonard somewhat in the HAFS, and artificially warming the tropopause too. But when you get a big, mature, strong storm, it dominates the environment. It becomes the killer of any weaker system. Leonard was intensifying too fast for the HAFS, I think. Once the model understands it's a mature storm that controls its environment, I think it could handle a hypercane."

Dr. Chandra himself had finally realized that his forecasters were clustered around Edward Kirby's desk, and he had devised a strong suspicion as to why. When he approached, he heard the tail end of that discussion, confirming his guess.

"All right, I'm sure Kirby's private model is very fascinating, but let's not neglect the data and operational model runs that we need to be focusing on," he chided them. "We have a five o'clock advisory to put out in half an hour."

"I don't suppose we're using Edward's intensity forecast in the product," Fisher joked.

"Only if you want to answer accusations of 'elitism' on *Morning Lark* in three hours for using his model but not the patchwork configuration of sixteen-year-old 'Tornado John' on the Internet. With a thunderstorm symbol for the 'r.'"

The Director's biting humor made them all, even Edward, laugh. "You don't even know what my intensity forecast is, Director," he chuckled. "Shall I show you? Everyone else has seen it."

"I heard enough. I heard the last word you said before I came over, and in all seriousness, the first four letters of that word are the only ones we're concerned with for now," Dr. Chandra said severely. "And around here, 'hype' is a four-letter word in the vernacular sense." He gave Edward a hard look. "And don't play with that model on government time."

"It isn't keeping me from my taxpayer-funded duties," he objected. "It's just like any other model. I can run it in the background. And you see that I brought my own laptop to do it." He considered how to phrase this. "Director, I know that I've been... rather enthusiastic... just now, but it's the excitement of a researcher who sees his topic possibly becoming relevant in the real world. And I mean that. We may *need* the output of this model for Leonard. I truly believe that it's a possibility."

The other forecasters all seemed to hold their breath to see if the Director contradicted him on this assertion. Dr. Chandra considered for a second. It seemed like forever.

"And I'm not going to say you're wrong that it's *possible*. Leonard and its future environment are unlike anything we've seen before."

Several forecasters' eyes widened in shock.

"So set it going automatically if you must, but don't mess with it when you're working on NHC's clock. We need you at one hundred percent for this hurricane."

"Aye, aye, Cap'n," Edward said the second time that morning, with a touch of sarcasm and a touch of self-deprecating humor. He managed a half-smile. He had carried his point. The Director might not want to openly admit it—at least yet—but he knew as well as Edward himself did what might happen. *Unlike most of our colleagues*, he thought, *Dr. Chandra isn't blinding himself to a dire possibility by normalcy bias.*

Chandra sighed. "I'm looking out for you all as best I can," he said, all scolding gone from his voice. "I'm your advocate."

"I know, Director."

"This storm is going to be terrible. Set aside Dr. Kirby's *hypercane* for the time being!" He almost didn't want to utter the word, spitting it out as if it were a bit of rotten food. "We are very likely going to be working a world-record Category Five hurricane! We need people taking us seriously. We don't need to be accused of sensationalism. Not now."

"You believe the trough will send it east, then, Director?" Dr. Evans asked.

"Yes," he said heavily. "The measurements that we have indicate that it'll be strong. Definitely strong enough to break the heat wave and rocket Leonard to the east. Definitely over the Loop Current and possibly over the body-temperature eddy."

These words hung in the air for a while, sinking in with all of the forecasters.

"If the trough cools things off, then the *air* will suddenly get cooler, but the water will still be human body temperature for some time after frontal passage," someone said, spelling it out explicitly. They all knew it, but it still somehow needed to be said.

"Yes."

This monosyllable hung in the air for a moment too.

"And the tropopause temperature... what do the models showing a strong front have for that over the Gulf?"

"They're now showing eighty-two to eighty-five below," Fisher said.

Someone swore vilely, which Dr. Chandra pretended not to hear. Most of the forecasters were grimacing.

"And that's why I should be running STCRS," Edward said, all trace of cockiness gone. "Eighty-five below zero C at the top and thirty-seven C in the Gulf? Those conditions are what it's built for." He gestured to the screen bleakly. "As you can see."

Chandra gazed sternly at them all again. "Run what you must, Edward, but do not post the output to the Internet. At least, not under any account that can be identified as yours."

"I won't."

"And this goes for all of you. Do not talk about this to the public—including social media—unless the storm actually does intensify in that manner. People on social media can babble freely, but we are official representatives of the National Hurricane Center. We aren't going to use that word unless the situation should come to warrant it." He paused darkly. "And if it does, may God have mercy on wherever it hits."

*   *   *

They all got back to work after that, Edward included. He decided to kick off another run of the STCRS once the Hurricane Hunters had finished their reconnaissance. In the meantime, several operational models would complete. Since Dr. Chandra had imposed a ban on the use of unofficial models for official forecasts, the predictions of the official models were of immediate interest to Edward.

Hurricane Hunters flew storms in a kind of starburst pattern, sampling every region that they could, instead of simply reaching the eye and staying in it. This meant that there would be periods of time when the storm's intensity could significantly change and they would not realize the extent of it until they made another eye fix. After their previous one, the one that had found 864 millibars and 205 miles per hour, they had left the eye to sample another quadrant. They were en route back to the eye and should be there in time for a final fix before the five A.M. advisory.

But the flagship model finished its run before the Hurricane Hunters got in their final leg. Edward—*and probably everyone else in the office*, he thought wryly—pulled its output up at once.

He whistled as he flipped through the images. HAFS was now taking Leonard over the hot eddy. It would not be long before other models followed suit. *And it's showing 770 millibars now*, Edward noted. *As Fisher said, it's done that before, but it's never verified. I bet this does verify, though. And then some.*

He took a look at the upper-atmospheric temperatures.

They were still, in his opinion, being artificially warmed a bit. *I wonder, though... could this model be seeing something that mine isn't? Mine is meant for research cases. It's tweaked and configured so that it does simulate the maximum potential intensity for a given set of conditions. But these are real values.*

He set it aside for now. Time would tell. He wasn't going to tell himself, even in his own mind, that it *didn't matter* if the storm peaked at 770 or reached the 600s, because in a crucial way, it probably *would* matter. *The stratosphere,* he thought. *The storm's height matters quite a bit for the region of ozone layer immediately above it, and it's very hard for a hurricane, even a 770-millibar one, to generate vertical updrafts strong enough to breach that barrier. So the intensity does matter for that.*

But despite his bitter, angry comment to Dr. Evans earlier —which he regretted now, since he thought he had probably frightened her—he knew that, for anyone who would be at the landfall location, the intensity would be so great either way that it wouldn't make much difference which model was right in the end.

*   *   *

As he waited for the Hurricane Hunters to penetrate the eye again, he then turned to social media. As soon as he had finished looking at the HAFS output, he realized what would happen once it hit the Internet.

People are going to go bananas, he guessed, pulling up a browser on his personal laptop to check. *Sixteen-year-old Tornado John... with a thunderstorm symbol,* he added in his thoughts. He smothered a laugh. It wouldn't do to start cackling to himself at work. People would wonder what he had found so funny.

When he pulled up his social networks, he was not surprised in the least by what he saw everywhere.

LEONARD: THE WORST HURRICANE EVER! blared the caption on a custom graphic that someone had made depicting a path into Miami, a track that not one single model was showing. Edward supposed that the statement probably wasn't wrong, though the image was amateurish and inaccurate.

NHC CONSIDERING CALLING LEONARD CATEGORY SIX!!! someone's handmade graphic wrongly declared.

Not to be outdone, someone else had announced in bold magenta text, **HURRICANE CENTER TO DECLARE NEW CATEGORY SIX AND SEVEN!** An obviously AI-generated image of a hurricane served as the background. The fake storm rotated clockwise, which was completely wrong for the Northern Hemisphere. Edward was actually offended on Leonard's behalf. *Is the real storm not impressive enough for you?* he thought. But that post still had over a thousand "likes."

This was either a disgraceful display of ignorance for a weather hobbyist or a cynical attempt to get more clicks and attention than anyone else. Perhaps some of both. Edward scowled, continuing down his feed.

Oh, just lovely. An account that he strongly suspected was not merely an overenthusiastic American teen, but was actually based in Russia, had posted, **Leonard: A Weather Modification Experiment with YOU as the Subject!** This post had over three thousand "likes" already and was approaching twenty thousand views. Edward desperately hoped that some of them were bots. If they were mostly human beings instead, that was not good.

There was no point in engaging with that sort of stupidity, though. He tried to focus on the posts that were at least made in reasonably good faith.

It didn't take him long to find what he was looking for.

World's First Hypercane?

This post had a lot of discussion, "likes," and views too. Edward scowled as he examined it. *Yes, it could become that,* he thought, *and it irritates me to no end that these... anonymous kids are chattering about it here. I should be the one leading this conversation. The researchers who first discovered this theory and invented this term are now either quite old or not with us anymore, so it should be me.*

He understood why Dr. Chandra had banned him from posting STCRS output. Social media would go insane with it. *More insane*, he amended, recalling the "weather modification" post. In fact, since he wasn't allowed to do it under his own name, it would only irritate him more to post it anonymously, unable to claim credit, and see these hyenas salivating and yapping over it anyway.

But he still hated not being involved. He scowled at his cubicle walls, a prison at the moment, a cell keeping him anonymous, preventing him from living out his research topic in the real world.

I'm going to get in that plane when Leonard looks like it'll make the jump, he vowed.

He forced his gaze away from his personal laptop and studied the screen of his work computer again. The Hurricane Hunters were almost in the eye for their final pass before the five A.M. advisory. Whatever they found would be the official values.

It then hit him that, however long it had seemed to him at the office, it actually hadn't been all that long. This was the same crew that had reported Leonard's intensification to a Category Five at two o'clock. They had been in the storm all along, though their mission was about to end. What an experience they must have had.

But I am going to have an even better one, he vowed again.

Edward refreshed the satellite imagery and gaped. Somehow, the eye was even clearer and drier than it had been before.

He kept refreshing until the Hurricane Hunters transmitted their fix, three minutes before the top of the hour: 842 millibars and 215 miles per hour.

"Just broke the world record," Edward said aloud.

* * *

Much of the forecast discussion had already been written, since everyone knew that Leonard was continuing to intensify, but they still had to scramble to rush the intensity forecast out. They had been waiting to see what the reconnaissance crew found before making the jump and endorsing the HAFS forecast in official products, but with Leonard now holding the world record for pressure, they all agreed that they had better respect the model. It had never been right when it had predicted such an extreme intensity, but that might change, they all concluded.

Huang Mei-shan, the forecaster who signed his name to the advisory and discussion, took a deep breath as he disseminated them. He grimaced. "I don't want this to verify, in one way," he confided as they all met in the coffee room to unwind, "but at the same time, I'm going to look like a fool if it doesn't."

"The Director will stand by us," Dr. Evans assured him. "I heard that he was going to go on *Morning Lark* at eight to talk about Leonard and try to calm the public. He knows this is a big, big deal."

"*Morning Lark*?" Fisher muttered. "Wow, he must really *be* worried."

They all murmured their agreement. That was the most-live-streamed morning show in the country, and its hosts, Rebecca Hall and Jason Brakeley, were well-known for trying to manipulate their guests into making on-air mistakes that would make them look stupid. But millions of people enjoyed seeing other people—particularly, it seemed, "elites"—bullied, as the show's ratings proved. It was rare for any television or Internet program to garner such near-universal popularity anymore, with the atomization of content and ubiquity of independent streaming media. That *Morning Lark* had done it was an impressive feat, in its way.

Edward left the break room. Before he could return to his desk, though, Dr. Chandra approached him.

"Can we confer privately, Edward?" he asked.

That was not the tone of someone who was displeased with his employee's behavior and wanted to reprimand him in private for it. Dr. Chandra wanted Edward's professional expertise at this moment, he realized. The irritation that he had been feeling decreased slightly as he walked with the

Director into his office.

Dr. Chandra shut the door as Edward sat down. He sat down behind his desk. "I was hard on you earlier this morning, I know, but that's because I want you to be mindful of the situation in a public-relations context. But now I speak to you as a scientist to another scientist." He leaned forward. "Off the record and strictly between us unless and until it becomes unnecessary?"

"Of course, Director," Edward assured him.

Dr. Chandra nodded. "Good. The fact is, I am *extremely* concerned about this hurricane, and I'm asking you for your honest expert opinion about it."

Edward took a deep breath as he organized his thoughts. Now was not the time for cocky, smug displays of his model output to try to impress his colleagues like a male bird showing off its colorful plumage. Now was the time to be serious.

"Unfortunately," Edward began, "Leonard is following the STCRS model's course almost perfectly, both for track and for intensity."

Dr. Chandra sighed, rubbing the top of his head. "I was afraid you were going to say that. And we know what came next."

"Yes."

The Director's gaze drifted out the window, where the dawn was breaking. "With the official models starting to get on board...." Chandra trailed off. He faced Edward again. "I'm going to go on the morning show and try to get this situation under control. Yes, I know as well as all of you what sort of foolishness is all over the Internet. Category Six, Category Seven, weather modification—you name it and it's there. We have to take command of the situation rather than turning the mic over to blowhards and fools. It's harder than ever to get good information out there. It gets lost so easily in the tsunami of crap." He cracked a wry, bitter smile. "Or should I say the storm surge of crap?"

Edward laughed, but he could not maintain it. The

situation was too serious. "I won't contribute more crap to the surge, Director. But I mean it very seriously—deadly seriously—when I tell you that I think STCRS could end up being right."

Chandra rose from his chair. "I fear the same. And even if it isn't, it'll be a catastrophic hurricane beyond all past storms we've ever seen. We're in uncharted waters now... and I know you aren't going to like to hear this, but I'm ordering all manned Hurricane Hunter flights into the storm halted for the time being."

Edward did not immediately process the Director's words. When their import hit him, he could not believe it. Rage suddenly spiked in him as sharply as Leonard's winds were spiking. "What?" he almost shouted. He was irate. "The Hercules can take what this thing is dishing out! You're going to keep me from—" He broke off.

But the damage was done. Chandra raised an eyebrow. "It's not about you, Kirby. You clearly want a metaphorical trophy on your shelf saying 'First Pilot to Fly a Hypercane,' but this is a matter of *safety*. The first *anything* is always terra incognita, to an extent. No matter how precise our simulations may be. We *do not know* what that kind of storm would truly be capable of, and I am not risking human lives unnecessarily. The Hunter craft will deploy drones into the storm's core."

Edward sucked his breath in between his teeth, trying to calm himself. "And if the drones indicate that we can fly it safely—that the planes can take it—I want to be the one to do it."

"We'll see, Kirby. But unless I say otherwise, this is my decision."

Chapter 11: Listen to the Experts

"Gooooood morning! The sun is up, the coffee's hot, and Morning Lark is live in New York to give you a harmonious start to your day—and today it's Labor Day!"

Rebecca Hall, a bleach blonde, the lead host of the show, smiled like a shark as the camera panned down on the artificially cozy stage that she and her co-host, Jason Brakeley, shared. Her red sheath dress was short enough that the camera angle could briefly show immaculately muscled calves onscreen before shifting to the hosts' faces. Brakeley had looks somewhat like those of Madison Chadleigh: brown curly locks and a clean-shaven face. But unlike Chadleigh, he didn't mar his good looks with rage-filled scowls.

"Good morning!" Brakeley said cheerily. "A world-record hurricane exploded seemingly out of *nowhere* in the Gulf yesterday, and the Hurricane Center says it may get even worse!"

Good morning everyone! A storm from hell is brewing! Chirp chirp chirp! Anne-Elise thought. She glowered at the nation's favorite morning show in the airline's premium lounge in Dulles International Airport. Edward had texted her telling her to watch it, because his boss would be on the show.

Brakeley and Hall smiled at the camera again, showing off perfect white teeth. Their coffee mugs rested before them on top of a maple-toned table. A third, unattended mug also rested there.

Either they don't drink their coffee or they're whitening their teeth every week, Anne-Elise thought.

"In fact," Hall continued, eyes and mouth both wide in absurd smiles, "we have the Director of the National Hurricane Center, Dr. Vinay Chandra, as our special guest this morning to talk about Hurricane Leonard."

"We all have questions about just how Leonard could have gotten so strong so suddenly, with basically no warning," Brakeley added. "Where was the NHC when this was happening? And what does the NHC's shocking forecast this morning mean for *you*? We're getting lots of questions over social media, and we'll be sure to ask Dr. Chandra about your concerns this morning. Oh—here he is! Come on and have a cup of coffee with us, Dr. Chandra!"

Since he needed to be at work, Chandra was interviewing from his Miami office, but they were able to project his figure seamlessly onto the set from his webcam. His figure shimmered into existence in front of the coffee cup as the hosts pretended to be amazed. Anne-Elise wondered what fool could possibly find such manifestly staged behavior entertaining. From the forced expression on his face, she would guess that Dr. Chandra felt much the same.

The hologram of the bespectacled, suited man faced what he must have known was the camera, even though he was undoubtedly looking at his hosts on his own screen. "Mr. Brakeley. Ms. Hall. Good morning to you."

"Oh, call us Rebecca and Jason." There was something predatory in Rebecca Hall's gaze and words. "We're friends here, Dr. Chandra."

He grimaced. "Very well. I'm glad to be here, and to share important information with the American people about world-record Hurricane Leonard."

"Yes," Hall said. "So let's begin at once!" She turned to him. "The first question we have comes from a viral post on social media. The most popular item about Leonard at this moment is a post alleging that the reason the storm seemed to erupt out of nowhere is that it was, in fact, a weather-modification experiment gone wrong."

"Or perhaps gone *right*," Brakeley added, smiling sociopathically.

Dr. Chandra's jaw momentarily dropped. He shut his mouth at once, gaping in disbelief and very evident outrage.

"So, can you address this concern, Director?" Hall needled. "I want to be clear, we aren't personally endorsing this view. But the fact that it has gone viral and is the most popular post on the topic means that people care about it. This is a concern that thousands have, and public concerns should be addressed."

Chandra almost seemed to be counting to ten under his breath. He took a quick intake of breath before steadying his temper. "All right. Let me make this crystal clear to everyone watching: We do not have the capacity to create hurricanes or significantly alter their intensity. Leonard formed in record-warm waters, and it is exploding in intensity because the upper-air conditions are very favorable for rapid development. I repeat, *we cannot create hurricanes or make them intensify or weaken.*" He took another deep breath. "We shouldn't give airtime to conspiracy theories."

It was clear to Anne-Elise that Dr. Chandra could not believe he was having to discuss *this*, of all things. Disbelief and disgust filled the Director's face and suffused his tone as he spoke.

Hall raised an eyebrow disingenuously. "Of course it is a conspiracy theory. But people are saying it, so it's important to discuss it—to debunk it, of course," she added. "I think I know where the confusion is coming from, though. Director, you must admit that it is very confusing to assert that we cannot change the intensity of hurricanes while also asserting that human-caused climate change has increased the intensity of hurricanes."

"It doesn't need to be confusing. Consider this analogy, which we can all understand: If a quarterback takes steroids, his performance will generally improve, but that same quarterback cannot inject just before a game and produce extra touchdowns on demand. It's the same with hurricanes—with extreme weather generally. We can alter the global system, and we have done so—to our detriment—which causes storms downstream to be different from what they otherwise would have been. But we cannot specifically alter individual storms."

"With all due respect, Director, this doesn't address the public concern about how this hurricane could have slipped under the NHC's radar," Brakeley said.

"It did not slip under our radar. We were watching it all

along. It simply developed and intensified at a record pace. Mr. Brakeley—Jason—I assure you that we have not been overlooking this storm." He addressed the camera, trying to keep this interview useful and helpful despite the hosts' conduct. "And neither should you, viewers. This is, as I have said, a world-record Category Five hurricane, and we have every reason to believe that it will continue to intensify even more. Our morning advisory and forecast call for it to reach 770 millibars and 260-mile-an-hour winds! If you are in the path, you *must* leave and take your family and pets with you!"

He was pleading with the public. Anne-Elise could tell that. He was doing his best to impart the urgency that the hurricane warranted. But to Hall and Brakeley, he might as well have been talking about a pleasant sea breeze. They just kept smiling those ghastly white grins.

In the airport lounge, two men near Anne-Elise were watching the interview. One of them turned to the other as the show cut to an ad break. "That was a good point," he said to his friend. "It sure does look like this hurricane sprang up out of nowhere."

"Yep," the other man agreed. "Very suspicious." He turned to Anne-Elise. "Don't you agree?"

She eyed them icily. "No, I don't. The Hurricane Center Director is right. We can't create hurricanes, let alone ones of this intensity."

"Hmph," scoffed the first man. "Well, I don't believe everything I hear. I think for myself and do my own research, and it sure looks odd to me that there was nothing, then—bam!—world-record Five."

"It is 'odd' in the sense of 'unusual,' but that doesn't make it a conspiracy. My brother does this for a living. That man is his boss."

"You sure your brother's telling you everything he does?"

There was no point in responding to such obnoxious arrogance, Anne-Elise decided. She gave the men a look of derision and turned back to the show.

Rebecca Hall was speaking again. She had not touched

her coffee. "Well, Director, this is a good digression to our next question. Category Five, you say. There is an argument, which has also been brought to us this morning, that storms such as Leonard should be designated 'Category Six.' And that if the intensification does continue as your forecast predicts, then it might even warrant 'Category Seven.'"

"There *is no* Category Six or Seven," Chandra said, impatience in his words. "Category Five is open-ended on the upper side."

Hall flashed him an insincere, contemptuous, glittery line of teeth. "But a storm like this is so *much* more intense than just a Category Five," she argued. A hint of menace suffused her voice. "There are people in your own field, Dr. Chandra, who have argued for a Category Six."

"Debates are the nature of research," Dr. Chandra said. "The point of categories is to convey to people the magnitude of risk that they face from a particular storm. The research question is how to convey that information in the most effective way for reducing casualties and encouraging responsible behavior."

"Exactly!" Hall agreed through that shark-like smile. "So isn't the National Hurricane Center being irresponsible by not creating a new category for storms like this?"

Dr. Chandra was visibly exasperated. He was speaking through clenched teeth as he answered her. "The question is not settled, but the current consensus is that it would diminish the perceived importance of Category Five status. We're only discussing this because the number of Category Fives has increased markedly. Because of climate change, they're as prevalent as Category Fours used to be, and the ones that would be designated 'Category Six' in the usual proposal—192 miles an hour or more—would then be as infrequent as Category Fives used to be. But this is all just a human shell game!" he emphasized before Hall or Brakeley could interrupt again. "Category Five hurricanes are just as strong as they always have been. If we make these storms *seem* weaker by putting a new category above Five, how does that benefit anyone in their path?"

"But Hurricane Leonard is *not* a typical Category Five," Brakeley said. "And it's going to get even worse, you claim."

Chandra was clearly offended. "Claim, Mr. Brakeley? We have issued a *forecast*, which state-of-the-art scientific models support."

"Nonetheless, if it does become what you say it will, we need another category for this storm. The fact that this is trending on social media proves that. And we the public pay for your work, *your job*, with our tax money. Shouldn't we get a say in this just as much as researchers do?"

"I agree," Hall said. She turned to Dr. Chandra. "I really think the Hurricane Center should reconsider—"

"It's an all-time world-record storm!" Chandra exploded, his patience finally at an end. "Isn't that dire enough? Don't the intensity numbers it *has* mean more than a category number? Winds over 215 miles an hour! And, frankly, I don't think it serves the public interest to take up valuable airtime with *this* sort of discussion, rather than providing actionable, useful information to those potentially in its path."

Hall cut in at once, still smiling ear to ear, the wide toothy grin of a demon in a horror film. *Don't the sides of her mouth hurt?* Anne-Elise wondered.

"I'm afraid we must agree to disagree, Director. An attention-grabbing category number *would* be actionable information. On air, we may refer to Hurricane Leonard as 'beyond Category Five.'"

"There is not—"

"I'm sorry, Director Chandra, but we have to leave some time for our next guest this morning." She turned to the camera. "Have we got a treat for you all today! Internet personality Zombie C. Rabbit, here to talk to us about the unexpected success of his surrealist podcast, *Purple Meatball Sauce!*"

Brakeley addressed the camera and spoke to the viewers. "But before we bid Director Chandra a fond *top of the morning*, one final word about Hurricane Leonard. Everyone out there in the storm's path, remember, there are people online who play at being experts and even twist legitimate research for their own purposes. Dangerous misinformation can easily spread. If you are in the path of this storm, listen to the experts and follow their advice!"

*   *   *

Miami.

"I got cut off to make way for Zombie C. Rabbit, host of the podcast *Purple Meatball Sauce*," Dr. Chandra said in stunned disbelief.

The forecasters gave him sympathetic looks. "You did what you could to get the message out," Adela Fisher assured him. "Brakeley and Hall are horrid people, but you were clear and concise."

"I suppose I should have known that I would be commanded to debate a long-running conspiracy theory and the 'Category Six' thing," he muttered. "I did try to get good information out."

"It's hard for us to accept sometimes," Dr. Evans said, "because our mission is to protect the public. But in the end, we can't force anyone to listen to us, believe us, or act on what we tell them. We just have to do our best. *Some* people will take action, at least."

Dr. Chandra managed a weak smile, but his thoughts were still elsewhere. "What *is* Purple Meatball Sauce? Why is it called that?"

"I have no idea and I doubt I really want to. Or you either."

He sighed, rubbing his eyes. "Probably not. All right. Never mind. Let's just focus on our world-record hurricane."

*   *   *

Edward had remained in his cubicle, stewing. He had insisted on working forecast duty, since he was barred from running up to Lakeland Airport to pilot a Hurricane Hunter into Leonard for now. The next forecast advisory would not go out until eleven o'clock local time, since there was little point in issuing another Special Advisory until they knew more of what Leonard was doing. To that end, Dr. Chandra

168

had ordered one of the Hurricane Hunter craft to dispatch a drone into the storm. The manned aircraft was flying around the periphery of the storm, sending drones into the core.

Meanwhile, the official models had locked onto a path for Leonard directly over the hot eddy now, and they were beginning to show the storm approaching the momentous 700-millibar level in their peak intensity forecasts. Edward himself had run STCRS several more times by the time the first drone reported its data, and the research model insistently showed hypercane-level intensities. In fact, each successive run of STCRS showed a stronger storm. The one he had kicked off at ten had accelerated the storm to 660 millibars and winds of 420 miles per hour.

He was starting to take note of the spread of landfall sites as well, and he did not like what he was seeing. Anne-Elise was on a plane back to Tallahassee at this moment, but a part of him wished she could have stayed in Washington. She couldn't, of course. She had left most of her things at home. And the models were showing Leonard making landfall at various sites west of the Big Bend region of Florida, rather than directly over it. The very worst part of the inner core would not strike her area if the models were right.

But Leonard was becoming *such* a big storm. The Gulf was full of moist air, and Leonard was taking full advantage of it. It was a monster now. The Hurricane Hunters had found the area of Category Five winds to be forty miles in diameter. It was massive. Tallahassee would take a bad hit even if it didn't take a direct one.

Edward had wondered if Anne-Elise was using the Wi-Fi on the plane, but she did not respond to texts, so he assumed she was not. She had to know what was happening, though. He had urged her to watch *Morning Lark* in the airport.

He eyed the clock. That drone needed to get its vortex fix in. He needed data for the eleven o'clock forecast.

"There it is!" Numbers began scrolling on the screen as it auto-refreshed. He examined them as people gathered around his desk again. They were all curious about what the drone would show.

"Well," Edward said to the gathered crowd, "here we are. Winds approaching three hundred miles an hour and pressure of 770, just as the model said." He was surprised at how unsurprised he was.

Dr. Evans shook her head in disbelief. "I can scarcely believe this is real, but the data have been quality-controlled and validated. I wish we could send in a manned flight to get human confirmation of this, but the Director is right: It's not safe."

Edward scowled. "I think the planes could take the g-force. But the Director's word is final, of course."

"Yeah. We have no choice but to use these data, shocking and unreal-looking as they are. They *are* real. We must use them. This will be quite a set of products."

Edward nodded. "But this storm warrants it."

"Sure does. You were absolutely right about Leonard."

He gave her a grim smile. "Not quite. Or perhaps not *yet*."

She grimaced. "Yeah."

The forecast discussion that Edward sent out was indeed one for the books.

Hurricane Leonard Discussion Number 9

NWS National Hurricane Center Miami FL   AL152051

1000 AM CDT Mon Sep 04 2051

Leonard continues its unprecedented intensification. The storm has rapidly grown very large, with a clear 10 nmi eye. Data from a Hurricane Hunter drone indicate that the internal pressure has fallen to 770 mb. This breaks the previous world record, which Leonard itself set six hours ago, by 72 millibars. This is also a 235 mb drop over 24 hours, which eclipses all previous records for intensification rate. The drone reported surface winds estimated at 260 knots. To say that Leonard is a very dangerous hurricane is an understatement.

At this point it is uncertain just how strong Leonard

can become. Its future intensity depends on its track, and models have begun to shift its projected path directly over a hot eddy in the Gulf Loop Current, en route to a potentially devastating landfall in the Florida panhandle. However, the storm is so strong that precise intensities make little difference to those in its path. Conditions at the landfall location will be unsurvivable....

*   *   *

Dr. Chandra's phone was ringing nonstop that morning, leaving him with little time to discuss anything with the staff. Some of the calls were sincere and important: emergency managers, local officials, and other agency chiefs. Others were less so. After the spectacle of *Morning Lark*, Chandra was resistant to giving any other media outlet an interview.

"I'm busy coordinating with Bay and Walton County officials," he snapped to the scheduler for a twenty-four-hour news channel.

"But we need a *statement!*" the man whined. "This is an unprecedented hurricane!"

"That it is, and that's why I am *too busy* to spend my time talking to the news today," he snapped. "If you want a statement, here is mine: '*Listen to the official forecasts and follow evacuation orders if you're given one, unless you have a death wish!*' There's really nothing else that I need to say." He reconsidered. This fool might well take him seriously. "The part about the death wish is not my official statement, on second thought."

"But we have a raging debate right now, a panel ongoing about whether Hurricane Leonard should be classified as a Category S—"

Dr. Chandra cut him off, infuriated. He had never been a drinker, but he really wanted a shot of strong whiskey right now.

*   *   *

"*Hurricane Center Director says to evacuate if ordered 'unless you have a death wish!'*" the chyron read.

171

"Do you think he really did?" Forecaster Huang asked his colleagues.

"Probably," said Fisher. She eyed the screen, where talking heads were buzzing disapprovingly at the Director's "unprofessional" words. The network had even found a pop psychologist to appear onstage to scold him and moralize over his frustrated statement.

"*It's a profoundly irresponsible statement that excuses and justifies suicide,*" the psychologist said haughtily. "*In this unprecedented event, the National Hurricane Center Director should not be making jokes about suicide-by-storm.*"

"You have got to be kidding me," Fisher said.

"Sadly, they're not. I have a niece just like this. No sense of humor at all, and always looking for something to be 'outraged' about if it means she can look down on others from her high horse," Edward said. He was eyeing the television with frustration. Leonard was intensifying to unheard-of levels as they all watched this trash, and he couldn't be in it!

At least he had managed to talk to Anne-Elise now that her plane had landed. She was very worried about the storm.

"*The fusion lab can stand up to quite a bit, but if we take a direct hit on the coast....*" She had trailed off.

"*There's not much that can stand up to three hundred miles an hour,*" he had agreed, "*and it's going to get stronger than that.*"

"*How strong?*"

"*Probably at least a hundred miles an hour stronger. But at this point, it doesn't really matter for those on the ground. It matters for the upper atmosphere, though.*" He had hesitated, feeling guilty about scaring her. "*But the models aren't showing the worst winds passing directly over Tallahassee. You'll see an impact, but if the lab can withstand normal Category Five winds, you'll probably be okay.*"

"*It was built near the Florida coast, so it can do that.*" She had paused. "*At least there's no risk of nuclear meltdown.*"

"*None at all?*"

"None. The worst that could happen is a neutron burst, and that's only if we lose control of the reaction. And it'll still be limited by the amount of fuel in the pellet."

"So there's no chance that Intensity Labs will accidentally turn the earth into another sun?" he had joked.

"No chance. Truly. There could be some local neutron radiation damage, but the worst that would happen would be bad public relations for the lab."

It had been good to talk to her and hear this reassurance, not because he had actually worried about the outcome he had named, but because it was a way for her to reassure herself about Leonard. He did expect Tallahassee to get a Category Five impact, but if she believed the lab could stand up to it, then she herself would be safe too. If nothing else, she could stay in the lab during landfall.

He brought his thoughts back to the present and his colleagues. Gesturing at the television again, he scoffed. "We should just ignore this noise box. Nobody gets alerts from TV anymore anyway."

He was still feeling put out at the Director for halting manned flights. He tried to avoid taking it out on his colleagues, but it was so frustrating to watch his favorite research subject likely become reality and be blocked from witnessing it firsthand! And all the more so because he knew that Dr. Chandra really had done this out of an abundance of caution. He really was looking out for them rather than just trying to protect himself from the spectacle of media and Internet sanctimony. *As a teenager, I just wanted my parents to look out for me and consider my safety before acting recklessly,* he thought, *but I'm not a boy any longer. I want to fly this storm. How often will we get such a chance?*

On second thought, with climate change, he wasn't sure the question had an obvious negative as the answer. *All right,* he conceded to himself, *but we'll definitely never get a second chance to fly the first-ever one. And this could be it. I should be there.*

He was tuning out the murmur of conversation around

him, getting lost in his own grievance and preemptive regret, when the voice of Director Chandra himself brought him out of it.

"Dr. Kirby? Could you come to my office?"

*　　*　　*

"The Hurricane Hunters who flew Leonard are back in Lakeland now," Dr. Chandra informed Edward as they shared a pot of coffee—decaf now, because they both knew they would get the shakes if they continued to consume caffeine. "It was apparently the most turbulent flight they'd ever experienced."

"That doesn't surprise me," Edward said. He leaned forward. "But they *did* touch down again safely. What g-force did they take?"

"Their systems reported four and a half g at peak. It was only for a second, though. What worries me is that the vertical acceleration in Leonard could be even worse now in brief spates... and that the four and a half g could be protracted now. The theory indicates that it could be."

"The theory of hypercanes?"

"Yes, Edward. I don't want you swaggering around the office declaring that I have said this. But we're both scientists and we know full well that the environment can support it. The storm has already dropped below 800 and it isn't even in the hottest spot yet, nor has it reached the area in the immediate wake of the frontal passage where the tropopause is coldest. If it does go hypercane, there'll be no need to swagger around saying it. You'll be right and you'll have the satisfaction of knowing that everyone realizes it."

Edward nodded, appreciating Chandra's words and the respect that Chandra manifestly held for him to hold meetings and confide in him like this about such an explosive topic. "The Super Hercules can take four and a half g easily. Obviously, since it already has today. In fact, even if Leonard ends up with vertical velocities of seventy meters per second —which my own model is *not* showing it doing—the plane could take the corresponding g-force from that."

Dr. Chandra studied him. "You really want to fly this, don't you?"

"I do, Director. You know I've studied extreme tropical cyclones all my life. And I'm a pilot. I should be in that cockpit if Leonard becomes what we both think it could become. It's not about attaching a plaque to my wall or placing a trophy on my shelf."

Dr. Chandra raised his eyebrows skeptically.

"All right, not *entirely* about that," Edward amended. "I do want this experience just to have it, rather than only to say that I have it. The plane can take the worst that I think Leonard could dish out, Director," he begged. "Please. Let us take off again. And let me have the cockpit."

Dr. Chandra leaned back in his executive chair, sighing. He rubbed his forehead in thought. "Leonard is the only hurricane in observed history to drop below 800 millibars. We do need data on a system like this, hypercane or not," he finally said, "and as good as our drones are, there's just something that a human can do that no machine can."

Edward's eyes sparkled with hope.

"All right. Get up to Lakeland. I'll task a crew. You like working with Cass as copilot, right?"

Nadya Cass was a NOAA aviator formerly of the Air Force who had flown many hurricanes with Edward. She was a lesbian, and Edward respected it and did not attempt to flirt with her at all, so they did get on well. "Yes," he told Chandra. "She's great." He paused. "Could you send Evans as one of the meteorologists? She could use the experience."

"All right," Chandra said. "I'll ask her. In the meantime, get on up to Lakeland and await further instructions. I'll send out another drone, and we'll see what it tells us. It should give us a vortex fix at two o'clock. If it looks safe, I'll give you the final auth." He paused. "Are you sure you're... *there* enough to fly? You really did get six hours of sleep last night?"

"I did, and I'm fine. I am running on adrenaline more than anything else. I couldn't sleep at this moment even if I wanted to."

"That's probably true for us all. In the most crucial moments of our lives, we tend to do what we must." Chandra smiled at Edward. "Get ready to fly your dream storm, Captain."

*   *   *

While Edward was driving to Lakeland, the drone's data came in just before two P.M. The Hurricane Center's staff gaped at it.

Leonard had, astonishingly, continued to intensify. It was now boasting 746 millibars in the eye and winds of 317 miles an hour.

"Well," Huang said philosophically, "it's not a you-know-what."

"It is a damn good thing that Kirby isn't here," Adela Fisher remarked. "'*You-know-what*,' honestly. It's still possible we'll need to use the word in official products."

"But we don't yet," he said. "Should we issue a Special Advisory?"

"Director hasn't authorized it, so I'm just going to call the one o'clock Central product 'Advisory 9A,' according to standard practice," she said. "There is nothing else Leonard could do to warrant a Special Advisory *except* become a hypercane, anyway. And if it does, it seems that Kirby will get to see it as he wanted."

"It may not. The rate of intensification seems to be slowing."

"It's not uncommon even in normal hurricanes for there to be a pause as it 'takes a breath,' so to speak."

"Surely it can't get much stronger than this. Maybe hypercanes cannot really happen. It was always just theoretical, anyway. Wasn't the theory originally meant to describe certain conditions after the Chicxulub event? But we don't have any actual geological evidence of hypercanes."

"That doesn't mean they couldn't happen, though. With plate tectonics and coastline changes, the evidence could easily be lost." She gazed at the computer showing a satellite image of Leonard. Its eye was as dry as the desert and starkly black in contrast with the white of the clouds surrounding the ferocious eyewall. "We're probably about to find out for sure if the theory is right."

Chapter 12: Flight of a Lifetime

Like all modern vehicles, Edward's car could connect to his phone, allowing him to take calls, have texts read out, and even dictate his responses. At two o'clock, the voice system sent him an incoming call from Dr. Chandra.

"Edward, the two P.M. drone just reported 746 millibars and 317 miles per hour."

Edward raised his eyebrows. "I'm not surprised."

"Nor am I."

There was a grim pause before the Director spoke again. "Satellite and drone data are showing no indication that this is its maximum intensity."

"So STCRS is probably going to turn out right."

"They're all 'going there' now, Edward. All the good models have jumped on the hypercane bandwagon... or the sub-700 bandwagon, at least. But yes, STCRS got there first." Chandra fell silent again, and this time, the pause in conversation continued.

Edward stifled a vile swear. Was the Director going to revoke his approval of a manned flight after all, since Leonard was still intensifying inexorably toward the hypercane threshold?

Chandra broke the silence at last. "Keep going to Lakeland and think this over along the way. This is not standard procedure, but it's as I said at headquarters: We are in uncharted waters."

"Or skies," Edward joked.

"*And* skies," Chandra corrected.

Edward chuckled. "Yes, thermodynamically uncharted waters and skies are both necessary."

Chandra laughed too, but it was clearly black humor now. "My point is, I'm breaking procedure this time. I'm not giving you an order. I am officially delegating authority to you about whether to take off, and I've told Lakeland Airport so."

Edward's eyes widened. "You're leaving it up to me?"

"You're the one who would be in charge of that plane. This

is your call. If you don't feel safe flying this storm when you get to Lakeland, you have full authority to call it off. If you want to go ahead, then unless I say no based on new data, you have my approval for that too."

Edward did some quick math in his head. "The first modeled hypercane was in a landmark 1995 paper. It went with *very* extreme conditions, far wilder than what we're seeing. Fifty Celsius at the sea surface. That storm simulation went to 225 millibars and something like 675 miles an hour." He felt that he could recite the insane numbers in his sleep, he had studied this subject so long. "Leonard won't do that."

"You're sure?" Chandra said darkly.

"I actually am," Edward said. "Even hypercanes have intensity limits, and they're controlled by the temperature differential between the sea surface and the tropopause just like hurricane intensities are. STCRS showed Leonard peaking at 660 and 420. But for the plane, of course, the most relevant issue isn't the horizontal winds. It's the verticals." He considered further. "Leonard will probably top out at fifty or fifty-five meters per second in the vertical. That's five and a half g of acceleration."

"Edward, you're simply dividing the updraft speed by Earth's gravitation. That's only valid if you're going from zero to fifty-five in the vertical when you fly into an updraft. You're assuming there are no downdrafts right next to an updraft."

Edward winced; the Director was right in his call-out. "Fair enough," he conceded, "but the plane can still take it. Because there *won't* be *downdrafts* of fifty-five or anything close to it."

Chandra was silent again. "Discuss it with Cass when you get there. Think it over, Edward. I'm not saying don't do it. I'm saying don't rush into it in a burst of bravado. Your lives are more important than the dataset you could get, and they're certainly more important than a trophy."

Edward sighed. "You're right. I'll let you know when I get there."

*　　*　　*

Nadya Cass greeted Edward with friendly gruffness. He gave her a thumbs up, but he could tell that she was nervous about Leonard's data. The crew included Flight Director Fred MacLean, a flight engineer, two electronics engineers, a navigator, an equipment operator, and three meteorologists—one of whom was indeed Dr. Sallie Evans, also arrived from Miami. She looked nervous but excited. Edward was pleased she had decided to come.

"We need to discuss this," Cass said to Edward immediately.

"There's been new data? Chandra told me along the way that the storm had hit 746 millibars and 317 miles an hour." He checked his wristwatch. "It's just after four. What did the drone report at the top of the hour?"

"There wasn't a four o'clock drone. The flight was only tasked to report data from ten until three."

"So we don't have recent data and won't know anything until we get into the storm ourselves?"

"That is correct."

Edward hesitated, suddenly having a moment of doubt. It was one thing to face a beast knowing in advance what kind of beast it was. It was another entirely to face a monster of unknown abilities.

"The three o'clock drone reported that Leonard has kept going. At that time, it was 736 millibars and 325 miles an hour."

It's going to do it! Edward thought excitedly. *Here we go!*

Cass noticed the excitement in his eyes and frowned. "Kirby, this is unheard of. You sure about this?"

"What are the vertical velocities?"

"Uh...." She glanced questioningly at the crew.

"Thirty-three to thirty-seven meters per second," Dr. Evans supplied.

Edward shrugged, his hesitation momentarily lifting. "What are y'all worried about? That's not a problem for this beast of a plane." He considered what he had heard before he

180

had left Miami. "They told me at the NHC that it was pulling four and a half g at two o'clock. This would be a bit less."

"So it's taking a deep breath before the plunge, from the sounds of it."

"It's pretty incredible to find myself among people who have no real doubt of what's about to happen," he remarked. "There have been times when I thought the only person at headquarters who actually believed me was the Director."

"Hard to ignore reality when this storm has the numbers it does." Cass stared at him. "Kirby, here's the thing. It's not entirely about what the *plane* can take. It's also what *we* can take."

"We are trained pilots. We can take extreme g-force."

"Yes, we should be able to take up to 9 g of acceleration before we start blacking out. But we had better be damned sure it won't exceed that. We have to be at a hundred percent if we fly something like this, not hypoxiated."

"You think Leonard is going to have ninety meters per second in vertical winds? No modeled hypercane has ever done that."

"It doesn't have to. Fifty in an updraft right next to forty in a downdraft... or fifty-five next to thirty-five... you get the idea."

Edward winced. The latter was not impossible.

"And, while the plane can take extreme g-force, it will start to strain. And if *we* are in rough shape already...." She trailed off pointedly.

"Do you not want to fly it?" he exclaimed.

"I want us to discuss this rationally. You're the subject-matter expert. Do you think this is a real risk? Put on your scientist cap."

Edward considered, trying to be rational and not let his excitement overpower his sense.

Cass's concern is legitimate, he suddenly thought. *Leonard won't reach ninety meters per second, but it is entirely possible it could have fifty-five next to negative thirty-five. Do I really want to pilot a plane in those conditions while fighting hypoxia myself?*

And there would not be one person on the craft to whom I could turn over the controls. This wouldn't be a matter of exhaustion or eyestrain in one individual. We'd all be subject to the same forces.

He gazed around at the crew. He knew these people. He'd flown with all of them through the years, even Evans a time or two. Their lives would be in his hands. *Dr. Evans's life would be in his hands.*

Do I truly want to fly a hypercane—because that's what it would be—if it means—

The excited, boyish bravado that he had maintained effortlessly through the day suddenly cracked. *My personal research hobbyhorse just got real,* he realized. *Chandra was right. I've been excited about the idea of flying a hypercane. Do I really want to take on the reality, with all that it could mean?*

For a moment, he was inclined to listen to that voice of caution and call off the flight, or rather, change its path. They could fly around the storm and dispatch drones into its core, as the last craft had done. That would still be important. If Leonard did what he expected, he would still be the pilot who had flown the Hurricane Hunter craft that confirmed the world's first hypercane.

But I could fly into the core myself. I could be in it. I've modeled extreme cyclones, including hypercanes, for most of my career during the hurricane offseason. Dr. Chandra may have been right that I was excited about wanting a "trophy," but I was right as well that this opportunity should be mine. And it is, if I muster my courage and take it.

With that, his hesitation evaporated for good. "This is a historic moment, whatever else happens with Leonard. This is the first confirmed sub-800 hurricane, if nothing else. It's potentially a once-in-a-lifetime opportunity to get data on a hypercane."

Cass was silent and impassive for a moment. Then she muttered, "It might not be under climate change."

"But it could be the first, and if we miss it—if nobody flies the world's first hypercane—I think we'll regret it. And you know, if there *are* more in the future, we'll need to know how to fly them. We could be the pioneers in that. We can't sit back at base and headquarters and cower in fear forever, if this is the first of a new kind of storm we'll be seeing. We have to learn how to face them."

Cass sighed, then gazed up at him with a weak smile. "Well, if we're going to do this, there's no pilot I'd rather be flying with."

He smiled back.

"Dr. Chandra left it up to us to make a flight plan, since all bets are off as to appropriate altitude levels. We'd usually aim for 850 or 700 millibars, but with the assumption that'll be fifteen hundred and ten thousand feet respectively."

"Yeah, 850 doesn't exist with Leonard, and 700 would be abject lunacy. It may not exist either anymore."

She grimaced. "Right. So, what's the ten-thousand-foot level in a storm like this?"

"My STCRS intensifies it to 660, and the operational models to 680 to 700. If that's the surface, ten thousand feet should be 450 to 500 millibars."

"You don't think it'll intensify *beyond* that, do you?" Meteorologist Patricia Cartwright asked.

He took a deep breath. "Nothing is showing that, not even my model. And while this is uncharted territory, my model's last run for Leonard has been dead accurate so far. I think 500 will be okay."

*   *   *

Without new data from Leonard, the Hurricane Center had to issue a five o'clock—or four o'clock Central—advisory with estimated values of 725 millibars and 335 miles an hour, acknowledging that "these values may be conservative." The center would not declare it a hypercane without proof of it, and Edward agreed with this decision. If they found that proof during their flight, it would indisputably warrant a Special Advisory. He wouldn't have to wait until eleven P.M. to see that historic advisory issued.

Also at five o'clock, the crew boarded the plane, with Flight Director Fred MacLean conducting the final checklist.

Edward tamped down his excitement as he and Cass took to the cockpit. This was a serious occasion, and he knew he could not be distracted. The flight out would not be too rough until they were well inside the storm, but Leonard was such an enormous hurricane that its outer bands were showing up in the sky at Lakeland. He had to be focused.

"The door is shut," MacLean called out over intercom. "All systems pass final checks, and all persons are aboard."

"Prepare to start engines!" Edward called back cheerfully. "Cass?"

"Roger that."

The people aboard the craft all took deep breaths as the engines roared to life and the plane tore down the runway for takeoff.

*   *   *

As the strong cold front passed over the eastern United States, conditions in the Gulf states dropped from nearly one hundred degrees Fahrenheit and sweltering humidity to a balmy, dry eighty degrees. By now everyone had the wherewithal to know about the unprecedented hurricane boiling in the Gulf. Evacuations were already underway, with Interstates 10 and 65 thoroughly backed up around the Florida-Alabama line. But those who were not directly in the storm's path were enjoying the cooler weather, a pleasant first taste of autumn—or it would have been in happier times.

With the strong trough steering it, Leonard's forward motion was picking up. It would be making landfall in a day and a half. The Hurricane Hunters did not have a very long flight.

The storm was so large that they were in clouds for the entire flight, and it wasn't long before hurricane-force winds began buffeting the plane. Edward glanced at the aviation radar, trying to find a smooth socket in the clouds. It didn't matter what the wind speeds themselves were as long as they were in one direction, the same direction that he was flying the plane.

"We're two hundred kilometers away from the eye!" Cartwright shouted. "I knew it was a big storm, but this is nuts!"

"Yep," Edward called out over intercom. "And we're going to be in Cat Five winds for thirty-three kilometers before we hit the eye."

"Un-freaking-believable."

Rattles and thuds battered the plane's shell as the turbulent winds got stronger and stronger. Edward tried to keep the craft flying with a tailwind whenever possible, but he knew well that intensifying hurricanes were turbulent, and his model had shown storms of this intensity—including Leonard itself—with updrafts and crosswinds throughout the core.

All along, the meteorologists aboard the plane were releasing dropsondes, pulling radar data, and taking in high-resolution measurements from the plane's stepped-frequency microwave radiometer. Every now and then, one of them would call out a particularly stunning report to the entire crew.

Edward believed that this was meant primarily for him personally, so that he would know what the storm he was flying—his dream storm, as Chandra had said—was doing. He was quite grateful to them for it.

"Surface winds of 280!" the third meteorologist, Dave Morales, called out. "And there's a red-hot radar signature just ahead!"

"It's the eyewall!" Edward called out, though everyone aboard knew that. "It'll be well over three hundred in that. Maybe four hundred."

He winced as a tremendous blast of wind rocked the plane. Crates and equipment clattered around. People bounced in their seats. But as he had proudly said back at headquarters, this plane was a beast.

He had kept the altimeter set to 500 millibars, but as they reached areas of lower pressure, their physical altitude dropped. That was normal and expected for any hurricane flight, but he did wonder just how low they would end up in the eye.

"SFMR just reported surface pressures below 800!" Evans said.

"We're still eighteen freakin' kilometers out of the eye!" Cartwright exclaimed.

"We knew it was down to at least 730," MacLean chimed in.

"Surface winds over three hundred!" Morales reported again.

Edward's heart was racing in anticipation. *This is it*, he thought. *We're doing it. We're going to be the ones.*

But despite the excitement of the situation, the hubbub of chatter around him, and the rattle of turbulence, he found himself slipping into a zone of profound inner peace and satisfaction. Neither the noise nor his own anticipation distracted him from his task at this crucial moment.

I am the calm eye of the storm, he thought.

WHACK!

The plane suddenly flipped ninety degrees from a blast of turbulent updraft wind. Papers, boxes, and crates bounced and rattled around, and several shouts and curses filled the air as the crew scrambled for purchase on any fixed object they could find.

Edward's heart thudded, his moment of inner peace gone. But he quickly righted the plane. Deciding to inject a little humor into the situation, he turned on intercom and called out in his best imitation of a commercial airline pilot, "Folks, we're going through a little bit of turbulent air at the moment, so please remain in your seats with seatbelts securely fastened—"

This was just what the crew needed. Laughs and chuckles erupted from them as they relaxed.

"Dropsonde, deploy," MacLean said calmly. "Prepare to capture the inner eyewall reading." This was standard operating procedure, to obtain a dropsonde report from the inner eyewall. Another—or possibly more than one—would then be released into the calm eye.

Cartwright released the dropsonde. The cabin crew all watched the rapidly incoming report. "Bloody hell," she said. "It's going almost halfway around the eye! Surface winds—366."

Whistles and exclamations of shock erupted around the plane.

"Okay, it hit the water now—surface pressure in the eyewall is—it's 738 millibars."

In the cockpit, Cass muted her intercom. "Shit. If it's 738 with winds of 366 miles an hour, what're we going into in the calm eye?"

Edward's heart was still racing. "We're about to find out."

The SFMR continued to report data as he piloted the plane through the intense turbulence of the eyewall. The pressures it was reporting continued dropping—729, 725, 718, 709—

The turbulent winds suddenly ceased. "In the eye!" Edward shouted.

"Dropsonde, ready an instrument for deployment," MacLean again said calmly and professionally.

"SFMR, what've we got?" Cass called out.

"Just dropped below 700," Cartwright reported.

The crew fell silent. They all knew what the models and the theory indicated that this pressure milestone meant. Edward's heart skipped a beat in excitement, but he kept his head and continued flying toward the center of the large eye.

"Dropsonde, deploy," MacLean commanded.

They all held their breath as Dr. Evans read out the data. "Calm winds," she announced. "Surface air temperature in the eye... 308 Kelvin."

They all goggled at this. That was over ninety-four degrees Fahrenheit. The cold front had dropped temperatures, but the storm was a heat engine unto itself.

"Surface pressure...." She hesitated for a moment, which seemed like eternity to Edward. "687 millibars."

Edward released his breath in a whoosh. "Yep. The readings back at the airport were the deep breath before the plunge," he said to Cass.

No one else in the crew had said anything yet. They all knew what the report might mean, but it seemed that they were waiting for something before they spoke. Edward suddenly realized what it was. "Cass, take the controls for a sec. I'd like to look at the data."

She understood. As soon as he had handed off control to her, he opened up a computer and looked quickly over the radiometer and dropsonde reports. There were certain values he wanted to see.

"Mixing ratio in the eyewall was forty-three grams of water vapor per kilogram of dry air," he said. "That's in line with all the research." He scanned further. "We took vertical updraft winds of thirty-seven meters per second coming in. Also in line. Surface heat flux in the eye... over seven thousand watts per square meter."

"Good God," Cass exclaimed.

"Yep. Hurricanes usually draw one or two thousand."

He would have to make the call soon, but there was one last thing he wanted to see first. He leaned forward and gazed upward through the plane's front window.

A masterpiece of Nature spread out in panorama before him.

He had been in many hurricane eyes before, including some Category Fives. Those were always well-organized: crystal clear centers surrounded by an inverted conical tower of clouds, a sight known poetically as the stadium effect.

The eye of Leonard was easily the most impressive one he had ever seen. The rolling eyewall towered as high as he could see, the clouds in perfectly striated layers. Frequent lightning flashes illuminated the eyewall. And the air in the calm eye was so thin, the pressure so low, that above them, the sky was a deep, dark blue.

Leonard was a magnificent storm, a triumph of Nature. But that ferocious, dark, frequently illuminated eyewall that enclosed the plane on all sides seemed to be sending a threatening message to the crew now: *You should not be here. No creature should be here. This place is not meant for mortal eyes to behold. You are ingenious to create a metal shell to shield yourselves from me, but you do not belong here. And I will make sure you remember that.*

Edward shook off the ominous feeling that had overcome him. *Superstition is understandable in such a moment as this, but I am a scientist first and last,* he told himself. He took out his phone and snapped some photos of this, just for himself.

"We're all waiting for your verdict, Judge."

Cass's wry voice brought him back to the present as he eased back into his seat.

"You're the expert, Kirby," she said. "Is it? Have we got one?"

The dropsonde and SFMR reports were stunning, but the crew had run quality control, and the readings were accurate. "Yes," he confirmed. "It's a hypercane." He couldn't believe the words that had come from his own lips—couldn't believe he'd actually had occasion to *utter* them about a real storm, rather than something in his model. "The theory said it would be, and everything we got from the sonde and SFMR supports it. Hypercane Leonard, friends. And we're in the eye to witness it."

They all took that in, awe, shock, and horror flitting over their faces to varying degrees. As Edward had said before they had taken off, this was a historic moment.

A horrific one, but nonetheless historic.

And the worst was yet to come for some spot on the Gulf Coast, they all knew.

From the cabin, Cartwright broke the silence. "And it's ten till eight—or seven Central. An advisory's about to come out."

"It'll be a Special Advisory," MacLean said.

"You know this?"

"They've advised me to expect one. Don't know what it'll say."

Edward's heart raced. Would the advisory say what he

believed it should? Would the NHC make the leap?

Since he had not commanded her to turn the controls back to him yet, Cass continued to fly the plane, now heading for the other side of the eyewall. "Brace yourselves for turbulence!" she warned as the plane entered the roiling mass.

The soundtrack of hell resumed once more, rattles and bangs and thuds, as the beautiful sights of the perfect eye disappeared into a gray haze.

Edward wanted to see the advisory and discussion, and now that they were in the eyewall, it was best not to turn control over to someone else until they were in an area of lower turbulence. He performed the co-pilot's duties mechanically as he waited for the crew to announce the NHC's transmission of the storm advisory.

"Special Advisory just dropped," Cartwright announced from the cabin. "And—my God. Kirby, you'll want to see it."

Cass was expertly flying the plane out of the ferocious eyewall and into a weaker area—though "weak" was a relative matter now—so Edward quickly refreshed his laptop. His eyes popped at the words that appeared on his screen.

Hypercane Leonard Special Discussion Number 11

NWS National Hurricane Center Miami FL   AL152051

700 PM CDT Mon Sep 04 2051

Leonard has crossed a meteorological boundary. Hurricane Hunters have found that the storm has obtained internal pressure of 687 mb and winds of 320 knots. Additional data from their ongoing reconnaissance confirm that Leonard has become a type of tropical cyclone called a hypercane. The NHC will use this term as long as warranted, and Saffir-Simpson Hurricane Wind Scale categories will be discontinued for Leonard while it remains a hypercane.

This is the first observed hypercane in human history. Modeling of such storms is theoretical, due to a lack of forecast verification data until now, so all intensity guidance should be considered uncertain. However, this guidance suggests that the storm may finally be reaching its maximum potential intensity. Based on research and modeling studies of hypercanes, which operational model guidance supports, NHC forecasts Leonard leveling off at 350 knots and maintaining that intensity until landfall.

Individuals in Leonard's path should not focus on specific wind speeds, pressure levels, or terminology. Weather conditions in the storm's path will be unsurvivable. Those in the projected path should evacuate immediately.

Additionally, the site may be hazardous for some time after landfall, due to high particle matter concentrations in the air from pulverized debris and possible ozone hole creation over the path from the storm's injection of water vapor into the stratosphere....

Edward read to the bottom of the discussion transmittal. At the very end, beyond the five-day intensity and track forecast, was a title-name combination that he had never seen attached to a forecast product:

Director Chandra

Edward felt a momentary pang for the fact that it wasn't his name on the first-ever hypercane forecast product, but he couldn't have that *and* be the first pilot to fly a Hurricane Hunter aircraft into one. He had chosen the latter, and he didn't regret the choice. *And with mine not an option, there's no one else whose name deserves more to be on that product than yours, Director,* he thought with some affection.

Chandra was a good guy, Edward thought. He was stern, but he looked out for the team, thinking of the public relations and politics as well as the science. He was cautious, but not to a fault. He knew when to hold back and when to take the plunge. Edward greatly respected the fact that

Chandra had not forced a forecaster to attach their name to perhaps the most important product the NHC had ever issued, a product that would be heatedly debated and would go into the history books, but had courageously and honorably stuck his own name on it. That said, "*I'm not throwing anyone into the fray or under the bus. I'm the leader, and I own this.*"

The whole crew seemed to have been reading it at the same time. As they all apparently finished, cheers began to erupt, Edward's loudest of all. He raised his fist to the sky and shouted a whoop. It was a shout of personal satisfaction at having been here for this moment and for having been right about Leonard from the start, but it was also a shout of awe, almost worshipful, at the storm for having achieved this milestone. Perhaps the cheers and whoops were inappropriate, and he did wonder if prim-and-proper Dr. Evans was participating, but the crew were all meteorologists and Hurricane Hunters. They were in their element. This was like climbing Mount Everest, setting foot on the Moon or Mars, confirming detonation of the atomic bomb in the Trinity test....

Or obtaining breakeven fusion energy, Edward thought, momentarily considering his sister and the fact that this monster was headed for landfall not too far west of her.

"What are we thinking for the landfall timeline?" Cartwright asked over intercom. "Still thirty-six hours from now?"

"Probably," Morales said. "Guidance shows a landfall around Panama City at six A.M. local time Wednesday."

"Panama City. My hometown. Naturally," Edward muttered. He raised his voice so that the crew could all hear him. "Hypercanes weaken *very* slowly if conditions remain favorable. Leonard isn't going to be much weaker when it hits. It might even be a bit stronger."

"What did your model show?" MacLean asked.

"The STCRS had Leonard peaking around 660 millibars."

"Do you think it'll do it?"

"I see no reason it wouldn't. Hurricanes often have, in the words of this great co-pilot, several 'deep breaths before the plunge,' several periods of rapid intensification. Hypercanes could too. But I don't think it'll drop below 600. The conditions don't really support it, based on available research."

"Like yours," Nadya Cass chimed in archly.

"Precisely. It's approaching its maximum intensity, I think."

"It's just after eight Eastern," MacLean cut in. "We can fly until midnight. The two eyewall interactions we've had so far don't seem to have done any harm to the plane. Let's see what Leonard continues to do. Over the course of four hours, we'll know if it's leveling off."

From the cockpit, Edward grinned. *This is not a one-and-done,* he thought gleefully. *I'm going to get very familiar with this storm. Five hours in the eye of the first observed hypercane!*

"The altitude limit of this plane is 40,386 feet," MacLean continued, "which would be lower for a storm with pressures this low. It's a shame we can't get much stratospheric data. For this kind of storm, we need to have that."

"You want me to climb?"

There was a pause. "Less than four hours to get all the data we can on an unprecedented, first-ever storm. If we climb to try to see how much vapor is getting injected into the stratosphere, we miss out on some eyewall data." MacLean sighed audibly over intercom. "We'll stay at ten thousand feet for three passes and follow standard procedure. We need obs of hypercane eyewall processes to feed into the models. Then, for the final pass, we'll climb to 150 millibars. That should tell us approximately how high convection is bursting, and it'll be as up-to-date for the eleven o'clock advisory as we can manage."

"Roger that. Cass, let me have controls back."

She turned the controls back over to him. He took a breath and closed his eyes in satisfaction as he resumed control of the plane. *Living the dream,* he thought. *This is going to be hell for someone, but there's nothing I can do to prevent that. It won't help them one bit if I am miserable and dour in this flight. Nobody has to know how much I'm enjoying this experience.*

*   *   *

For the next three hours, they sampled the storm in all its quadrants, gathering as much data as they could. Edward was not in charge of data acquisition—that was the crew—but he knew the importance of this part of the mission. Leonard was the first hypercane ever seen. They needed this data.

At nine o'clock Eastern, Leonard had intensified to 681 millibars.

Intensification once again seemed to level off, as the storm "took another deep breath." Its pressure remained steady at ten. But its winds had caught up to the deepening and now thrashed the sea at 380 miles an hour, far faster than the strongest tornadoes ever observed.

By eleven, the time of the next full advisory from the NHC, Leonard had 678 millibars of pressure. Deepening did seem to be leveling off—at least for this spate. But the winds were now whipping away at 410 miles an hour.

"It's stopped rapidly intensifying," Meteorologist Morales observed from the cabin, "but it's still *steadily* intensifying. That normal, Kirby?"

"I don't know," he confessed. "None of us do. But it's what the hypercane research models predict, so I guess the answer is 'yes.'"

"I thought your model took it to 660."

"It did. And it might turn out right. Wouldn't take much. At this point, the storm is so strong, and pressures are so low, that eighteen millibars is little more than Leonard farting."

He had thought this was funny, but the joke fell completely flat as the cabin fell silent. The silence quickly became awkward.

Then Morales spoke up again. "I was going to tell you to show more respect, but...."

Edward then understood. "No, you're right," he agreed.

"It's just a weather system. It doesn't care what we say."

194

"Still, it deserves... reverence," Edward agreed. "You're right."

"Final pass, Kirby," MacLean intoned, cutting in. "Let's see what's going on in the lower stratosphere. Initiate climb to 150 millibars... unless that is beyond the plane's safe operating limit."

"Roger that. Beginning climb."

Chapter 13: An Angry God

This is bad, Edward thought as he flew in the low stratosphere.

Although they couldn't fly to fifty thousand feet, the eyewall clearly towered at least that high. That wasn't unheard of even in normal hurricanes, but there was a difference between normal hurricanes and Leonard. Normal hurricanes could only reach such heights if the troposphere itself was extremely thick. They could not continue to expand vertically very far into the stratosphere, because in the stratosphere—and in contrast with the troposphere—the atmosphere quickly became warmer than the rising air.

The only thing that could overcome the unfavorable thermal conditions of the lower stratosphere was an immensely powerful vertical updraft. Normal hurricanes couldn't muster updrafts of the necessary strength. But hypercanes had been theorized for over sixty years to have that ability.

The Hurricane Hunter crew were now witnessing confirmation of that theory.

The troposphere was not unusually thick in the central Gulf of Mexico, so fifty thousand feet was unambiguously the lower stratosphere. But Leonard had vertical updrafts befitting the hypercane that it was, so the sheer force continued to send moist air upward in defiance of the stratospheric thermal gradient.

We shouldn't be flying this high, Edward thought with disquiet as the plane struggled. *This is under forty thousand feet, but it's still probably beyond the plane's safe limit. The air is too thin, and the engines are fighting it. Gasping for breath, in a sense.*

The winds in the eyewall were still two hundred miles per hour at flight level, and vertical velocities were twenty meters per second at this altitude. Edward had to focus on the controls, with the plane threatening to stall, but he imagined all this vapor around him being shot higher still by such powerful winds.

The ozone layer begins at around forty-seven thousand feet, he thought ominously. It was bad, bad, *bad.*

But the only thing he could do was provide data about it.

I respect you, he thought, as if offering a repentant prayer to Leonard. *I have wanted to "conquer" a hypercane, I now realize. Dr. Chandra was right. I wanted a trophy on my wall, like a hunter wants a trophy of his successful kill, but you are too powerful for anyone to conquer. I understand that now. I salute you. I'm glad to have had the experience, and I respect your inestimable power.*

Then he smiled as he reflected on the fact that he was offering up thoughts to an inanimate force of nature. Leonard had a name, but that was a human conceit. It was just a physical phenomenon, not a god. It didn't have feelings.

And yet, at the same time, there was something almost godlike about the fact that this beast would exist no matter what humans called it. Wasn't that inherently divine, in a way? The names and words that people gave to gods were just conveniences. A god either existed or didn't. If it did exist, it had a certain nature, and the name by which humans called it had no bearing on that nature.

But would this storm exist at all—at least as a hypercane—if there were no humans?

Edward knew the answer to that question. *We created Leonard, in a way, but we cannot control or defy it.*

There was a momentary pause before Patricia Cartwright spoke. "Radar confirms water vapor and vertical updrafts well into the lower stratosphere. Probably, yes, into the ozone layer."

"So maybe we should've brought some astronaut suits?" Edward joked darkly. Black humor was the only way he could cope with this appalling data point and what it portended.

"Go to hell," she said, but dark amusement was also in her tone.

"We're already in hell," Dr. Evans put in. "We're in a hypercane. And we've probably overstayed our welcome. Not to be superstitious, but...."

"I was thinking the same thing," Edward agreed. "So let's get back to ten thousand feet and get out. We've seen the tropopause and lower stratosphere, and it's what we all feared. Let's respectfully take our leave of Hypercane Leonard." He marveled inwardly at the fact that he, a scientist who took pride in being rational, was viewing the storm as a person—or an angry god.

"You're the pilot," Morales added to the banter.

"Sure am."

Their raillery was interrupted by a shock. The plane began to shake and shudder, though there was no turbulence in the eye. Cass gasped and clutched her seat. "Shit, Kirby! We're stalling!"

"I know!" Edward was now focused singly on that. Blocking everything out but the storm and the control panel before him, he initiated a descent. "Hold on to your seats, everyone back there! Beginning descent to a safe altitude."

The plane continued to tremble as Edward brought it down as rapidly as he safely could do. Negative g-force was far more dangerous to the human body than positive. Positive g-force could cause lightheadedness and hypoxia, but that would pass once the acceleration ended and the heart's own muscular action reasserted itself as the dominant force. *Pilots* who blacked out mid-flight faced the deadly risk of crashing, but the body itself could usually recover from positive g-force. But negative g-force could cause blood clotting and vessel rupture in the brain as excessive blood was pushed upward.

Edward gritted his teeth as the eyewall of Leonard loomed. This was not good with a plane threatening to stall out. He could bank to try to avoid it, but that carried its own risks—

The hell with it, he thought. He banked hard to the left.

Not fast enough.

The right wing tip caught in an area of rapid counterclockwise winds.

It was not zero to two hundred miles an hour in that short a distance, but the speed difference was significant enough to jerk the plane to the right and slightly upward.

"*Kirby!*"

The plane spun in a half-circle. Edward swore, trying to regain control of it, as the forces of Hypercane Leonard hurled it fully into the roiling eyewall, *tail first*. Flying at four hundred miles per hour from its own engine thrust, the plane was deep into the swirling clouds in a mere second. And Edward did not have control.

In this moment, as the plane was jerked around in the eyewall by its tail, Leonard had control. And Edward knew it.

The plane was dropping, and not by the pilot's intention in a controlled descent. It wasn't in a tailspin—the updrafts were too powerful for that—but it was being thrown from side to side, rocking, tossed about in the hypercane winds like debris. Edward heard thunderous thuds, clatters, shrieks, and screams of unvarnished terror from the cabin—but he could not focus on that. He had to get control of this plane.

A tremendous shearing metallic sound slammed their eardrums. "That's bad," Cass said, eyes wide.

"*Dr. Kirby!*" screamed Dr. Evans. "We've lost engine number two! It's dangling! I see it!"

Another thud.

"It *broke loose!*"

Cass took the intercom, aware that Edward couldn't right now. "Copy. Status report on the other three engines."

WHAM! Turbulent winds began battering the plane again. The shaking recommenced, and exclamations of fear from the cabin mingled with clatters and thuds as cargo was tossed around.

"Kirby, we're at twenty thousand feet and dropping!" MacLean called out.

MacLean—calm, professional, unflappable MacLean—was upset. Edward had already been frightened, but he was now terrified.

"I'm trying to find a socket of steady winds!" he shouted

199

above the din. The menacing threat that he had attributed to his anthropomorphic Leonard returned to his thoughts.

"There's a smooth spot just ahead," Morales called out.

"I see it too! Roger that. Heading for it!"

"Status report on the remaining three engines!" Cass insisted.

Edward barely heard the response. He certainly didn't register what it was. The plane was now at fourteen thousand feet and tumbling fast. He had at least managed to pull it from Leonard's grip, and was flying it again, but they were not clear yet—far from it. The shaking and banging continued.

There was nothing else in Edward's mind right now. He was focused solely on steering the plane toward the area where straight-line—incredibly strong, but not turbulent—winds beckoned. Even better, it was a tailwind. Taking a deep breath, he navigated the craft toward the comparatively safe place.

The shaking and rocking did not cease but did seem to lessen. Edward released the breath he had been holding. "Everyone okay back there?" he called out over intercom.

There was silence. Instead of anyone from the cabin, it was Cass who responded. "Edward, we have *one engine*."

A stone seemed to sink down his throat. "What?" he sputtered.

"I'm glad you weren't paying attention. You did what you needed to do. But we are flying on a single engine, number three. We lost one, two, and four in that."

Edward was stunned silent.

"NHC knows," MacLean cut in. "They've ordered an immediate mission abort."

"We're at the end of the mission anyway."

"Kirby, we're on the south side of the storm. It's moving north. Continuing on this heading will mean the least amount of time in strong winds."

"Copy. Continuing at 179 to 181 degrees." He lowered his voice. "Chandra is going to kill me," he mumbled, but Cass grimaced and turned away, and he then realized what she was thinking: *You'd better hope that Leonard doesn't do it first.*

It was possible to fly the plane on one engine, but it was far more challenging. The thrust was imbalanced, and the engine was struggling, having to do the work of four.

And Leonard was intensifying again. The instruments still worked, having recorded data all along without a gap. It would be invaluable for understanding hypercanes, Edward comforted himself. That was worth it. But now those instruments were telling him that Leonard's pressure was still dropping.

With only one engine, horizontal winds were now a major issue. The plane needed to stay in a tailwind all the way out of the storm, and that was not easy. Their course couldn't remain due south, since the storm was rotating. A headwind —or, worse, crosswinds—would overtax the engine, Edward feared.

He held his breath, heart pounding, as he navigated through the hypercane core—the winds of three hundred miles an hour or more. There was still a vast ring of Category Five winds beyond that, and the thunderstorms comprising this ring were intensifying.

WHACK!

A fist of wind tossed the plane out of its safe tailwind groove. Crosswinds immediately began battering it, and a horrendous lurch upward—then downward—made everyone scream.

Another pair of jolts, these even stronger than the first. Even Edward bounced in his seat, his control over the instruments momentarily gone. From the cabin, groans of people and thuds of tossed-about objects resumed again.

"What was *that*?" Cass exclaimed.

"Updraft and downdraft," Edward replied, gritting his teeth. The plane was still bouncing, and worse, it was dropping. He knew it. The engine—that last engine—was struggling.

"We're not in the eyewall!"

"It's an intensifying thunderstorm."

"Captain, report," MacLean said, his voice oddly toneless. "Engine three is smoking."

Edward gazed at the altimeter and nearly threw up. They were descending.

And now they had lost all their engines.

"Kirby?"

Edward stared at the radar. There was another socket of straight-line southeasterly tailwinds. He jerked the plane as hard as he could into it, feeling relief as the storm—finally—did not fight him. They were descending, but there was nothing he could do about that now. At least they were not being tossed about like a cat toy. If he could just keep them in this socket—if there were no more surprises—they could continue southeast and get into the weaker winds. Maybe, maybe, they could manage a water landing—

"*Kirby, do you copy?*"

"Yes, I copy," he replied dully. "I'm going to stay in this socket of tailwinds on a general southeasterly course into... hopefully into tropical-storm-force winds. The storm is too big to escape fully before we hit the surface." He took a deep breath, steeling himself for what he was going to have to say. "Prepare the cabin crew for an emergency water landing."

No one onboard dared speak for a few seconds. But time was critical now, and they all knew it. MacLean said, his voice cracking, "Roger. Crew, prepare life raft for deployment. Gather emergency supplies and the backup data box. And strap on your life jackets."

"You've got this, Edward!" Morales suddenly called out over the intercom. "You can do it!"

"And this is not your fault!" Dr. Evans added.

Yes, it is. I made that left bank that threw us into the eyewall and cost us three engines.

But if I hadn't banked, we would have gone into the eyewall anyway. Was there a way to avoid this? Was this inevitable?

He couldn't focus on blame. He had to get the plane down on his terms, rather than letting Leonard dictate the terms.

And he had to do it in an area of possibly-survivable winds and waves.

The cabin crew undoubtedly hurried to prepare what they could. Edward couldn't think about them. They had their job to do, and he had his. If he could just do it, they might be okay. The life raft was tough, the same kind that the Navy used. It would stay afloat in all but the worst waves. It had compartments for supplies: their food, water, sunscreen, first-aid kits, and the waterproof data box containing single-use, write-once memory. They had transmitted all their data back to the NHC as it came in, but it was also recorded to this box.

Edward expected Leonard to have one more surprise for them, a fatal one this time, to punish them for their hubris. But he managed to stay in the socket of tailwinds without any unmanageable updrafts or downdrafts.

They entered Category Four, then Three, then Two, then One winds, as the plane inexorably descended. It was now basically a glider. Then suddenly the gray slurry filling all their windows changed. They had descended below the cloud deck, merely a thousand feet above the turbulent sea surface.

"SFMR, winds?" Edward asked.

"Transmitting peak winds of fifty knots here," Morales said.

"Well, damn." Edward had hoped the winds would be weaker. "All right. Brace for impact and prepare to evacuate the craft."

He wondered if the cockpit would shatter on impact. He was trying to slow the plane down with the flaps, and without a four-hundred-mile-per-hour tailwind, it was flying at about 150 miles an hour. Too fast. Cass adjusted the flaps to maximum position as Edward tried to land parallel to the surface.

The dark, angry sea rushed up to meet him. He closed his eyes, hoping this wouldn't be the last thing he saw.

THUD!

Edward realized in two seconds that he was not dead, nor

was he hurt. He opened his eyes. The plane was bobbing—or at least, it was trying to. The waves were tall even in this area.

But they had to try to make it. Edward and Cass hurried into the cabin, where MacLean was preparing to open the emergency exit door. They had hooked up the life raft to a near-instant air pump.

MacLean opened the door. Seawater rushed inside, and gale-force winds battered their faces. But they pushed the raft out, inflated it, and scrambled on. MacLean did a head count.

"All crew accounted for. Co-pilot."

Cass gave him a nod and scrambled onto the raft, attaching her life vest.

"Captain."

"You first." Whether he was to blame or not, Edward was not going to let anyone but himself be the last off this plane.

MacLean shrugged. "As you wish."

Edward gazed at the interior of the plane one last time. Instruments were beginning to spark and short out as saltwater flooded the cabin. Darkness suddenly fell as the main circuit fizzled. *What a disaster. I didn't want this. It was a good plane.*

At least no one died.

Yet.

A sad expression on his face, he saluted the plane and got aboard the life raft.

They were all waiting for him, having quickly stuffed the necessary items into the waterproof compartments of the raft. The waves were fierce, and Edward just had to hope that nothing more than about twenty or thirty feet tall would slam them. The storm would continue on its course, and the winds and waves would lessen. If they could just survive the immediate term, they would probably be okay. The NHC knew where they were from the final data transmission. Someone would be sent out to get them.

Edward realized that his family would learn about this, and his heart skipped a beat. He reached for his cell phone, which was in a waterproof case. That advertising claim had not been a lie, either. The phone still worked.

But this far out at sea, there was no signal.

And it wouldn't take that long for the battery to drain.

"Well," he said, "this sucks."

"Understatement, Kirby," Nadya Cass replied, rolling her eyes.

*   *   *

Indifferent to the fate of the Hurricane Hunter crew who had so courageously—or foolishly—entered its domain, Leonard barreled relentlessly toward the coast, as strong as ever.

In fact, it became a little stronger.

Director Chandra had halted manned flights into the storm's core once more, and everyone at the center knew better than to ask for them to be resumed now. Drones would suffice. Drones would *have* to suffice.

As the fourth of September became the fifth, and dawn broke over the panicking Gulf Coast, a drone dispatched into the eye found that Leonard had achieved almost the exact intensity that Edward's STCRS model had predicted it would. The instrument returned readings of 663 millibars of pressure and winds of 430 miles per hour.

That was the reading at seven in the morning.

"So Kirby's model basically nailed it," Fisher said at headquarters. "He would've been so proud, the crazy man."

The entire NHC staff was in a state of catatonic disbelief, both at the storm's intensity and the fact that they had lost a Hurricane Hunter crew for the first time in a century.

Dr. Chandra was insistent that they had *not* received any indication that anyone was dead. They had made a successful water landing, based on the data. Edward Kirby might indeed be crazy in some ways, but no one could deny that he was as good a pilot as he believed he was. He had navigated an unpowered plane out of a *hypercane* and landed it on the water in tropical-storm-force winds. They could survive. They had the means. Dr. Chandra was determined not to assume the worst.

But this hope—and hope was all that it was for now—did not lessen the shock and anxiety that they all felt.

*   *   *

Dr. Chandra had no choice but to appear on the media that morning. Since the plane's communications had gone dark, he had practically lived in his office, doing virtual interviews all through the night. He really needed sleep, but that was not happening.

"This was an extremely experienced and skilled Hurricane Hunter crew," he insisted to Rebecca Hall and Jason Brakeley on *Morning Lark* at eight. "The pilot, Dr. Edward Kirby, has flown many Category Five hurricanes. And more importantly, before the plane's communication systems shorted out from contact with the water, they were able to transmit data indicating that they had made a successful water landing and deployed their raft."

"But Leonard is such an unprecedented system," Hall replied. "Its winds are, as your own products have said, 'unsurvivable.' How could this crew survive the conditions at sea even if the plane stayed intact?"

Hall fixed her bullying gaze upon the hologram of Dr. Chandra, just as she had done yesterday morning. Had this all really happened in one day? It seemed like an eternity to the worn-out Director. He sounded weary as he replied. "Dr. Kirby landed the plane in an area where the instruments were reporting just gale-force winds. And while there would be a surge and tall waves, the life raft can withstand the conditions that the final data transmission reported. The crew have personal life-saving gear, too. And they would have thought to get their potable water and nonperishable food off the plane, and the raft has storage compartments." He tried to infuse his voice with optimism. "We have every reason to hope that the Hurricane Hunter crew who courageously flew into Leonard are still alive. I am coordinating with officials right now to get a rescue mission deployed. In the meantime, what viewers at home need to do is stay alert and informed, and if you are in Leonard's path, *get out now.*"

"But what does this catastrophe say about the Hurricane Center?" Jason Brakeley interjected, his perfect coiffure shining and his smile broad and insincere. "About NOAA as a whole, in fact? Political leaders are asking whether this mission should ever have been approved. You *were* sending flights that released drones into Leonard, Director Chandra. Then suddenly you gave the approval for a manned mission—*this* mission. Why?"

"The data that the drones reported indicated values within the plane's tolerance. Unfortunately, Leonard continued to intensify—"

"But knowing that it was possible the storm would do that, why did you allow this flight?" Hall insisted, eyes gleaming predatorily.

"Hurricane Hunter flights are inherently riskier than standard commercial or general aviation," Chandra said. "It's impossible to gather data on every single location in any storm, and there could be tiny pockets of very sharp vertical acceleration in any strong system, even just an intensifying Category Three. The vertical velocities in Leonard are comparable to those in severe thunderstorms like we'd see on land. We simply cannot mark out every single pocket of vertical updraft in a tropical cyclone, *and* its precise intensity, without data from within the storm."

Brakeley pounced at once. "So it's possible this disaster could have occurred even in—as you put it—an 'intensifying Category Three'? This raises the question of whether we should have manned Hurricane Hunter flights at all!"

Hall agreed before Chandra could respond. "And as Jason asked you, why not continue sending drones?"

"I'm glad you mentioned our drones," Chandra said, trying to seize the narrative back from them. "The final drone report before the crew entered the storm was from three P.M. They took off from Lakeland at five. They didn't reach Leonard's inner core until seven. We might have decided not to fly Leonard if we'd had data from that gap." He did not actually believe Edward Kirby would have ever made that decision—he was certain that the self-assured aviator would have found an excuse to justify a manned flight into the eye no matter what the data showed—but Edward Kirby wasn't here right now to contradict him. And he himself could have ordered the crew to stay out of the core, if nothing else.

"Who's the Director of the National Hurricane Center, Dr. Chandra?" Brakeley said with sneering sarcasm that he did not even try to hide. "Who has authority to order a drone mission?"

"Contrary to what you seem to believe, even I cannot order twenty-four-hour drone coverage of a hurricane, or even a hypercane like Leonard," Chandra snapped. "We have restrictions on resource usage. I would like NOAA to have more flights and equipment, but it is up to Congress to approve that."

Hall smiled nastily. "Dr. Chandra, it sounds to me as if you are using this tragedy—"

"We don't know that it is a tragedy, and as I said, we have every reason to hope this crew is still alive."

"They made a water landing in gale-force winds and seas churned up by the most extreme storm ever observed on planet Earth," she said contemptuously. "As I was saying, it sounds to me as if you are using this tragedy to ask for more money for an agency that, frankly, should have serious inquiries made into how it spends its *existing* funds."

"That," Dr. Chandra said through clenched teeth, "is a matter for Congress to decide according to their constituents' needs and formal analyses of spending. It is not something any media personality should decide. Again—we need to stay focused. There will be a rescue mission to find the missing crew. What viewers right now need to know is that if they are in the path of this storm, their time to evacuate—to *save their lives*—is running out!"

*　　*　　*

Dr. Chandra tried to ignore the media storm around the loss of the Hurricane Hunter craft and focus instead on the physical storm that was about to blast a spot of the Gulf Coast back to its constituent particles. Taking matters into his own hands, he appeared virtually in a midday conference with President Harry Phillips and some emergency officials from his administration.

The President pledged the support and assistance of the United States Navy to find the downed Hurricane Hunter crew. Hopefully, he said, they could be found soon, since the Navy had a very clear idea of where they had gone down.

Unfortunately, few media outlets carried the press conference. President Phillips was not a very photogenic person, as Richard had boorishly pointed out on the night of August 29, and a conference with a "dull" president and assorted federal bureaucrats was not very entertaining.

The twenty-four-hour news did cover the press conference, but not many people watched that anymore. People generally viewed specialized independent streaming shows at their leisure and obtained up-to-the-moment news from social media.

The NHC had a social-media division, and they did their best. Hopeful posts about the Hurricane Hunters alternated with dire ones aimed at people in Leonard's path, urging them to evacuate. The center even posted short videos featuring a staff meteorologist who had worked in television broadcasting. Only someone with that background could explain the storm's path, intensity, the reason for the term "hypercane," and the danger it posed all in five minutes.

But the NHC's social media might as well have been a bird flying amid the wrath of Hypercane Leonard. At the bottom of every post that the center made were hundreds—often thousands—of hate-filled, conspiracy-mongering comments. These far outnumbered the "likes" that the posts received, let alone reposts—the metric that the NHC had most wanted to see increase, as a large number of reposts would mean that people were sharing their warnings widely.

But instead, people were spending their online time attacking the center itself.

You are criminals! one user accused the NHC after a video about the storm.

You should be Investigated for Murdering the Hurricane Hunters! someone else said, odd capitalization and all.

My cousin told me that his engineer friend said that it's impossible for surface winds to go over 250 mph on earth, someone else officiously claimed. *Friction becomes too much. You are lying!*

It's because they can't scare anyone with Category 5 anymore, someone had replied to that comment while also "liking" it. *We've figured out that a Category 5 isn't so bad. That's why they have to invent this new word. It's nothing but fear-mongering.*

On and on it went. The social media team at the NHC, three young staffers, finally took a break, emerging from their office and going into the coffee room to commiserate.

"I did see a cam of I-10," one of them said. "It's packed with vehicles. People *are* evacuating. I just have to hope that these... accounts... online are just the usual idiots mouthing off."

"There seem to be an awful lot of them this time."

"Yeah... that's true. Well, then, let's hope that the people in the storm's path aren't listening to them."

Chapter 14: Hype-er-cane

September 5, Tallahassee.

Anne-Elise had been shell-shocked ever since the grim phone call from Edward's boss yesterday. She had clung to Dr. Chandra's insistence that the crew had made a successful water landing in relatively low-velocity winds and had deployed the large, robust raft. She had also gone online and checked the Hurricane Hunter data for herself. It showed what he had said it did, though of course he would not have lied when the truth was so readily verifiable.

But no one has heard anything from them since then, she thought in agony. *They touched down in stormy seas. Even if the winds weren't "that bad," relatively speaking, the surge that this storm would produce would be....*

She didn't want to think about that.

They could ride the surge, though. Surge is dangerous onshore, but not so much at sea.

But they can't ride fifty-foot waves.

They can strap themselves to their raft. If it stays afloat, they would stay afloat.

It was at this point that she had to stop speculating. The plane's instruments were certainly shorted out, and, while the Hunters undoubtedly had waterproof cases for their personal cell phones, there would be no way for them to obtain coverage at sea. Meanwhile, the batteries would drain. Even if they had solar charging adapters—and she had no idea if they did—there would be limited sunlight with the cloud deck of a storm as large as Leonard.

Their only chance was to get to shore or be rescued, she knew. And she also knew that she would not hear a word from Edward until that happened.

If that happens.

She had prepared herself for landfall as well as she could. Unless conditions were expected to be truly impossible to survive—and Tallahassee was not supposed to be in the four-hundred-mile-an-hour eyewall, so conditions there should be

211

"merely" Category Five—someone had to keep watch on the fusion lab. Anne-Elise decided to be among those people. She would hunker down there. It was sturdier than her home.

Beyond that, she just had to hope that her brother had survived.

*   *   *

The governors of Louisiana, Mississippi, Alabama, and Florida scheduled a joint video call to coordinate the interstate response to Leonard. The Florida panhandle would see the worst impacts, but all the Gulf states except Texas would take damage from landfall.

Anne-Elise had little use for any of these governors, but she had still intended to watch the videoconference to learn what there was to be learned. She had thought that the governors would stream it—over Florida's official video social media channels, perhaps—as a public service to anyone, and that the conference would be nonpartisan and information-focused. In days past, state governments would have done that. Indeed, in days past, it would have been an immediate outrage for them not to do it.

But times had changed over the course of Anne-Elise's life. The four governors agreed to hold their call exclusively through the for-profit political streaming show of Madison Chadleigh. Anyone who wanted to watch the state governors discuss emergency preparations for their states would have to endure the aggressively demagogic *Attack Dog*.

Reluctantly, Anne-Elise invited Chelsea and Vera to her house to watch the show. Richard, mercifully, was in Washington right now, working for Speaker Gilbertson. *Vera and I often don't agree,* Anne-Elise thought as she awaited their arrival, *but maybe we can team up this time against Chelsea. My sister is more passive-aggressive and whiny than actively hostile like her vile husband. Maybe we can keep this discussion on our own terms if he isn't here. Maybe Chelsea will even be a little bit reasonable without his horrible influence.*

When Chelsea and Vera arrived at Anne-Elise's

townhouse, their expressions were deeply concerned. This seemed hopeful to her. Perhaps Richard Mellor really was the problem. Perhaps without his toxic presence, she and Chelsea could be like sisters again, and Vera would not feel the need to stake out an extreme position just as a defiance of her right-wing mother.

Anne-Elise hoped so, anyway. Because as much as she wanted to hope for Edward's survival, she could not ignore the bleak possibility that the three of them were now the only close blood relatives in the family anymore.

She instructed her assistant to turn on the television. She'd renamed it back to Omnia now. The urge to provoke had gone out of her. The *Attack Dog* show began, the camera panning down to the stage as it did to begin every episode.

To viewers, the governors appeared in a large screen next to the host's currently empty chair on his dog-paraphernalia-festooned set. Chadleigh stalked onto the stage, pumping his fists, posing for the camera, and sneering at the screen as the drumbeats and barking dogs sounded in the background. He took his seat just before the call began.

"Today we have the governors of Louisiana, Mississippi, Alabama, and Florida videoconferencing live as Hurricane Leonard barrels toward the Gulf Coast!" Chadleigh announced to his audience. "We're going to watch and listen to their call, and after that, the governors have agreed to take questions from this very show!" One of the governors gave a thumbs-up to Chadleigh. "And it looks like it's time for their call to begin." He addressed the screen. "Governors, can we expect anyone else to join the call? Harry Phillips, for instance? Or any federal emergency management officials?"

His voice was faintly sarcastic, and Anne-Elise could tell from his tone that this was not a sincere question, but a choreographed opening intended for them to disparage the President.

Louisiana Governor Roger Deschamps answered, doing exactly what Chadleigh had intended him to do. "We don't think it would be appropriate to have Phillips or anyone from his administration here," he declared. "We're coordinating this effort together, a partnership of our four states."

Florida Governor Corey Sandoval chimed in his agreement. "Phillips has asked us to request a federal major disaster declaration, but we're not going to do that, because we know what'll happen. It would be an opening to let federal agents barge in and dictate what we all do. We can handle this storm ourselves."

"To be clear," Chadleigh said, smiling because he already knew the answer, "you are not requesting any federal support?"

"No. We can't trust the federal government under this administration. They won't treat our voters fairly."

What about the residents of your states who didn't vote for you? Anne-Elise thought sourly. *You don't care about us, do you?*

The other governors agreed enthusiastically. "We'll share state resources," Mississippi Governor Zach Harwell said. "I pledge your state, Governor Sandoval, all the aid that Mississippi can spare."

Deschamps and Alan Eggles, the governor of Alabama, both did the same proudly, aware of their audience.

"What about that aircraft crew supposedly lost at sea off the Louisiana coast?" Harwell asked Deschamps. "Personally, I fear they're dead, but we can't confirm it officially, of course."

Deschamps scoffed. "I need all hands on deck for landfall. We all do. I can't send the Coast Guard out for this. Harry Phillips has said he'll send the Navy after them. That says a lot about his priorities, that he's more focused on finding reckless federal scientists who put themselves in danger than in helping storm victims."

"I thought you didn't *want* federal support," Anne-Elise said to the television. Chelsea and Vera did not respond.

"And frankly," Harwell added, "I'd be shocked if they were alive."

Governor Sandoval then spoke up. "If they *are* alive, in my opinion it raises serious questions about the truthfulness of the National Hurricane Center. How could a crew survive a storm with the winds that they *claim* Leonard has?" Sandoval shook his head.

"Well, whatever the truth is about *that*, the Hurricane Center was reckless to send out that flight. I saw that on *Morning Lark*—I know, I know," Harwell added as Sandoval scowled. "It's mainstream. But I think they got this right. They really called that federal bureaucrat to account this morning. The government shouldn't be spending money on manned flights into hurricanes when it can just send drones. And it *was* sending drones into this one. I think we need an inquiry into this."

"The center is located in my state," Sandoval said. "To the extent that I can use state resources to investigate it, I'll do so. But we should also have an inquiry into the data they're alleging about this storm. I'm not denying it's a strong hurricane. You can look at the satellite and see that for yourself. Doesn't take a Ph. D. to see that it's a bad storm. But the claims they're making about it...." He shook his head. "In any case, our focus needs to be on landfall, not fishing foolish pilots out of the sea."

Anne-Elise felt as if she had been slapped. She turned to her sister and niece, hoping that they were as outraged and shocked as she was. To her horror and disgust, Chelsea was staring at the television with a mildly sorrowful, but also resigned and self-righteous, expression on her face. Vera had lost interest and was fiddling with her phone, scrolling social media mechanically.

Anne-Elise wondered if steam was coming out of her ears like in classic cartoons. She tried to focus on the call, even though it was abundantly clear now that the governors had nothing of value to say and merely regarded this as an opportunity to play politics.

She was right. The governors continued the call a bit longer, preening and posturing about how they would help Florida and each other, until finally, mercifully, they ended the discussion.

Chadleigh, who had been sitting in his armchair next to the doghouse and bulldog model, pumped his fist into the air in approval. "Thank you for taking valuable time out of your busy schedules to appear here, governors," he declared. He then turned to the camera as the screen that had been showing the governors went dark and was lifted out of the studio by an unseen mechanical attachment. "Don't leave yet, though, viewers. The governors have raised several excellent points, and I have more to say on these points. And unlike these public servants who have to focus all their time on preparing for a disaster, I'm just a political talk-show host!" He smiled in faux self-deprecation.

With this, a chyron appeared at the bottom of the screen, a red bar with white text shouting the question, "HYPE-ER-CANE?"

For a second, Anne-Elise could scarcely believe her eyes. *Oh, he is not. He is not going to do this. Not for this storm.*

The moment passed, as the truth hit her. *He is. They're going there. That governor said that, starting this, because this is a coordinated plan to attack the Hurricane Center's integrity.*

"The government was sending drones into this hurricane," Chadleigh continued, pointedly not using the correct word. "Then suddenly it wasn't. Then the plane goes down! My friends, I concur with the implication that Florida Governor Sandoval made. There's supposedly data indicating that this crew performed a water landing. *How?* In the alleged conditions, how?" He pounded his armrests. "Either that data was faked, or the storm's alleged intensity was faked! You can't have it both ways!"

"Yes, you can," Anne-Elise snarled at the television, startling Chelsea and Vera into looking at her. She ignored them. Her heart was thumping in dread. Millions of people undoubtedly had watched the governors, hoping to learn useful information about the storm and the intended emergency response. Instead they had heard conspiracy-mongering from one of the governors, now seconded and amplified by this demagogue. What would come of this? She feared the consequences of this disgusting spectacle.

"Frankly," Chadleigh continued, "I think the government should defund and disband this whole agency. Not just the Hurricane Center, but its parent agency too. That would have to happen under a *future* administration, of course, since Harry Phillips won't do anything about the climate-alarmism syndicate. He's part of it!"

"*Climate-alarmism syndicate?*" Anne-Elise sputtered.

Vera finally set her phone down. She regarded her aunt coolly. "Phillips and Romano are too moderate. They should have pursued revolutionary change to solve the climate crisis rather than trying to appease people like Chadleigh. He obviously can't be appeased."

"They have never tried to appease Chadleigh! They supported 'moderation,' as you put it, because that's *what most people want*. People don't *want* to tear apart the social fabric for a 'revolution.' They just want to go on living their lives without chaos and disruption! And clean energy was meant to help them do that!"

"Well, it hasn't worked out."

Anne-Elise turned away from her in disbelief. Against her will, her gaze was drawn back to the blathering Chadleigh, who continued to expound on his conspiracy theory.

"I will just say it," he declared. "I think there should be an investigation into whether this 'hypercane' is a lie, a way for the NHC to gin up fear about 'climate change.'" He quirked his brows and tilted his head. "Representative Taverner, House Energy Committee Chair? You might want to look at this."

The thought of that smirking weasel made Anne-Elise's face grow hot with anger. "There's a conspiracy, all right," she snarled. "And *they're the ones perpetrating it.*"

Suddenly Chadleigh looked surprised—or pretended to— as something happened, or was choreographed to happen. He blinked and put his hand to the headset in one ear.

"Well," he announced, "Representative CG Taverner

himself was listening, and he's decided to call into the studio! So it seems that we have another visitor tonight, an unexpected one!"

"*Totally* unexpected, I'm *sure*," Anne-Elise snapped. But at the same time that her fury towered, so did her fear. What was going on? This was obviously a highly coordinated effort.

The chyron continued to read "HYPE-ER-CANE?", but another banner appeared onscreen just above it, which read "ON THE PHONE: REP. CG TAVERNER (R-IN)."

That smarmy, know-it-all voice then sounded over the studio, maddeningly familiar to Anne-Elise's ears. As hard as it was to believe, this—this *kid*, she decided—had summoned her before his committee just a few days ago. So much had happened—was still happening.

At this moment, Anne-Elise felt like her world was spinning out of control, the vortex of insanity and chaos intensifying as rapidly as Leonard's vortex of wind and water had.

"I agree that there's something suspicious in all this," Taverner agreed over the phone. "I'll definitely launch an inquiry. Those planes cost the government tens of millions of dollars apiece."

"Oh, *that's* what you're worried about," Anne-Elise snarled. "Not Edward, not his crew. You pathetic waste of skin—"

"And I will make sure to introduce legislation to end manned hurricane flights. This crash occurred because of a reckless pilot joyriding in a storm on the taxpayer's dime," Taverner continued, "with the Hurricane Center's endorsement."

"They were claiming outlandish intensities before that plane went down. Might this whole thing—making up insane data, letting that jackass thrill-seeker of a pilot take a joyride, as you put it—"

Anne-Elise burned in fury for Edward. She stole a glance at her sister and niece. Vera was immersed in social media still, and Chelsea merely looked sad.

"Might this all have been a stunt to promote climate

alarmism?" Chadleigh insisted. He switched his voice to a mockery of a "feminine" voice, high-pitched and fluttery. "Oh *my*, the *world's first hypercane*, and they lost a Hurricane Hunter crew for the first time in a century! The climate fear-mongering *has* to be true!"

"Oh, we already know they're climate fear-mongers, but if there were *crimes....*" He trailed off menacingly, the threat unspoken. "You raised a good point, though. Earlier, I mean, when you said that the parent agency should be disbanded. Why are we spending so much money trying to predict what is inherently unpredictable? Weather forecasts are flat wrong half the time. We've all been told it wouldn't rain and then got caught without an umbrella."

"I bet *you* haven't. I bet your body man holds one over you every time you get out of a vehicle in the rain," Anne-Elise snapped. "And I've never seen it rain when the forecast was 'zero chance.'"

Taverner continued. "And every time there is a tornado, *every single time*, there are people interviewed who say that they had no warning! It makes you ask why we even have a Weather Service?"

"Those people always get quoted because the media think it's 'dramatic' and don't care how irresponsible it is," Anne-Elise snapped at the television.

"My belief," Taverner concluded, "is that they promote climate alarmism because they know they are trying to do something that can't be done, and they have to have some way to try to justify their existence and keep tax money flowing in. I will certainly be investigating everything about this accident and the purported 'hypercane,' my friend."

With that, the phone call ended. Chadleigh turned back to the camera, addressing his viewers. "Well—I'm afraid we're out of time today. But in closing, I have this to say to those in Leonard's path: Don't believe everything you are told. Do your own research and make your own decisions. Your governors are looking out for you, and the *state* emergency response will put *your* well-being first. In fact, I would advise those of you who aren't in the direct path of the eye to stand by, hunker down, and guard your property instead of running away. I do not think this storm is what they're claiming it is. But don't take my word for it! Research it yourselves."

"*This is criminal!*" Anne-Elise practically roared. "He is going to get people killed!"

Chelsea finally spoke up. "They have the right to make their own decisions. The official information is out there. It's not being suppressed. They can choose to believe the Hurricane Center's data or not. They aren't children, Anne-Elise."

"But they trust him, and he is abusing that trust to endanger their lives—" she sputtered, shaking her head.

Chadleigh was still speaking, though his atrocious "advice" was about to end. "Buy a gun—several, if you can afford to—if you don't have one. Though why don't you have one?" he laughed. "My point is, things could get ugly. So take care of yourself and your own."

And with that, the show finally ended.

Anne-Elise did not drink, but at this moment, she wished she had some wine. She had a terrible feeling that something very bad was happening—and not just the storm—but was it just a panic reaction to the utter chaos of the past few days and the miserable uncertainty about Edward?

She breathed deeply, trying to steady herself. *He landed the plane. They deployed the raft. He was smart. He had taken the plane south of the worst winds, and the storm was heading north, so the winds that they face will decrease further as the storm continues on its path. It's coming closer to me, but... it's moving away from him.*

If they made it.

She tried to speak at last. "Chadleigh is a disgrace, and I don't know about you, but everything about this feels choreographed and planned. Taverner didn't just *happen* to be listening to that show. His call was planned. All of this is planned."

Chelsea raised her eyebrows skeptically. "Was the storm

planned too?"

"Of course not. But they're working around the clock to try to control the narrative about it." She took another deep breath, organizing her thoughts. "And why? Chadleigh gave the game away himself. Leonard, the world's first observed hypercane, is a proof of climate change that *nobody* can deny."

"They're trying," Vera put in.

"Exactly," Anne-Elise agreed, pleased with her concurrence. "In the past, climate skeptics could say things like, 'Well, *we've always had Category Fives, and maybe there are more of them now, but we don't know that for sure because we don't know how common they were before the satellite age.*' But this is different."

"I heard somewhere today that one could form if an asteroid struck or an underwater volcano erupted," Chelsea said hesitantly.

"Which didn't happen. That leaves climate change as the reason the extreme conditions existed. Accept that Leonard is a hypercane, and you have to accept climate change." She gestured to the television screen. "And they've figured that out too."

"I've found that when people speak of a nebulous 'they,' it's usually a conspiracy theory."

"I suppose you would know. Your husband does it all the time."

"I don't agree with everything Richard says, and I don't agree with what you are implying either. It's not a conspiracy. Chadleigh is just a loudmouthed show host. It's just entertainment."

"CG Taverner isn't, and he's listening to this crap! A major politician basically just endorsed someone who claims that there's a conspiracy to falsify data and *down aircraft*—a plane that *our brother* flew, Chelsea!—to 'fear-monger' about climate change. And Chadleigh told his viewers to *stay put!* They'll die if they do! They will be ground to puree! There will be *nothing left of them*, not even a sandblasted body. Maybe a skeleton—*maybe*—but no more." Her gaze hardened. "I'm at the point of saying Phillips should declare a state of emergency, send in troops to remove everyone in the direct path, and tell anyone who doesn't like it to go to hell. *Anyone who stays behind will die.*"

Vera cut in again. "This is just bluster. When it comes down to it, those governors will ask for federal aid. They always do. They rant and rave against the federal government, but they always come begging in the end."

"Not always."

"I think they will this time," she insisted. "Though frankly, if they actually did let things fall apart, it might be exactly the wake-up call that people desperately need." She pulled up her phone and began scrolling again.

Anne-Elise gaped at her. "You're on their side?"

"Of course not, but we have to undergo revolutionary change for the climate crisis to be solved, and if they let the coast fall into chaos, it would speed that along. The Phillips-Romano administration would try to 'help,' and it would ease the pain in the immediate crisis, but it would just prolong the long-term one."

"You—*you*, a climate activist, or so you claim—see the Phillips-Romano administration as a bigger enemy than far-right climate-change deniers, who seem *right now* to be orchestrating a conspiracy to destroy hurricane forecasting?"

"The enemy is the status quo."

"Oh, my God!" Anne-Elise got up from her seat and stalked over to the window. Staring out at the billowing, striated gray clouds that heralded the protracted arrival of Hypercane Leonard, she breathed deeply.

They don't even want to talk about Edward, she thought. *Chelsea is his other sister and Vera is his niece, and they don't even want to talk about him.*

And *I'm aiding and abetting it,* she realized with shame. *I've let myself get distracted in a storm of my own rage. That show—this godawful media world we live in—I'm as much an object of prey to it as anyone, for all the airs I give myself. I too let this stuff distract me.*

She turned back around to face her relatives. "We're all focused on the wrong things. Edward has, hopefully, survived a plane crash and is at sea on a life raft this very moment. That is what we should be focused on. I take back what I said about Phillips. He shouldn't send troops to the coast if these hicks don't want them there. Take them at their word and make them beg! I hope you're right, Vera! Make them beg. But at least he is directing the Navy to find Edward and his crew!"

Chelsea looked up sorrowfully at her sister. "Anne-Elise, Edward is probably gone." Anne-Elise opened her mouth to object, but Chelsea continued speaking, holding up her hand for silence. "I hate this, but I have accepted it. I comfort myself knowing that at least he died doing what he loved, and he got to achieve his dream of flying a true monster of a storm."

"They transmitted their coordinates and a confirmation of the successful deployment of that raft," Anne-Elise insisted.

"You and I both know that they are in an environment of very tall waves and strong winds. It's not good, Anne-Elise." She scowled at her lap. "If he is dead, as I fear, then he died doing what he loved. But I can't say I didn't warn him about flying. I expect he insisted on flying that storm. That's why they stopped sending drones. I would just about bet money on it. Edward wanted them to stop so that he could be in the eye himself."

Anne-Elise cringed. That did sound like their brother.

"We all bring our fates upon ourselves," Chelsea continued in a philosophical tone. "All of us, in one way or another."

Anne-Elise gaped at her. "You are talking about our *brother!*"

"Edward is no more an exception than I was. Or our parents."

"You know, for once, I agree with you," Vera said.

Anne-Elise could not believe her ears. Just as it had done years ago when her parents had ordered her out of the SUV, something snapped in her. It wasn't precisely the same—she didn't, even now, wish either of these women dead—but it was similar.

"Out," she said abruptly. She stalked back over to the couch. "Get out of my house!"

Chelsea *was* shocked now. "Anne-Elise! I didn't mean—"

"Yes, you did. You meant it, because it's as I've said before—the only person you've ever truly cared about is yourself! So fine! Go to your own home. If you're going to speak this way about our *brother*, you are not welcome here."

Chelsea was sputtering. "Anne-Elise, please—*sister*—I'm sorry—"

That only provoked her further. "No, you aren't. You're only sorry that I reacted this way. You speak so self-righteously of *consequences*, but you don't want to face your own!"

Vera raised her eyebrows at her aunt in derision, her gaze not leaving the screen of her cell phone as she scrolled her social media feed. "Middle-aged women, acting this way. You both are only proving my point about societal rot. It has to end—"

That was it. Anne-Elise grabbed the phone from her niece and held it aloft. "You first! Unhook this *thing* from your veins!"

Vera leaped to her feet. "Give me that back!"

But Vera was short, and Anne-Elise was tall. She held it high, taunting her niece. "You want it? Then take it from me!"

"You think I won't try?" Vera reached for Anne-Elise, long lime-green fingernails digging a red scratch on Anne-Elise's arm.

"Ow!" Anne-Elise dropped the phone and clutched her arm. Vera retrieved it and shoved it into her expensive handbag.

Chelsea gaped at them both in abject horror and murmured something inaudible to Anne-Elise. With a quick, appalled single jerk of her head, she rushed for the door, Vera not far behind her.

As the door slammed, Anne-Elise suddenly remembered.

Another scene involving a middle-aged adult, a young woman, a stolen phone, and a scratched arm came back to her.

"Oh, God," she gasped out as she rinsed the scratch. "Oh, God."

Despair practically choked her as she bandaged her arm. She sank onto her couch and put her hands over her face.

You were right, actually. Both of you. We have all brought our fates upon ourselves. And maybe the only way out is collapse.

Did we ever truly stand a chance?

She wondered if she was referring to the Kirby-Mellor family in particular or humanity as a whole.

Maybe, she thought, it didn't much matter. Like a fractal, patterns at the largest scale continued down to the smallest.

Edward, I hope you made it. You're a madman about storms, but your joy in what you do is beautiful compared to the ugliness that we have all created.

Misery overwhelmed her as she remembered a time when she too loved something beautiful. *I wanted to save the world with clean fusion. My "beautiful golden future," that's what I called it then.*

She gazed out the windows, where Leonard's wrath was beginning to rage. *Maybe Vera is right, but only partly. Maybe what we need isn't a total collapse, but just a good shock. This could do it. Maybe this will be the dark night before the dawn.*

I know you made it. You had to have made it. You're too clever not to. Be safe out there, brother.

Chapter 15: Landfall/Landsmash

The sun had risen on the morning of September 5, but no one on the central Gulf Coast got to see it that day—and if the shocking afternoon message of the Hurricane Center proved accurate, it might be quite some time before anyone in that area saw it again.

Anne-Elise could scarcely believe what she was reading, but the situation warranted it if anything ever did.

Hypercane Leonard Advisory Number 17

NWS National Hurricane Center Miami FL   AL152051

400 PM CDT Tue Sep 05 2051

TIME IS RUNNING OUT TO EVACUATE... THOSE IN THE DIRECT PATH OF THE EYE WILL NOT SURVIVE....

Hypercane Leonard, the world's first observed hypercane, continues toward a landfall near Panama City, FL early Wednesday morning. Conditions will become unsurvivable earlier.

Maximum winds are 350 knots... 400 mph... and pressure in the eye is 681 mb. No significant weakening is expected before landfall.

CONDITIONS WILL BE UNSURVIVABLE IN AREAS WITH WINDS OF 250 MPH OR HIGHER. NOTHING WILL REMAIN IN AREAS WITH 325 MPH OR HIGHER WINDS.

People in areas of 160-250 mph winds will require an engineered shelter to survive.

In the path of Leonard's eyewall, the following will occur:

Bodies likely will not be recognizable after the storm and may not exist at all in areas impacted by the inner core, due to high-velocity sandblasting down to the skeleton.

Buildings, including large well-constructed homes and mid-rise towers, will be swept from foundations and the debris shredded. High-rise towers will likely fail and collapse. Windows will blow out and glass reduced to sand.

Multiple layers of soil will be blown away. All vegetation will be destroyed and shredded.

Electrical, water, and fuel infrastructure will be destroyed.

Emergency responders will not be present during and immediately after the storm. They would not survive the conditions either. No superheroes are coming to save you.

An immense amount of debris, produced by Leonard's winds and ground to the size of dust particles, will be rocketed into the atmosphere, creating a toxic cloud. Air quality will likely be at Hazardous levels for weeks.

Leonard's injection of large amounts of water vapor into the lower stratosphere is expected to be depleting the ozone layer in the path of its inner core. Until the ozone layer regenerates itself in this location, harmful solar ultraviolet radiation will threaten the surface.

All in the path must evacuate to survive. Persons, pets, and livestock will face certain death in the hypercane winds.

Anyone attempting to remain in the path of the eyewall had better have access to a deeply buried watertight shelter with weeks of supplies of food, water, and sanitation.

If you are in the eyewall's path and you don't have your own fallout shelter, your choices are evacuation or death.

Director Chandra

Anne-Elise had heard from Edward of the famous "doomsday warning" that a local office had issued decades ago for Hurricane Katrina. With climate change causing ever more unprecedented disasters in the years since that historical storm, the Weather Service had issued similar warnings when a situation was dire enough to warrant one. Most of the text of this one followed that unfortunate but necessary semi-recent tradition.

But the "superheroes" comment and the next-to-last paragraph were not graphically terrifying. They were sarcastic. That was new to Anne-Elise. She'd never seen blatant sarcasm in an official Weather Service product for an incoming weather disaster. It certainly drew people's attention, which was what mattered these days, but a part of her hated that such language was necessary. But such was the world of the sound bite, the world they'd all built.

In any case, Chandra's irritation was blazingly clear to her, and she couldn't blame him. The media's obsessive focus on vilifying the NHC over Edward's flight and the political right's determination to deny Leonard's intensity had to be psychologically devastating.

Anne-Elise realized that she was barely functioning herself. She needed news about Edward, but she knew there would not be any until they were rescued, made it ashore... or time ran out for the possibility of survival at sea. Instead of fixating on something about which she could do nothing, she tried to focus on preparation.

The eye was expected to pass right over her hometown. If she were more superstitious and narcissistic, she would believe there was a twisted but appropriate irony to that. But she knew that Leonard was just a physical phenomenon, and that there were tens of thousands of people in its direct path. It wasn't aimed at her, and it definitely wasn't aimed at her past.

But the lethal three-hundred-mile-per-hour winds extended fifty-five miles from the eye in all directions. Tallahassee was about ninety miles away from the expected landfall spot, and it would be in Category Five winds, which extended about 115 miles in every direction from the eye.

Leonard was truly a monster storm.

She had nonetheless decided to sit it out. There were too many who simply *had* to evacuate or face death. This included hospital patients, nursing-home residents, prisoners, animal shelter and veterinary clinic patients, and others who did not have a means of evacuating on their own—as well as all the irreplaceable pets and personal possessions that those who *did* have vehicles would take with them. It was an unprecedented evacuation effort. The evacuees were having to go very far inland indeed to find shelter, and Anne-Elise did not want to contribute to the problem. She would normally evacuate for a Category Five impact, but in this case, there was a far worse impact expected just to her west.

As Director, she had opened up Intensity Labs to everyone employed there and their immediate families. As a nuclear facility, it was built to withstand a Category Five hurricane—and it wasn't as if they would be doing fusion tests during landfall anyway. Anyone employed at Intensity could shelter there, along with their dogs, cats, caged small animals, household members, and relatives who had no other shelter or means of evacuation. Comparatively isolated as it was from commercial districts, the lab had a small cafeteria, so she decided to offer free meals. Some of the food wouldn't keep if they lost power. It would need to be eaten.

She tried to feel good about what she was doing, but the storm and her terrible uncertainty about Edward were too bleak for her to think of anything positive.

The day dragged on. Anne-Elise gave orders to her staff to prepare the building, as people rushed in with their "entourages." Those who had aggressive, sick, or easily frightened pets had to keep them separated from other people or animals. Those with young children were supposed to keep their kids away from infants, the elderly, and the frail.

One worker showed up with a child who had measles. To Anne-Elise's fury, further inquiries revealed that the child was not immunocompromised. Rather, the entire family was unvaccinated by choice, because they believed it caused harm.

Wouldn't people who worked for a nuclear fusion research facility have more respect for science than this? she wondered. Clearly not—or, at least, their respect for science was very field-specific. *Or perhaps it's just respect for the paycheck that Intensity provides,* she thought cynically.

"I'm not going to turn you out of the facility and into Category Five conditions," she said harshly, "but you aren't going to be around anyone else with your son infected with the measles."

The man instantly became furious. "I have a *right*—" he began hotly.

"You *do not* have a 'right' to shelter in this lab!" she exploded. "You have the *privilege* of doing so because Deputy Director Gleason and I have *chosen* to open it up! And that means you will follow our rules. There are infants here who can't be vaccinated yet. You absolutely *don't* have the right to infect them! Your choices," she decided, "are to shelter in the third-floor single-stall handicapped restroom—all three of you—or to head out. The restroom is clean and you'll have exclusive use of it. And you will have meals brought to you from the cafeteria like everyone else."

The man sneered. "Consider this my two-week notice," he spat.

"You're leaving, then? Braving Category Five winds rather than sheltering here in a clean bathroom to avoid infecting other people's infants with the measles?"

"Yes. I'm not endangering *my* child for the comfort of other people's kids, and I'm not going to be *quarantined* in the cripples' bathroom like a prisoner because of our family's choices."

Then go to hell for all I care. I don't have time for this, she thought. "Suit yourself, then," she snapped.

"And I'll be sure to come forward about this discrimination," the man threatened as he turned away.

"There are vulnerable infants here, and even if their lives don't matter to *you*, I am protecting their health and lives from your sick child. You'll lose in court if you sue."

"Who said anything about suing? The real court is the court of public opinion. A viral *scandal* is a bigger problem for you than the piddling measles virus that Sandy has."

Then may 180-mile-an-hour winds silence you first, Anne-Elise thought darkly. *All of you. Your kid will grow up just like you otherwise. I know all too well that kids usually become their parents in some way.*

After the family departed back into the already howling winds, Anne-Elise shut herself in her office. She gazed at the photograph of the deceased Dr. Vince Hailey, the lab's first director.

You believed in the power of science to make people's lives better, she thought as she studied her mentor. *So did I in those days. But what if people don't want the gifts that science offers?*

On one level, that interaction shouldn't annoy me as much as it does. It's frustrating, to be sure, but it's a minor thing. Just one family out of everyone who works here.

But this vignette of arrogant, anti-science stupidity in conjunction with the far broader conspiracy to attack the science of weather and climate? Which is probably going to cost people their lives in this storm?

And the willful, oblivious blindness of the mainstream media and mainstream podcasts to the way that they are helping it along with their attacks on the Hurricane Center?

And the fact that this anti-intellectualism is present even in a cutting-edge fusion research lab?

And this on top of the landfall itself, my dread of the conditions and news that will follow, my frustration with my sister and niece, and the fact that I don't know if Edward is dead or alive.... It's almost too much for one person.

She put her head on her desk, trying to take deep breaths until she was able to return to her tasks. It wasn't easy to put this aside even in the short term, but she knew she must.

*   *   *

Drones continued taking measurements of Leonard overnight, as the fifth became the sixth, up until landfall. The storm fluctuated only tiny amounts, confirming theories that mature hypercanes in ideal conditions experienced only blips.

687 millibars and four hundred miles per hour. Then 690. Then the winds dropped to 390—briefly, and absurdly, provoking giddy joy in the foolish media that Leonard might be "weakening." There was a lull in drone missions after that, allowing this irresponsible coverage to continue for several hours.

The illusion was shattered with the next drone. The pressure was steady, but the winds were back up to 410. And in the report after that, the drone reported that they were holding steady.

Time was running out. People on the Florida Gulf Coast had not had much time to evacuate, since the storm had intensified to unprecedented levels so rapidly. The authorities opened up all lanes of traffic to outbound drivers, since there was no reason for anyone to go in the opposite direction.

But Leonard was as indifferent to the fates of the evacuees as it had been to the Hurricane Hunters' fate. The storm continued inexorably northeastward toward the doomed area of coast.

Traffic thinned out as most people made their escapes, but there were always some who waited too long.

*   *   *

Dangerous winds of Category Five intensity began to reach a small part of the coast by midnight. As more of the inner core came inland, those winds fanned out, whipping ever more coastline.

But it was possible to survive Category Five winds. The lethal hypercane winds, those of three hundred miles an hour or more, began blasting the coast by three A.M.

The storm surge accompanied the winds, inundating entire beaches and beach houses that had been built on twenty-foot pilings. But even a forty- or fifty-foot surge could go only so far inland. Where it stopped, the storm's winds ripped the exposed ground and everything on it to shreds.

Those buildings that had not failed in the Category Five winds came apart rapidly and catastrophically in the hypercane winds. In mere seconds, Leonard's forces pulled roofs off, collapsed the walls, ripped the structures off the foundations, pulped them, pulverized them into debris and dust, and then ground the foundations themselves down to concrete particles.

At certain high velocities, particles of dust and grains of sand flew so fast that they became electrically charged, producing an unearthly glow. The eerie phenomenon had been observed in the 1935 Florida Keys hurricane, which had long held the record for the lowest pressure and highest winds for a United States landfall. Had anyone been able to survive the onslaught to record it, they would have observed the phenomenon with Leonard too.

At six o'clock A.M. Central time, the center of the eye came fully onshore: the definition of a landfall. Its pressure was 682 millibars, which the drone flying high above reported. The drone's stepped-frequency microwave radiometer reading of surface winds was 419 miles an hour.

But the drone could not be deployed in the hypercane any longer, now that the storm carried a large volume of solid particles. It could fly with a tailwind and survive the fast-moving water vapor particles Leonard carried when it was at sea. But the storm was now packed with the pulverized, particulate debris of terrestrial habitat and human civilization. That would gum up the drone's propellers and motors. This would be the last drone reading of Leonard, and the last measurement of any kind taken while it remained a hypercane.

*   *   *

In the conference auditorium of Intensity Labs, Anne-Elise sat onstage with the other senior staff. Some of the rows of chairs had been dismantled to allow families some space and a barrier between themselves and others. Some were eating. Others were staring at their devices, fixated on the horrible event that was unfolding to their west, even though there was no information to be had after that final drone report.

Dr. Gleason gave her a sympathetic look as he sipped some tea. "I'm sure your brother will know where to go. He's probably going to make for the Louisiana coast. That would be closest to where the plane went down, and it will be out of the worst parts of this storm."

"I know," she said. "And the President will send the Navy out to get them as soon as he can. I know that Edward and his crew have what they need to survive on that raft... as long as they don't capsize." She sighed. "This storm must have whipped up record waves."

"Undoubtedly," Gleason agreed, "but they didn't go down in the worst area. And the storm was departing the spot where they bailed, rather than heading in."

She nodded. "I know. But all it takes is one."

Dr. Gleason nodded as well. "You'll know soon, one way or the other. It's bad now, but it won't last indefinitely." He paused. "What about the rest of your family?"

"My awful brother-in-law went to DC. My sister and her daughter live in Tallahassee, so I assume they either evacuated or sheltered somewhere. What we're facing is bad but survivable, at least if one is smart."

"At least there's that."

"I wonder what conditions are like at Ground Zero. I don't suppose we'll ever know. There'll be no eyewitness reports." A lump suddenly, embarrassingly, formed in her throat. She swallowed. "The only people to ever go inside the inner core of a hypercane and emerge from it are Edward and his crew."

*   *   *

Some people, determined to believe Madison Chadleigh or some anonymous account on social media, had indeed decided to stay. They were so sure that Leonard was just another Category Five hurricane and that the federal government was falsifying its intensity for some nefarious purpose of its own. They'd been through Category Fives before. One seemed to strike somewhere every year. It was almost like Easter, a holiday that did not fall on the same date every year. It was just *impossible*, they thought, that Leonard could explode from a tropical storm to a hypercane in so short a time.

This was what the family of Joseph P. Hitchfield believed. They were professionals. They had money. They had a nice brick mansion in a very good neighborhood. They had all the latest electronics, including a huge television in their home theater room. They had a boat, which bore a flag declaring their status as "Dog Pack," the unofficial fan club of Madison Chadleigh. They even had an interior tornado shelter, a reinforced safe room.

When a piece of debris shattered the large patio doors of the Hitchfield home, Joseph, his wife, and their teenage children decided that they had better hunker down in that shelter. Surely it wouldn't need to be for very long. Their safe room was certified to withstand winds up to 250 miles per hour. When—*when*—it survived, that would prove that the government was lying about Leonard, the Hitchfields were sure.

They took their cell phones in with them. The signal wouldn't go out. The storm wasn't strong enough to take down cell phone towers. The Hitchfields would prove it. They would report live as they *personally* proved to *all the world* what a filthy lie the climate-alarmism syndicate was peddling with this ridiculous word, "hypercane." Mad Dog himself—or at least, whatever staffer was in charge of his account—had even "liked" a post by Joseph declaring his intentions. It was such an honor.

*   *   *

On the highways, those people who had waited too long to start their evacuation still tried to escape. The handful of cars were moving at speeds of a hundred miles an hour, fighting winds of comparable intensities.

But all it took was a single bad gust to send a vehicle careening or a tree crashing down in the road.

The winds whipped ferociously as panicked, frantic drivers tried to drive through Category Three or higher conditions on Highway 231. Several vehicles had hydroplaned off the road or blown over. Nobody stopped to help them. There were no ambulances now, since the hospitals in the landfall zone were closed, and other drivers were too focused on saving themselves to waste a second of precious time trying to get someone else out of a wrecked vehicle.

The winds were blasting at least 110 miles per hour when a tall, thick pine tree crashed down across every lane. The first vehicles to encounter it had no time to stop. They slammed into the fallen trunk or each other, creating a barrier across the highway—and there were no crews out anymore to remove the trunk or the cars.

People began blowing their horns and screaming, all futilely. Someone in a large pickup truck with huge tires was more rational, if brutal. As if this were a monster-truck rodeo, this driver drove right over a smaller crashed vehicle and the fallen tree. The pickup truck continued on its way north at a hundred miles per hour, a grim display of the strong crushing the weak. But it was brutality or death now. The law of the jungle had asserted itself here.

Leonard's winds were already so strong that it was almost impossible for a person to stand upright, but some still tried. A couple threw their car doors open, ran through the blinding rain—nearly tripping—and leaped over the fallen tree. Where they intended to go on foot, they could not have said. They would not get far; Leonard was moving inland at eighteen miles per hour, and it would overtake them soon with the very worst of its core. But they would be no better off against hypercane winds in their vehicle, so perhaps they had merely wanted to die fighting—however futile that fight might be—rather than giving up.

Others had different irrational panic reactions. One woman became so furious at the drivers who had crashed into the tree, even though everyone on the road this late bore responsibility for their fatal choice, that she got out of her car with a rifle in hand and began shooting directly into the parked cars. What she thought that would accomplish was equally a mystery.

She was not the only person in that volatile, panicked crowd of stranded drivers who was armed.

Perhaps the bloody free-for-all that followed was a mercy.

*   *   *

Back in the Panama City mansion of Joseph P. Hitchfield, horrendous crashes and thuds sounded all around him. He and his family had lost their electricity, and from the sounds of it, not much of their mansion remained standing except the tornado shelter. Somehow, they still had a cell signal. Apparently the nearest tower still stood—for now. But he doubted much else did.

He couldn't believe this. What Category Five hurricane could tear down his brick manor? It had withstood them all. It was engineered to do so.

Something very heavy smashed into the side of the shelter. The wall started to crack and bend.

"This isn't a hurricane," he said to his wife. "This is a nuclear blast or something."

She did not respond. She was staring at their teenagers, guilt washing over her face.

The next slam against the tornado shelter was accompanied by metallic screeching noises. The force of Leonard's four-hundred-mile-per-hour winds sheared the not-so-safe room entirely off the foundation, lofting it airborne. The Hitchfields screamed.

The winds slammed debris into the bent side, caving it in. A tiny crack allowed the wind to penetrate. Within a second, the shelter was shattered. Within five more seconds, everything and everyone it had contained was simply part of the debris cloud.

*   *   *

Animals in the path of the eye had advance warning that something very bad was coming. Leonard was a monster storm, and winds were fierce long before the unsurvivable core struck. Any creature that could get out had done so.

Not all could.

Nesting parents had to choose between guarding their nests and abandoning their defenseless young.

Creatures that traveled too slowly, such as turtles, couldn't escape in time.

Some species had as their instinctive survival behavior to burrow deeply into the earth. This would work in normal hurricanes, as long as their burrows didn't flood.

But one would have to dig very deep indeed to escape the maelstrom of four-hundred-mile-per-hour winds. These winds carried so much fine-grained debris that they stripped away entire layers of soil.

Plants couldn't go anywhere. They stood no chance. Reeds bent like in the proverbial fable, but this time, unlike in that fable, bending to the wind did not save them. The wind was carrying so much sand and dirt, and at such a high speed, that it shredded leaf, stem, and flower. Then the hypercane's winds sandblasted the soil away, exposed the roots, and shredded them too.

The same thing happened to softwood trees. It took longer, but the end result was the same.

Hardwoods, particularly old, gnarled ones, put up the greatest resistance, but even they stood no real chance.

The strongest tornadoes ever observed tended to carry winds of three hundred miles an hour. Such extreme force could strip the bark off trees and snap off all but the thickest branches. Denuded of their protective bark, trees died quickly.

Hypercane Leonard was stronger than any tornado had ever been. Even the strongest trees could not defy it. And the air that immediately blasted their vulnerable wood once the bark was gone was filled with salt and debris. Any tree that wasn't killed on the spot was doomed from salt damage.

There would be a biological dead zone in the path of Leonard's inner core. Nothing could survive such horrific forces except something very deep in the earth.

238

And while hell was breaking loose at the base of the storm, an equally hellish event was occurring at the top: an event that would make it hard for life to thrive in the eye's path of destruction even after the storm had dissipated.

*   *   *

As the Hurricane Hunters had observed during their ill-fated climb, Leonard was a tall storm. The ferocious updrafts that rocked their plane had blasted moist air high into the atmosphere, forming clouds of supercooled water and ice. Most of this convection occurred in the troposphere: the "weather" layer, the surface layer. The tropopause, the top of this layer, was supposed to be a "stop sign" for any significant additional vertical movement of air.

Normally, it would be. Normally, rising air would stop at the tropopause and only barely enter the stratosphere because the temperature of the surrounding stratospheric air would abruptly become warmer than the rising moist air, rather than cooler.

But Leonard's fierce, moist updrafts were strong enough to overcome this by sheer force. They ran the stop sign.

As the plumes of sublimated ice bloomed into the stratosphere far higher than they were supposed to go, the chilled water molecules encountered a new gas, one that they had not chemically encountered in large amounts along their path until now. This gas was ozone.

In the natural oxygen-ozone cycle, high-energy ultraviolet light would split the oxygen molecule—O_2—into two atoms, a process called photolysis. Normally, these atoms would bind quickly to O_2 molecules to form ozone, O_3. This was how the ozone layer continually regenerated itself.

But water vapor interrupted that process. Ultraviolet rays inexorably continued to photolyze O_2 into O, but when that atomic oxygen encountered water vapor, it drew away the hydrogen atoms from the water molecules, combining with the hydrogen to form hydroxyl radicals, or OH.

The hydroxyl then initiated a reaction with the surrounding ozone that resulted in oxygen molecules and hydroperoxyl, HO_2. Shot upward and outward by the hypercane's intense winds, the hydroperoxyl reacted with the ozone elsewhere in the ozone layer to split it into O_2 and yet more hydroxyl radicals.

Thus the cycle of ozone destruction continued until the winds of Hypercane Leonard had weakened too much to transport more hydroxyl-containing vapor to another part of the stratosphere.

But the damage was done. Wherever the hypercane's updrafts shot water vapor high enough that it reached the ozone layer, the destructive reactions occurred and an ozone hole formed.

*   *   *

In the immediate aftermath of the hypercane's passage, there was nothing alive on the surface—except microorganisms—to be killed by the suddenly unfiltered blasts of high-frequency ultraviolet solar radiation that the ozone layer normally would absorb. There was also so much dust in the atmosphere that it would be some time before the usual levels of solar radiation would reach the surface.

But some ultraviolet rays reached the ground anyway. The particulate-matter cloud was not a solid shield.

Ultraviolet C, or UVC, radiation normally did not reach the earth's surface. Ozone blocked much of it, but oxygen gas could too. However, with ozone depleted over the path of Leonard's inner core, fairly significant levels of these highly damaging, mutagenic rays were reaching the ground. Ozone also absorbed UVB radiation, and now, with the hypercane-induced ozone hole over the eyewall's path, far more UVB was reaching the ground than humans—or any other life form —would be used to when they could populate the area again.

The ozone layer would eventually regenerate itself, but it would take time. For the present and immediate future, the sun was no longer a friend to this part of the Sunshine State.

*   *   *

The Gulf of Mexico.

The Hurricane Hunters were bruised, exhausted, hungry

240

from rationing their food, and most of them were thoroughly sick of each other. Edward could not believe it, but he was even sick of Sallie Evans. She was dour and grouchy. He could not understand how he could ever have thought he wanted to be married to her. They would be a terrible match. *Thank you, Leonard, for showing me what a bad idea that was*, he thought.

There was no privacy on the raft. When anyone had to perform their bodily functions, it was in plain sight of everyone else, so the others just looked away. But it was still humiliating.

They had families on the Gulf Coast. Edward's sisters and niece were fairly close to the center of Leonard's track. They all wanted to be off this accursed raft, out of this accursed water, and back onshore. And where were the Navy, the Coast Guard, or *anyone*? Surely someone did know that they had made a water landing?

The only saving grace was that fresh water, at least, was not yet a problem, nor was the risk of unfiltered sunlight. Leonard was so large that their course northward kept them in a steady drizzle of rain. They collected it in their water containers as it fell. It was dreary and unpleasant to be wet all the time, but it was better than being baked and drying out. At least no one appeared to be sick.

Edward tried to keep the mood as upbeat as he could.

"So," he proposed after a sparse breakfast the morning of the sixth—*the morning of landfall*, he knew, though they were not receiving transmissions anymore without a plane—"is this when we're supposed to start thinking about cannibalism? That trope usually turns up in these 'survival' stories 'round about now."

Patricia Cartwright chuckled, but it was bleak.

"I don't know that it should go up for a vote," Edward continued with faux seriousness. "I'm not sure I'd like the outcome. Even if y'all don't blame me in words, I'd be shocked if you didn't in your thoughts." That, he realized, *was* serious. His smirk fell.

"Edward, enough of that," Nadya Cass cut in. "We all

241

agreed to fly, and you shouldn't blame yourself for that disastrous bank. You were going into the eyewall no matter what."

"And I was the one who called for a high-altitude fix," MacLean said. "We could have entered the eyewall without trouble if we hadn't started to stall. We did it several times at ten thousand feet."

Edward sighed. "So we can't decide who should be eaten. All right. What about our superpowers, then?"

"Superpowers, yeah, I *wish*," Morales grumbled.

Edward tried to keep the joke up. "But it's possible that the ozone layer was ionized even here. The vapor penetration into the stratosphere occurred over a large area. So if we're being bombarded with UVC, shouldn't we start mutating?"

"There's really nothing funny about this situation, Dr. Kirby," Evans said.

No one was in the mood for jokes, even black humor. Edward sighed and gave it up, settling himself in "his" spot on the raft. The waterproof data backup box, with single-use write-once media containing all their in-flight observations of Leonard, rested in his pack. He wondered why they had taken it. The NHC already had the data. Maybe this was his "trophy," he thought bitterly.

"I think we should make for the Louisiana coast," Edward said abruptly. "That won't be the location that we transmitted back to Miami, of course, but when we get closer to New Orleans, there'll be a lot of shipping. And there's all that naval activity on the Mississippi coast. We're more likely to encounter vessels there."

"I agree," Cass said. "And we really have no idea what's happening onshore except that Leonard is ruining a lot of people's lives right now. There may truly not be enough military personnel to spare a rescue attempt."

Edward sighed again. "I didn't want to face that, but... you're right."

"New Orleans area it is, then."

242

After

Chapter 16: Relief for the Suffering

September 7.

Tallahassee was in the dark, and there was quite a lot of damage—no surprise for a city that had experienced Category Five winds—but compared to what lay to the west, it was in reasonably good shape. The capital of Florida was still functional, more or less.

It hadn't seemed that way to Vera and her polycule. They had lost their electricity and cell phone service yesterday in the 170-mile-an-hour winds, and it was still not back on. They had experienced strong hurricanes before; it was nearly impossible not to in twenty-first-century Tallahassee, but the city was inland enough that they had not experienced Category Five winds until now, so past outages for them had always been brief.

Vera was pretty sure this was the first time in her life that she had been without power and phone service for over a day. It was a traumatic experience—but it was also an enlightening one.

"This feels like drug withdrawal," she complained to her friends. They were all slouched in the living room with battery-powered LED "candles" switched on, but no one had an idea of what to do.

"What do you know about drug withdrawal?" Sohrab scoffed.

"I drink coffee. And it *sucks* to miss a cup." She scowled; that had happened just today. Without power, they couldn't run the coffeemaker. And of course, no coffee shops were open or delivering. To fulfill her body's craving, she had had to resort to one of Butterfly's caffeine pills. They contained no acetaminophen or any other drug, just caffeine. That had been a surprise; she'd had no idea that Butterfly used those. Indeed, Butterfly had them stashed, contraband-like, in a sock drawer. But Vera supposed it made a certain kind of sense. Butterfly *was* hyper.

"I agree with Vera," Butterfly then put in. "I don't know what we're supposed to *do* without power and phones. How are we going to *eat*?"

Channing was annoyed. "We have sandwich ingredients, and we ought to eat them before they spoil anyway. We're not *helpless*."

"But we have no phone service, no Internet, no TV...."

"I didn't use the analogy of drugs to compliment us," Vera said coolly. "Realizing it was 'withdrawal' was kind of a wake-up call, actually. We *shouldn't* be so reliant on devices. Look at us," she exclaimed, gesturing around the living room. "Sitting here *wasting* the batteries powering these candles, while we do *nothing* but grumble and complain. This is pathetic. We are pathetic."

"What are we *supposed* to do?" Butterfly whined again. "What *is* there to do?"

"I don't know! Play a board game, maybe?" The idea suddenly took hold of her. "Yes, let's do that. Let's make sandwiches and start a game. It'll be fun."

"Why are you so against phones now?" Butterfly insisted. "You said your aunt tried to *steal* yours because she thought you were spending too much time looking at it. Do you agree with her now?"

This was, in fact, what Vera was thinking about. The inter-action had infuriated and scared her at the time, but after she was out of her aunt's house, some uncomfortable realizations had hit her. Her uncle was lost at sea, possibly dead, and she had been obsessed with her phone. "She didn't have the right to do that. But... maybe I do spend too much time looking at it."

"But there's a horrific natural disaster just to our west. We need to know what's going on there."

"How are we going to find that out? The storm had four-hundred-mile-per-hour winds. There won't be anything alive to give a report."

"Somewhere there will be survivors. Maybe not in the area where the worst winds were, but at some point, there will be people. Somewhere between here and Ground Zero.

We're alive, after all. Most of Tallahassee is okay. There's got to be a place where there are people alive but in really bad shape. People who need help." Butterfly seized upon this idea. "We should be out there helping them! We should be in the thick of things."

Mike finally spoke up. "You know, they're right," he said, speaking of Butterfly with preferred pronouns. "We *should* be in the thick of things. But you're also right. We shouldn't be obsessed with our phones and electricity. We wanted revolutionary change. That means things break and shatter." He paused. "I'm glad we didn't put up solar panels on the roof. They'd be ruined now."

"But we might have power stored up if we had collected enough," Butterfly insisted mulishly.

"It'd still be a major expense to get a solar array repaired or replaced. We need a reliable source of energy that doesn't go down in bad weather."

"That sounds like fossil-fuel propaganda," Sohrab said.

A startled look passed over Mike's face as he realized what he had said. He flushed. "Uh... that is...."

"It doesn't have to mean fossil fuels. My aunt's blasted *lab* is probably what it should mean," Vera grumbled. "I guess she was right about that. I saw online that she had opened it up to employees and their families before the storm hit. They probably have emergency power. And if they're as close to 'net-positive' as she likes to boast... someday they'll be always-on." It was a hard admission for her to make, but she couldn't avoid it.

Butterfly glowered. "Then I wish Tallahassee was hooked up to *that* for its power source. We would have Internet. I just want to know what's happening at the landfall site! There is profound human suffering *very close to us*, but we're stuck in this room!"

"I agree that we should go to a hard-hit area and help out where we can," Vera agreed, "but... can't it wait until tomorrow? We need to eat. And it's dark."

"It's dark there too."

246

"There is a curfew until the city clears the roads of large debris. We could get arrested if we drive out there. That doesn't help anyone. Sometimes getting arrested is a good way to draw attention to a cause, but not this time. No one will even know about it. Let's at least wait until the city lifts the curfew."

Mike sighed, but he could see her point. "Fine. Sandwiches and Cards Against Humanity?"

"Might as well," Butterfly muttered miserably. They lowered their voice. "I miss my *phone*...."

"You're acting like someone you love died," Channing scolded. "It's... improper... when there is so much tragedy to our west."

"I just wish I could know what it's like there."

"How does it help them for you to know that? There is *nothing you can do right now*. There's nothing any of us can do to help them by gawking at their suffering. That's all we ever do! We gawk at people's pain, stream it to more people who *also* gawk at it, and pretend that it helps the victims! It doesn't! It just gets *us* attention on the Internet and makes *us* feel better about ourselves!"

Vera's gaze snapped up to Channing. She had reluctantly come to the same conclusion herself, and she hated it. It was shameful to have to view herself as the progressive-activist version of a motorist gawking at a deadly car crash, but she couldn't ignore that unpleasant realization. And in addition to being shameful, it was demoralizing to imagine that most of her life's work had achieved nothing.

She rose from her chair sharply. "You're right," she said. "I'd realized the same thing. Here's what I think we should do. We'll play a game and eat sandwiches tonight. As soon as we can, we will head west and do something *real*. And the point won't be to live-stream it. The point will be to *help* Leonard's victims, even if no one but them ever knows about it."

They all agreed on this. Vera then headed into the kitchen with Channing and Sohrab, while Mike and Butterfly looked for the game. It was a relief to prepare sandwiches and fruit cuts. She had been on the verge of striking some of her friends. It unnerved her how quickly she got sick of these people once none of them had electronic distractions to steal away some of their attention.

*   *   *

The Leon County and Tallahassee authorities restored power overnight. Internet and cell service soon followed. Vera and her friends woke up on the morning of the eighth not to the rising sun—indeed, the sky was so dark from clouds and dust that it looked like the apocalyptic sky after a wildfire—but rather to the familiar alarms on their phones, which they had left plugged in just in case.

Vera got out of bed and stared out the window at the appalling sky. It was a ghastly dark reddish-grayish-brown slurry. Vera shuddered as she realized what this was. She hadn't found the NHC's advisories very interesting, although the "doomsday" one was something of an exception, but she realized that their emphasis on dust clouds had lodged in her mind anyway. This was the debris of nature, of civilization, of life itself.

This is what it looks like when everything is torn down. This is what that truly means. The unwelcome thought forced itself in.

The smart lights came on with her phone's wake-up alarm, providing her with enough illumination that it didn't feel like she was getting dressed in the dark. Mechanically she put some clothes on. She needed a bath, but that should probably wait until after they had visited the hard-hit areas. They might have to get into the muck. If nothing else, this dust would dirty them.

Butterfly and Mike were already watching TV in the living room. The set was streaming *Morning Lark*. Everyone, it seemed, watched that.

"Gloom has settled firmly over the Florida panhandle," Rebecca Hall announced on the show. "Leonard made landfall two days ago as of this morning, and it is now unleashing wet, windy misery on Georgia and the Carolinas, but it is no longer a hypercane."

"Assuming it ever was," Jason Brakeley added. "Leaders in Congress and the governments of the affected states are raising questions about that."

Vera's eyes widened. "This crap from *Attack Dog* has gone mainstream?"

Sohrab emerged from the kitchen and sat down. "Looks like it."

"But no one can deny that it *was* a record-breaking storm, whatever its true intensity was, and it has left untold damage in its wake. The National Hurricane Center has declared it an extratropical storm, merging with the very cold front that had enabled it to intensify so explosively. But its mark remains," Hall concluded somberly.

"We're sharing a clip from a weather cam in Tallahassee. Take a look at this sky," Brakeley said, as the clip began to stream. "This looks like it's taken from a wildfire in California, doesn't it? But it's what the sky looks like over the Florida panhandle."

"We can certainly confirm *that*," Vera muttered, gazing out the windows.

"We do not yet have reports from the areas believed to be hardest hit," Hall said, "but we do have Governor Corey Sandoval of Florida live on the phone this morning. He may know something new. Governor?"

The screen changed to display a chyron identifying the telephone speaker. "Morning," he said crisply over the phone. "I don't have long—very busy here—"

"Of course," Hall said, smiling that dazzling, predatory, artificially whitened smile for which she was famous. "We wouldn't want to take up much of your time, Governor."

"We haven't been able to get into the hardest-hit areas either, but reports are bad. There is a stretch where the roads simply don't exist. We've sent out a helicopter, before it got too dusty to keep flying safely—"

Brakeley chuckled cruelly. "Good to know that *Florida* isn't taking any chances with flights, unlike the NHC!"

Sandoval laughed too, equally nastily. "And we don't have any joyriding thrill-seeker pilots, because they know that the state of Florida won't indulge their urges! We use taxpayer money wisely here. But to get back to the point, state emergency management officials in that helicopter found visual evidence that there might have been a major tree fall leading to a huge car pileup on Highway 231. It's hard to say for sure, because the asphalt itself is eroded, but there seemed to be a lot of crumpled cars in that area."

"*Can* anyone get into Ground Zero?" Vera wondered.

"We'll go as far as we can," Mike vowed. "I figure if the roads are gone in an area, there probably aren't any survivors anyway."

"True."

"What is the plan going forward, Governor Sandoval?" Hall asked. "Are you and the other Gulf state governors going it alone?"

"Yes. Eggles of Alabama, Harwell of Mississippi, Deschamps of Louisiana, and now Hale of Texas have agreed to follow Florida's lead in the recovery. Alabama and Mississippi have some significant damage too, in fact. We're pooling resources and coordinating this ourselves. We've also had donations pour in from churches, to the tune of millions of dollars."

"Millions? It'll take *billions*," Channing said as she entered the living room, toast and orange juice in hand. "Probably *trillions*."

Sandoval, of course, did not hear her, and Hall and Brakeley were nodding along with smiles on their faces and sympathetic eyes. "We are sure that we can handle this with state resources and charitable donations," Sandoval declared. "We don't want Harry Phillips's federal goons in here."

"So you are not requesting a federal major disaster declaration?" Hall asked.

"We are not. The federal government proved it was incompetent and reckless with human lives by losing the Hurricane Hunters, and we also, as you know, have serious

250

questions about its truthfulness about the intensity of this storm. It's bad," he said hurriedly. "Our visuals from the helicopter and the handful of reports and photos we've gotten prove that. Leonard was a very bad hurricane. But we just see no real evidence that it was what they claimed it was, other than their own assertions. I'm not going to help Harry Phillips and Natalia Romano look good."

"He'll change his mind," Mike said. "He'll go back on that. Just wait and see. He'll be begging Phillips for help in a day."

Vera had believed that too as of three days ago, but she was no longer sure.

*　　*　　*

The county lifted curfew soon after that, so Vera and her friends prepped to head as far west as they could that day. It was bad outside—Vera and the others instantly started coughing when they stepped outside, and face masks did almost nothing—but Mike's rich father supplied them with five respirators. He had purchased them in bulk before the storm hit, taking the warnings about dust clouds very seriously.

"Got fifteen more at home," he said, handing them over.

This troubled Vera. "Shouldn't you give them to emergency officials? There may be a shortage, and people will need them."

"I'd rather not give Corey Sandoval's people anything for free."

"Aren't they just civil servants, though? Emergency officials?"

"They're working for him. It makes *him* look good if his 'state and church operation' goes well. I won't be complicit in that."

"*Thank you,* Dad," Mike said pointedly, giving Vera a dismissive look. "We'll put these to good use."

"There's also a load of food in those bags!" He pointed at several brown paper grocery bags. "Make good use of that too."

"We will. See you later, Dad."

251

*   *   *

The sky grew darker and browner the farther west GCCF's SUV went. Branches, shingles, palm fronds, political signs, and flamingo lawn ornaments—the debris of Florida homes after a tropical cyclone—soon gave way to smaller and harder-to-identify debris. Some of it *was* still identifiable: a cooking pot, the handlebars of a bike, a child's toy. Other debris required a second look and a guess: Perhaps that wood block was a piece of a drawer; that wadded-up cloth was surely someone's shirt. The closer they drew to Ground Zero, the more of the latter they saw.

Channing's gaze was suddenly averted. "Look!" she exclaimed in horror. "That's got to be a human skull!"

Everyone except Mike, the driver, clustered around the windows to stare at where she was pointing. Vera flinched. Indeed, an object that sure looked like a skull rested in a patch of flattened grass. Butterfly whipped out their cell phone and instantly snapped several photos of the grisly object to share on social media.

"But we're not at Ground Zero," Sohrab said, appalled.

"The storm must've picked it up and carried it all this way," Vera said, eyes wide. She was appalled too. "I mean... obviously it did, since the... the person whose skull that was...." She broke off. That had been a human being. Taking a deep breath, she continued. "They were sandblasted down to the bone, and then the skeleton itself must've been... pulled apart. So this person was in very strong winds." She broke off again.

The storm had undoubtedly disrupted phone service in the path of its inner eyewall, and it was impossible that it would be restored this soon. The towers themselves were probably gone in such extreme winds. But while they still had coverage, everyone who was not driving was glued to their phone, getting caught up with everything they had missed.

"The governors of Massachusetts and New York have offered to send their emergency officials south," Sohrab remarked.

"Well, that happens a lot, doesn't it?" Channing said. "Lots of states sent people out West for the fires earlier this year."

"Because the western governors accepted the aid." Sohrab's expression darkened. "These pricks have refused it. Sandoval has accused them of being 'in collusion with the federal government,' whatever that means."

"My aunt was right," Vera muttered. "They really *aren't* going to accept anyone else's help. They will let people suffer rather than accepting help from anyone they disapprove of politically."

"Well, we'll go around them. We won't give them a choice. We'll take our support directly to the afflicted, and if anyone asks, we'll make sure everyone knows who we are."

The roadside debris was rapidly becoming more granular, and the plants were more often flattened or stripped bare. They were approaching some of the hardest-hit areas that might still have survivors.

"The road's about to run out," Mike observed, slowing down the vehicle. "I don't think we can go much farther."

He pulled off the road, which, sure enough, dwindled rapidly to ground-up asphalt ahead of them. A media outlet from Panama City had also arrived and parked a large van there. Local news channels were practically an endangered species these days, but it made sense that local people would be among the first to cover this event. Mike parked next to this van. They all prepared to put on their respirators.

"Look at this!" Butterfly suddenly exclaimed, shoving their phone in front of the others' faces. "My post with the photos of the skull is going viral!"

Vera and her other friends gathered around Butterfly and peered at the phone. Sure enough, the graphic images had garnered tens of thousands of interactions just in thirty minutes. It was currently one of the most-trending posts on the Internet.

"And I've picked up a lot of followers from it! I'm going to see if I can leverage this into relief for the suffering," Butterfly continued.

"Butterfly," Channing said, "that was part of a *dead person.*"

"I know, but what can I do about it? Nobody knows who it was. It's not like I'm posting photos of an *identifiable* dead body."

"They'll find it and run DNA on it, and it probably won't be long now that it's all over the Internet."

"Well, then, the family will be glad I posted about it. It would be lost otherwise," Butterfly said stubbornly. "And it was a viral post," they added in a low whimper.

Channing just shook her head. "Whatever."

They put on their respirators, got out of their SUV, and began heading toward the area where people, perhaps, still lived, just waiting for relief from their suffering. As they walked into town, they quickly found a mixed-use area, with storefronts and shuttered restaurants intermingled with small houses. None of the buildings were in great shape, but most were still standing.

"Look!" Channing suddenly exclaimed, pointing at a drugstore with shattered windows and debris littering the parking lot. "People are coming and going!"

"I'm sure the media would call this 'looting,'" Vera scoffed, "but it just looks to me like voiceless, marginalized, and desperate people who are taking what they need."

"Exactly," Mike agreed, hurrying to keep up. "Stores will get insurance payouts for everything inside. The companies will throw the entire inventory out if people who need it don't take it."

"Drugstores usually sell a handful of groceries," Butterfly put in, "but never anything fresh. But thanks to your dad, Mike, we have produce! We can help them!"

As they approached the drugstore, they noticed that its condition was not as good as it had seemed from a distance. Pieces of ceiling hung in strips, but at least the roof was mostly still able to keep water out.

A man was running out of the store with an armful of body washes and hair products. Vera's lips thinned. Perhaps the people taking things they needed had already been there and left. She hoped that was all it was. The man stopped for a moment, eyeing the young adults as if to size them up. He laughed dismissively and continued on his way.

They ignored the implications of that look and continued inside. A scene of absolute chaos greeted them.

Shelves had been thrown over, whether by the wind or by humans. Products filled the floor as people frantically tried to scoop them up, often fighting each other. Screams and shouts filled the air. Someone was gurgling, as if choking to death—or *being* choked.

The grocery aisle was stripped bare. Vera decided to take comfort in that. Those who needed food had found it, she told herself.

A few aisles over, someone was screaming. Mike ducked down and ran over to see, Vera quickly following him.

Two women were fighting over the meager contents of the seasonal aisle, which currently carried end-of-summer clearance items. One of them had grabbed a beach umbrella and was trying to stab the other one. The other woman had picked up a barbecue grill lighter and was trying to get in close enough to set her adversary on fire.

Mike and Vera ducked away quickly, instinctively aware that no good would come of getting involved. Their urge to "help" was absent right now.

Glass shattered somewhere in the beauty aisles, followed by a tremendous thud that sounded like a human body falling. That was just an aisle or two over. Mike and Vera hurried back to their friends, who were already heading for the medical section.

This was even worse. There were few over-the-counter medicines remaining, but people were fighting ferociously for those that did remain. Blood spattered and pooled on the floor in places.

But the worst of all was in the back, the pharmacy area.

The pharmacists had apparently locked it before Leonard had struck, which explained why it had not been looted already. But the locks were shattered, the pharmacy—with all its controlled drugs, including narcotics, pseudoephedrine, medical cannabis, and some prescriptions that were even stronger—was being sacked, and a bloody knife fight was currently underway.

Vera peered anxiously as one man sank his knife into the chest of another, grabbing at the bottle of pills the latter held. Blood spurted through the air. The other man shrieked but still fought back. He reached for the face of his foe, gouging an eye.

A gunshot then silenced one of them—which one, Vera could not immediately tell, as her first instinct was to duck down and hope *she* hadn't been shot.

"We need to get the crap out of here," Channing finally said, voicing the thought that they were all having.

All five young adults ran for the exit. They were outside before they realized that they had abandoned their bags of food.

*   *   *

Vera and her friends emerged into the parking lot to find that a news crew had arrived there too.

"Tara Harper with WJHG Panama City, temporarily based in Fort Braden," a reporter announced. She too wore a respirator. "Do you live in this area?"

"No," Vera answered. "We're from Tallahassee. A climate nonprofit here to offer food and relief to the victims."

"Did someone send you here?"

"No, we're volunteering. We have nothing to do with Sandoval's... whatever he is doing. Doesn't look to me like he's doing much of anything," Vera said scornfully, gazing at the damaged buildings and debris.

"Yes, this seems to be one of the 'hot spots' for looting and theft. I suppose you have learned that firsthand, if you just came from the drugstore."

Indignation filled Vera at this comment, but she decided to see this as an opportunity to set the record straight. "It's true that there is violence in there. That's why we're running. People were fighting over drugs, and someone was *shot*." She shuddered. "But the grocery aisle was already empty when we went in. Some people *are* just taking what they need! Things that would be thrown away anyway! There are a few bad apples, but it's *not* the majority."

"You're correct that much of the inventory would be thrown out—" Harper began.

"See? But people *need* this stuff. There won't be any relief for weeks. Let them have it! Better than *wasting* it!"

"That is true, but the problem is that—that *this*"—she gestured at the drugstore, indicating the lawless violence —"doesn't help get it to people who need it. People in that store weren't peacefully lining up to take only what they needed; they were violently fighting over anything they could, probably to resell it at very high prices. This is simply the strong preying on the weak."

Vera couldn't argue with that. She had seen it for herself. Trying to organize her thoughts, she took a deep breath. "This *should* be done in a more organized way," she conceded. "Store owners will claim losses on their inventories, so they should donate it to charitable relief. But there isn't any! There is no one organizing anything peacefully to ensure it gets to those who need it. And that is the government's fault! Corey Sandoval has *abandoned* these people to make a political point."

"We've just received news from Washington that President Phillips is considering declaring martial law in this area and fighting it out with Governor Sandoval in the courts."

Vera scowled at the idea of armed military troops patrolling here. Her progressive core revolted at the thought. "I see no evidence that we need the military here," she declared. "It is a violent institution, and violence begets more violence. There's *one* store that has a problem with violence, and I suspect that's because there are controlled drugs in the back." *And Tylenol, and shampoo, and beach umbrellas,* her mind supplied unwanted. *It's not just controlled drugs.* Vera tried to tamp this voice down, but she could not quite succeed.

Harper barely avoided scoffing on her live broadcast. "It's not just one store, I'm afraid. We have footage showing that wherever there are shops, people have been scooping up whatever they can." She shook her head. "And it's also spreading beyond stores. We also have an interview with someone who was robbed at gunpoint in her own home."

"Nonetheless," Vera continued doggedly, "an example of additional violence—the military coming in and menacing these people—won't help. What they need is an example of peace and charity. They don't need violent force. Violent force is the *problem*. They need *help*. This only proves that Harry Phillips is no better than Corey Sandoval."

Sohrab stepped up. "Yes. These politicians are all the enemy. Our group is here to offer *real* help. We brought food—"

Before he could finish, something—or someone—slammed into Vera's side, knocking her to the ground. Butterfly caught her before she hit the pavement, but the attacker had what he wanted: her phone.

Mike saw the attack, and he was a large, athletic man. He was also brash and aggressive, perhaps more than was good for him, so he did not hesitate to take off running after the assailant. In a second, he had overpowered the man, shoving him to the ground, wrenching Vera's phone away from him, and—to her shock—slamming the man's head into a curb until he was knocked out.

He returned the phone to Vera, not even looking back at the man he had attacked. Vera gaped at him. "There are no doctors around here," she said. "And those people in that store are violent. You've probably killed that man."

Mike's gaze was hard. "He shouldn't have attacked you."

Vera was shaking from the aftermath of the attack—and the sights she had witnessed in the drugstore—as she put her phone back into her purse. But she was still able to think of other things, and she knew that Tara Harper and her crew had recorded the entire interview and attack.

Whether it was being live-streamed, she did not know. If it wasn't, she would ask the reporter to cut any footage that included her or her friends.

"Is this live?" she asked the reporter, her voice trembling.

"Yep."

Vera cringed. *It won't be long before this is all over the Internet,* she realized glumly. *The far right will have a field day with it.*

"I think we're done here," she informed the reporter. "We've lost our food, anyway. We need to regroup before we try this again."

"We are planning to head to residential areas on the other side of town to interview them," Harper said. "Have you been there?"

"No, we thought to go to the commercial area," Channing replied. "But maybe we could still ask the local people what they need and bring it back to them another day. That might be better than offering food or whatever to them if we don't know *their* needs."

"That's an excellent point," Sohrab agreed. "Let's find out what people need and then come back."

"So could we follow you?" Channing asked Harper, smiling. "We don't really know where to go."

"You may accompany us, but don't interfere with our broadcast."

Chapter 17: Radioactive Meltdown

They fell in with the reporters and walked toward the wholly residential part of the small community. Towns like this often had mixed-zone downtowns where businesses were built right next to homes, but even the smallest places had single-family-only zones too. They headed to the closest such neighborhood on foot, since the roads were a mess.

Here, it was easy to tell that a major storm had struck. The damage was much worse than it was in the mixed-use area, perhaps because the owners of these private homes were clearly not affluent and therefore their homes were of poorer construction quality than the commercial businesses. The buildings in this area were battered, often missing roofs and porches, and debris was everywhere. Cell service had also become spotty. It was hard to maintain a signal, and it was nearly impossible to stream video. Even photo uploads and downloads were delayed.

A few people were seated on cinder blocks, stumps, or battered porches, rifles and shotguns laid across their laps as they glared at the reporters and young adults.

"Sir," the reporter called out to one man. He had neither a respirator nor a mask over his face. "WJHG Panama City. Are you all right? Do you or anyone in your home need any assistance?"

"We can bring you food," Butterfly chirped. "Or shampoo, or... anything you need."

"I got food," the man snarled. "I got what I need. And anyone who tries to *take* what I've got will be introduced to this gun."

"We're not going to take anything of yours, sir. Do you know if anyone else in your neighborhood needs assistance?" Harper asked.

"I think you should mind your own damn business if you know what's good for you."

Harper withdrew at once, gesturing for her crew and GCCF to come with her.

They continued down the street, or what remained of it. It

was cluttered with nails, wood fragments, leaves, pine straw, and assorted trash from human dwellings. They passed several more houses, all sandblasted and soaked. In one of them, several pairs of eyes watched out a window as they walked down the street.

They stopped again at the first house that seemed to be out of the hostile armed man's line of sight. A male-and-female couple, these two wearing medical face masks, were affixing a spray-painted piece of plywood bearing the message "LOOTERS WILL BE SHOT" to the front of their house.

"Sir, ma'am," Harper tried again. "I'm Tara Harper with WJHG Panama City. Are you all right? Do you need any assistance?"

The man nailed the plywood and turned around to glare. "We're *fine*. You're the news? Bet you won't report the *truth*."

"What do you mean?"

The man eyed them all suspiciously. "What's going on is not what we were *told* was going on."

The reporter maintained her impassive, calm demeanor. "Could you explain what you mean? What do you believe is going on, sir?"

"We still have phone service out here, and Kiley and I saw the truth on the Internet," he replied, referring to his wife or girlfriend. "The government caused this."

"The storm? Sir, the government didn't cause Hypercane Leonard."

"Yes it did," he declared. "Maybe they aren't letting you media people know the truth, but we did our research. The government has a secret weather-modification program called Stormfury."

"Sir, that was an experimental project to determine if hurricane eyes could be collapsed by cloud seeding. It was shut down in the twentieth century."

"That's what they *claimed*, but it went on in secret," he insisted. "That's where the word 'hypercane' comes from. It really means 'government-modified hurricane.'"

"But the experiment didn't entirely work. This thing didn't have no four-hundred-mile-an-hour winds. The real problem is nuclear," the woman, Kiley, said. "I've never seen a hurricane do *this*"—she gestured to the brown sky—"nor have I ever been told to be afraid of *radiation* because of some hurricane. And Jim and I have lived in Florida all our lives. We know about hurricanes better'n anyone."

Harper tried to explain calmly and respectfully, even though Vera did not feel that these people deserved any respect. "Ma'am, sir," she said, "the government did not intensify the storm, and there was no nuclear incident. If you fear that, you can rest easily on that score. The dust and radiation that you've been told about are concerns precisely because Leonard *was* a hypercane, and it became one because of preexisting environmental conditions, not human storm modification. Hypercanes can do things that regular hurricanes cannot. The theory always suggested it, and now, unfortunately, this tragedy has proven it."

"How can any storm cause radiation?" Kiley sneered. "Dust, okay—but radiation? It's nuclear. I'm no fool and neither is Jim."

"Nuclear radiation means gamma rays. The radiation you've been warned about is ultraviolet, from the sun," Harper explained.

"I've never been afraid of the sun before. People get sunburned sometimes. It's no big deal. Why're they telling us to be scared of the sun all of a sudden?" Jim scoffed.

"It is a threat because Leonard probably damaged the ozone layer. That's one thing hypercanes can do and hurricanes cannot."

"The ozone layer. So we're bringing that up again? That was the big greenie scare before 'climate change.' It was before our time, but Mad Dog said so on the Internet. He knows his history."

Vera exchanged exasperated looks with her friends. So that explained it. That monster was doubling down on his lies.

"'*Oh no, there's a hole in the ozone!*'" Kiley mocked. "It's enviro crap." She folded her arms over her chest. "How's our house standing if it had four-hundred-mile-an-hour winds?"

"You weren't in the area of the strongest winds."

"Yeah, nobody can get in where they claim that was, and why is that? Nuclear. I saw something online that proves it."

Harper was trying to keep her patience, and Vera could tell that it was becoming difficult. "There are plenty of false reports and AI-generated videos circulating, no doubt—"

"It wasn't fake. It was a live-stream of someone from inside Panama City," Jim said. "Mad Dog shared it. A guy whose last words on the video were that this was no hurricane, but a 'nuclear blast.' Then hell broke loose and the video cut off. I'm sure he died then."

"If he was in Panama City, he likely did, sadly. But that was because he was in the core of the four-hundred-mile-an-hour winds. There was no nuclear blast, meltdown, or any other sort of nuclear incident, I promise you."

"There's a nuclear lab not too far away," Kiley said. "The radiation and nuclear material got into the hurricane, and the government is trying to cover it all up."

Harper finally gave up. "Thank you for your time. If you do not need assistance, we must keep going."

Vera and her group decided to leave the reporters after that. She was profoundly demoralized. Where were the poor marginalized people who cared deeply about climate change, tried to live sustainable lives, knew that the reckless unsustainable lifestyle of the privileged was disproportionately harming *their* communities instead, and bore the brunt of the storm? These people were just trashy, willfully ignorant Floridians. Where were the *real* victims?

*   *   *

The five friends were sad and sour as they walked gingerly back toward their vehicle. At least they could get the map app to appear on their phones to help them retrace their steps. Some roads were completely washed out.

"You know, we didn't actually get into the worst areas,"

Channing said in a low voice.

Vera had realized that. "This place probably took winds of two hundred or so. There are a lot of debarked trees and leveled houses. But other stuff is still standing. It kind of looks like pictures from a really bad tornado, and my uncle has said that the worst tornadoes start at two hundred miles an hour."

"So the hardest-hit areas...." Channing trailed off.

"That's where the skull came from. We don't want to go there."

"We'd have to go on foot. The roads will be scoured away."

"There's no point, anyway. There won't be anyone alive." That was abundantly clear to Vera now. "It's entirely likely that some of the debris we see everywhere in *these* areas isn't actually from here. The storm would have lofted a lot of crap and dropped it wherever."

"Panama City is probably gone, then." Channing shuddered. "That would account for the volume of debris. A whole city."

They fell silent, letting the horror of that sink in. It was difficult to accept. No one knew what to say after that—what *could* follow such a terrible observation?—so they continued onward in silence.

Mike was leading the way, as the biggest, brawniest, and toughest of them. After the attack on Vera in the parking lot, they had all collectively realized, without saying it, that he needed to be in front in order to frighten and dissuade any additional would-be attackers. Sohrab was slim to the point of boniness, and Butterfly, Channing, and Vera were all visibly female. Mike was the only one who could menace people with nothing but his own body. When he tensed like a nervous scout and held up his hand in the sign of a halt, they all did.

"*I'm trying to help!*

"*You're covering up for them!*"

"*I wanted to bring your Maw some insulin!*"

"*You want to poison her! That's what you want!*"

There was a pause. Then the first person sputtered,

"What is wrong with you?"

"You didn't get us all with the radioactive meltdown or the storm you stirred up, so now you're trying to pick off those of us who figured out the truth!"

"What the hell are you talkin' about? There's no radioactive meltdown, and nobody 'stirred up' the storm!"

A gunshot then rang out, followed by rapid footfalls.

The five young people hesitated, debating rapidly in their minds whether to pursue this. Someone might have just been shot. If the person was still alive, they might be able to save them. But if they involved themselves in a gunfight, they could be shot too.

A groan burst through the air. Yes, someone had been shot.

Mike took a deep breath and sped up his pace, following the sounds. The other four hurried to keep up. In a minute, they stood before a sprawled, bleeding man who lay in the fetal position on a patch of grass.

Channing knew CPR and some first aid. She quickly recognized that the bleeding was coming from the man's left upper arm. With swift dispatch, she stripped off her belt to tourniquet the wound.

The bleeding slowed from a gush to a manageable trickle. He still needed to be hospitalized, but they would just take him back to Tallahassee. Hospitals were functional there.

"Thanks, kids," the man croaked. His face had gone pale. "Surprised at this point to see any human kindness around here."

"We came from Tallahassee to try to assist," Vera explained as Mike lifted the man in his arms. "The hospitals are open there. You'll be okay." She paused. Based on his voice, this man was the one who had offered insulin. He was probably the "good guy" in the altercation they'd overheard. "Were you trying to provide insulin to someone's mother?"

He nodded quickly. "Neighbor's Maw."

They had almost reached their SUV. Sohrab unlocked the doors and helped Mike ease the patient in. Vera debated for a moment about whether they should lower a seat, soon deciding that it was best for his injury to be elevated. He should sit upright.

They all got into the vehicle. Mike started it and sped out of the battered area quickly.

"Your neighbor is insane," Butterfly proclaimed.

The man grunted. "This crap is spreading around. It's nuts, but...." He took a deep breath, trying not to faint. "Going around the Internet. And I'm FEMA, so...."

"But they're your *neighbors*," Vera exclaimed, horrified. "They *know* you!"

"Don't matter. I think it might even make it worse. They see me as an infiltrator. An enemy within. Something got twisted in these people over the past two days." He took another deep, painful breath. "When things get bad like this, the mask goes down and people show what they truly are." At this, he passed out.

They were all alarmed, but Channing reached for him to check for a pulse. "Steady," she reported. "And he's breathing. I'll monitor him. We do need to get to a hospital as fast as possible, though."

Mike hit the accelerator.

*　　*　　*

The hospitals in Tallahassee were full, but Vera and her friends still managed to get the man admitted to an emergency room. He was carrying a Florida driver's license and a Department of Homeland Security employee badge, both with the name Greg Paulson. The doctor believed he would recover.

"Well," Vera mumbled as they headed back to their vehicle at last, "at least we did one good thing for *someone*."

"What a miserable day," Butterfly agreed.

They got inside and shut the doors. Then Channing said what she had apparently been holding back until they had privacy.

"Someone needs to take out Madison Chadleigh," she declared. "He's the one who's been telling all those people

266

that this is a government conspiracy."

"I've found the video that that crazy person was talking about," Butterfly said, already on their phone.

"*Which* crazy person?" Vera muttered.

"The one who said that there was a guy in Panama City who live-streamed landfall. I found the video. Chadleigh did repost it. It looks real. The guy's stream does end with him saying 'This isn't a hurricane. This is a nuclear blast or something.' Then stuff blows all over, and a half-second later, the video ends."

"Then it was an idiot who didn't believe it was a hypercane, tried to sit out landfall, and got killed for it," Channing said harshly.

"Of course, but Chadleigh says it could be the 'shock wave' from a meltdown."

"I don't know if a meltdown at a fission plant *can* cause a shock wave," Vera said, "but even if one could, the *fusion* lab couldn't, and besides, the guy was at Ground Zero! That's not where the lab is! Their own conspiracy theories aren't even consistent."

"I don't think that bothers them."

Vera shook her head. "This is insane. There is certainly a meltdown around these places, but it's a meltdown of rapidly spreading radioactive *stupidity!*"

*　　*　　*

With power restored, the five friends were back to their usual habits. Vera was vaguely sad that her moment of enlightenment had passed, but there was also comfort in the familiar routine of scrolling and watching. Maybe, she thought, it was better just not to think of that moment when she and some of the others had to face their dependency on social media. They lived in the modern world, and it took a hypercane landfall, after all, to snap the cord—and then only temporarily. Better just to accept it, she reasoned.

It was never a pleasant activity. Television and feeds always stirred up anger and feelings of helplessness, even while addicting Vera and her friends to the urge to *know*, however futile "knowledge" might be in this case. But tonight, the ritual was exceptionally grim.

President Harry Phillips and Vice President Natalia Romano appeared in a brief press conference, which was currently the top news item on their streaming package. It was not the most popular item of all categories—that, Vera noted from the onscreen Top Ten, was the show *Webcammers of New York*, about the daily lives of self-employed porn performers in that city—but at least people interested in the news had watched an official source enough to vault it to the top. That or it was short enough that people were not put off watching it. It was only a few minutes long.

Vera clicked on the press conference, remembering Tara Harper's claim that he was considering declaring martial law around the landfall site over Governor Sandoval's objections. She wondered if this was what he had indeed decided and that was why it was the top news item.

The President was not an exceptionally old man, but he had not aged well, and the past few days had taken a toll on him. He also had never been good on camera. This press conference was no exception. The Vice President looked awkward and tired as well, with heavy dark bags under her eyes.

"Mr. President," a White House correspondent asked him, "have you made a decision about martial law in the hardest-hit counties?"

Phillips gazed out at them wearily. "I...." His voice was scratchy and quiet. He cleared his throat, not a good look on camera when he needed to appear strong. "I have decided that the Vice President and I should go to the hard-hit areas first and assess conditions in person before making that call. Reports are that the situation on the ground is very bad, but we want to confirm that ourselves."

"But is it safe? If conditions are so bad, should you be there?"

"We have a responsibility to the American people and especially the people of Florida. I don't want to dispatch soldiers into their communities without having seen for myself that it's necessary."

Another reporter spoke up. "Mr. President, we've been told that emergency officials—federal, not just state—are concerned about security in areas surrounding Ground Zero and don't think you should be there. What is your response to this?"

"I appreciate their concern, but we will have the best security that the United States government can provide the President and Vice President. Our concern needs to be focused on the victims."

"When do you intend to go, if you're determined to do this?"

"We have a big event planned in New York with some of the survivors of the 9/11 attacks. There aren't many adult survivors left, and it's important for us to be there for the fifty-year remembrance. But we think we can get down to Florida on the thirteenth, a week after landfall. If the situation is as dire as we're hearing, we need to give the state time to get things in order." He held up his hands and turned aside, indicating no further questions would be accepted.

Vera turned off the television.

"He's really going to do it," Sohrab exclaimed. "He really is going to send in troops."

Channing agreed. "He's just looking for a pretext. That's what this 'visit' is about. That and it looks bad for him to be AWOL."

"He would do better—both of them would do better—just to stick with people who want to reminisce about a terrorist attack that occurred before our *parents* were even born. That's what they should focus on: chattering with other old people about historical events. Nobody wants them in Florida."

"That's true enough," Butterfly observed, looking up from the phone.

"What's going on, Butterfly?" Channing asked.

"Well, three things. One, everyone is panning that press

conference. I see why. It was really boring. Two, that conspiracy theory we heard about today is all over the Internet."

"Nuclear material and a 'stirred-up' storm?"

"Mmhmm. Chadleigh dug up some old history, something called 'Project Stormfury' from, like, eighty years ago where people tried to modify hurricanes, and they're saying it's still going on—and that it *works*. Also, a lot of people are convinced that the *real* reason no one is allowed in the areas where nothing is left is that it's radioactive. And that your aunt's lab, Vera, was responsible somehow. The conspiracy theory is inconsistent, as you pointed out, but they all agree that there was a nuclear incident and a hurricane. But it looks like nobody survived the very worst winds, and the lack of survivors makes it easy for conspiracies to spread."

Vera shook her head. "It's stupid, but you know what? It's my aunt's problem. It's her lab. We need to focus on the real victims, not on doing public relations for Intensity Labs."

"What was the third thing that you referred to, Butterfly?" Channing asked.

Butterfly winced, gazing sheepishly at Vera. "The interview with that reporter and the attack—that guy trying to take your phone—have gone viral all over right-wing spaces. It's bad. I don't even want to repeat what they're saying."

Vera sighed and turned back to her phone to see for herself. She supposed she wasn't surprised. She had expected that as soon as the reporter had said it was being streamed live. She had known it would be bad. She knew that she did look somewhat stereotypical, with her short dyed hair, nature tattoo, and casual androgynous clothing. Many right-wing accounts mocked her mercilessly for her appearance. It was infuriating, but she expected it.

But as she clicked on the trending topic and scrolled through the feed, her eyes widened in shock. These were not just stupid, petty personal comments. Those existed, but there were other posts that truly upset and even frightened her.

Pity that thug didn't rape her. It would teach her a lesson.
Can you blame him? I wouldn't touch that ugly thing.
Well of course he didn't rape her. He's white.

Vera had to look away from the thread of racist vitriol that followed this comment, all of it stating baldly—not even implying, declaring outright—that a Black looter would have raped her and bashed her head in.

"We should respond to this," Channing suddenly said. "These evil people are using the action of a white man to condemn people of color."

"Why is it our responsibility to respond to that?" Vera grumbled. She didn't even want to think about it. It was too vile.

"We have a platform now, with this video going viral. We should use it to take a stand against racism. The man who attacked you was white. And most of the people in that drugstore...." She trailed off, frowning, as she tried to remember.

Vera combed her memories too. The truth was, she hadn't paid attention to the races of the people fighting in the drugstore. It hadn't seemed important. It *wasn't* important. What had struck her was the violent, uncivilized behavior of them *all*, not the color of their skin. And it had been a traumatic series of memories. She'd been attacked. She'd seen or heard two people get *shot* today! That kind of event tended to blot out unimportant details. To the extent that she could remember at all, she believed that the people in the drugstore included white, Black, and possibly Hispanic people. Maybe others. She really didn't recall clearly.

"I do think there were people of several races in the drugstore," she said gingerly. "So we shouldn't say that we only saw white people being violent. But we certainly did see some."

"Are you going to post a statement, then?"

"No. Not from my personal account. If it has to be done, use the GCCF account for it." She gave Butterfly a pointed nod.

271

"On it!" Butterfly said.

In a minute, the statement hit their feeds. **Generation Climate Catastrophe Florida unequivocally condemns attacks on people of color for the violent behavior of a white man in a widely shared video. Leonard's landfall and the cruel policies of our governments are disproportionately affecting marginalized communities. We urge those who are disturbed by the video and the vile display of racism to donate to reputable and ethical recovery efforts.**

Butterfly and Sohrab smiled in satisfaction as the "likes" for this bland statement piled up. GCCF's followers almost all shared their politics, so the statement didn't even reach the centrist or apolitical parts of social media, let alone the right. Its audience approved of the statement, and two of the GCCF approved of the audience reaction. The ouroboros of online interaction continued to feed on its own tail.

But Vera was not so sanguine, and she could tell that neither were Channing and Mike. Channing's outburst from last night blasted back to the forefront of her mind:

"It just gets us attention on the Internet and makes us feel better about ourselves!"

Once the power came back on, it didn't take long for us to revert right back to that, Vera thought.

"We have to go back," she said abruptly. "Online statements just aren't enough. There is real suffering out there."

"Yes," Channing agreed. "As you said, Vera, there were people of all races fighting in the drugstore. But those weren't the oppressed and marginalized. Neither were those trashy conspiracy theorists in the town. The real victims are in the shadows, being preyed on by their own neighbors. Their governor has abandoned them. And now, their president, who claims to be an ally, is probably going to send the military after them. He may say it's to 'keep order,' but that just means 'attack marginalized folks while letting their oppressors off the hook.' They have no one else to stand up for them, so we must."

Mike was glowering at his phone. "I agree we need to go

back, but I don't want to walk into that again unprepared."

"What do you have in mind?" Vera asked.

"I think we need to get a lot more people with us, and I think we need to be armed." His gaze hardened. "My dad can get us guns, for those who are comfortable carrying them, and the rest of us should have Molotov cocktails ready to whip up."

Vera gaped at him. "Isn't that just *looking* for a fight?"

"Vera, y'all must not be reading what I am. There is a right-wing militia stirred up by Madison Chadleigh's conspiracy-mongering, CG Taverner's determination to egg it on and give credence to it, and this damn fool idea of Phillips and Romano to show up at Ground Zero. They're planning to gather there. Fascist terrorists, gathering near the landfall site."

"I haven't seen that," Butterfly exclaimed.

"Then look harder. You won't see it on our organization's feed. Let me show you." With that, he switched the television input to be a wireless capture of his phone screen, so that they could all see on the large set.

Vera gasped at what appeared on the television.

This is the critical moment, Taverner's personal account declared. **We will put Phillips, Romano, and the entire climate-alarmism syndicate on the spot on September 13. We will demand the truth: about patriot Joseph Hitchfield's video, about the real reason that plane crashed, about the data that the NHC won't let anyone audit. Fellow truth-seekers, stand with Mad Dog, Speaker Gilbertson, and me at Ground Zero!**

Thousands of "likes" and comments had followed, many of them from people declaring their intention to show up. If even half of these people followed through, there would easily be two hundred militia members there.

"We need to be there," Mike said gravely, "and we need to be armed. I'm not going to limit this to GCCF. There are only fifteen of us. I'm going to call in everyone I can think of. And I think that once they see that we are standing up for them, the real victims of Leonard will stand with us. We'll have strength of numbers then. They're out there; they just understand their own vulnerability better than anyone, so they keep their heads down most of the time. They need to know that we have their backs." He smiled, his eyes slightly wild. "This could be the start of the revolutionary change we've all wanted."

*   *   *

The Hurricane Hunters came ashore at Port Sulphur, Louisiana, on the ninth of September. A small unincorporated community in the wetlands, it had not fared especially well in enormous, ferocious Leonard. But then, few places on the Gulf Coast had emerged unscathed.

Edward and his crew really needed to shower. They were filthy. They also needed to plug in their phones somewhere to recharge their batteries. Unfortunately, they did not have charging cables; they had not thought they would need them for the few hours they had expected to be on the plane. They had their wallets with them; their credit cards and driver's licenses, at least, were not lost. But they could not make reservations, either for transportation or hotels—assuming any could be found—without phones. A quick search of the handful of stores proved that chargers were sold out.

Port Sulphur also had no shelters available. Sighing, the Hurricane Hunters trudged back into their raft and continued up the river to New Orleans.

*   *   *

They arrived at New Orleans the next day. They had to scramble up a dock on foot, but at this point, Leonard refugees doing that weren't an unusual sight anywhere on the Gulf Coast, so the port authorities didn't even blink.

The Crescent City was funereal. New Orleans had taken a Category One or Two impact, Edward believed—nothing they couldn't handle—but they knew all too well what had happened to their east, and they were mourning their fellow Coast residents.

It also became apparent that either there were no hotel rooms available in New Orleans, or nobody wanted to let these stinky, disreputable-looking characters in. Edward suspected the former; the hotels had to be flooded—he cringed inwardly at that word—with stinky, disreputable-looking evacuees.

Phone chargers seemed to be a hot item; the Hunters tramped from store to store looking for them, but chargers were among numerous items that had sold out.

Finally they decided that they would try to find a bar just to have a place to rest and get some news. They selected a divey-looking one downtown, hoping that they wouldn't be thrown out of such an establishment because of their stench.

The wait staff did want to keep their distance, but they were clearly accustomed to people in various states of hygiene, and a functional credit card was a functional credit card. Since it was a bar, several televisions were on, and since it was after a horrendous storm landfall, half of them were actually tuned to the news instead of sports or entertainment.

One screen, in perfect sight of the Hunters' table, bore the chyron "*Devastation after Leonard hits Florida with 420 mph winds.*"

Edward glanced at the images of misery before sighing and turning away.

"You're the Hurricane Hunters who went down?" the waitress asked them as she brought them their orders. "We all thought you were dead."

"We're the ones," Edward said, "and none of us are dead yet." He picked up the extra drink he had ordered, a single shot. Sighing, he poured it out over a saucer. "To the people on the coast who didn't make it."

They all stared at their drinks glumly.

"So," the waitress continued, "y'all flew out of Tyndall?"

"No, Lakeland—inland from Tampa," he explained. As he considered the location of Tyndall Air Force Base, horror suddenly overcame him. His eyes widened and his lips parted.

"Yeah," the waitress confirmed, observing his face. "It's gone."

"God," Nadya Cass whispered. "But it was right at Ground Zero. It took the worst winds of anywhere, probably."

"They evacuated the base," the waitress said. "Nobody died there—well, unless they had squatters after the officials left. But yeah. Nobody can confirm it for sure, because the roads are gone after a certain point, but there has been no word out of that area."

"The area where the winds were three hundred or higher," Edward said. He recalled the television chyron. "Or... 420. Nothing will stand up to that. Was that the strongest that it was along its whole path? If you don't remember, that's okay," he assured her.

"I think it did briefly get stronger at one point."

He sighed. "I suppose there are no vacancies in town?"

The waitress shook her head. "Everything's booked."

"Shelters?"

"I doubt there's any space left anywhere."

"Anywhere we can get a phone charger?"

"Unless you're inclined to rob someone for theirs—which has actually happened a lot here, and this *isn't* a recommendation, I will note—good luck with that. But if you just need to make a call, you can use my phone."

Edward's eyes lit up and his mouth broke into a smile at the offer—but his expression froze, then changed to one of dismay as he realized that he did not know anyone's number. He had never needed to. He had been dependent on his phone's convenient contact list. Now that he did need to know his sister's number—or the number of Dr. Chandra—he didn't have access to them. His phone was in his pocket, holding the information he had not deemed necessary to remember, but currently it was a brick.

The bleak, ridiculous irony of the situation suddenly became too much. He fell back in his chair, laughing bitterly. His crew were all looking similarly shamefaced and cynical; undoubtedly they were in the same boat. Embarrassed chuckles escaped from Cartwright and Cass.

Edward raised his glass of beer. "To the late, terrible,

glorious Hypercane Leonard. We deserved you."

The waitress, Dr. Evans, and a few others looked reproachful at this, but no one spoke a word of disagreement.

"Right, then," he finally said. "We'll just book bus tickets. I'll show up at my sister's in person."

Chapter 18: Debris Field

Mike and his father had really come through, Vera thought.

Through his contacts, Mike had managed to rustle up over 150 people to join their counter-protest. These were a different breed from the comparatively bland activists associated with public-facing nonprofits and collectives like GCCF—people who focused on public outreach, document production, and media spectacle. These were the sorts of people who wore black from head to toe and masked their faces—because they carried bats, clubs, flamethrowers, Molotov cocktails, and sometimes even guns to their demonstrations. Indeed, "demonstrations" wasn't really the correct word for what they did. They set fires. They did not just spray-paint property with washable paint; they often destroyed it. And they were not afraid of fighting. These were, for all intents and purposes, leftist militia.

GCCF might be provocative in the eyes of people like my aunt and uncle, Vera thought when these people began showing up at the agreed-upon meeting point outside the Ground Zero areas. *But it just shows how little they know.*

She had known that Mike had ties to these groups, and that in fact, this history was why he was brash and aggressive. But it was still surprising to see the numbers.

Mike's dad was an enigma to Vera. A very rich board member of a private for-profit hospital, he nonetheless gave Mike—and the polycule—all the money they wanted for their progressive causes, and he eagerly supported *and armed* them to stand with these... she had to admit it... kind of scary leftist militia.

She supposed she could somewhat understand Mike's dad if he acted as he did out of guilt. She certainly felt guilty enough herself for being the daughter of Richard and Chelsea Mellor. But she had rejected their financial support. Mike's father was still on that hospital board.

Nonetheless, he has provided us with the means to protect ourselves, she thought. Not everyone in GCCF wanted to pick up a gun, but Vera and Mike didn't object to pistols. They also knew how to use them. Teaching Vera about gun ownership as a teen had almost been a point of pride to her right-wing parents. She rather relished the idea of using their tutelage for *her own* political cause.

Not, of course, that she wanted to have to shoot anyone. But she would not hesitate to defend herself or her friends if any of the far-right fascist militia threatened them.

*　　*　　*

The GCCF group and Mike's... other friends... congregated in Blountstown, a small town that seemed to be on the very edge of the region where survivors still could be found. On maps, a person could draw a finger-shaped core, matching the track of Leonard, where the winds had likely been unsurvivable. There had been no reports and no survivors to come out of this region, and even on satellites, the dust cloud was extremely thick. Blountstown was just outside the eastern edge of this area. This was where the President and Vice President would touch down. They had wanted to be as close to Ground Zero as they could, rather than making a comparatively comfortable photo-op in Tallahassee—which, for all that it took a Category Five impact, had weathered it pretty well.

GCCF carried their gas masks in their backpacks, but none of them wanted to wear them just yet. They were inconvenient and made it hard to be heard and understood. In addition, with Mike's friends around wearing full masks, they might be mistaken for those people. They would make do with KN95 masks for as long as they could stand it.

Vera was uncomfortable around Mike's associates. They seemed to be looking for a fight. In any case, the right-wing militia that they had come to defend against had not yet put in a major appearance. The leftists outnumbered them, so for now, to Vera's relief, she and her friends would rove around and talk to locals.

The area was in terrible shape. The town they had visited on the eighth seemed comparatively well-off in contrast. In some neighborhoods, most houses were piles of rubble. In others, houses were leveled down to the first floor, or a single room on the first floor. Trees were stripped and snapped. There was hardly an intact vehicle in sight; every one that GCCF saw was mangled.

It didn't take long for GCCF to find a subdivision—or what had once been one—where people were willing to talk.

"The Publix is still standing—sort of—but it's emptied out of food," one woman with filthy hair and dirt smudges all over her face and clothes informed them. "You don't want to go there. These outsiders are coming in, people nobody around here knows—"

The woman's boyfriend or husband cut in then. "Nobody knows these people you're talking to either, Tammy."

"But they look pretty harmless to me, don't you agree, Mike?"

Mike—Vera's friend—bristled at the fact that this man had the same name that he did. —*Or perhaps at the declaration that he looks harmless and weak,* Vera thought. She remembered the loaded pistol under her jacket. Mike carried one too. It was probably for the best that these paranoid people did not know that, though.

"I mean, no offense, but y'all would get squashed if you went to the Publix," Tammy said to the young adults. "You said you're from Tally, and you obviously are. You sound Floridian. These new people don't speak like they're from around here... people wearing skulls and shit like that... and they're taking places over."

The far-right militia, Vera realized. *They're in the Publix. That's why nobody on our side has been able to find many of them.* "Did this start recently?" she asked.

The woman nodded. "Just last night. It got real bad today."

"It is a fascist militia," Mike cut in. "They're here to protest the President's visit."

Tammy glowered. "I wish he'd stay the hell out. Nobody needs him here. And now he's just attracting wackos to our town."

"Have you seen any sign of Sandoval's 'recovery' effort?"

280

"Nope. No church people, no state people. Just the locals, and now, Nazis in the Publix, you tell me. Don't nobody care about us. Before they took it, it was local gangs there and in every other store that still had a wall or two. Roving around and taking everything they could." She scowled. "Another gang set up in the Walmart to sell stuff that they'd stolen. It's outrageous what they're asking. Nobody can afford it. It's like a Florida version of the Mafia."

"Have you considered banding together as a community to fight back?" Butterfly asked eagerly. "The authorities *have* abandoned you, but you could organize your own peacekeeping—"

Tammy snorted. "*Peace* ain't gonna solve our problems, girl."

The woman's male companion, the other Mike, cut in again. "But there's community organization, you might say." He smirked knowingly. "Over in Tropical Breezes—that's the new richy-rich subdivision, just five years old—there's a 'compound' setting up."

"What do you mean?" Sohrab asked.

"It's Fred Warrington. Multimillionaire. Made his fortune in real estate development. His mansion is something like thirty thousand square feet, and it went through the storm pretty well, word has it. Took off the roof and little else. He's offering 'protection' to people if they work for him, like servants."

"And he's got a line of guards around the perimeter of his estate," Tammy added, "people who accepted his offer. Sent them after the Walmart gang. It got bloody in there, we hear, but Warrington's people won. Seized some of the food. Allegedly he's gonna plant a big garden that can feed everyone who now works for him." She snorted, but her laughter was dark. "They say he's accepting sexual services from some of the prettier women, too."

Vera was outraged. "That's a regression to barbarism. He's setting himself up like he's a lord in the Middle Ages or something."

"Well, most of us don't have a lot of use for it or for the people who took his 'offer.' Weaklings, they are. Those of us out here, where things got bad—we just deal with the gangs in our own way."

Her man hefted his gun, a high-velocity rifle. "Got a couple of these. If somebody comes at our property and they look like a threat, I give 'em one warning to clear out and then I shoot if they don't. That's what all of us around here do. We don't need the help of some slimy rich bastard takin' advantage of the situation."

"I haven't noticed any dead bodies around," Vera said hesitantly.

"We strip off anything of value they have and leave 'em for the critters. Or I guess there might be cannibals now. Not my problem."

That was all that Vera cared to hear. She'd just about had enough of this grim narrative. And worst of all, the traitorous thought crossed her mind that her Mike wasn't really that different from Tammy's Mike in some respects. Yes, it was time to move on.

They thanked Tammy and Mike, then left the... neighborhood, though it was hard to consider this wasteland as that.

*   *   *

Moving deeper into what had once been the town, they soon found another local who was willing to talk: a man who introduced himself as Nate Abercrombie and said he was a local lawyer. Vera looked forward to a productive conversation with an educated person this time.

"Yeah, Warrington has his little 'fief,' and that's a good way of putting it," Abercrombie declared when they asked him about that. "I think it's sleazy, and I have more respect for people who stand up for themselves independently. Seems more like the true American spirit than seeking help from a guy who wants to make himself, as you put it, a medieval lord."

"But none of this should be necessary," Channing emphasized. "The fact that things have fallen apart in the course of a week... this is really bad."

"Civilization is a fragile thing. We're all just a few days away from *Lord of the Flies*. This town has had proof of it lately."

Three blank faces stared back at him. Vera and Sohrab were the only ones who got the allusion.

"It's a book about teenage boys who fall into violent, barbaric patterns when they're lost in the wild," she explained to the others. Their expressions cleared.

Abercrombie was amused. "Schools aren't what they used to be, it seems. But my point is, it's gotten bad here. You've heard about Warrington, the vigilantes, the Walmart gang—oh, and these fascist gangs coming in today and taking over Publix. Those are places you don't need to go. Just take it from me. But...." He hesitated. "If you kids are wandering around the town asking for information, you also need to know about Domino Point."

"What's that?" Channing asked.

"Area to the southwest. It used to be a fairly nice subdivision, but there's nothing left now. And I mean *nothing*. Even foundation slabs are gone. It's a no-go zone."

"Why?"

Abercrombie leaned in and lowered his voice, as if he were afraid that someone else was listening. "I've heard that nobody who's gone out there has returned."

Mike's eyes narrowed. "Do you know for sure that these people actually *went* there, and aren't just dead from the storm itself—or the violence?"

"Well, I don't know any of them personally, but that's what I've been told. And you need to get off your high horse, mister, because it's not just rumors. Even drones go down when they approach Domino Point."

Vera was angry too. Was even an educated person going to expound on conspiracy theories? "How could anyone send a drone in the first place? You've had no power for a week. How could anything have a charged battery?"

"Look, I know for a fact that a drone flew out there and

went down. I saw the video—while, yes, we still had batteries. It's online. You could find it when you get back to Tallahassee. The drone went out there and then suddenly fritzed out and went down."

"Its battery probably ran out."

"Maybe, but the guy who sent it was one of my neighbors, and he insisted that it was not drained. We think it was EMP."

"Electromagnetic pulse? By who?" Mike scoffed.

"The government." Abercrombie lowered his voice further. "There's another rumor about Domino Point, that there is a giant super-intelligent alligator prowling the area, and that's why nobody returns. It hunts them. Said to be mutated to be fifty feet long from nuclear radiation." He rolled his eyes. "I don't believe that, of course. That's just a stupid conspiracy theory. A week obviously isn't long enough for anything to mutate and grow that big. But the government could be doing things with EMP. That's rational."

*　　*　　*

"You know," Vera said to her friends when they were out of earshot of everyone else, "I don't really want to talk to any more of these yokels."

"This is... really something," Channing agreed.

"I'm trying to cut them some slack. They're living in very rough conditions, and they're clinging to whatever notion of stability they can, whether it's a nasty real-estate developer setting himself up as a feudal lord, private vigilantism, or conspiracy theories to make sense of things. But I'm really running out of patience with it."

"Yeah. Let's just wait for the President to visit. We should get back to the area he's supposed to touch down. There will be news media there now and probably some local officials."

That sounded like a good idea to everyone, so they headed back.

*　　*　　*

"This is Tara Harper with WJHG News. We are live from Blountstown, Florida, where we await the arrival of President Phillips and Vice President Romano for their first visit to a hard-hit area since Hypercane Leonard made a devastating landfall just seven days ago. Protesters from both the left and the right have gathered to express their opinions to the President and VP. And local conditions are, frankly, terrible," the reporter emphasized. "Leonard brought winds of three hundred miles an hour to the southwestern side of this town. Nothing can stand up to that, and it is believed to be—this is very grim, but I don't know how else to say it—one of the dividing lines between no survivors, in this case to the west"—she gestured in that direction—"and devastation, but a handful of people who survived the storm, to the east." She paused to let that sink in. "One survivor was the Director of City Water, Mr. Foster Kenyon. Mr. Kenyon, we understand that the water is not safe to drink?"

Foster Kenyon, a harassed-looking Black man in dirty jeans and a short-sleeved collared taupe shirt, agreed. "We've put out a boil-water notice, but there's two problems with that. One, it's hard to get information out except by word of mouth. People still have cell service in places, but they don't have electricity, so phone batteries are mostly dead. Even a solar hookup is no good with this dirty, dusty sky. Though I hear the sun's rays would be a problem now."

"I'm afraid they would be, Mr. Kenyon. I appreciate your difficulty, too, in spreading the word about the water."

"And the other problem with boiling is that you can't do it unless you can make a fire. People could do that with matches and kindling, but we have shut off the gas lines for people's own safety. There are too many breaks in the pipes. So water is a big issue. People are getting sick. We've had reports just this morning of people getting dysentery, people getting cholera, amoebas, E. coli—all sorts of things. It's a bad situation."

"This morning Governor Sandoval promised that there would be an airlift of fifty thousand gallons of bottled fresh water to the hardest-hit areas. Has that happened yet?"

"Yes, it came in today, but *we* didn't get fifty thousand gallons. That's *total*, for all the areas that don't have water. It just isn't enough. And it doesn't help with the people who got sick. We need medicine. We need people airlifted to doctors and hospitals. I hear there are hospitals open in Tallahassee, but there just aren't that many people that can get out there. You've got to have a working car, with the tires not damaged —and a lot of them got sandblasted down too thin to drive on without blowing—and you've got to have roads that aren't full of nails and other sharp things. It's hard."

Harper's eyes were wide. "We can only imagine, Mr. Kenyon."

He glowered at the reporter's camera. "And I just wanted to make a statement. I hear there are conspiracy theories that this was a nuclear accident, or that the government modified Leonard to become stronger and that's what 'hypercane' really means. If that is what you believe, any of you watching this, I want to tell you some facts. This was the worst thing I've ever experienced. They say we had winds of three hundred in the south of this town, and I believe it. Anyone who tells you that the damage wasn't caused by the storm itself, that the Hurricane Center downed that plane on purpose, that there is some nuclear crap going on, or that there is any government on Earth that could *control* a storm like we had, that person is either a liar or a fool."

Streaming the interview on their fully-charged phones, Vera and her friends nodded in satisfaction. *Here* was an example of the kind of victim—or survivor—that they had been looking for: a person of color who understood the situation fully, and who profoundly resented the vile behavior of the privileged.

Harper nodded. "Thank you for that statement, Mr. Kenyon. It is a breath of fresh air and a moment of bleak but plain truth that was desperately needed. And please know that America stands with you in your difficulties. Do you have hopes for President Phillips' visit today? Do you think that a federal response might change things?"

"I'm glad that he and the Vice President are coming. Personally, I think they should send in the military. Things are bad, Tara. Local authorities simply do not have the resources to keep order. We lost cops and officials ourselves. And if nobody else will maintain the law out here, we need soldiers to do it. It may be hard, but what's going on out there is a lot worse. Trust me."

At these words, Butterfly stifled a gasp. Sohrab and Channing scowled. Mike's eyes narrowed in anger. He muttered something that Vera did not catch, but it did not sound like a compliment.

As for Vera herself, her thoughts were in turmoil. The catechism that she had long repeated suddenly seemed like a cruel joke, given the terrible reality this community and many others faced.

Mike motioned to his friends. The five core GCCF members huddled together. Mike was furious as he spoke in low tones. "The media want to promote the agenda of structural oppression—the status quo—and so they seek out people like that man to put a Black face on it. It's a duplicitous game they're playing."

There was a time not too long ago when Vera would have agreed with that view herself. But she was no longer sure she did. Foster Kenyon didn't look like an oppressor to her. He was trying to help his community. He, a middle-class local government official from a small town in Florida, was speaking the truth about Leonard in the face of a media whirlwind to spread misinformation and outright lies. That took courage. And when they had visited the other community on the eighth—a town that hadn't even suffered as much damage as this one—Vera had not seen one person who fit her idea of a perfect victim.

Maybe the reason for that wasn't a conspiracy to silence and conceal those people. Maybe it was that they didn't exist. Maybe, just maybe, the problem was with her—their—ideas of what "perfect" victims should be.

And after all, who were they to determine what a perfect victim should be like and what such a person should think? Vera glanced at her expensive handbag and her phone with a grimace, as if seeing them for the first time. Their polycule consisted of five white young adults from affluent families. Tallahassee had weathered Leonard relatively well. The worst thing that had happened to them was that they had lost power for a day. Who were they to judge Foster Kenyon for wanting the military to come in and stop human predators from exploiting innocent people?

She took a deep breath. "Mike, I don't think we need to condemn him. He's experienced things we can barely imagine. And he's got a firm grasp on reality when it comes to Leonard. He seems like a rational, well-meaning person to me."

Channing gasped. "Vera! This is *what they do!* They find people of color, LGBTQ people, people with disabilities, anyone who is marginalized but still supports the oppressive status quo. It makes it look 'respectable.' But these people only have views like this because things are so bad for them that even the idea of military occupation seems better... and because they don't know about the community-based alternatives that are available."

Vera knew the argument. She would have made it herself a few days ago. But right now, it just seemed arrogant and patronizing. "So they hold these views because they're too ignorant to know better? Is that it?" she scoffed. "Look, maybe ideally there *would* be community peacekeepers. But this place is in no position to have that right now! Look around you! It's hell! These people need something to protect the vulnerable right now, not something that'll take time to organize."

Mike was about to argue further—but a sudden rush of movement cut off the fight.

"Move! *Move!* Marine One is landing—"

Vera and her friends were shoved back in a wave of people as the helicopter appeared and began final approach.

"Look!" Mike suddenly exclaimed. "It's starting!"

Vera whirled around to see where he was pointing. His black-clad, masked, armed friends were rushing forward, puffs of smoke in their path and sparks flying.

Behind them were the right-wing militiamen, emerged from the half-demolished Publix. Vera squinted through the smoke to see.

Her eyes widened. She had expected them to look like Nazi storm troopers, uniformed and bedecked in swastikas or other white-supremacist symbols. They were not.

Well, okay, there were some with the Confederate flag on their jackets, Vera observed. But most just looked like... people.

Some of them did wear tactical vests and helmets. Most of them carried guns. Some held poles that they'd sharpened into pikes.

But the right-wing militia mostly wore t-shirts and jackets with a variety of iconography on them. Vera saw the Punisher skull symbol, angry eagles, stylized lion heads, lots of American flag prints, and the snarling dog that she knew to be the Dog Pack symbol—the fan club of Madison Chadleigh. Was he here?

As if reading her mind, that familiar voice suddenly boomed out over a bullhorn. "*Friends! Antifa is here to try to start a fight!*" Chadeigh announced. "*Don't put yourselves in the wrong!*"

Another voice, hateful to Vera's ears, resounded over the roar of Marine One's propellers. "*Defend yourselves if you have to, but don't attack unprovoked!*" Representative CG Taverner shouted.

"What is *he* doing here?" Sohrab exclaimed. "He's from Indiana!"

Vera then remembered the message that Mike had found and displayed on their television on the eighth. "He said he would be!" she shouted. "And Chadleigh... and Gilbertson." Instantly she began looking around for the Speaker of the House. If there was any figure she would definitely recognize, it was her dad's boss. And in this moment, it did not even cross her mind to deny that Richard Mellor was her father. Was he here too, she wondered?

She couldn't find her father, but she quickly located Gilbertson.

The Speaker, Taverner, and Chadleigh had had their people set up a stage about a hundred feet away from GCCF to protest President Phillips and Vice President Romano. They were ascending this stage to address the right-wing crowd that they had summoned, security guards and bulletproof glass in front of them.

Chadleigh raised his fists to the sky. The right-wing interlopers who weren't engaged in fighting roared their approval of his signature gesture. "*Patriots!*" he roared over his bullhorn. "We are here to demand the *truth!*"

Another roar resounded from the crowd. More smoke billowed up, as the skirmishes continued.

CG Taverner then took the stage. "For Joseph P. Hitchfield, who would want us to discover *exactly* why he and his family died!"

The crowd went crazy. More smoke billowed up, more sparks and flames flew, and gunshots began erupting—accompanied by screams, as those bullets undoubtedly found marks. The smoke reached the area where Vera and her friends stood. She ducked down, hoping that if a stray bullet made it here, it would strike someone else first.

The crowd of enraged rightists and leftists surged closer. Marine One had landed now, its propellers still roaring, but the President and Vice President had not emerged. The media and the locals had already scampered away to what they undoubtedly hoped was a safe distance.

Was there a safe distance in this place?

Gilbertson, suave and mature with his salt-and-pepper hair, then got onstage. He raised his fist. "For the Floridians here, in *my district*, who are suffering! You have the right to know why! You have the right to know if you've been lied to! And we will *demand* that Phillips and Romano answer your questions!"

A sense of impending doom came over Vera. The right-wing demonstrators, whipped up to a frenzy by these people.

The black-clad associates of Mike, who might or might not officially be Antifa but were definitely armed to the hilt. The politicians swooping in. And the powder keg that the community itself already was....

Vera felt as if she was momentarily taken out of time. *This is going to be very bad very soon*, she thought, as if having a precognitive glimpse of a dark future.

But then she was abruptly brought back to the present for the worst kind of reason.

"Get off me! Let me go!"

Vera whipped her head around to find Channing, who was screaming. There were so many screams, shouts, and bangs—so many people moving in all directions, and so much smoke to obscure it all—that she couldn't immediately find her friend. But then she saw through the smoke.

A right-winger in a tactical vest with a Confederate flag emblem on his chest was grabbing at Channing, pinning her arms away from her body with one huge gloved fist and trying to force her jeans down with his other hand.

Vera and Mike reacted at once. They drew their pistols and did not hesitate. The only thought that momentarily crossed Vera's mind was *Aim for the head; don't hit Channing.* Her friend only came up to the would-be rapist's chest level.

Two tremendous blasts rocked them both, their eardrums unprotected from the explosive sounds.

The man holding Channing went limp and collapsed to the ground, pulling her down with him halfway, but she pulled free of his heavy arms to stand upright.

Vera looked at the man's head—and then looked away. There was blood—his face wasn't right—a ragged two-inch-wide exit wound had removed his right cheekbone and eye—

I just killed someone, Vera realized dully. It didn't matter that Mike had contributed. That wound was the doing of them both; a single shot from a pistol couldn't create an exit wound that large. But she knew she bore some responsibility for the death.

Oh, no, I don't, she thought suddenly. *That monster*

brought it upon himself by trying to rape Channing. I wouldn't have shot him otherwise.

Another shot popped. Mike shouted, then collapsed to the ground in a terrible spray of blood. His pistol clattered aside.

Vera could only get a brief glimpse of the gaping red wound in his chest before she felt a thud in her right shoulder and then a sudden surge of horrendous pain. Her knees bent as she crumpled. The ground was rushing up to meet her face, and she could only try to brace her fall with one arm. The other... wasn't working.

Channing, Butterfly, and Sohrab were screaming and kneeling down. Despite having nearly been raped just a minute ago, Channing was recovered enough to clutch at Vera's bleeding shoulder to try to tourniquet it as she had done for the FEMA agent five days ago. Vera wondered numbly why no one was trying to assist Mike. He was injured worse, from the looks of it....

She caught a glimpse of his face. His gaze was glassy, his eyes open but not seeing, his skin already paling. A flood of blood pooled under his body. Vera understood then.

Her arm hurt so badly. Channing was squeezing it, and that made it hurt worse even though Vera knew on some level that it was necessary to save her life. She had never experienced pain like this. And hell was unfolding around them, and Mike was dead.

She knew that she was fading to unconsciousness—the FEMA guy had done that too in their vehicle, she thought idly, her mind wandering—but she tried nonetheless to stay alert and conscious. Her gaze shifted to the stage, where Taverner, Chadleigh, and Gilbertson stood smugly behind their bulletproof glass, watching the carnage unfold around them. Fury surged in Vera's chest.

About fifty feet away from the stage, an altercation was occurring at the presidential helicopter between the President and his Secret Service detail. Vera could not say how she understood what they were saying. She supposed, vaguely, that it must be the large loudspeakers that they had set up. What was powering them? The helicopter's own electrical system? *The things we wonder about when we're on the verge of passing out*, she thought.

"Mr. President, you and the VP have to get back inside! This is out of control and we cannot secure your safety—"

"Shut up!" Harry Phillips roared. "You know what'll happen if we do? '*President and Veep flee Ground Zero chaos in fear while Gilbertson, Taverner, and Chadleigh get the riot under control*'! That'll be the headline! I'm not going anywhere—"

"This is bigger than a bad headline, Mr. President!"

"No! It's not! This is the ballgame! This moment is why I became President! Now, *get out of our way!*"

Don't, Vera pleaded with her thoughts. *Don't do this. Flee. Get the hell out of here.*

But of course, no one could hear what she was thinking.

Vera watched helplessly as the President and Vice President emerged from Marine One, almost forcing their way through the Secret Service. Harry Phillips, never photogenic, was now angrier and more disturbed than she had ever seen him. His face was lined with anxiety. Vice President Natalia Romano still sported dark bags below her eyes, and her face seemed to be more aged than it had been a few days ago as well. But she was also determined and resolute.

Get back in the helicopter! Vera thought.

She knew, preternaturally, what was about to happen—so when it did, she was shocked, but she was not *surprised.*

Gunshots pierced the air in rapid staccato. Someone had an illegal automatic weapon, apparently. *Probably several someones*, Vera thought. Several bullet dings appeared in a row on the side of Marine One.

The President and Vice President collapsed to the ground.

Screams erupted from the crowd, particularly—it seemed to Vera—the locals. The shouts coming from the right-wing militia seemed gleeful to her.

No, she thought as dark spots finally popped over her field of vision. *No. I didn't ever* actually *want—*

She passed out.

Chapter 19: Grim Reaping

Chelsea and Richard hurried out of their car and rushed to the parking garage elevator that would take them to the hospital lobby. Richard had flown to Tallahassee on the thirteenth to support his boss at the Ground Zero event, but events had turned catastrophic. Harry Phillips and Natalia Romano were both dead in a horrific double assassination, leaving Hal Gilbertson as—

Chelsea's breath caught in her chest as it hit her that her husband would be the White House Press Secretary. Hal Gilbertson had been Speaker of the House. With the loss of both the President and Vice President, *he* was next in the Constitutional line of succession.

He was President, though he had not yet officially taken the oath of office. He was already giving orders as if he had, but he had to do that. The United States could not be headless. The oath was just a formality in situations like this, though—a comforting ritual, which would be needed most in tragic ascensions. According to the Constitution, he already was the President.

She had prepared for the possibility, since he had planned to run for the office next year. She had expected that she might have to move with Richard to DC full-time. She had *not* expected it to happen *this* way, this soon.

She wondered whom Gilbertson would nominate as his Vice President. He had to pick someone, and Congress would have to confirm that person. Perhaps Corey Sandoval, Governor of Florida... but no, that might be impolitic. The VP customarily would be from a different state. Perhaps he would bury the hatchet with his primary rival, Jim Barnett Hale of Texas?

The elevator stopped at the lobby level, and Chelsea's mind returned to the reason why she was at this hospital. Vera was here. Vera had been shot in the riot.

As if reading her thoughts, Richard spoke up, frowning. "We're here because she was injured and we're her parents. It's our duty. But I've received some extremely serious news, which you need to hear from me rather than anyone else. One of her 'mates', a thug who died in the riot, brought in Antifa. That's who started the riot. It wasn't our people. They were peaceful, Gilbertson and Taverner assured me, until Antifa started attacking them. And I'm sure that's who assassinated Phillips and Romano."

"One of her *friends* invited in Antifa?" Chelsea exclaimed.

"The rich prick whose dad bought their house for them. I've been told that the father and son both have—or *had*, in the case of the dead one—Antifa ties and that they invited those goons, and brought in a ton of guns and Molotov cocktails too. And video evidence is that Phillips and Romano were assassinated by a fully automatic weapon, most likely an illegally modified AR-15."

"Oh, this is not good." Chelsea instantly understood what would likely follow. Her daughter would be criminally charged. It was nearly impossible that she wouldn't be.

"No, it's not. We'll have to distance ourselves from her. It'll be a major problem for the Sp—the *President* otherwise."

"She's our *daughter*, and I'm sure *she* didn't bring in Antifa.... She just knew someone who did, someone who owned their house, who had financial power over her... so how could she be culpable?"

"She's an accomplice after the fact. She had to have known who they were and what they were there to do, and she showed up anyway." His gaze was hard.

"*Out of the way!*"

To the shock of the Mellors and everyone else in the lobby —which included quite a lot of people, since there were still many Leonard victims hospitalized, as well as the riot survivors—three police officers stormed through the doors, bearing an older man in a bespoke suit and shined shoes that probably cost several thousand dollars. The rich man was handcuffed.

"What the—" Chelsea broke off.

"That's probably the dead rich boy's father. He's a board

member of this hospital." Richard's gaze became smug and malicious. "Good riddance. He'll die in prison for this."

"If he did fund those Antifa thugs and equip them with illegal weapons, he should," Chelsea said firmly. "But it sounds like he is the one the law should bring to account, not our daughter or her surviving friends."

"The law will do what it must do," Richard said in hard tones. "We have to stand by the President as he restores order."

Chelsea thought he was being unfair to Vera. Chelsea strongly disagreed with Vera's political views, and she didn't approve of her living with four—*three*—other people in some sort of strange harem, even if Vera said that they weren't in sexual relationships. That, in a way, made it even more bizarre and unnatural to Chelsea. But she didn't want her daughter imprisoned if Vera didn't deserve it, and it was hard for Chelsea to believe that Vera had wanted any of this disaster to happen.

She certainly wouldn't have wanted Hal Gilbertson to become president, she thought.

Richard had gone to the front desk and was now speaking to the receptionist, who seemed resistant for a moment, but then Richard said something visibly aggressive, and the woman relented. He returned to Chelsea looking grimly satisfied.

"Let's go see her."

*   *   *

A surgeon had operated on Vera's arm to remove the bullet fragments and patch it up as well as he could.

"There's a fair amount of tissue damage," the doctor reported. "I think it was a .223 round, which is usually shot from—"

"I know what that likely would have been shot from, and I know what it can do," Richard growled. "Did she lose her arm?"

"No, but she may have limited use of that arm in the future. We're hoping the nerves reconnect fully, but this kind of high-velocity impact does a lot of very messy damage. She's lucky to be alive. If it had hit the subclavian artery, she probably wouldn't be."

"Well, I'll thank God for sparing her, then," Chelsea said.

The doctor's lips thinned, and it crossed her mind that he probably didn't have much use for declarations that God had spared this or that person when he must have seen innumerable Hypercane Leonard victims in the past week and heard of even more who were not spared. She grimaced.

"She's awake and... willing to speak to you. For a few minutes."

The doctor stood aside as Chelsea and Richard entered the hospital room. He closed the door behind them.

Vera was lying on the hospital bed, hooked up to an intravenous drip. Her right arm was bandaged and splinted to limit movement.

"I'm surprised you came," Vera croaked. "Channing, Butterfly, and Sohrab... they could only come here briefly. The cops wanted to question them."

Richard glared at her. "You are in a great deal of trouble now, far worse than you ever were for spray-painting buildings and blocking traffic. Your dead friend and his dad set Antifa on Phillips and Romano and armed them with Molotovs and AR-15s illegally modified to be fully automatic, and one of the Antifa goons—we can't determine exactly who did it from the bad video that's available—assassinated them both!"

Vera gaped at them. "I don't believe that! There were right-wing militias too, and they were definitely armed! Mad Dog Chadleigh and CG Taverner had been stirring them up, too, with lies and conspiracy theories about Leonard! *They* are far more likely to have assassinated Phillips and Romano than anyone Mike contacted!"

"*President* Gilbertson has personally assured me that they were peaceful—"

She tried to sit upright in her hospital bed, falling back in pain when she couldn't. "He's a *liar!* You want to know something, *Dad?*" she snarled at him, finally owning the term, if only because she could throw it in his face this time. "You actually *are* talking to a killer. I *personally* killed someone! A right-wing militia thug died by my own hand!" She glanced at her injured arm. "The one I can't use anymore, but it did good work."

"What are you talking about?"

"I shot someone through the head, and so did Mike, and you know why? Because this fascist piece of crap was trying to *rape* our friend Channing! He was attacking her and trying to rip her pants off, and we were armed! So we shot a big hole in his skull!" She glared at her parents. "So you go tell Hal Gilbertson *that! Tell* him just how *peaceful* his fascist militiamen really were!"

Chelsea was horrified. She and Richard were very familiar with guns, of course, and they had taught Vera how to handle a gun, but they had never actually killed another human being. And now Vera was under suspicion of being an accomplice to the *assassination of the President and Vice President*, and here she was proudly confessing to killing someone!

"Oh, Vera, this is bad," Chelsea exclaimed, hurrying to her bedside. "Have you told anyone else that?"

Vera gaped at her mother in disbelief. "Are you implying that Mike and I did anything wrong? That monster was going to rape Channing, and probably kill her afterward, if we didn't act! He got what he deserved! And defending someone who cannot defend themselves is always acceptable in the law."

"But it looks so bad, Vera," Chelsea mourned. "Mike's father has been hauled out of the hospital already, under arrest for whatever he did to fund and illegally arm Antifa...."

"That's Mike's dad's problem," Vera said mulishly. "I didn't do anything wrong."

"You did, though. You should have gone to the authorities as soon as you learned that there would be illegal guns and Molotov cocktails at the Ground Zero event...."

"*What* authorities?" Vera scoffed. "The people in that

town told us about roving gangs taking over Walmart, taking over Publix—until Chadleigh's militia ran them out—some multimillionaire creating a little 'fief' for himself where people 'serve' him in exchange for 'protection,' and vigilante homeowners shooting anyone who 'looks threatening'! There *are* no authorities! It's a lawless hellhole just west of here!" She glared heatedly at them. "And Chadleigh and Taverner whipped up a bunch of right-wing loons to assassinate Phillips and Romano, hoping the chaos would hide them, and it looks like they'll get away with it. It looks like Gilbertson is going to blame us for it! Me! Did you tell him to do that, *Dad*?" she mocked.

Richard bristled. "I didn't tell him anything. The evidence speaks for itself."

Chelsea shook her head. "So it's all a right-wing conspiracy? You sound like your aunt did before landfall, when we were all watching the governors—"

"Then she was right!" Vera burst into tears. "God. What has *happened*? I didn't want this. I just wanted to make the world a better place...."

"Let's go," Richard said quietly to his wife. Chelsea gave Vera an apologetic look before heading out the door. Somehow, she knew she would not see her daughter again for many years. Even if Vera did not go to prison, they would be profoundly estranged after this. There would be no more family gatherings, no more mother-daughter visits with the aunt and uncle. However spiteful, bitter, and reluctant those visits had been, they still had taken place, because Chelsea knew that Vera still felt some modicum of affection and loyalty to her mother, if not her father.

That was probably gone now. Chelsea closed her eyes momentarily as a memory from long ago flooded her brain.

An SUV, driven by an angry drunk, ambling down a bridge.

Anne-Elise, fourteen years old, had suddenly frozen and gone numb. It was unnerving enough to garner even Chelsea's attention. Something, she realized, had broken irreparably in her sister then.

Something similar had happened just now, she knew.

The thought saddened her. *Hal Gilbertson is president,* she thought, *but my family is torn apart over it. I wanted to have a family. All these years, since my abortion, I advocated for family. That was why I decided to identify with Richard's family, adopt his politics, and champion conservative candidates like Gilbertson. Now I'm on the verge of seeing that pro-family vision succeed, but at what cost? Gilbertson isn't president because he won an election. He's president because the previous President and Vice President were assassinated. And yes, it's possible that one of his own supporters did that.* She hated admitting it, but she knew it was true.

And I may have gained a platform to advocate for family nationally, but I've lost my own. Again.

Is this really worth it?

No, her inner voice whispered. *It's not.*

But she also knew it was too late to fix anything. The time to change this terrible outcome had passed.

*   *   *

Anne-Elise gazed listlessly at the computer screen. She could not stand watching... these events... unfold on television, and she no longer wanted to be glued to her phone for streaming and social media. In fact, in recent days, she had come to like the idea of a retrogression on phones: using hers just for calls, texts, email, and emergency alerts. Nothing else.

She doubted she could achieve it, but it was worth a try. People had managed to quit various highly addictive chemical drugs through the years. This was just a psychological addiction.

There was no confirmed news about the Hurricane Hunters. A rumor had made the rounds that a bartender or waiter in New Orleans had met them, but Anne-Elise dismissed that. Why would they have gone to a bar in New Orleans? That would have been a foolishly frivolous thing to do, given the circumstances. And even if, for some reason, they had, why wouldn't Edward have called her? He had a waterproof phone case; this she knew, and they would be able to charge their devices somewhere, surely.

No, Anne-Elise had accepted that time had run out for her brother. He should have come ashore by now if he had survived. A wave had most likely capsized them, as she had feared. She couldn't stand to look at social media, where false rumors were rampant, and be tempted to purchase the counterfeit currency of false hope. The cruelty of the New Orleans bar rumor had been the final straw for Anne-Elise, the moment when she decided to delete her social apps and clean her browser history of these sites.

She glowered at the news article before her, which described the confirmation of CG Taverner as the new Vice President. That smirking, condescending little troll, summoning her to Congress, disrespecting her, and threatening the lab—all because of the ravings of a TV host.

The lab had weathered Leonard well, suffering only some roof damage. It was, after all, engineered to withstand Category Five winds, and so it had. They'd sent the employees and their families back home, had the janitorial staff clean and scrub everything down, and by the fifth day after landfall, they were back to work.

The revolutionary new fast-ignition laser design that she had thought of twelve years ago was finally working. Dr. Vince Hailey would be so pleased and proud if he could see this. The cone method of fast ignition had long had problems —placing the heavy material of the cone very close to the fusion fuel pellet caused unwanted atomic interactions to occur in the reaction, lessening its efficiency significantly— but her ideas about shielding had resolved the issues.

It had been a very challenging engineering feat to create a tiny magnetically shielded cone. The magnetic fields used in tokamak fusion chambers were very powerful, and they required very large magnets. The Intensity Labs ignition laser had multiple layers of material comprising its cone: the metal cone itself, microscopic circuits controlling the flow of electricity that activated the magnetic field, and very strong carbon shielding to protect the delicate circuits from melting from the proximity of the laser beam.

It had taken years of microcircuit design to get it right, but it was working. Energy loss in the reaction was low. They were on the verge of producing enough energy from fusion to negate the power expenditure to get the ignition laser to full power. Within days, they would have a predictable, reliable, *truly* net-positive reaction.

Anne-Elise had planned to continue development on the proton-boron reaction, a harder nut to crack than deuterium-tritium, but for their "production-line" power, things were almost ready to go. They'd have to have government approval, but Anne-Elise had not worried about that with the Phillips administration.

But with a slick-as-oil fossil-fuel backer as President and a vicious, unqualified culture warrior as Vice President, Anne-Elise now feared for the future of Intensity Labs. Government approval to enter the power grid was almost laughable to consider now. Anne-Elise was no longer sure that Intensity would even stay open.

There was apparently a ridiculous conspiracy theory making the rounds in the hard-hit areas that Intensity had somehow caused a radioactive meltdown and Leonard had sucked nuclear material into its clouds to deposit it all over the coast. But that would pass once it became apparent that the lab stood with minimal damage and no one had radiation sickness. The threat that she feared Gilbertson and Taverner posed to her lab wasn't that they believed that nonsense. No, they believed a different kind of nonsense, a conspiracy theory far subtler and less easily debunked.

It wasn't fair, she thought. The expression might be childish, but it was true. *I have dedicated much of my adult life to this,* she thought bitterly, *and now, when it's on the verge of becoming real, these malevolent fools swoop in and threaten to tear it all down.*

Gilbertson was already issuing a blizzard of executive actions to demolish things that Phillips and Romano had done. Traumatized by the horrors of Leonard's landfall, the flood of videos of the lawlessness on the Florida Gulf Coast, and the shocking double assassination, cowardly federal bureaucrats were hurriedly complying. It was sickening to Anne-Elise.

Meanwhile, CG Taverner was on social media, taunting his political enemies like the Internet bottom-feeder he was, rather than acting in accordance with the dignity of the office he held.

They had not won an election. They had no mandate to serve in the executive branch. They were in office because of a double murder and a Constitutional requirement for continuity of government. They should not be acting as if they had just received a popular-vote landslide victory. But they were.

One intrepid White House correspondent had daringly asked the new Press Secretary, Anne-Elise's own brother-in-law, about that. She read the article text again that detailed his smug, sneering, contemptuous response.

"When people voted for the President's party to take Congress in the midterm last year, they voted for the Speaker that this House chose to be next in the Constitutional line of succession. Gilbertson was already Minority Leader at the time, so he was clearly in line to be Speaker. The voters knew this. Yes, he does have a mandate."

Anne-Elise knew that Richard Mellor—indeed, the entire gang of rogues and rascals that Gilbertson and Taverner were bringing in—didn't really believe this. But she also knew that they didn't care. The country's electronics-induced short attention span was their greatest ally. In a couple of months, few would remember that they had objected to this administration's entitled behavior.

Anne-Elise recalled her final meeting as Chelsea said farewell to her before flying to DC. Richard had been there too.

"You'd better look for new work soon," he'd gloated to her, that obnoxious smirk on his face that so many of his compatriots wore. It was the Taverner smirk, the Chadleigh smirk. That was all that these people cared about, it seemed: bullying others. But then, they were Internet trolls all grown up—so to speak. Of course that was important to them.

So much for the assertions that "the Speaker's bill doesn't affect me at all," Anne-Elise thought, recalling the evening that they had all spent watching Gilbertson pontificate on that show. What a lie. You knew all along it was a lie, too.

Intensity Labs could have changed the world, but it had to start in America, and what if America doesn't want forward change anymore?

People know they're unhappy, but they are looking to the wrong solutions. They don't want to blame these eternally-damned devices they're all addicted to, nor the web of hate and ignorance that keeps them ensnared and hooked to the screens that deliver it, nor the hit of trauma after trauma that climate change has inflicted, culminating with a hypercane now. Instead they blame the doctor who's coming with medicine. They have turned against science.

What if the people of this country have become so ignorant and delusional that they no longer want to move forward? What if the fusion breakthrough simply happened too late?

A sharp knock on her front door interrupted her dark musings.

That knock was familiar. It couldn't be—no, she would not deceive herself, even for a minute—this was just a charity drive or something—

She got up to answer the door, her heart pattering in spite of herself. The door, still swollen from moisture, balked for a moment, but she managed to wrench it open.

The smell almost knocked her down at first, and she did not immediately recognize the man who stood on her doorstep with a scruffy beard. But in the next second, she did.

"Edward Kirby!" she roared, pulling him inside and slamming the door. "I thought you were dead!" She made to hug him but instantly drew back, repelled by the scent of body odor, unwashed scalp, and days-old sea salt.

He chuckled, aware of why she had pulled back. "Not dead. I thought I'd never get here, though. There are apparently no roads on the shortest approach from Louisiana, so the bus we were on went far out of the way to get here."

"'We'—meaning your crew?" She did not know how to ask him if they had all survived, which was the question she truly had.

He understood, like the twin he was. They had always had a preternatural understanding of each other's thoughts. "We all made it," he said. "It was unpleasant, but we survived. We came in at Port Sulphur and then continued on the raft to New Orleans."

She blinked. "You *were* in New Orleans?"

"Yes. Why?" Something then occurred to him. "Wait. We went to a bar to have a place to sit and watch the news. It got out, didn't it?"

"I didn't believe it could be true," she admitted. "But why didn't you call, since you did go to this bar and later booked a bus ticket?"

"I had my wallet, but my phone is dead."

"And you couldn't charge it?"

"Believe it or not, I couldn't. It seems that phone chargers are the hardest-to-find items on the entire Gulf Coast."

"I... suppose that doesn't really surprise me, now that I think about it. Well, you can charge it here. While you get a shower."

"I'll be in the bathroom for a while, probably."

"I am *extremely* glad to hear that." She managed a smile at their banter. "Edward... I don't know how much you've heard...."

"I know that Phillips and Romano were assassinated." He had heard this shocking piece of news from another bus rider. "I'm sure our brother-in-law is thrilled."

"The less said about Richard Mellor, the better." Her expression darkened. "That was the main item, but there are several things you need to know. Things involving Vera, but also, things about the Hurricane Center... and about the absolute, well, hypercane-level shitstorm of lies and conspiracy theories that raged while you were at sea. It's still raging, and now, people at the highest level support it. But for now, just get cleaned up. I'll catch you up later."

* * *

He emerged from the bathroom an hour later, scrubbed pink and clean-shaven again. Physically, he was back to normal, but Anne-Elise noticed something in his eyes that had not been there before, even after that hideous walk home over thirty years ago, their parents' violent end, or the failure of his two marriages: a dark, haunted look, the look of someone who had experienced things that he could not bring himself to describe.

With that in mind, she knew not to ask him about his experiences. It must have been harrowing beyond words to have to bring the plane down in a storm, knowing that the life of everyone aboard was in his hands, and also knowing that he had been the one to push most for the flight to occur in the first place. If he wanted to talk about these things—or anything that came later—she would leave it up to him.

He yawned. "I meant to talk to you, but I'm really tired. The last time I slept in a real bed was the evening of the third. Very early morning of the fourth too, I guess. Chandra called me back to the office because Leonard had rapidly intensified to Category Five"—he laughed at how quaint that sounded now—"and then I worked the forecast desk all day, living on coffee, and flew the storm that evening. I slept... sort of, a few hours at a time... on the raft, and on the bus, but—"

"You don't have to explain," Anne-Elise assured him, pushing him toward the small guest room. "Get some rest."

* * *

His clothes were in rough shape, but she had no men's clothing in her home, so she decided to put these in the laundry overnight so that he would at least have something clean to wear. He slept for thirteen hours. The next day was,

306

mercifully, a Saturday, so Anne-Elise woke up the next morning at nine, as she did on weekends. She let him continue to sleep as she made coffee and breakfast.

He finally emerged from the guest room, wearing the freshly washed clothes that she had put in front of his door, and trudged into the kitchen.

"I haven't wanted to think about it," he acknowledged over breakfast, "and I actually think I went into deep sleep as soon as my head hit the pillow, so I didn't have the opportunity to—"

"To upset yourself by doomscrolling?"

He nodded shamefacedly. "I know I shouldn't do it, but the phone was charged enough by then that I could use it. I'm glad I didn't. I need to call the boss, but that can wait a little longer. Someone else in the crew might already have reached out to him."

"You should still call him. But before you do, you need to know everything that's happened. And I'd rather you heard it from me than from the thrice-damned Internet."

She then caught him up on what had happened on land since then: the vicious attack on the Hurricane Center from both political and mainstream media, the Gulf Coast governors' malicious negligence, the ensuing violent lawlessness in hard-hit areas, the rampant conspiracy theories, the falling-out with Chelsea and Vera, and the involvement of Vera's dead friend in inviting armed leftists to the Ground Zero scene knowing full well that armed right-wingers would be there too.

"*Were* they Antifa?" Edward asked.

"Who knows?" Anne-Elise said, throwing her hands up. "That's what the right calls every militant leftist who picks up a weapon. Maybe they were; maybe they weren't. It doesn't really even matter. That's just a term that people like Mad Chad use to demagogue."

Edward considered. "It's not impossible that one of them could have assassinated Phillips and Romano, but odds are, it was one of the people that Taverner and Chadleigh brought in. From what you tell me, Vera's hothead friend wanted people who could fight the right-wing militia. That was why he and his dad brought them, to fight 'fascists.' Chadleigh and Taverner are the ones who stirred up the right against Harry Phillips."

"That's my conclusion too—and Gilbertson used them as his stalking horse, in my opinion. He got to look slick and handsome while they got down in the mud for him—not that they objected, of course. They are true products of this time. They love the mud."

"Do you think...." Edward broke off, that haunted look in his eyes darkening yet further. "Here's what bothers me about all this, what I can't look away from. Hypercane Leonard was an in-your-face, impossible-to-ignore proof that climate change *had* to be addressed. The conditions that hypercanes require to form *cannot develop* without an asteroid or comet strike, a major underwater volcanic eruption, or extreme climate change. And this being the mid-twenty-first century, we have enough around-the-clock full-earth observations that we can cross two off the list for Leonard." He glowered at the dark TV screen. "And Harry Phillips was headed for defeat in the polls, but then this storm hit, providing him with an opportunity to shepherd a recovery, comfort a shocked and grieving nation, and bring the country into a new era for climate resilience and clean energy."

Anne-Elise nodded sadly. "With Intensity and the rest of the clean-power sector leading the way."

"It could have happened like that. So it makes me wonder... was there a sudden concerted effort to make damn sure that it did *not* happen like that? A 'break glass in case of emergency' moment for climate deniers? Everything that could go wrong did. The Gulf state governors conspired together to screw over their own people, people like Taverner and Chadleigh whipped up conspiracy theories so determinedly that the mainstream media felt they 'had' to cover them, and then this catastrophe at Ground Zero."

"It has occurred to me too. I can't decide, though. I think

there was certainly enough human stupidity and proud ignorance on display that there didn't need to be a conspiracy."

"They're not mutually exclusive." He sighed, rubbing his forehead. "If I hadn't taken that plane into Leonard, they wouldn't have had *that* point to demagogue about."

"But then they would have claimed that the drone reports were unreliable without human measurement to confirm them. They always would have found some excuse."

"That's true." He chuckled bleakly. "You know, I have the data box. Not sure why I felt the urge to keep it. I guess I really did want a souvenir or a trophy, just like Dr. Chandra said."

"What data box? The plane's black box?"

"No. So," he explained, "you know how the planes transmit observational data in real-time back to Miami? And it instantly goes on the Internet?"

"Yes."

"Well, in case a transmission got corrupted or lost somehow, we needed a backup record. That's what this is. It's a weatherproof box with single-use, write-only media inside. And the instruments themselves write directly to it. Tampering—whether environmental or human—is impossible." He picked up his backpack, which rested on the floor. "It's in there. Proof of what Leonard was. Guess I'll return it to the NHC when I head back."

"You're still motivated to fight?"

He raised his eyebrows. "What, you aren't? There's an election next year. Gilbertson and Taverner will have to answer for what they're doing, and they'll have to do it very soon. Yes, I'm motivated to fight."

Anne-Elise laughed darkly. "You're very optimistic."

"They can't cancel elections."

"They can destroy an awful lot before the election."

Chapter 20: A New Era Dawns

After breakfast, Edward remembered that he needed to call Dr. Chandra. He trudged back to the guest room to find his now fully-charged phone. His eyebrows lifted at the sight of a torrent of text messages.

Some of them were backlogged from his time at sea and on the bus, but others had arrived overnight and this morning. Judging the latter more important, he scrolled through the messages.

Edward, no one can get in contact with the boss, Nadya Cass had reported. **Phone calls go straight to voicemail and he doesn't respond to texts.**

The other recent messages were all from his crew—not a single one from Chandra—and they were all similar. No one could get a hold of the National Hurricane Center director.

"What the bloody hell?" Edward muttered. Why would Chandra be completely inaccessible *now*, of all times? He continued scrolling through his texts, then opened his email.

"Huh. That's strange."

There were a few frantic messages and hopeful emails from his colleagues in the aftermath of the crash. These dwindled as the days piled up. But after the thirteenth, there was not a single email or text from *anyone* in Miami. Not Chandra, not Fisher, not Huang—no one. There were not even any messages from the past day, when the crew would have been able to inform their coworkers of their survival.

That was *odd*. That was really freaking bizarre, Edward thought—and as he headed back to the kitchen, a very dark explanation presented itself as to why it might be.

Surely not, he thought, sitting down. *Surely these—people—now in charge aren't putting gag orders on the Hurricane Center.*

Anne-Elise was not in the kitchen anymore. She had moved to the living room. Edward sat at the eat-in counter, brooding, his thoughts becoming darker by the second.

It's not just the boss. I don't have anything from anyone at

NHC since the 13th, he texted to Cass. **Do any of you?**

A minute elapsed. Then the message appeared ominously.

Nope.

Edward stared at the word, wondering if he would sound like yet another paranoid conspiracy theorist if he asked the question that was practically exploding out of his mind right now. He decided to just chance it. **Are you thinking what I'm thinking?**

Two minutes. Then—**Don't know what else it could be.**

I feel crazy even thinking it, he said.

Me too. But the whole country has gone crazy, so maybe this is normal.

Edward hesitated again. **Are all of you safe? Able to contact each other?**

Cartwright and I are at her place. Evans is hanging out here too. We warned her not to go home alone until we get an answer about WTF is going on at NHC.

Edward could hardly believe the conversation he was holding. The implication, of course, was that Dr. Evans—a small single woman in her twenties—might be grabbed in her own condo and "disappeared" because she knew the truth about Leonard. He could not believe they were saying this. It seemed deranged. Edward kept shaking his head, convinced that the days on that raft and the surreal events on the Gulf Coast had addled his reason. People did sometimes go paranoid and lose their grip on reality if they were away from civilization for too long. Surely that was what had happened to them all.

But if this really was just all in their heads, then why, *why*, weren't their colleagues at the Hurricane Center replying to their texts or taking their calls?

The guys are all holed up with MacLean or Morales in their homes, Cass continued. **Nobody wants to be alone. We're way ahead of you, Cap.**

I slept in, he pleaded.

Better wake up now.

Edward winced. That was dark. He took a deep breath and

decided, at last, to go into the living room where his sister sat.

*   *   *

At noon today, Hal Gilbertson was giving his first speech since being sworn in. In past years, noon on a Saturday might have been an odd time for a presidential address, but anyone could stream it whenever they wanted, so timing of the live event did not matter.

Last night, when he had announced his intention, the credulous media had already decided that the speech would "calm the nation's frazzled nerves" hours before he had even spoken a word. Anne-Elise doubted that, but it seemed that they would declare it had happened anyway, no matter what reality might be—until their assertion *became* reality simply because people all assumed *they* were the odd ducks and conformed to what they were told.

She was holding the remote when Edward entered the living room. He marveled at this; she had a voice assistant like most people, but sometimes she still wanted to have manual control.

"I don't want to say it," she said to him, understanding that look in his face without needing to ask.

"'We're conversing with our devices instead of human beings'?" Edward said, a hint of mockery in his words for that old platitude.

She laughed darkly. "There are individual exceptions, but in the general case, I don't think conversing more with other human beings is the solution. Om... *the assistant*"—she carefully avoided activating it by saying its name—"isn't nearly as big a problem as, in fact, all those *conversations* that human beings have with each other. The past two weeks have proven that beyond all doubt. All the conspiracy theories, lies, hate, and willfully arrogant stupidity? Conversations between humans."

He winced again. "Fair point."

"These devices have allowed people to *have* all these 'conversations' far more widely than we otherwise could

312

have, to be sure. They've encouraged us to 'speak' the dumbest, most worthless thoughts that we have to a vast audience all over the world, and they allow and encourage that audience to provide instant reinforcement for these thoughts. But ultimately, the human brain, not an AI program, is responsible for each and every one."

"That's bleak... but I can't really argue with it."

"So it's not about devices. I just don't want to utter *this specific request*." She flipped to the stream of Hal Gilbertson's speech.

"Ah," Edward said, understanding now.

The new executive took to the stage. He did look as photogenic as Richard had always claimed, Anne-Elise begrudged. He was inherently handsome and also knew how to work the camera to his advantage. She supposed that this country would give him five extra approval points just for that.

"From ashes and dust, a new era now dawns," Gilbertson declared, "and the clouds will always part to reveal the sun!"

Edward barked out a bitter laugh. "And then you get fried to a crisp. I exaggerate, of course, but UVC is now going to reach the surface in places—and a lot more UVB than people are used to—and it will be very bad until the ozone regenerates itself."

"There will indeed be an ozone hole?"

"I'll need to check the monitoring instruments, but I'd be shocked if there wasn't one. In that plane...." He blanched for a moment, remembering that the climb and the stall were the reason why he had lost control. "Leonard towered into the stratosphere. It definitely would have been able to inject water vapor into the ozone layer."

"Bring it on. Maybe some of these idiots will stand under it to 'prove a point' and get cancer. But no," she instantly corrected herself, "that won't matter. Someone will tell them that the government irradiated them with secret technology to silence their 'truth-telling,' and they'll believe *that*."

He raised his eyebrows at that vicious cynicism, but he

did not respond.

They continued to watch the new president, his smug, cocky young vice president standing next to him.

"I ask the nation to observe a moment of silence for Harry Phillips and Natalia Romano," Gilbertson said, pausing. Taverner continued to smirk.

"Even in a moment where one should be respectful, he can't bring himself to say 'President' and 'Vice President,'" Anne-Elise observed bitterly. Edward sighed yet again.

"Federal law enforcement are currently reviewing footage, but we expect to charge members of Antifa with numerous felonies, including seditious conspiracy, terrorism, and various gun crimes. State officials may also issue state-level gun charges," Gilbertson said. "These thugs came to Ground Zero to attack a peaceful event that the now-Vice President and I helped organize to protest the previous administration's response to Hurricane Leonard."

Hurricane Leonard, Anne-Elise thought, noting that. Edward glowered as well. That couldn't be accidental.

"These militant leftist thugs had a long history of violently attacking moderate Democrats," Gilbertson continued, "of which we have seen evidence in video footage. Recently, in fact, some of their associates held an illegal protest, blocking Florida commuters en route to work, and deliberately singled out Phillips-Romano supporters to verbally assault. One person who took part in that protest, who was killed at the Ground Zero assassination and riot, was in fact the one who —with his father—invited and illegally armed Antifa. They brought these people in with the intention of attacking peaceful, patriotic Americans. But I assure you, my fellow citizens, justice *will* be done."

Disgust filled Anne-Elise at this. CG Taverner was smirking like the ass that he was, and in that moment she became absolutely convinced that they knew full well that one of *their* "peaceful patriotic Americans" had been the assassin.

You don't deserve to be charged with crimes that you didn't commit, Vera, she thought about her niece, *and unlike this jerk, I do actually hope that justice is done. I hope that you aren't convicted of anything you didn't do. But you've probably ruined your life nonetheless. And you did bring this upon yourself by treating allies as enemies and being a consummate hypocrite about your stated beliefs.*

"And now, my administration must turn to the Leonard recovery," Gilbertson continued. "We will be working closely with state partners in the affected states—"

"Ah yes, now that *you* are there, Sandoval and his gang will work with the federal 'gubmint,'" Anne-Elise said acidly.

"—but enough questions have been raised about Leonard's intensity that we have decided that we must also immediately undertake a comprehensive review of the storm."

"So is *this* why nobody at the NHC is responding to my texts?" Edward wondered.

Anne-Elise turned to him with raised eyebrows. "*What?* Nobody at all?"

"Not one soul, and the other members of my crew have said the same thing. It's like they've been put under a gag order... or had their devices seized."

As if to confirm his guess, Gilbertson said, "I have therefore ordered the creation of a Blue Ribbon Storm Reanalysis Panel. Vice President Taverner will be the chairman. The panel will be staffed with independent investigators, experts in computer science and engineering, and they will have full authority to forensically inspect all National Hurricane Center computer systems with data pertaining to Hurricane Leonard, as well as employees' government-issued and personal devices. Panel members will be looking specifically for evidence of data tampering."

Edward sank back, stunned. "They're really doing this. They're going to drag the center through the mud—" He broke off. "Well, they'll see for themselves that there was no tampering. Let them look. They're not going to find the conspiracy they think they will. Then they'll be the ones who will have to apologize to the nation for persecuting and defaming the real heroes in this disaster."

"You're very optimistic," Anne-Elise said again. "It seems to me that the point of this is to *fabricate* evidence of tampering."

"I think they actually believe there's a conspiracy," he disagreed. "I think they're high on their own supply, Taverner especially. They'll look awfully embarrassed once their forensic computer analysts tell them that there's nothing wrong."

"Then are you going to turn over that data box that you salvaged?" she said pointedly.

He grimaced. No, on second thought, he didn't really want to do that anymore. That data box contained an unalterable record of the proof that Leonard was a hypercane. If Anne-Elise was right in her cynicism, and these people did tamper with the NHC's computers, the box might soon be the *only* such record. There was another data box in the plane that dispatched the drones that had provided storm observations from the time of the crash until landfall, but if Anne-Elise was right, these people would "make it disappear."

Edward understood the political and scientific significance of having accurate data, but a part of him—the part that had, in Chandra's words, "swaggered around" the office, pleaded to fly Leonard, and exuberantly cheered the dire NHC advisory proclaiming it a hypercane—wanted to protect "his" storm from being denied and dismissed. Leonard was the first observed hypercane, and Edward had gotten up close and personal with it in a way that few still alive today—only his crew, in fact—could boast. In Edward's mind, the storm genuinely deserved its human name, and he was keeping its records safe like someone might preserve the photos and correspondence of a deceased relative. He knew he was anthropomorphizing it, but he couldn't entirely help it. His work was truly his passion.

But at the same time, the practical consideration of scientific integrity remained. That was perhaps a better reason to hold onto the box, he supposed.

"Yeah. Didn't think so," Anne-Elise said, interrupting his

thoughts. "And I'm not advising you to. Hold onto it like you're a political refugee escaping over the Berlin Wall."

"Well, that's dark. But yeah... I think I'll just hang onto this. They have no way of knowing that it wasn't lost with the plane, unless someone in the crew tells them. And I don't think the crew will do that. They texted me that they're all basically hunkering down."

"We are also going to reassess the question of whether the government should, in fact, be conducting weather forecasting and research at all," Gilbertson said.

Edward gaped again, his face paling at this bomb. "They *wouldn't—*" He broke off once more, eyes wide with shock as the magnitude of the political disaster sank in fully.

"My view is that, while this is an important function, it is one that states should do. Why should Florida fund forecasts for wildfires in California? Obviously, as Hurricane Leonard proved, Florida's needs and California's needs are different."

"Oh, right," Edward scoffed sarcastically, "because the weather systems that affect California stop at the state border! That front that intensified and picked up Leonard *totally* didn't cross state boundaries, not at all!"

"The findings of the Blue Ribbon Reanalysis Panel should also be taken into account," Gilbertson said. "If it finds that the federal operation was in any way deceptive or fraudulent, that is a strong data point in favor of turning weather forecasting over to states. There could be no conceivable motive for Florida, for instance, to deceive its own people about the magnitude of a storm."

"*We are Floridians!*" Edward roared indignantly. "Many of us were born here, and those of us who weren't still moved here, settled here, and *became* Floridians! That's how it is everywhere!"

"Yes, but are you listening to this, Edward?" Anne-Elise asked him anxiously. "I mean *really* listening? They've already determined what this 'panel' will find."

He stared blankly at the screen. "It does sound like that." He heaved a breath. "Yeah. I'm going to hold onto that data box like it's a priceless treasure. They can put out their predetermined lie, and when they do, the crew and I will put out the truth."

Anne-Elise decided not to respond. This still seemed far too optimistic to her. She hoped she was wrong.

*   *   *

A vast stretch of coastline was virtually annihilated, lawlessness and barbarism were rampant in the areas where people did still survive, a toxic cloud darkened a whole region, urgent answers were needed about whether the sun would be a menace for certain areas soon, and the nation—or at least, a part of it—was grieving the assassinations of the previous president and vice president. So naturally, the new executives decided to appear on *Attack Dog* that night.

Anne-Elise did not want to watch this show. She blamed Chadleigh more than almost anyone else for the political disaster, and she thought it was disgraceful that these people deemed it appropriate to appear on this show in a time like this. Were people truly so obsessed with entertainment and sound bites that they had lost all sense of when that fixation was improper and callous?

But it seemed to be the only way to hear what they had to say, and, as angry and despondent as she expected their remarks to make her, she did need to know what they were planning. So she reluctantly loaded that horrible show at prime time to watch. At least Edward was there... and at least their *other* relatives weren't.

The bass drums and snarling dogs assaulted her ears. The camera panned down to the set, which seemed ridiculous now. Props of a doghouse, a fence, a "BEWARE OF DOG" sign, and a bulldog model. Such laughable affectation, but millions ate it up.

Edward was glowering as the new president and vice president appeared on stage. Gilbertson, suave as ever, waved to the audience. Taverner had a look of malice in his young face. Both twins wondered what that portended.

"Mr. President!" Chadleigh exclaimed as they sat down. An

extra chair had been added for Taverner, since there were now two guests. "Mr. Vice President! I cannot tell you how long I've wanted to speak those words to you!"

Nope, no sense of propriety at all, Anne-Elise thought.

Gilbertson chided his host. "Now, let's remember the occasion," he said—but to the twins, it sounded insincere, a false assurance as deceitful as their banter two weeks ago about how they didn't really mean to call their foes "lizard people."

"Of course," Chadleigh said, sounding as scripted as Anne-Elise had anticipated.

Taverner then spoke up, his voice ponderous and grave. "For most of the nation's history, in times of national crisis and trauma, the political leadership has tried to transcend politics and speak for—and to—all Americans," he began. This tone from him was very strange to Anne-Elise's ears, and she instantly was on her guard.

Then he broke into that hateful smirk. "Well, I can't speak for how anyone thought in historical times, but *today*, that's a mug's game," he proclaimed. Leering at the camera as Chadleigh laughed, applause sounded in the background, and whistles erupted in the midst of it, he continued, "The President and I have taken office with half the country insistent that we have no right to be here. We followed the Constitutional order, but our opponents seem to have a problem with that. They repeat the baseless conspiracy theory that it was one of *our* supporters who assassinated Phillips and Romano! Our supporters were there to hear us speak—and I include you in that, Mad Dog—and protest Phillips peacefully!"

"Of course," Chadleigh agreed.

"You and I have some things in common," Taverner continued to the show host. "Your show is *Attack Dog*, and as Vice President, it's conventionally my role to be the attack dog for the President. I see that he's looking at me reproachfully," he said to Gilbertson. "I'm doing this—I'm saying these things—so that you don't have to."

Gilbertson managed a smile. "CG mentioned conspiracy theories. Unfortunately, many are flying about the assassination *and* the storm. Our administration wants to reassure Americans regarding Leonard, as our predecessors failed to do, and there are two theories in particular about the storm that I must address."

"Oh, so this is where you try to make yourself sound 'reasonable' and rein in the chaos you cheered on when it was useful to you. You have this all worked out, don't you?" Anne-Elise snarled.

"First, the idea that the government modified Leonard to become more intense. That 'Project Stormfury,' an endeavor from the 1970s to weaken hurricane eyewalls, continued in secret. Nothing about this is true. The word 'hypercane' was coined in 1988 in a research paper that was unrelated to Stormfury. Hurricanes are just too big and powerful for any human technology to modify them. I think you yourself worried about this one, Mad Dog?"

"Well, since *you* are saying this, Mr. President, I trust *you.*"

"Thank you. Viewers out there—the government did not modify this storm. Now, the second conspiracy theory."

Then, demonstrating the fact that this was scripted, a still of a very familiar building appeared on the heretofore blank television screen on the set: Intensity Labs Advanced Fusion Testbed.

"There is a lot of fear that this facility had a nuclear meltdown," he said, "and that radioactive material got sucked into Leonard and deposited all over the Florida panhandle. This is not true. I repeat—*this is not true.* Could we switch to the drone footage?"

The still flipped to a video of the lab taken from a drone during... well, what passed for daylight now. It was clearly taken after the storm; tree and roof damage showed up on the footage, and Leonard's winds had scooted several parked cars around the lot, causing some minor fender-benders. But it was equally clear that the lab had not suffered a nuclear incident.

"This lab is intact, and there has been no meltdown," Gilbertson said firmly. "I personally want to reassure everyone on this point. It's a fusion lab and *can't* have a meltdown. That only happens in fission reactors. Leonard's rains were not radioactive, and neither is the cloud of dust that hangs over the Gulf Coast."

"And I suspect, now, that they're going to double down on the conspiracy theory that the NHC falsified data," Edward growled.

He was very quickly proven correct. Gilbertson continued, "We have enough real concerns without worrying about false ones. While the dust certainly did come from Leonard's debris, questions remain, as I said at noon today, about the storm's real intensity. That's what the Vice President's Blue Ribbon Panel will look into."

"Could you tell us more about that? Mr. Vice President?" Chadleigh turned back to Taverner.

"The panel will be independent, of course—we aren't going to influence its findings—"

"Then that means you won't need to. I'm sure you'll pick people who know to say exactly what you want to hear," Anne-Elise said.

"Leonard was certainly a very strong hurricane," Taverner continued. "Probably 250 miles an hour. I don't dispute *that*."

"Could winds of 250 create this debris cloud?" Chadleigh asked.

Taverner struck the obvious softball. "Of course they could. Tornadoes can level buildings down to the foundation and pulp the debris with winds of just 210. This storm very easily could have had winds of 250. But four hundred or higher?" He shook his head. "I have personally seen an engineer assert that it's impossible for winds at the earth's surface to go past approximately three hundred. Friction becomes too strong."

"It certainly is *not* impossible," Edward said heatedly. "Friction does produce drag, but a strong pressure gradient is still the biggest influence on wind speeds."

"So why would the Hurricane Center have claimed that Leonard was so much stronger than it was?" Chadleigh asked.

Another softball. "Well, two things, I think! First, to hype the claim of climate change. Then, after that crazy pilot downed the plane, the Hurricane Center realized they had a public-relations disaster on their hands, so rather than admit that their joyriding cowboy pilot cost the government millions of dollars, they doubled down on this wild intensity claim—this word, 'hypercane'—to lift blame off his shoulders, and hence their own."

Edward groaned, putting his hands over his face. "I didn't want this. I never wanted this. I just wanted to fly that storm. And I'm glad I did! I have the data box, and it looks like I'll need to keep it safe from these vandals."

Taverner was still speaking. "But the climate motive came first, of course. They were already claiming insane intensities before the plane went down. The thing is, we can engineer structures to stand up to 250-mile-an-hour winds. Tornado shelters can do that. So the climate-alarmism syndicate—I have to hand it to you, my friend, for coining that term a couple of weeks ago—had to have something scarier. Something that nobody could survive."

"If that's the case," Edward snapped, "then where *are* these survivors? How come no one has emerged from the area where the eyewall passed? *Because anyone who didn't leave was killed. Because the winds were three and four hundred miles an hour.*"

"They're in a bind," Anne-Elise agreed. "They needed the weather-modification or the nuclear conspiracy theory to account for that. But they knew they couldn't maintain the nuclear one, and they knew they would be called upon to 'prove' the Stormfury one, now that Gilbertson is the president. These theories were useful to them to whip up a violent mob, but now they would be a problem. That's why Gilbertson is trying to kill these conspiracies now."

"What about the video of Joseph Hitchfield, streamed live from his tornado shelter?" Chadleigh asked. "I shared it, of course, and you seemed to endorse it at the fateful event in Florida."

"I endorsed the implication that there were unanswered questions about it," Taverner said. "Of course, Mr. Hitchfield was incorrect that there was a nuclear strike. He was in the eye of the storm; he would have been terrified and spoken whatever came to his mind in those final moments." He shook his head sadly. "The shelter that he used was rated for winds of 250. It's possible Leonard exceeded that—though not, of course, to the extent that the Hurricane Center claimed. But even if the winds were just 275 briefly, that would do it." He smirked, unable to maintain a facade of grief even for one of his own supporters. "The problem is that the claims the NHC made were so outrageous that they ceased to be believable, and people like Hitchfield, who saw through it, disregarded *everything* they said as a result. If you're going to tell a lie, at least make it plausible!"

"But that cuts back to what you said about fear-mongering," Chadleigh pointed out. "If the lie is plausible, it isn't as scary."

"Exactly. The point is, we really need to get to the bottom of just how strong Leonard truly was. These questions must be answered."

"There have been reports that at least some of the Hurricane Hunters made it ashore," Gilbertson said. "We'll definitely be tracking down the truth about this and questioning them if these people are who they claim to be. They may have important information to provide the Vice President's Blue Ribbon Panel."

"I'll speak to your panel when hell freezes over," Edward snarled.

"Yes, we'll certainly be looking into these reports of their survival," Taverner agreed.

"Well, as long as they aren't part of a cover-up themselves," Chadleigh said dubiously.

"The computer forensics experts we're bringing on will be responsible for the panel's core findings," Gilbertson said.

"Any testimony will be secondary."

"Naturally," Chadleigh said. He faced the camera. "Well—that's all we have with the President and Vice President, I'm afraid! They must get back to work for the American people. But what a relief it is to have people in charge who are looking out for *true* Americans' best interests, at last!"

With that, the interview ended. Anne-Elise switched off the television, disgusted, furious, and frightened.

Edward was silent for a while. She then remembered that he had been at sea for days and then cut off from the world until his phone was usable again. She had been hearing this sort of thing for over a week, but it was new to him. He needed time to assimilate it.

But finally she had to say something. "Edward, you know that if they do have your NHC colleagues' phones, they already know you're alive, because you have been calling and texting them."

He blanched. "Shit."

"This 'panel' is not going to be honest. Its outcome is already decided. I joked about going over the Berlin Wall this morning, but you and your crew might *actually* need to disappear. I don't know... maybe they'll be okay... but you have that box, and you're their scapegoat, the 'joyriding, reckless cowboy pilot.' You'll be charged with something if you stick around. You shouldn't be, but they'll invent something."

He sighed yet again, rubbing his forehead. "Well... unless they've seized my plane, it's still in Miami. I suppose I could fly to Mexico or the Bahamas until the election next year. And don't tell me I'm 'being very optimistic,'" he added as she opened her mouth. "I'm an innocent man, but I'm considering fleeing the country to protect myself from false charges and protect scientific data from politically-motivated destruction."

She closed her mouth. She could not argue with that.

*   *   *

Anne-Elise was paranoid that someone would track her phone signal—or her car—but she supposed that she'd be questioned anyway. She would just say that she had driven her brother to his home. Any "crime" they might charge him with would not be such that her driving her brother home would make her an accessory.

It was a long drive from Tallahassee to Miami, and Edward did not want to have the kind of "long conversation" that implied that it might be the last for many years. He truly believed—or wanted to believe—that he would be back in the States in a year and a half. She hoped he would be right about the election and that Gilbertson and Taverner would pay a price for their actions. But hope had not served her very well the past two weeks, so she did not trust it.

Edward "parked" his plane at a private general-aviation airstrip when it was in Miami. It was fortunate that he had it there, rather than at the international airport, because then he would have to get clearance and announce his presence. Here, he could just take off in the dead of night. He'd show up on flight radars, but hopefully he would be well to the west— or east, if he went to the Bahamas—by the time anyone figured out who it was.

Despite her warnings that there might be alarms or devices planted, he insisted on visiting his home first to pick up some of his belongings. She remained in the car.

He emerged with three packed bags, his laptop, and a look of profound sadness on his face.

"No signs of a search," he reported. "And I don't think they would have left the laptop if they'd been there."

"You'd better be sure they don't have it bugged."

"Anne-Elise, they would have *seized* it, not bugged it. I guess even these goons have to follow the law and get a search warrant, and they haven't charged any of us with anything... yet."

She sighed. "I hope you're right."

They continued to the airstrip, Anne-Elise making sure to turn off her phone and switch off her car satellite connections for this part. This actually *might* make her an accomplice, since it indicated Edward's intent to flee rather than simply go home.

It was dark when they arrived at the small hangar. The plane was there, pristine and unmolested. Edward breathed a sigh of relief as he got in. He placed the data box on the copilot's seat reverently. "You know," he said to her just before he started the engines, "I took some photos of Leonard's eyewall when I was in it. They should still be on my phone." He smiled weakly. "I haven't even thought to look at them. Maybe when I get to Nassau, I'll do that... and try to remember how it felt."

"You've decided on the Bahamas?"

"It's much closer than Cancun."

"True."

"Maybe the next time we see each other, I'll have found a hot islander wife. Third time could be the charm."

She groaned. "Edward, I have no idea if you're serious... but if you are, you do you, I guess."

"That's the best thing any of us can do."

"Yeah." She choked up as she hugged him, she hoped not for the last time. "Stay safe. I know you probably shouldn't text me...."

"I'll send a message over a secure app when I'm there."

"Oh, that would work." Relief passed over her. "Good." She heaved a weary sigh. "Take care. Of that box, but also of yourself."

"You too."

*   *   *

The drive from Miami back to Tallahassee seemed even longer than the one down. Perhaps it was because she was alone now. She stopped overnight midway and checked her phone. She opened up the encrypted message app first, smiling at Edward's message of a safe touchdown in the islands. To her surprise, there were no texts or calls from her sister.

She tormented herself along the long, dreary trip with thoughts of her pretty Space Age Revival townhouse being sacked while she was away. Of agents waiting in ambush to arrest her—and she didn't derive any comfort from the fact that she had not done anything wrong; she had simply driven her brother to his home, and he had not been charged with anything. That, she feared, would not make the slightest difference.

At last, she turned down her quiet street, scanned her home, and took a deep breath as she parked. She had to do this, so might as well get it over with. She unlocked the door.

Everything was as she had left it. There were no signs of searches or planted cameras. She would go through the place thoroughly, but she didn't think anyone had been here when she was gone.

Then she steeled herself to look over her call log and texts. One message after another from her sister stared back at her.

Anne-Elise, Richard says that the President thinks Edward is alive and that you may have seen him. Is this true?

Anne-Elise scowled and continued reading.

Sister, I'm not trying to get him in trouble! The VP's Panel just wants to question everyone. That's all. It's not like Vera's situation!

I promise, Edward is not in trouble yet, but he's acting like he has something to hide. Have you seen him?

If Edward comes forward, the President may privately urge the attorney general to drop all Vera's charges except concealed carrying without a permit. Which is FL, not federal. Please respond.

That last message was from just two hours ago. Anne-Elise was thoroughly steamed now. It was hard for her even to describe all that was wrong with this. —That this worthless "administration" was so determined to attack science that it would drop charges related to an *assassination*, for one. —For another, that the President would interfere with the Justice Department so brazenly. —Third, that Vera had been charged with anything other than illegally carrying in the first place. —And finally, that these supposed pro-family advocates— Chelsea included—would actually threaten one member of a family in order to make a collaborator out of another, at the expense of his scientific integrity.

Anne-Elise typed up her message.

Yes, Edward was here. He had come ashore with his crew in NOLA and finally got to Tally. He wanted to go home, so I drove him to Miami. I'm disgusted that you'd think he "has something to hide." He survived a plane crash in a hypercane! Survived days at sea! And if Taverner wants him to say that Leonard wasn't a hypercane, he'll be disappointed. It was, and Edward is a scientist first and last, as he'd say himself. He will never lie about science for politics.

Frankly, "sister," I'd tell you to go to hell except that you're already there, because you made your own. And so am I, for the same reason. One condemned soul can't pull the other out. You were right: We do bring our fates upon ourselves.

She hesitated for a moment before sending the message.

Chapter 21: Climate Justice

September 18.

Now that Edward had disappeared, it seemed that all chances for leniency—or, in Anne-Elise's opinion, *fairness* and *justice*—for Vera Mellor had vanished.

The Justice Department, with its new political appointees running things, was announcing charge after charge against Mike's father, and Anne-Elise believed that he did deserve some of them. But the Justice Department had not actually accused any specific person of assassinating Harry Phillips and Natalia Romano, and Anne-Elise suspected that if the administration believed it *could* win a conviction on those charges against one of the leftists—justly or not—it would have charged someone. Instead, the charges were all gun felonies, seditious conspiracy, and terrorism-related.

However, not a single person from the right-wing group was charged with anything, even a gun crime. It was too brazen, Anne-Elise thought. They could have charged someone from "their" crowd to at least give the appearance of fairness and justice. That they hadn't was essentially proof positive to her that these were political prosecutions. It also circumstantially suggested that they knew the assassin *had* been one of their crowd.

But as the daughter of the President's press secretary, Vera was one of the best-known figures from the fatal riot. The media were obsessed with her case and the "family drama" involved.

She did have a lawyer, and the person was not a public defender. A nonprofit had agreed to fund their legal defense, insistent that the charges against GCCF's surviving members were excessive and that Vera and the law firm's other three clients—her housemates—were innocent of everything except, in Vera's case, the state-level concealed-carry charge. Her lawyer was trying to enter a plea bargain to get the other charges dropped in exchange for a guilty plea on that one.

Anne-Elise hoped it would work. Maybe the justice system

wasn't corrupted beyond hope. Perhaps. It would certainly be one in the eye of Chelsea and Richard Mellor if Vera got the false charges dropped *without* a slimy deal involving her uncle. But Vera had still ruined her life for the foreseeable future.

Anne-Elise had not learned about any of her niece's woes from her sister. She had learned from the news. Chelsea still had not replied to Anne-Elise's long message, and at this point, Anne-Elise didn't expect her to. It was disgusting that Chelsea had decided to aid her husband's bosses in harassing Edward and even more disgusting that she had helped these vile politicians threaten her own daughter to achieve their political agenda. That, Anne-Elise believed, said everything that needed to be said about Chelsea's "family values."

*　　*　　*

The nature of the administration's anti-science agenda became clearer than ever to Anne-Elise when she read the afternoon news. Gilbertson had issued two executive orders that Monday: "*Eliminating Questionable Politically Motivated Claims from Federal Weather Products*" and "*Auditing Unproven Power Sources.*"

She was sure that she knew exactly what these would mean, and she was not wrong. In the first, he had imposed a ban on the use of the term "climate change" in National Weather Service forecasts and also banned the word "hypercane" in all federal products relating to Leonard. The order allowed the latter term to be reinstated if "the Vice President's Blue Ribbon Storm Reanalysis Panel determines that the storm Leonard merited the word."

So it obviously won't make that determination, she thought cynically. *It's predetermined, as I said. But this slimeball gets to say that he's being "reasonable" and not "banning" anything, just making sure that it truly applies.*

The second order was more pertinent to her. It ordered the creation of another panel to audit all solar, wind, and nuclear power facilities in the country for "safety and reliability."

Never mind that this is an ongoing audit process that the government already does, she thought. *He doesn't get to control that process, so he must create his own personal little political panel to do it and override the experts.*

The staff at Intensity were very nervous about the second order. Anne-Elise and Dr. Gleason discussed how to handle the rising anxiety at the facility, and she soon learned that they had very different views on that subject.

"I think they're right to be nervous," she declared, "and I think we should level one hundred percent with them. In the end, it's better to be honest about a bad situation than to lie to people and pretend everything is okay until it's obvious it isn't. Then people just feel shocked and betrayed, and they've lost all the time that they would've had to prepare. It's like concealing a hypercane forecast from them until it makes landfall, in a way."

Dr. Gleason's eyes widened. "That seems extremely grim to me," he said. "That order affects plants that are hooked up to the power grid. We're not, so this doesn't necessarily even affect us."

"You know very well it's just the beginning."

"I *don't* know that, and neither do you. I think we should just tell them to keep doing their work," he argued, "and reassure them that lots of people appreciate them and value what they are doing."

Anne-Elise could not go along with this. "That may be true, but it also doesn't matter, if the people with power aren't among the ones who appreciate their work. Ten thousand 'likes' on social media for a post 'appreciating all that they do' won't make a dime's worth of difference if Hal Gilbertson is on the other side."

Gleason gaped at her. "But for morale...."

"Bobby, the question I think we face is whether we are merely in rough waters, or whether we are the crew on the *Titanic*. If it's the latter, it doesn't matter what our morale is. In fact, high morale is just a twisted joke if this is the *Titanic*. The orchestra playing as the ship goes down is a longtime analogy for a reason."

"That's dark," he sputtered.

"Yes, well, times are dark. It doesn't matter who appreciates us if those with the power to shut us down do not. That's the ugly truth, but it's nonetheless the truth."

"But Anne-Elise... what do you want to *do*? You surely don't want to shut down tests?"

"No," she said. "Let's keep operations going. Maybe we'll get net-positive soon like we expect and have a flash-bang headline for a few hours, until something knocks us off the 'Trending' list and people forget about us in a day. At least people will get to enjoy the brief dopamine high of that flash-bang headline, I suppose."

Dr. Gleason gaped again, shocked at her cynicism. She had always had an acidic tongue and a wry way of looking at the world, but this was astoundingly dark.

"But I cannot tell everyone who works for us that things are going to be okay in the long term. We're managers, Bobby. They'll assume that they can trust what we say, so I'm not going to abuse that trust and tell them things I don't believe myself."

*   *   *

Late in the afternoon, Gilbertson issued a third executive order. This one lifted all sun protection factor caps on sunscreens. Previously, there had been a cap of SPF 60 on products that could be sold. Now there would be no cap.

Anne-Elise knew that Dr. Gleason considered *her* cynical, a charge that she didn't deny, but this order seemed breathtakingly so. There would not be a need for such extreme sun-protection products if the ozone layer remained intact across the country, so Gilbertson obviously understood that it was *not* intact over areas that included the district that had elected him to Congress. But admitting that there was an ozone hole there meant admitting that Leonard had been a hypercane.

Therefore, the executive order did not admit that this need existed because of an ozone hole. Instead Gilbertson—

or his staff, most likely—had declared that *"the previous cap of SPF 60 is artificial, arbitrary, and restricts the free market."*

Under the order, products could immediately go on the market making any SPF claim they wanted, as long as they provided "publicly accessible research" to back it up. Companies could conduct such "research" themselves, rather than putting their claims through an independent review.

It was likely to unleash a "Wild West" situation on the sunscreen market on the Gulf Coast. Undoubtedly scores of products would soon flood the market that could not do what they had claimed. Skin cancer rates would skyrocket as people purchased such products and believed they were protected from UVB and UVC when they were not.

But Anne-Elise could not stop thinking about the cynicism of this order. *If you know there's a need for such products, then you know what Leonard was. That's the only way that there could be an ozone hole. You just can't admit it officially because that means admitting other things about why it formed.*

*   *   *

That evening, CG Taverner announced the composition of his Blue Ribbon Reanalysis Panel. Anne-Elise had not had high expectations for this, but even she was shocked at his staff choices.

"Antonio Travanti, age twenty-one," she read aloud to herself, shaking her head. "Certification from the 'Xavier Tsatsos Institute.' What is that?" She quickly searched, then shook her head. This was an unaccredited "coding school" founded by a venture capitalist. It seemed that Taverner himself had accepted campaign donations from Tsatsos. It would figure. Then Anne-Elise noticed something else. "Oh— and Travanti also calls himself 'Morphallus' online. Ha ha, how clever."

She continued down the list. Every single member of the twelve-person "Reanalysis Panel" was a young man. The youngest was twenty and the oldest was twenty-nine. Six had college degrees. Not a single one was an atmospheric scientist, geoscientist, or physicist. Most had ties either to Xavier Tsatsos or to another venture capitalist named Harold F. Orczy.

And many of them had proudly declared, usually on their social media, sometimes even on their professional profiles, such online nicknames as "Morphallus," "Kilt Up," and "TupHerWares." The entire panel appeared to be composed of online trolls like Taverner himself had been, but very well-connected and rich trolls.

And now, very powerful ones.

*　　*　　*

September 19.

"Blue Ribbon Reanalysis Panel demands testimony, records from NHC staff," the headlines read.

That didn't take long, Anne-Elise thought, glowering. In her opinion, these little boys—as she called them—should not be able to compel anything without subpoena power, which they did not have. But to her absolute disgust, Gilbertson's Acting Secretary of Commerce, whom he had appointed after firing all the high-level political appointees from the previous administration, was eagerly granting them everything they wanted, including forcing scientists to testify in an "investigation" with a predetermined conclusion.

This Acting Secretary had also put the entire NHC staff on administrative leave. The Hurricane Center was currently nonfunctional, even though hurricane season continued. Another storm was already brewing in the open Atlantic, but that didn't matter to Gilbertson's administration either. The computer models were run from another center, and they continued to operate, but there was no official authority to interpret and analyze them with respect to tropical cyclones.

Anne-Elise had checked the model output herself. The potential storm was a typical Atlantic tropical wave, gradually making its way across the ocean. The models were indicating that it could strike Texas by the month's end as a hurricane. Anne-Elise wished it would be another hypercane, just to prove a point to the "Blue Ribbon Panel" and those who supported it, but the conditions no longer existed to support one. Leonard itself had injected enough dust into the atmosphere that the Gulf of Mexico was cooling down rapidly to normal hurricane-season levels of heat. But it was too far out to be sure where this tropical wave might strike, and the Weather Service offices on the Texas coast were not comfortable working tropical cyclone concerns into their forecasts yet.

That left an opening for fools on the Internet to issue their own "forecasts" from their uninformed interpretation—or outright dismissal—of the models, and they eagerly took it. It was a disgusting spectacle. Things had been bad enough on that front with Leonard, but at least the NHC had been issuing official, authoritative products then. Now, there was a void.

Precisely as Gilbertson, Taverner, and the rest of them want, Anne-Elise thought bitterly. She turned back to the article, trying to finish reading it, despite how enraging and depressing it was.

Edward, somehow, maintained his resolute optimism that things would turn around. He continued to keep her updated from the secure messaging app that they now used instead of texting.

The Hurricane Hunters who flew with me have all gone to safe locations. We're keeping in touch. Let Gilbertson and Taverner overreach; it won't take long at the rate they're going. When they do, and the tide turns back to reason, we'll make our big, dramatic reveal with the truth. I've got the data box!

A series of emojis of a lock and key, an island, a tropical drink, an airplane, and a hurricane then followed. The string of cute, cheeky icons seemed like overkill to Anne-Elise. He was trying too hard, she thought.

She hoped she was just being too pessimistic and cynical. Perhaps he really did hold onto some hope. Edward had always had a tendency to see himself as a heroic, important figure. His aviator persona had never been a false front, and neither had the sense of mission that he had told her he'd felt about being the pilot to fly into the world's first observed hypercane. Perhaps, she supposed, he truly did see himself as a heroic truth-teller in this situation, just a different variety from before.

He had certain traits in common with Vera, she now realized. Or at least, Vera as she had been before her own "cause" fell to pieces.

But Anne-Elise knew that she... did not see the world the same way. She used to, but no longer, she realized. She was profoundly pessimistic that the tide was going to turn back soon. Sighing, she tried again to finish the article.

"*Our work is not secret or classified*," Dr. Vinay Chandra was quoted in it. "*We have nothing to hide and will gladly explain how our data-gathering systems work, the quality-control mechanisms, error checks, and protections against tampering or damage. We hope that the panel and any Americans with concerns will be reassured.*"

It was the sort of statement that he undoubtedly felt he had to make, and maybe he even believed that he could convince these people if he just spoke honestly, eloquently, and thoroughly enough. Anne-Elise was a scientist; she understood that impulse all too well. Just a couple of weeks ago, she had fallen prey to it herself, telling CG Taverner about the risk of a neutron burst simply because she was trained to be honest and open about her work as a scientist. She knew that science *had* to operate on honesty and openness, on full—even over-the-top—explanations, for the scientific method to work.

But she also understood that some people would simply take advantage of a scientist's honesty and inclination to "explain." She was not sure Dr. Chandra and his staff did understand that.

A *neutron burst*, she suddenly thought again. *In the midst of all the stupid "nuclear meltdown" ravings about Intensity Labs, I didn't give much thought to the actual risk that the lab's work entails.*

It would require all the safeties to fail....

A dark, horrible, vindictive idea was germinating in her mind. She quickly tried to shove it out, but she could not banish it wholly.

*　　*　　*

September 21.

Cheers and whoops erupted in the corridors of Intensity Labs, spreading from one to the next as the news itself spread.

The final inefficiency had been resolved. The fusion reactor had achieved net-positive power, *truly* net-positive, with the output from the reaction overpowering the amount needed to get the ignition laser to full power.

"*Eureka!*" scientists, engineers, and technicians had shouted, acutely self-aware of the cliché of using this phrase, but that very cliché was why they were doing so. For a moment, Anne-Elise wondered if Edward and his crew had felt the same when their measurements had confirmed that Leonard was a hypercane. Probably. And in the case of Intensity Labs, the joy would have been—could have been—*should* have been untempered with any dread of what would come next.

But no longer was that the case.

She had been present outside the ignition chamber, standing by Dr. Gleason to watch as the numbers ticked ever upward, finally passing the level of power that the laser itself was pulling.

Twelve years ago, she would have been the loudest of all. Now, the most enthusiasm that she could muster was a brief, weak smile.

"Congratulations," she said almost tonelessly. Dr. Gleason glanced at her, surprised that she couldn't even manage excitement now, with the success of her life's work. But Hal Gilbertson, CG Taverner, Madison Chadleigh, and her own horrible brother-in-law had destroyed that for her.

She realized that her presence would just be a drain on the mood of everyone else here, a black hole sucking all particles of matter and energy away to crush them into a singularity. She smiled again. "This is a bit overwhelming for me," she lied. "I'll be in my office."

*   *   *

Intensity's fusion chamber was the most advanced kind that existed. The only risk of deuterium-tritium fusion was the release of a free neutron in each atomic reaction, and a lithium lining captured these neutrons, preventing them from escaping.

The "blanket" would become very hot from neutron capture, so it would have to be cooled while fusion continued. This, Anne-Elise thought, was one thing that could *actually* melt down if something went wrong, but it would not be the kind of radioactive meltdown to which old-fashioned twentieth-century fission reactors such as the Chernobyl reactor had been subject. And the problem if the lithium blanket melted would be that there would then be nothing except deuterium-tritium fuel pellet availability to prevent the fusion reaction from sending out wave after wave of free neutrons.

She considered history as she pondered those safeties. *Apollo 13's oxygen tank blew up because a thermal gauge got locked in place, allowing the tank to become superheated during the oxygen mixing process and all the protective coatings of the electrical wires to be melted. So the next time the astronauts mixed the oxygen, an electrical spark caused the whole tank to blow up.*

At Intensity Labs, reaction safety depends fully on that lithium blanket being cooled before it can become damaged from heat. The cooling systems are automated, and there are multiple layers of safety checks in the software. If the cooling system shuts off, the software will also shut off the ignition laser and lock it from being restarted unless someone with root access manually overrides it. And then if the cooling still doesn't start, or if the blanket is heat-damaged, it'll detect that and shut off ignition again.

I am the Director. I have root access.

She tried again to cast out the horrible idea that had once more occurred to her, but she could not ignore the fact that it did keep occurring to her, even now, in Intensity's moment of triumph. In what should have been *her* moment of triumph.

She believed she understood what was going on. Like a dark obsession, it kept popping into her mind to torment her. *Then I'll try to exorcise it,* she decided. *I'll give it what it wants.*

Taking a deep breath, she opened up the software that the development team used. There were multiple versions: the many "development" branches, which had access only to simulations of the reaction rather than the real thing; but also the "production" branch, which was locked down with root-only access.

Anne-Elise copied the production code to her own machine.

Her team—which, back in the day, had included her—had written the code to be easily understandable. Scientists had an unfortunate history of writing dense, disorganized code, with critical functions sometimes buried in places that were not intuitive. She had not wanted Intensity's software to be written like that. Functions were quite easy to find, such as the module "safety_lithium_cooling."

I'll write something, Anne-Elise vowed. *That'll satisfy this dark fantasy I have: just writing it, not actually executing it. Just knowing that I could sabotage it, that I have that power, would be sufficient.*

*   *   *

That evening, she brought her copy of the code home on a portable USB drive. She would continue to work on it there. She didn't want to leave any evidence of this on her work computer. These days, she was becoming rather paranoid.

It did not take long to put in a bit of code that would break the safety mechanism. She soon found a weak point that she could exploit. The thermal monitoring system activated the cooling system when the lithium blanket reached a certain temperature, and it shut down the ignition laser if the cooling *shut off*, but not if the cooling ran but didn't work correctly. The cooling system itself was supposed to shut off if its fluid overheated or ran low, triggering the ignition system to shut off as well. If it did not, the thermal monitoring would detect that the temperature of the lithium blanket kept rising, but it did not have a "cooling is running but isn't working right" emergency kill switch. The system checked for heat damage as the ignition laser first powered up, but no other time. There should have been a redundant check; there wasn't.

If she were feeling productive and responsible instead of destructive and vindictive, she realized that this would actually be an Apollo 13-level flaw that she would insist on having fixed.

But the breathless, relentlessly cheery jabber on TV in the background was changing her mind about this being just a dark fantasy. Determined to "elevate the nation's mood," as if that were their job rather than reporting on the news, the media were treating the Gilbertson-Taverner administration as a much-needed breath of fresh air, or a digestive cleanse, rather than the pathogen—or cancer—that it was, in Anne-Elise's view.

If this is what this country is hellbent on doing, turning its back on science and seeking comfort from ignorance, then it does not deserve this gift, she thought sourly. *These are people who were told two days in advance what Leonard would be, and what did they do? They believed conspiracy theories and lies instead. They decided that the government was using weather modification to experiment on them, that the reason there were no survivors was a nuclear accident rather than a hypercane, and now, that the government has falsified data about its intensity as part of "the climate-alarmism syndicate."*

And why would it do that? There's a conspiracy theory about that too! They believe scientists are "night-crawlers" who "push" climate change and clean power in order to destroy the American man and the American family.

340

You know what? Fine. If people want to keep burning fossil fuels and then denying the consequences, even unto death and literal disintegration in four-hundred-mile-an-hour winds... then fine. If they don't want science to save them from their own malevolent, arrogant, willful ignorance, then science shouldn't try.

These people do not deserve clean fusion.

In bitterness, fury, and—although she would not admit it to herself—profound grief, Anne-Elise finished her code that night. Once activated, it would remove the checks on the level and efficacy of the cooling fluid. The system would continue running even as the fluid became less and less able to cool the hot lithium blanket. Low or hot fluid would never result in a shutoff signal being sent to the cooling system.

And as a result, the reaction would not shut off either.

You want a nuclear meltdown, you stupid Florida hicks? Anne-Elise thought in incandescent anger as she ran a simulation with the code to see if it would work. *I'll give you one. You survived a hypercane, but you don't want to face that, do you, because of what the hypercane's very existence implies: that humans have messed up the planet and are deeply vulnerable to the inevitable consequences.*

You could have regained a sense of control and power, you know. You could have vowed to do something about the conditions that created Leonard. But rather than taking responsibility for climate change, you decided to cosplay as "courageous truth-tellers," imagining that you'd survived a government-caused nuclear event. Fine, then. I'll make your conspiracy theory true, and you can see just how much you like the real thing.

*   *   *

September 28.

"Hurricane Leonard's intensity was intentionally exaggerated, panel finds."

Anne-Elise glowered at the Thursday morning headline that so rudely dominated her computer. She navigated her mouse over the app to try to tell it that she didn't want to see political crap, but unfortunately, this only had the effect of loading the offending story for her to read the entire opening paragraph.

"In his second major press conference, President Gilbertson announced that the Vice President's Blue Ribbon Storm Reanalysis Panel has quickly determined that intensity claims about Hurricane Leonard made by the National Hurricane Center during the previous administration were exaggerated to the point of scientific fraud."

Ten days? Anne-Elise scoffed in her thoughts. *So your band of Internet trolls could "reanalyze" a hypercane in ten days, CG? What a pathetic joke... except it isn't funny. The media is reporting on this with barely any skepticism or concern at all.*

Her gaze then shifted from the computer screen to the USB stick that rested, like a grenade without the pin pulled, beside her keyboard.

For the third time in her life, something snapped and broke inside her. Her brow darkened. She grabbed up the drive and shot to her feet like a rocket.

Her gaze shifted to the window. The dust had definitely decreased. It was clearly daytime. Since Leonard's landfall, she had had to look at a clock to tell what time of day it was. The sun would soon show itself, a blast of highly damaging ultraviolet rays baking the surface where Leonard's eyewall had burst too high.

If any spot on Earth deserves that, it's the district that put this horrible man in Congress, she decided.

Without even bothering to power down her computer, she stomped out into the living room, where the television was blaring into oblivion.

"The dust over the Gulf Coast is subsiding at last. Visibility has increased in Tallahassee to half a mile as of the top of the hour," the weatherman announced in a neutral tone.

The tone of the reporting anchor was not neutral. It was bubbly, obnoxiously so to Anne-Elise's ears. "Thank you, Jake!

It does feel like we have been in mourning, and Mother Earth has mourned with us, but now the black veil is lifting. We may even see the sun again in a few days!"

*   *   *

The Director's office, Intensity Labs Advanced Fusion Testbed.

Anne-Elise opened a terminal window with superuser privileges and typed "/mnt/usb/cooling_fix" into the prompt. She did not press Enter. The cursor at the end blinked, waiting for her to execute a command. Blink, blink. Enter or Ctrl-C.

If she ran this script, the code would execute, overwriting the existing production code. Before long, the cooling systems would malfunction, but the safety system would not know it. Fusion reactions would continue, bombarding the lithium blanket with free neutrons until it overheated and melted. Then neutrons would start escaping the chamber. This would continue until someone figured out what had happened and shut the laser down—or the fuel ran out. But the damage would be done—to the facility, to the workers, and to the public perception of fusion as a clean, almost miraculous power source.

How am I even considering this? she thought. *How did it come to this?*

Vera had always insisted that society was sick, decadent, broken, and—though she did not use the language of religion —had to be punished for its sins. That was fundamentally what she had believed and why she had wanted to "tear it all down," though, like so many religiously motivated hypocrites, she had not wanted her purge of "sin" to include herself.

You were right that society is sick, Vera, but for the wrong reasons, Anne-Elise thought grimly. *The problem isn't the things that made modern life good. It's not modern medicine, atmospheric science, advanced energy technology... and it's not the Internet. Nor is it really even social media, for all that I've hated it the past couple weeks. Whether the Internet and social media were good or bad always depended on how people used them.*

343

That's the key: people.

Humans are the problem, and we always have been.

She considered the profound irony of the fact that she, a human, was considering acting as judge, jury, and executioner.

This breakthrough comes from an idea I had, but many more people worked on it. This wasn't a case of the lone scientist having a "Eureka" moment in a private tower. Many people shouted that a week ago. They contributed too. I couldn't have done it all by myself.

I'm contemplating doing the very thing to them that Gilbertson and Taverner might do to me: unilaterally destroying their work.

For a moment, she hesitated.

Her last text to Chelsea suddenly returned to her thoughts. **He will never lie about science for politics**, she had told her sister. But was she not currently considering lying about science for politics? The reaction was safe. They had foreseen the risks and accounted for them. She was considering intentionally breaking that in order to punish people for politics.

But then a realization hit her, hardening her again.

The very fact that I'm thinking of this, even knowing what a villain and a hypocrite it makes me, is evidence against humanity. There is a darkness in us, a selfish vindictive cruelty, that we will probably never be rid of, because we evolved this way. Long ago, in the mists of time, it probably benefited us.

My sister said, that miserable night when we believed we'd lost Edward, "Edward is no more an exception than I was. Or our parents." We all bring our fates upon ourselves, she said.

I'm not exempt either. I'm no better than anyone I condemn. Humans are the problem, and I am a human.

We're part of the earth's biosphere, she reflected, and the earth system, like any other biophysical system, has ways of purging itself of problems. Tropical cyclones themselves form because the atmosphere is out of equilibrium. They're merely physical phenomena that form because the laws of thermodynamics require them to form. The hypercane and other disasters could be the earth's own way of restoring equilibrium. Leonard's dust cloud is already cooling the Gulf of Mexico back to normal September levels.

The earth's method of solving the climate crisis will spare no one, but this, perhaps, is what "climate justice" truly means. Justice is simply an attempt to restore balance when there is an imbalance.

Her index finger lingered over the Enter key. She took a deep breath and prepared to press it.

Bzzt! Her phone vibrated, interrupting and preventing her from acting on her dark urge—at least for now.

Annoyed, she unlocked the phone, expecting to see a marketing text or an unwanted notification from the social media apps that she had neglected for days, urging her to return.

It was neither of these. Instead, it was a secure message from Edward.

Saw the news today about that joke of a "reanalysis." It's bad, but don't let it get you down. They're only doing this because they're desperate. Lots of people don't believe that report, and the "authors" are a total joke. I'm not just saying that because I want it to be true. My Hunter colleagues have told me that lots of people are disgusted. Hang tight and don't give up hope. I haven't.

How can anyone be this optimistic? she thought. She typed a despondent reply: **Edward, they're going to target clean power. That'll include Intensity. It's not just that report that's the problem.**

In a moment, his reply came. **Well, are you going to let them get you without a fight? I was up against a hypercane and I didn't give up. And I didn't require perfectly calm winds. I just landed the plane in winds that we had a chance of surviving... and here we are. We survived, because we told the storm, "You're not getting us that easily." Gilbertson, Taverner, and the blue-ribbon trolls don't have the dignity and don't deserve the respect that Leonard did, either.**

She drew back, considering this.

Did she just want to tear down Intensity—melt down her dream—so that someone else couldn't do it to her? If so, she had given up.

But he had not.

Edward had taken the data box with him to the Bahamas as an investment in a better future, a future in which the truth mattered again. He had taken it even though the present looked grim.

He had a point. It was hard for her to admit now, with her brain settled into this dark swampy morass, but he did.

We also refused to let our abusive family get us without a fight, she realized. *We said no, and in the end, we survived them.*

Anne-Elise turned back to the computer screen. The terminal prompt continued blinking, awaiting her answer.

Appendices

Supplemental: Hypercanes

For my first novel, *The Inheritors: A Climate Fable*, I invoked a theoretical type of extreme tropical cyclone, dubbed by Dr. Kerry Emanuel (who has made it his life's work to study extreme tropical weather) a "hypercane" (Emanuel 1988). This type of storm has never been observed, but the equations that govern tropical cyclone intensity via thermodynamic processes predict that it would form under certain conditions.

Until recently, it was believed that those conditions could only occur from an asteroid or comet strike or the eruption of an underwater volcano. And, to be sure, hypercanes of the most extreme possible intensity *could* only occur under such conditions (in which case, particularly with a bolide strike, we'd have a lot of problems to worry about in addition to the storm!). But less extreme conditions could produce "less extreme" hypercanes, and these "lesser" conditions are entirely plausible under anthropogenic climate change.

Without going into too much granular detail on the subject, a tropical cyclone has a maximum potential intensity that it can reach. The storm's actual intensity will usually be further limited by factors such as wind shear, the entrainment of dry air, and sea surface upwelling, but the *potential* intensity that it can reach is governed by the *temperature at the tropopause* (this is the limit of the troposphere, the slice of the earth's atmosphere where most weather occurs), the *surface air humidity*, and the *sea surface temperatures*.

For the same surface air humidity level and tropopause temperature, hotter seas mean higher potential intensities.

For the same sea surface temperature and surface air humidity level, colder tropopause temperatures mean higher potential intensities.

The tropical storm or hurricane essentially acts as a thermodynamic heat engine. It draws hot, moist air from the near-surface, vents some of it upwards through the "chimney" of the eyewall, dissipates some in rainfall and near-surface evaporation, and dissipates some through radiation as this air

348

descends again to the surface. A tropical cyclone seeks thermodynamic equilibrium, and in those that we have always seen, they achieve it through these processes. When a storm is taking in more heat from the ocean than it is currently dissipating, it intensifies. When it is dissipating more heat than it takes in, it's weakening. When it is dissipating exactly as much as it takes in from the surface, the storm is in thermodynamic equilibrium. This is why its maximum potential intensity is controlled by sea surface temperature and tropopause temperature.

At least, that's how it's supposed to work, and how it always has worked within recorded human history. Hypercanes are a different theoretical beast. In the hypercane case, the storm *cannot* reach thermodynamic equilibrium through the typical processes, because the temperature difference between sea surface temperature and tropopause temperature is too great. It takes in too much heat too fast to vent it out through the eye or dissipate it through surface fluxes. In this case, the equations predict that the storm would experience runaway intensification. The factor that would eventually end up limiting its intensity in this case would be its own internal friction from the high winds it obtained. This is a much slower and less efficient process than the usual tropical cyclone processes, so the storm would reach a far greater intensity than anything we've ever observed, and it would maintain it for a long time.

A hypercane would be defined by its internal heat-dissipation processes and whether it was "supercritical" (the technical term for "no equilibrium through fluxes and venting"), rather than having any specific wind speed or surface pressure. It is not "Category Six" or anything of the sort. Indeed, there's a good case that it should not really even merit the term "hurricane" (or "typhoon" or the equivalent), since it would be a different kind of tropical cyclone, and should not be considered on the Saffir-Simpson Hurricane Wind Scale, if one ever were to form. But on planet Earth, the "weakest" hypercane would probably have central pressures of 700 millibars and winds over 400 mph, based on a solution of the thermodynamic equations for tropical cyclones.

Dr. Emanuel's early research papers on the topic, "The Maximum Intensity of Hurricanes" (1988) and "Hypercanes: A possible link in global extinction scenarios" (1995), for which he had co-authors, focused on the most extreme scenario: In the case of the 1995 paper, a hypercane formed in 50°C seawater. This, fortunately, cannot happen under even the worst projections of climate change. (It could happen with a bad enough asteroid strike, but again, we'd have pretty serious problems of *many* kinds in that case!) The hypercane that Dr. Emanuel et al. modeled from these conditions reached almost 200 mb and nearly Mach 1 winds, as Edward Kirby says in the story.

That is not what happens in this novel. It is meant to be hard science fiction about climate change, and climate change is not going to do *that* to us. However, the tropical cyclone intensity equations indicate that, at surface air of 75 percent relative humidity, a borderline hypercane *could* form with merely 35°C water and -70°C to -80°C upper atmosphere temperature.

In my modeling of this storm with the WRF-ARW model (the flagship weather model for research, updated regularly), I was unable to reproduce that. That doesn't mean the equations are incorrect. They are not. What it means is that the *implementation* of the WRF model imposed certain compromises and restrictions on how the storm was simulated.

But I was determined not to write anything that could not be explicitly backed up with a simulation to support it, so I used slightly more extreme initial conditions in order to get a hypercane from WRF. Those conditions were 37°C seawater (human body temperature) and -85°C tropopause temperature. *These conditions, and an appropriate vertical air profile all the way up, caused the flagship weather model to generate a storm that sure looks like it's a hypercane, and which the equations predict should be a hypercane.*

Sea surface temperatures in the Gulf of Mexico have routinely reached 34°C in recent years. It happens every year. And upper-atmospheric temperatures over Florida have reached at least -78°C, with surface air only 3° warmer in a real atmospheric sounding than the sounding that I used for my WRF storm simulation.

We've never managed to draw the "inside straight from hell," as Edward Kirby puts it, all at once before. But there's no reason we couldn't in the future.

On my website, https://www.eleanorthorne.net, you can view slideshows of various fields of my simulated Hurricane/Hypercane Leonard. The intensities of these fields, which include surface pressure, surface winds, vertical velocities, and more, strictly follow the story timeline. If you have the computing resources to do so, you can even learn how to simulate "Leonard" yourself and obtain the configuration files that will generate it.

I have also provided a table of pressure and surface wind values for Leonard in this book. All the pressure and wind values in the Leonard Timeline table are drawn directly from the model's output. These values are what a research-quality weather forecasting model produced for the input values noted previously and mentioned by characters in the novel.

Hypercanes are soon going to be possible... *if they aren't already*.

Supplemental: Leonard Timeline

Date (CDT)	Pressure (mb)	Surface Wind (mph)	Events
09/03 1 PM	1004	41	Tropical Storm
09/03 2 PM	1002	58	
09/03 3 PM	1002	75	
09/03 4 PM	1001	76	Flight crew in eye; Category 1
09/03 5 PM	998	74	
09/03 6 PM	985	82	
09/03 7 PM	982	99	Category 2
09/03 8 PM	972	108	
09/03 9 PM	964	117	Category 3; flight leaves storm
09/03 10 PM	953	126	
09/03 11 PM	947	145	Category 4; flight crew in eye
09/04 12 AM	934	156	
09/04 1 AM	915	181	Category 5; Edward called back
09/04 2 AM	881	197	
09/04 3 AM	864	204	
09/04 4 AM	842	214	World record; flight leaves storm
09/04 5 AM	833	217	
09/04 6 AM	830	236	Manned flights halted
09/04 7 AM	815	282	*Morning Lark* Chapter 11
09/04 8 AM	797	289	Unmanned flight dispatched
09/04 9 AM	780	304	
09/04 10 AM	770	303	Drone reports begin
09/04 11 AM	762	302	Edward leaves for Lakeland

09/04 12 PM	757	311	
09/04 1 PM	746	317	
09/04 2 PM	736	324	
09/04 3 PM	725	342	Edward arrives at Lakeland
09/04 4 PM	714	346	Edward's flight leaves
09/04 5 PM	703	359	
09/04 6 PM	694	357	Edward's plane reaches the core
09/04 7 PM	687	366	Hypercane confirmed
09/04 8 PM	681	363	
09/04 9 PM	681	381	
09/04 10 PM	678	410	
09/04 11 PM	675	420	
09/05 12 AM	672	413	Edward's flight downs
09/05 1 AM	672	415	
09/05 2 AM	668	418	
09/05 3 AM	665	418	
09/05 4 AM	669	414	
09/05 5 AM	667	406	
09/05 6 AM	666	417	
09/05 7 AM	663	430	Peak intensity
09/05 8 AM	664	402	
09/05 9 AM	666	414	
09/05 10 AM	669	388	
09/05 11 AM	673	373	
09/05 12 PM	675	388	
09/05 1 PM	673	400	
09/05 2 PM	676	412	
09/05 3 PM	681	408	
09/05 4 PM	681	401	"Doomsday" Advisory
09/05 5 PM	681	399	
09/05 6 PM	681	414	

09/05 7 PM	687	406	
09/05 8 PM	690	401	
09/05 9 PM	691	390	
09/05 10 PM	694	387	
09/05 11 PM	691	392	
09/06 12 AM	689	407	
09/06 1 AM	687	410	
09/06 2 AM	686	410	
09/06 3 AM	686	412	
09/06 4 AM	685	417	
09/06 5 AM	685	422	
09/06 6 AM	682	419	Landfall

Bibliography

Emanuel, K. A., 1988: The maximum intensity of hurricanes, *Journal of the Atmospheric Sciences*, Vol. 45, No. 7, pp. 1143-1155.

Emanuel, K. A., K. Speer, R. Rotunno, R. Srivastava, and M. Molina, 1995: Hypercanes: A possible link in global extinction scenarios, *Journal of Geophysical Research*, Vol. 100, No. D7, pp. 13755-13765.

Li, S., Jaroszynski, S., Pearse, S., Orf, L., Clyne, J., 2019: VAPOR: A Visualization Package Tailored to Analyze Simulation Data in Earth System Science. Atmosphere. 10(9):488. https://doi.org/10.3390/atmos10090488

Lin, J., and K. Emanuel, 2024: Why the lower stratosphere cools when the troposphere warms. *Proceedings of the National Academy of Sciences*, Vol. 121, e2319228121, https://doi.org/10.1073/pnas.2319228121.

Skamarock, W. C., J. B. Klemp, J. Dudhia, D. O. Gill, Z. Liu, J. Berner, W. Wang, J. G. Powers, M. G. Duda, D. M. Barker, and X.-Y. Huang, 2019: A Description of the Advanced Research WRF Version 4. NCAR *Tech. Note* NCAR/TN-556+STR, 145 pp. doi:10.5065/1dfh-6p97

Visualization & Analysis Systems Technologies, Visualization and Analysis Platform for Ocean, Atmosphere, and Solar Researchers (VAPOR version 3.8.0) [Software]. Boulder, CO: UCAR/NCAR – Computational and Information System Lab, 2023. doi:10.5281/zenodo.7779648

About the Author

Eleanor Thorne is the pseudonym of an atmospheric scientist on the Gulf Coast, near the landfall location of Hurricane Katrina. A native of the Southeast United States, she has experienced hurricanes and tornadoes for as long as she can remember and has been fascinated with hypercanes since graduate school. She has worked with the National Weather Service, Environmental Protection Agency, environmental nonprofits, and in national politics.

She is a classical liberal, a cat person, a baseball fan, and enjoys a nice walk on the beach.

As *The Inheritors* makes clear, she *doesn't* like infotainment, pseudo-populism, or political extremism that much. She thinks real, serious (and really serious) problems call for real, serious solutions, and that such problems should not be opportunities for would-be social engineers to try to remake real people's lives by force and deceit.

In addition to being a scientist, she has also dreamed of being a novelist since she was seven years old. *The Inheritors* is her first novel.